THE ELIOT GIRLS

The
Eliot Girls

KRISTA BRIDGE

Douglas & McIntyre

13 14 15 16 17   5 4 3 2 1

Douglas and McIntyre (2013) Ltd.
P.O. Box 219, Madeira Park, BC, VON 2HO
www.douglas-mcintyre.com

Cataloguing data available from Library and Archives Canada
ISBN 978-1-55365-982-2 (pbk.)
ISBN 978-1-55365-983-9 (epub)

Editing by Barbara Berson
Copy editing by Pam Robertson
Proofreading by Shirarose Wilensky
Cover design by Anna Comfort O'Keeffe and Carleton Wilson
Cover chalkboard background courtesy of freestock.ca
Text design by Carleton Wilson
Printed and bound in Canada
Distributed in the U.S. by Publishers Group West

We gratefully acknowledge the financial support of the Canada Council for the Arts, the British Columbia Arts Council, the Province of British Columbia through the Book Publishing Tax Credit, and the Government of Canada through the Canada Book Fund for our publishing activities.

For Peter

The light there was like a blow, and the air smelled as if many wonderful girls had just wandered across the lawn.

—John Cheever, "The Common Day"

Prologue

THE STAFF TEA PARTY carried on down the hall—at a reassuring distance she could hear the clinking of china, the music of voices and laughter—but she had made her escape, unnoticed, to the solitude of her cool office. She was not altogether against the niceties, the polite mirth, of such gatherings. Parties were necessary procedures, she understood. The teachers needed to bond (how she despised that treacly word), to recognize in the eyes of virtual strangers the intimacy of shared purpose, the elevating ambition that had built the very walls that held them. She had stood to the side, observing the delicate dance, sipping her tea at rhythmic intervals in an effort to calm her fraught nerves. And then she had slipped out, made her retreat across the gleaming hardwood of the corridor as quietly as she could manage.

In her office, her breaths slowed to their ordinary tempo. The copious leaves outside made shadows on the window, and she was drawn to them. In moments of wildest emotion, she tried to stay quite still. Happiness was a state she distrusted. Too hinged did it seem on the external, too erratically greedy, too connected to childish indulgences ill-suited to a woman of her station. But she had to grant that no other word sufficed at present to describe the replete pleasure inside her, this queer and bridal feeling. Everything was coming together. Construction had been completed, the last of the trucks cleared out, the mounds of mud replaced by tidy flower beds. The edifice that now housed her was not merely a school. It was George Eliot Academy. Her vision brought splendidly into being.

Looking out over the grounds, she braced her gaze against delights too numerous to be met with moderation. (Had she been happy in quite this way since those Sunday afternoons across the ocean long ago, when her mother had allowed her one chocolate-covered biscuit at tea time?) The long, tree-lined driveway stretched out before her, the freshly mowed lawns on either side lapping the distance to the high wrought-iron fences. In her heart, she felt certain that her school had already achieved in its infancy the standing of its future, an irrefutable place in history.

It was just for a second that her eyes wandered, to the kaleidoscopic film of glass cleaner lining the borders of the windows, but it was then that two small figures appeared at the top of the driveway. The phone rang, startling her back into acuity. That was when she saw them. Ruth Brindle and the girl. (What was her name? Amy? Emma?) She frowned. Although she was not entirely surprised to see Ruth—she had remarked Ruth's absence from the tea party, made a mental note to have a word—she couldn't imagine what had possessed her to appear so tardily, and toting her daughter. She had put the girl on the waiting list simply as a kindness. But really, there was no question of her acceptance. During her entrance exam, she had tried to place an edge piece in the centre of a puzzle.

Ruth was gesturing to Devon Hall, smiling nervously, trying to draw the girl in, but of course the girl was looking the wrong way. Up at the sky, it seemed. She let go of her mother's hand and set off on an unfortunate, disorganized sort of run, then stopped. What damn thing was she looking at, her mouth agape?

From the bulwark of her office, Larissa McAllister leaned very close to the window, so close that her nose nearly grazed the glass, and peered out. A red balloon, caught up by a weak wind, was drifting over the sparse pink rose bushes. It paused mid-air, then floated over the giant willow tree, lingering above the highest branches. Ruth followed the girl to the edge of the lawn and looked up, her face a prism of wonder. Then she kissed the top of her daughter's head.

Larissa blushed, leaning back into the asylum of the long crimson curtain. She stifled an urge to rap on the window, to remind them of themselves. But they were breaking no rules. The girl wasn't streaking through the flower beds. No blaze of hyperactivity had thrown her feet into anarchy. They were simply looking at the wrong thing. The marvel here was the buildings, their grand poetic decree. Ruth ought to have known better. Yet how close she stood to her daughter, mirroring the drift of her quiet disobedience. Even after the balloon had vanished behind the modest steeple of the chapel, they continued to watch the invisible path it had taken.

Larissa closed her eyes against the interlopers. The acoustics of her empty chamber were such that the silence was dense, almost tactile, and she let her mind stray, just for a second, to her mother's best parlour, those perfectly round biscuits on the lily-of-the-valley plate (she had not meant to chip it, she had been so careful), the smell of rainy summer days and the spines of her favourite books. Then, crouching, she opened the roomy bottom drawer of her desk and beheld the old record player she had secretly stored there. The records, well kept in their cardboard sleeves, were still in a box, and she sifted through them until she found just the one she had in mind. Gilbert and Sullivan, always, when she wanted a lift. She wouldn't go so far as to dance, no, but she could allow herself a little music, here in the place she alone had brought to life.

Chapter One

THE FLOWERS WERE CONGRATULATORY, but seemed to point to an irony. Audrey Brindle's acceptance letter from George Eliot came late, in early August, after she'd spent several wearying months on the waiting list. While the two women of the house danced around the kitchen, Richard Brindle, who had submitted, albeit beneath his breath, that his daughter should sneer at Eliot's belated approval, had stood stiffly by the refrigerator, despairing of her lack of pride. The following day, however, a lavish bouquet was delivered. On the card was simply "Congratulations," written in Richard's sloping lefty penmanship and punctuated with an austere period. Without the exclamation point that gave *congratulations* its customary zeal, the celebratory gesture seemed somehow insincere, a sly allusion to the silliness of her excitement over a place that didn't much want her. The flowers carried the whiff of paternal censure. They were a raised eyebrow at a slutty dress.

But because she had never received flowers before and feared she might never again, Audrey kept the arrangement long past the decline of its blooming health, until the water in the glass vase was a putrid green cloud and the petals came away in her hands. In spite of their provenance, the flowers felt like an ode to hope, and though officially dead, they were still sitting in the middle of the kitchen table on the first day of school.

The early morning light was pooling on the long marble counter, but the room was far from peaceful. The family dogs, Stevie, Marlow, and McGill, surrounded Audrey like shameless sycophants, brightly engaging her in eye contact to convey their hunger, felt at every meal as passionately as if for the first time. Spotting a squirrel in the backyard, Stevie suddenly broke away from the pack and flew at the back door, barking. Audrey gave the lingering animals noncommittal taps on the head and turned an unfriendly back to the din. She had been up long before her alarm, and the amount of day that still lay before her was vast enough as to seem almost cosmically unfathomable. By seven o'clock, she was already dressed in her uniform and staring at her reflection in the streaky mirror of her dressing table. She had run through the day in her mind countless times, each attempt at positive imagery challenged by a more compelling scenario of disaster. Every moment alone made her less convinced that things would turn out well. Yet in the public light of the kitchen, matters were no better. The heat of the September morning was already seeping through the tall windows. Moisture gathered at her neck, tightly bound in her new tie. She was no better than a child playing dress-up. If she couldn't even make herself believe that she was an Eliot girl, how could she hope to persuade anyone else?

"Look at you!" came the exclamation from the stairs.

Light-footed and smiling, in a white silk bathrobe that added to her oppressively seraphic glow, Ruth descended. As she entered the kitchen, she held her arms out as though presenting Audrey to an audience. "Wow," she whispered, shaking her head. "Just look at you."

"Oh, please," Audrey said disagreeably.

Ruth cocked her head and frowned. "What's the problem?"

But Audrey couldn't articulate the problem. She understood her own ill humour too poorly to explain it lucidly to herself, let alone to her expectant, beaming mother. A decade was a long time to want something out of reach; she had grown used to looking at George Eliot through the eyes of a marginalized lover.

The history of her long-withheld acceptance to Eliot was not easy for Audrey to consider. Because Ruth taught in the Junior School, the Brindle family had taken for granted Audrey's un-eventful acceptance. Yet the most explicit warnings had failed to prepare them for the tangle of rejection that obstructed their path. Having conceived of a school that would be a breeding ground for enlightened thinkers, that would honour the flavour and appearance of tradition while liberating girls from the mind-shrivelling path of learning set by men and for men, Larissa Mc-Allister, Eliot's principal and creator, had installed as a barrier the most suitably gruelling entrance exams her team of writers could devise. At five, Audrey had insisted in the interview portion that one plus two equalled zero; at nine, she had proven unable to write a satisfactory five-hundred-word exposition about her fa-vourite book. On round three, after several years of after-school tutoring, she had finally made it onto the waiting list for grade ten. Today was meant to be the reward for all her hard work. But whatever inadequacy the admissions procedure had been de-signed either to awaken or expose, it had done its job. How could she have known that dread was to be the consequence of so much hope?

"I can't get this tie right."

"It looks perfect," Ruth said. "So. Breakfast then."

Ruth was not a breakfast person, but in recognition of Audrey's first day she had resolved to make something special. She had been torn about how to handle the morning. Although she would never have confessed her own nerves to Audrey, she had been awake for most of the night. For as long as she'd taught in Eliot's Junior School, she had always loved the first day of the school year. Nothing made her feel younger, more brimming with a sense of possibility. She wanted that feeling for Audrey but had seen with an almost visual clarity, like the systematic movement of the second hand of a clock, the decline of her daughter's happiness the closer they got to Labour Day.

That morning she had stayed in bed, her anxiety and excitement overlapping, until light began to escape out the sides of the closed curtains. Then she leapt up, grabbed the bathrobe—a gift from Richard, not at all her style, with *"Mi amor"* sewn in loping white cursive onto the chest—and threw it on in an effort to convey that this would be a morning of leisure. Still, she doubted herself. Was it better to honour or ignore the momentousness of the occasion? Celebration ought to have seemed fitting, but Ruth worried, especially confronted with Audrey's dispirited face, that revelry only underscored the years of failure. Ruth didn't want to contribute to her daughter's jitters, yet she felt she ought to do something. She couldn't keep herself from doing something.

As she breezed past Audrey to the stove, the light material of her bathrobe flapped open below the waist, revealing that she had not yet put on underwear.

"Mother, come on," Audrey said, shielding her eyes.

They were watched by their own images, lining the stairs in a parade of moments better worth preserving. Audrey graced the gallery wall with a doting frequency befitting her only-child status, in various posed and candid photographs: being pushed on a swing by her grandmother, sitting in the park as a toddler with fists of grass on the way to her mouth, dressing Marlow in an apron and a shower cap. She and Ruth smiled outside the house of Charlotte Brontë on a rainy day in England; they lounged in their bathing suits on the deck of a catamaran in Antigua; they lugged their own Christmas tree on a farm in Mount Albert; they jumped off a cliff into a lake at a friend's cottage in Parry Sound. Richard despised being photographed and so often ruined pictures by lurking in the shadows at the edge of the frame, his mouth pursed sourly, that Ruth finally gave up trying to include him. He appeared in only three pictures: in a black-and-white high school shot, his wavy hair neatly cropped in the style of the fifties, though he graduated in the seventies; in a morning suit under a blossoming pear tree on his wedding day; exhausted and perturbed in a hospital chair as he held his newborn daughter.

And then there was Ruth, who, unlike her husband, loved looking at photographs of herself. She didn't care whether an image was flattering. For her a photo album was a map of her emotional world, and she could often remember exactly what she had been thinking as she sat before the indifferent gaze of the lens. And so she appeared on the wall not only in the requisite photographs—smiling conventionally in her graduation cap and gown, taking wedding vows in a dreadful lacy concoction, cradling her baby below newly immense breasts—but also in moments seemingly irrelevant—drinking iced tea on the porch of her mother's house, sitting on a lawn chair with their dogs at her feet—moments when images of tranquility belied the turbulent thoughts in her head.

Standing now over the stove, she pushed her long hair out of her face and twisted it up into a precarious, loosening bun, then lifted a cookbook from the shelf and opened it to a hardened, batter-speckled page. "Okay. A cup and a half, a cup and a half." Scowling, she rooted around inside a cupboard, then let the door bang shut as she moved to its neighbour and began a search there. "Am I losing my mind? Where on earth is the flour?"

Ruth often griped about the newly renovated kitchen. It had been done according to Richard's specifications, and, in a fit of materialistic largesse, he had wanted to do everything as expensively as possible. The large kitchen, with a southern exposure overlooking the untended garden, and its white Shaker cabinets, white Carrara marble countertops, a custom stainless steel apron sink, gleaming steel appliances, was everything Ruth knew she should have desired in a kitchen, but its sleekness oppressed her. The perfection only made her feel as though she was a guest in someone else's house.

Audrey could find it in her to do nothing more than stare dejectedly at the pears piled high in the green glass art deco bowl too valuable for its current purpose as a holder of fruit. Ruth's efforts would oblige her to eat, but she was doubtful that she could manage a bite.

"Aren't you just so excited?" Ruth said. For days, she had been harping on how excited Audrey must be, irritated with herself for the repetition—especially when Audrey was clearly about as far from excited as a person could be—but unable to staunch the gush of her pleasure. She smiled. "You look so pretty."

"Whatever."

"You do! Haven't you looked at yourself?"

"Unfortunately, yes."

"I wish you would trust me when I tell you how much you're going to love Eliot. We've worked for this for so long."

Audrey nodded glumly.

As Ruth cracked two eggs into a bowl, the dogs, spotting Richard on the stairs, stirred in unison to mount a repeat performance of their best impersonation of starving animals. Ruth peered up into the cupboard again. "The flour has to be in here. Am I staring right at it?"

From the doorway, Richard cleared his throat. "This looks promising."

Ruth looked at him and smiled, a hand on her hip. "Did you rearrange everything to irritate me?"

"Of course," he said, kissing her on the cheek as he breezed into the kitchen.

The dogs bumped their noses eagerly against Richard's bottom as he poured out their food. He stood well back as they stormed their bowls, then sat down at the table and spread the *Globe and Mail* out before him. He laid his tie neatly beside his placemat and tried to settle in for a heartening read—there was an editorial on a minor MP scandal that was just the kind of item to inspire his enthusiastic scorn—but his usual cheer was absent. Mornings generally found him refreshed and sanguine, likely to whistle, emitting both the scent and the spirit of a man just out of the shower. Now he fidgeted with a corner of the paper. His eyes rested, inert, on a single spot, his usual running news commentary silenced by this global scowl.

"Why is everyone in such a bad mood?" Ruth cried. "I'm making a nice breakfast."

Marlow, finished his food, approached, loudly licking his chops, anticipating the morning's next pleasure. Richard took a biscuit from his pocket and held it in his palm before Marlow's mouth. "I just don't think it's right to see a dog dead over one small snarl."

"Oh," Ruth said, her face falling. "I forgot about that."

On Richard's agenda that day was the euthanizing of a pit bull who'd been adopted the year before by a young family in a fit of philanthropic idealism about the beleaguered breed. Less than an hour after the pit had growled at the four-year-old boy, the father had slammed it into the trunk of the car and dragged it by the scruff of its neck into Richard's vet clinic and demanded that he put an immediate end to its life. Richard had advised a night of reflection, but the man had called from home two hours later to say that he was terrified of the animal and it was spending the night in the garage.

Richard tried to be sympathetic to the family's anxiety: he knew that the worst a golden retriever could inflict couldn't rival the damage when a pit bull flipped. He had seen first-hand, luckily just one horrifying time, the permanent disfigurement. But still. The flimsiness of these owners' open-mindedness, their preening and ignorant saviour-complexes, made him angrier than if they'd never wanted to touch a pit bull in the first place. He understood why some people feared pits, but the self-importance of these paper-thin do-gooders inflamed his moral sensibilities. He had told this family many times that pits needed a firm, alpha hand. Everyone knew that children should be supervised around animals. Yet this child had a history of pulling the dog's tail and trying to ride it like a horse. The father had once laughed, recounting a story about the boy securing an elastic band around the dog's muzzle. The family had gotten it wrong in so many ways, yet vilified the dog for giving a mild warning. At the very least, he felt, the owners should have the decency to locate another family for the dog.

"I'm thinking about refusing to do it," Richard said. "Force them to have the deed done elsewhere, if they insist. But if I do that every time I disagree with someone's choice ..."

"You know people are awful. You've seen worse."

"Mostly, I've seen better."

"He might yet change his mind."

"I hate pit bulls. They freak me out," Audrey said.

"I don't think you're really that narrow-minded, are you?" Richard frowned. "Doesn't that generalization trouble you?"

Audrey shrugged. "At least the guy is being honest. Isn't that better than trumping up some stupid injury he supposedly can't afford to treat? Like those people whose dog had a torn ligament?"

Richard returned an unconvinced, conciliatory smile. "I'm not sure any argument can be made for this guy's honour."

Ruth began ladling batter onto the sizzling frying pan. "Okay, okay. Let's not forget what good things this day holds. Have you not noticed your daughter this morning?"

Audrey shuffled to the fridge and took out the orange juice. She scowled at the neatly laid out pancakes, then reached over and drew a long hair out of one.

"Oops," said Ruth.

"I'm sorry," Richard said. "Of course I haven't forgotten. You're looking very attractive, Audrey. Very proper. Deceptively proper." Her father's smile was a hair grudging, without the bullying radiance that made her mother's so stifling.

Ruth, detecting ambivalence, stared at him meaningfully. "Audrey's going to love it," she said.

"I'm sure you will," Richard said.

"Yeah, yeah, "Audrey replied.

"Just get through the day and it'll be smooth sailing."

Audrey turned back to Ruth. "This tie looks like it's choking me.

Did I do it right?"

Ruth pointed the spatula at Richard. "That reminds me. I just saw Leslie at the clinic yesterday for the first time in months, and I barely recognized her. Has she gained a ton of weight?"

"So kind of you to notice."

"How could I not notice? It's an enormous amount, isn't it? Enough that we could describe it in terms of 'stone.'"

Smiling, Richard coughed into his hand. "Yes, I would say that Leslie has—how can I put this?—increased her allotment of herself." He turned back to the newspaper and flipped through the front section absent-mindedly, not staying long enough on any page to do more than scan the articles, then stood up and slung his tie around his neck. "You know what, I think I'll head out and grab some breakfast later. I need to get to the clinic early so I can get my bearings."

"But the first batch is ready."

He passed Audrey's plate to Ruth and kissed first her, then Audrey, on their cheeks before hurrying out to the front hall, holding up his hand in a backwards wave.

"Brush your teeth. And don't forget your tongue!" called Ruth.

"Done, and done," he said. "Best of luck, kiddo." And he slipped out the front door before another word could be said to suck him back into the unproductive diversions of the kitchen.

With his exit, the house was unsettlingly quiet for a minute, and Audrey was reminded of the imminence of her own departure. She returned to the table and sat heavily. She knew that she ought to be savouring her anticipation—that the lead-up was the best, and certainly the easiest, part—but all the things that made the day important also made it seem insurmountable. She just wanted everything to be finished.

Ruth dumped four slightly burned pancakes onto the plate, delivered them to Audrey's place, and spread a napkin across her lap with a playful flourish of servility. "My dear."

"I'm not hungry."

"But you need the energy!" She glanced at the clock. "Oh, shit. I've got to get dressed. Can you be ready in fifteen?"

In Ruth's absence, Audrey occupied herself by staring at the loudly ticking clock. Morosely, she took in the kitchen, sentimentalizing even the most insignificant household objects: the dusty linen curtains, the stained and dripping dishcloth, the licked-clean dog bowls. She felt that she was leaving it all forever, that the day's experience would form a barrier between how she felt now and how she would feel for the rest of her life. There would be no return to the shelter of this banality.

Ten minutes later, Ruth returned in the outfit she felt most presented her as the person she wanted to be, a crimson pencil skirt and pressed white blouse, her sapphire necklace falling just to the centre of her clavicle. Standing at the hall mirror, she fussed with her hair, which had been messily swept upwards and clasped in place with a tortoiseshell clip. She grumbled under her breath. "Ugh, I can't do anything with my hair in this weather." She looked past Audrey into the kitchen, where Audrey's pancakes sat untouched, and a shadow of poutiness flitted across her face. "But your special breakfast. I worked so hard."

"I'm sorry." Audrey put a hand to her stomach. "I just can't."

Ruth took a step forward, her arms lifted a little, but then let them fall to her side, a vague sadness on her face, as though Audrey had rebuffed a hug. Opening the front door, she gasped at the humidity already descending. "We better get a move on. The last thing we want is to be rushing."

Audrey had hoped for longer at home—not to prepare herself, exactly, but to stew in her apprehension. Procrastination could only make her feel worse, she knew, but logic and emotion had never set off in her more discordant desires. Ruth wanted her to luxuriate in the archetypal profundity of all first days, to experience that view of Eliot, looming at the top of the long driveway, but the impossibility of her mother's ambition had never been more clear. She stepped onto the front porch and looked down the long treed hill, past Queen Street to Lake Ontario stretching out into the boundless distance like the ocean.

Inside, in the living room, Marlow and Stevie erupted into a chorus of barks and bombarded the couch to offer an explosively confused—equal parts exultant and irate—audience for the passage of the poodle next door, out on a walk.

"Ugh!" cried Ruth as McGill rushed to join them, leaving a trail of saliva on her skirt as he brushed past. Her glow was substantially mediated now, but she persisted in her pleasure. She joined Audrey outside and pressed her hand. "We're finally at Eliot together! But don't worry, I promise I won't embarrass you."

And with that, they headed off into the sticky morning.

Chapter Two

AUDREY STOOD AT THE top of the driveway, delaying her move forward into the throng. Madness lay before her. Shiny Volvos and minivans swished past, and advancing on Devon Hall was a swarm of students, each girl's distinctiveness devoured by the multitude. The crowd travelled as one happy, undulating beast, and hovering above it, as if in protection, was a cloud of laughter that seemed its own entity. Audrey braced herself and moved forward, trying to look indifferent and distracted—unpersuasively, she repeated to herself that her solitude was not a liability—but she was sinking into terrible regret. Ruth had insisted that they part ways at the gates. She was, after all, a teacher and feared her position made her a social handicap for Audrey. Audrey knew her mother was right. She wasn't a child. But to be so quickly—indeed, callously—abandoned left her floundering.

It was a day when everything was apt to look pretty, and Audrey couldn't fail to be mesmerized by the radiant swirl of Eliot girls. The beauty came from their cumulative power—not one girl in her navy-blue kilt and white shirt, but at least a hundred, milling on the pristine grass under the expansive shade of the towering trees, streaming towards Devon Hall, as poised in its place as if it had risen up from the grassy field through the sheer magnitude of its will and ambition. Though the shops and restaurants of Yonge Street were mere blocks away, George Eliot Academy sat on a tidy parcel of bucolic land that brooked no threat of urban intrusion. The school's exact location had long been a source of contention among parents. Those who hoped George Eliot would take a place amidst Toronto's chief girls private schools alleged that it was in Rosedale, while those who hoped it would provide quality education but with a more daring curriculum with courses in women's studies and Russian literature insisted that it stood on no-man's land. Those who thought the school's headmistress, Larissa Mc-Allister, was a traditionalist averred Rosedale, and those who said she was a feminist protested. And on it went. But what everyone agreed was the school couldn't have been finer and more elegant, even if it were old. (Larissa McAllister had consulted with the architects at every step during the school's lengthy conception. Later, unable to hide how gratified she was to read in the *North Toronto Post* that George Eliot looked like a compressed version of Upper Canada College, Larissa admitted to Ruth Brindle that she had indeed, rather cheekily, taken that old boys' club as her inspiration.)

For as long as she could remember, Audrey had imagined her own form in the shadow of those Georgian-style buildings, in the sunlight on the pristine lawns. But now the loveliness of the vista only made it more impenetrable.

The scene inside was no better. The front door swung closed behind Audrey with a mute heaviness that shut out the sunny day with the humourless authority of a chastising librarian. Standing to the side of the roomy octagonal foyer, she had only a second to contemplate her approach before another wave of girls propelled her forward. She had been in this hallway many times before, but she had never seen it from just this perspective, the change in her own status having in turn changed all her views. The maelstrom of voices echoed off the panelled walls and high ceilings. Outdoors, the open spaces and wind had diffused the volume, but enclosed in the broad corridor, the noise became a commotion, a deafening flurry out of which burst the occasional squeal. Groups of girls cluttered every foot of space. There were the predictable conversations about summer activities, the shrieked greetings, the theatrical hugs. Near the door huddled a group of prefects making half-hearted efforts to corral the incoming students into some kind of order. (*Hey guys, you know what? Guys, if you could just…*) Beyond them, the groups broke down more imprecisely: a squat, sporty brunette chattered aggressively upwards into the Nordic landscape of her friend's face (*And would you believe he had the nerve to be like, "Sorry, I think we were always better as friends." As if I invited myself…*); four nearly identical blondes resuming an argument apparently left unsolved before the summer months (*No, because you told her before exams, no, don't give me that look, no, I'm totally sick of you lying about it, Jen told me…*). Crouching by a shiny ficus was a girl as overwhelmed as Audrey, searching for something in her knapsack, on her face the terrified alarm of a cornered dog.

Down the length of the hall, huge pendant lights like golden orbs blanketed the scene in a warm, old-fashioned glow that made it look like a still from another time. On the long wall hung portraits of Larissa McAllister's favourite feminist thinkers, flanked by calligraphic renderings of what she considered their most gleaming philosophical aperçus. In the prime position of glory at the beginning was George Eliot herself. The words "ADVENTURE IS NOT OUTSIDE MAN; IT IS WITHIN" made a grand pronouncement next to her grave likeness and encapsulated what Larissa McAllister felt to be the theme of her own life. After George Eliot, the women formed a pictorial assembly line, their words, their sketched faces, offering nothing so common as inspiration; their ideas were to be the students' sustenance, their very breath: Mary Wollstonecraft ("Nothing contributes so much to tranquillizing the mind as a steady purpose—a point on which the soul may fix its intellectual eye."); Simone de Beauvoir ("I am incapable of conceiving infinity, and yet I do not accept finity."); Virginia Woolf ("I would venture to guess that Anon, who wrote so many poems without signing them, was often a woman."); Eleanor Roosevelt ("Remember always that you have not only the right to be an individual; you have an obligation to be one."); Betty Friedan ("The feminine mystique has succeeded in burying millions of American women alive."). At the end of the gallery was a portrait of Larissa McAllister herself—an audacious placement meant to convey that she was assuming her rightful place in history—wearing a smile of Mona Lisa reserve, surveying, with modest approval, the scene of her creation.

Audrey edged through the crowd to the grand central staircase and made her way up past the mahogany panels with the names of all the head girls and prefects etched in gold. At the landing window, she paused: her gaze fell on the swing set in the Junior School playground. Although not the site of her earliest memory—that involved something less pleasing, a running crash into a giant pillar in a neighbour's basement, a splitting pain in her forehead, a babysitter's rank breath, her orange teddy bear, tucked against her chest—its significance, bound as it was in her evergrowing Eliot mythology, came in time to surpass the status of that first recollection. She was on the swing, propelling herself ever higher. Ruth, ordinarily overprotective, was off attending to school business, and Audrey was alone, perhaps for the first time ever, in this place perceived as entirely safe, sheltered from the threats—the thieves, the perverts, the dangerous drivers—of the city. Even now, on the bustling landing, Audrey could remember that feeling of being alone—astoundingly, marvellously—out in the world. She could see herself on that swing, looking down at her childish legs, athletic and determined. It seemed that at that moment she became aware of herself. She moved her legs because she chose to, because her brain sent a signal. She was not just living—running over the moist grasses, noticing a purple bruise on her shin, leaning back and looking up at the clouds—but conscious of living.

Ruth had taken her inside after that. As they made their way down the corridor, its empty glass cases awaiting awards that had yet to be created, everything so clean that they seemed to have been the first people to set foot inside, Ruth glanced furtively around, then pulled Audrey into a shady classroom. "Next year, this will be your room," she said. The curtains were drawn across a wall of windows. In the corner, a child-sized Paddington Bear stood guard over bookshelves crammed with a kaleidoscopic array of illustrated volumes. Framed watercolours were hung in a row across the top of the blackboard—children skipping down a cobbled road, a young boy curled up in a window seat with a book, a girl napping with her head on the stomach of a watchful St. Bernard.

Audrey was wearing the new dress bought for her upcoming entrance interview. When she'd woken up in the morning, it was hung up on her closet door like an empty person, new patent leather Mary Jane shoes with a pretty rose buckle positioned underneath. She walked up and down the aisles, stepping lightly, as though afraid to awaken the spirits that would banish them for trespassing. Finally, she stopped at the side farthest from the door. "I want this desk," she said.

Ruth crouched down beside her. "It's yours." She started to get up, then, but a thought dawned on her. "Want to engrave your initials?" She drew her new Montblanc ballpoint pen from her briefcase.

Audrey shook her head, scandalized.

"Come on, Auds. Show a little daring. You're A.B. The first two letters of the alphabet. No one will ever guess."

Audrey laughed and took a step back, disowning participation, as Ruth applied the pen to the wood. The desks were antique, joined in a line of six, and they had recently received a shiny new coat of thick varnish. Ruth chipped at the wood, barely managing to draw a short diagonal line, before measured footsteps sounded in the hallway.

As students now dashed this way and that, Audrey considered how sure she had been, so many years ago, that she would fit in here. She had been destined an Eliot girl well before becoming an Eliot girl. Now life was going on everywhere around her, but she was shut out of it. She could locate no entry point, and although she had never been more anonymous, she had never felt more conspicuous. Every glance felt like an attack.

Audrey forced herself to keep moving, to seem to have a purpose. On the second floor, she headed for the bathroom and found it empty. Facing her reflection in the long wall of mirrors, she closed her eyes and opened them again. She had imagined herself disappearing into the crowd, but it was becoming obvious that even the coveted uniform couldn't stimulate such a swift and sly metamorphosis. The clinical brightness of the bathroom did no kindness to her face. Her eyes were shadowed and bloodshot from nights of fitful sleep, her wavy hair was frizzy, her cheeks were still flushed from the walk. Anxiety had fixed her in a state of permanent, wide-eyed vacancy, as though she spent her life on the brink of unwanted revelations, perpetual astonishment her only mode.

Audrey blinked at the strange girl staring back at her. In the past month, she had grown somewhat used to looking in the mirror and failing to recognize herself. In August, vexed by every facet of her appearance, she had cut her hair. Although Audrey was forever being told she resembled her father, her long, unruly hair had been one attribute she shared with her mother, and chopping it off had been just one in a series of attempts to differentiate herself from Ruth. The change had been meant to help her grasp some new, defining image, but all it had accomplished was to make her feel more alien in her skin. She thought that feeling less like herself would help set the tone for this new chapter in her life; it would catapult her into the role she was preparing to play. But she missed being able to hide behind the plenty of her old hair. Too much was her face now laid bare. Her features, she was sure, took up an excess of space against too pale a backdrop: her olive eyes overly large, her lips inelegantly full.

She was still frowning at her reflection when the door swung open and two girls burst into the room, shattering its hermetic serenity. One girl doubled over, laughing noiselessly with her mouth wide open, while the other was alternately seized by laughter and hyperventilation. They opened the door again and the taller girl threw what looked like a mashed orange wedge down the hall.

"Oh, you are in some deep, deep *merde*! I almost pity you. I really do!" she yelled, still barely able to hold herself up under the force of her paroxysmal laughter. The orange was whipped back at her; she grabbed it and reared back like a professional pitcher and returned it down the hall.

Again the orange was hurled back by a distantly cackling phantom, and again it fell with a damp thud at the yeller's feet. This time, she stepped gingerly over it and let the bathroom door swing shut behind her.

The two girls turned at once to Audrey in the spirit of dissection. They leaned slightly into each other, their elbows touching as though they were exchanging messages with a series of nearly invisible nudges. Indistinguishable from the neck down—both uniforms were arranged in a state of conscientious chaos, the kilts a hair shorter than allowable, the Oxford shoes scuffed at the tips, the white blouses crumpled and half-tucked—the girls were otherwise a study in contrasts. The thrower of the orange gathered her brown hair into a messy bun, exposing ears dotted with tiny silver-adorned piercings, and cleared her throat. Her review of Audrey was undisguised and penetrating, and though her lips revealed no smile, her eyes twinkled, either in the aftermath of the orange throwing or in the discovery of something amusing in Audrey's bearing. The other girl, neck stiff and arms folded, a single blonde braid hanging tidily over her shoulder, took in Audrey more coldly, as though she had long since conducted her appraisal and discarded the subject.

"What grade are you in?" asked the dark-haired girl.

"Ten," replied Audrey. "You?"

"We're in grade six!" she answered in a shrieky falsetto meant to sound childlike.

She skipped towards a cubicle and paused before going in.

"God, it's the first day, and already this bathroom reeks of shit."

Audrey's nose had picked up nothing other than the overpowering antibacterial smell of industrial cleaner, but she knew that she must be the prime suspect in the creation of any fecal odour and that the smell, even if fictitious, was as real as they chose to believe.

The girls stepped into cubicles simultaneously, then locked the doors and dropped the seats of the just-cleaned toilets, their earlier titters resurfacing.

"Listen, Whit, listen," came the voice from the dark-haired girl's cubicle. "Your pee is soprano and mine's alto.

They listened without laughing for a second.

Then came the voice again. "Whit, you have, like, the opera singer of pees."

"Then yours is, like, R&B," returned the blonde. "Your pee has soul."

They flushed at the same time and emerged from their cubicles, delighted by their synchronicity. As they washed their hands, they smirked at each other's reflections in the mirror, then left without giving Audrey another glance. The second the door swung shut, they burst into laughter out in the hall.

Audrey planted her hands on either side of the sink and stared down her reflection again, enjoying the briefly empowering flicker of anger that illuminated her features. A gush of nostalgia for her old school came over her. How she missed the very featurelessness her mother had taught her to deplore. The homely serviceability of the building itself, the banana-yellow lockers and speckled linoleum floors, the smell of pot lingering in the back hallways, the worn and scratched surfaces. The harmless indifference of the crowd, its exchange of apathetic chit-chat. All the things that had inspired her scorn now kindled a spasm of sadness. It had been a forgivable offence, being a forgettable girl there.

But a good school was the key to everything. Before she even knew how to read, she was taught this essential fact of life. There was no getting around it. Here she would have to stay.

IN THE CLASSROOM, THE mood was the frantic joy of a drunk just before he spills over into belligerence. It was a madhouse of noise. Nothing so discernible as conversation was taking place. Girls were perched on desktops or standing in clusters, flooding each other with incoherent delight. As Audrey was gathering her nerve to enter, a series of hoots preceded a happy gasp, and a girl with her hair in pigtails toppled ecstatically off a desk to a swell of applause.

There came a shout from the other end of the hall and Audrey turned to see Moira Loughlin, the art teacher and a former friend of her mother's (the allegation, never voiced directly to Moira herself, was that she had become intolerably conceited since finally selling a painting and introducing the term "fan base" to her everyday vocabulary), bouncing towards her, nearly tripping over her long purple peasant skirt, tousling the asymmetrical bob she considered her trademark.

"Audrey!" she cried, clapping. "Check *you* out!" She came to a skipping halt in front of Audrey and placed her hands on her hips, nodding with exaggerated approval. "Looks like I didn't get the bulletin! So…you excited?"

Audrey smiled uncomfortably. "I guess."

"Well, you're about to become part of one heck of a group," she said, beaming into the classroom and then back at Audrey. "I can't tell you how good it is to see you here, finally."

Audrey glanced away, willing Moira to stop talking. All the effort she'd put into getting accepted at Eliot only made her feel less deserving of her spot. This was the secret, the shame she imagined written all over her. It was the blemish no uniform could hide. A girl seated just inside the doorway cast an aloof gaze out at them. Audrey tried to judge how much of the exchange she might have heard.

"I kept reassuring your mom that you'd show that Ms. McAllister what you were made of when you were good and ready. She may have been worried, but I never was, not for a second." She thumped her hand insistently against her chest, drawing attention to the creased, sunburned cleavage visible through the unbuttoned front of her oversized denim shirt. Suddenly, a thunderbolt seemed to rip through her body, and she exclaimed, "Suze!" Her eyes leapt to the girl just inside the door. "Did you have a good summer?"

"Awesome," said Suze lifelessly.

"You been taking your sketch pad with you everywhere, like we talked about?"

"Absolutely!" Suze replied, her voice now dripping with sarcastic enthusiasm that seemed to escape Moira, who continued to smile with uncontainable pleasure.

"Will you do me a favour, kiddo?" asked Moira, now gripping Audrey's shoulders and shoving her in the direction of Suze. "You take care of my friend here. It's her first day, and we all know how those can be."

Offering an apologetic half smile, Audrey allowed herself to be foisted on the reluctantly rising Suze, and they stood there staring at each other helplessly until Moira, happy with her matchmaking, finally retreated. Upon Audrey's entry, the room went instantly quiet. A funeral procession of two, Audrey and Suze made their way slowly across the front of the room under the now-whispering scrutiny of the surrounding girls.

"You can sit there, I guess," offered Suze, biting her thumbnail while listlessly gesturing with her head at a pair of unoccupied seats. "Most of the seats are taken. The thing is, like, pretty much everybody has planned already who to sit with."

"This is okay," said Audrey, setting down her knapsack.

Suze nodded and, considering her duty discharged, her unfairly extracted pledge to Moira honoured, retreated sluggishly to her own desk. There, still chewing on her nails, she became embroiled in an intense, low-voiced conversation with her deskmate.

As Audrey sat and began to unpack her bag, there came from the hall a stampeding sound, and the two girls from the bathroom burst in, dancing around the front of the room in a frenzied tango. They twirled each other like drugged ballerinas, then finished with the blonde lowering the brunette into a low and wobbly dip.

"My unmentionables!" she shrieked. "Everyone will see my unmentionables!"

"Your unmentionables get mentioned pretty often," replied the blonde. "Especially at St. George's."

Bunches of girls scattered around the front of the room made an appreciatively hysterical audience.

"Oh, oh! The bitterness! And not even nine o'clock!" said the brunette, pulling herself up. "Don't worry, Whit, there's someone for everyone. Some guys like girls with dicks."

As Audrey watched them, the hazy alarm of the preceding weeks came into focus. She had never been good at this brand of teasing. Nor was she the adult teen, precociously challenging her teachers on the finer points of various philosophical or political ideologies. At her former school, she had once sat in glazed awe as a fellow student engaged the history teacher in a half-hour debate about whether the roots of communism and fascism were ultimately the same.

But the kind of safe vacancy she had relied on before wouldn't go over at Eliot. There was more to life, surely, than the fear of being embarrassed. Ruth was forever telling her that now was her chance, and though the precise character of this chance was never articulated, Audrey sensed that her mother was talking about a lot more than education. It was a matter of reinvention. No one knew her at Eliot. A new life, a new identity, seemed almost to be within her reach. Now was her opportunity to be something other than herself. She could choose to be more than the girl who sat quietly in the middle of the room. The difficulty was that the means of creating the delicate details of that persona were as murky as ever.

With five minutes remaining before the bell, the dancing girls began to lead a crew of others in the creation of a list of cryptic reasons grade ten was to be the most awesome year yet. After deciding amicably upon number ten, "Après-school aerobics with you know who," the group was now fighting over number nine. Audrey was pretending to have some important matter at hand in the bottom of her knapsack when a voice from above offered an enthusiastic, "Hey!"

Audrey looked up with wary hope. Leaning towards her with an intimacy that suggested long acquaintance was a petite girl smiling so assertively that her presence commanded the space between them and bestowed the illusion of considerable height. She asked if Audrey minded if she took the seat beside her, and entrapped by her own politeness, Audrey nodded weakly. The girl set a shiny black briefcase on the desktop and snapped it open as she settled herself. From its organized interior she drew a Ziploc bag of dried apricots, which she offered to share. "I'm Seeta!" she said, digging apricot out of a molar with her tongue. She extended a hand, which Audrey stared at in momentary confusion, never having had someone

37

her own age suggest shaking hands. "Are you new here too?" Seeta asked.

Audrey nodded, glancing away. She tried to project a certain distractedness, not wanting to engage too fully with this new seatmate. (Was it really settled then? Was this to be her lot for the rest of the year?) She supposed there should be some comfort in the neighbouring desk not remaining empty, but emptiness at least meant possibility, whereas this felt shatteringly like the end of possibility. Futures were decided in a split second. Alliances, even if unwillingly formed, were hard to shake.

The one-sided conversation that followed confirmed Audrey's gloomiest suspicions. With the volume, both of voice and gesture, of someone wanting very much to be noticed, Seeta offered a detailed comparison between George Eliot Academy and her old high school in Scarborough. There was very little about this old school that didn't inspire her derision, from the perpetual smell of egg salad in the classroom to the buffoonish males who insisted on taking over every class with their stupidity: "I mean, how could any person over the age of twelve not know what existentialism is?" Taking in her surroundings with rapturous glances, she marvelled in her escape from that hell of mediocrity. "At least everyone knew I was a serious scholar," she said. "No one bothered me."

She might have been pretty, had there not been so many elements of her appearance that defied prettiness. Her black hair was thick and shiny, but greasy at the roots, and so long it reminded Audrey of a horse's tail. In the corner of her eyes was a dusting of sleep. Her full lips were slightly chapped. As her monologue continued, her tone grew somewhat shrill in proportion to her escalating enthusiasm, and she began to draw the attention of girls seated nearby. The general consensus seemed to be that ignoring her would be safest, but she proved difficult to ignore. Her roving eyes sought the other girls out, and she aimed a forceful smile of good cheer at anyone whose gaze drifted towards her. Glances were exchanged behind her head, but she noticed nothing.

Finally, she stopped talking and let out a long sigh, as though her outrageous admiration of everything in sight had exhausted even her. "I'm sorry," she said. "I completely forgot to ask your name."

Audrey unwillingly released the information.

"It's fate, then! *Breakfast at Tiffany's* happens to be one of my favourite films."

Audrey's stomach made a screeching sound like a car racing around a bend.

"What was that?" cried Seeta, looking around excitedly.

The second bell rang then, and the stragglers in the hallway rushed in and took their seats, followed by the homeroom teacher, who would shepherd the class to assembly. The day was just beginning, but Audrey had a bad feeling that something had already been decided.

Chapter Three

THE ENDURING MONOTONY OF the morning staff meeting was one of Ruth's most reliable pleasures. In that half hour were housed the only mindless minutes of her day. As announcements got underway and handouts were distributed, Ruth sank into a quasi-attentive trance, grateful to be cradled in others' more competent palms. Nothing was required of her but to listen, or to appear to listen. She could be the audience rather than the guide, the student rather than the teacher. In her many years at the school, she had never ceased to be uplifted and amazed by the elegant proficiency of the machine of Eliot running around her.

But on this morning, as she headed to the staff room, her body resisted the usual decompression. Anxiety about Audrey had been plaguing her from the moment they left the house. In the car, they had listened to the news and exchanged few words. Ruth had fought the urge to reach out and grab her daughter—whether to embrace her or shake her she wasn't sure. Ruth hated silence, and during that drive, even more than usual, she felt crushed by it. No words of encouragement, it seemed, could disarm Audrey's malaise.

When they had reached Eliot, Ruth let Audrey out at the base of the driveway. Her impulse was to hover, shadowing Audrey to the classroom, making introductions, but she knew that that would be the worst thing she could do. It was a kind of agony: her hopes for her daughter were immeasurably outsized by her helplessness. After they parted, Ruth parked in the lot behind the school, then doubled back to the front and took up a partially hidden post by an old oak tree so that she could observe Audrey's approach. It was a moment before Audrey came into view, dawdling up the long driveway, then weaving her way through the constellations of girls spread across the circular drop-off area. She walked without purpose, as though uncertain she was even in the right place.

Outwardly, there ought to have been little to distinguish Audrey from the other girls, but Ruth noticed, even more than she usually did, how the old-fashioned school uniform made Audrey seem as though she had stepped out of another generation. In August, she had cut her wavy brown hair into a twenties-style bob, which accentuated the elegant length of her neck. (Audrey received compliments so poorly that Ruth was reluctant to tell her this.) In the past year she had grown noticeably taller—though her posture was terrible, perhaps to compensate for her unease at this new height. Yet Ruth's heart broke at the sight of her, looking not straight ahead, but wonderingly up into the sky, as though marvelling at the clouds.

Now fifteen, Audrey was losing the unawareness that, in childhood, had given her a kind of unaffected charm. In its place had grown an almost insistent awkwardness. Ill at ease in her body, she was perpetually slouching and fidgeting, glancing away from eye contact. Ruth was sad to witness the change, though she knew that she shouldn't be surprised by it. A part of her was even grateful for it. She had always thought there was something a little vulgar about supremely confident teenagers. She could not help thinking that there was something beautiful in such awkwardness.

Audrey stood out as one of the few solitary girls. The sight made Ruth realize—she couldn't believe that she had never thought of it before—that she had rarely seen Audrey in one of those happily squealing girl groups. On the occasions that she had fetched Audrey from her former school, she would sometimes find her on the less crowded side of the school, in conference with one other girl. Ruth had interpreted the seeming smallness of Audrey's social world as her response to the chaos of the overpopulated public school. Ruth herself disliked large groups. If there were other signs of mild melancholy in her daughter, she chose to read them as the typical disaffection of adolescence. But where, then, she wondered, was the equally typical ebullience, the giddiness that descended abruptly, brilliantly, leaving girls inarticulate with outrageous joy?

At Audrey's age, Ruth had been brimming with the kind of reckless confidence that was the hallmark of happy youth. Her mother, who had made it her personal mission to extinguish the power associated with good looks, had never told Ruth that she was pretty. Ruth still remembered the moment when she was fourteen: she had glanced in the bathroom mirror and seen her face as if for the first time. The recognition was petty, yet transformative. She saw herself, then, rushing headlong into life with a spirited resolve that no one would be able to destroy. Of course she had met obstacles to her self-esteem, but that was part of the point. In her was a secret, almost furtive, fund of strength.

Ruth had never been inclined to look for herself in her daughter. When Audrey was a child, Ruth had watched her little girl picking her way around the garden singing to herself like a benevolent drunk and understood that this was why people became parents. Surely there lay the magic of creating a life. To observe the distinctness of your child was to discover the power of sorcery in yourself.

She didn't understand those parents who boasted total genetic ownership of their children's every frown and blink, assigning the son's laboured pedalling of his bicycle to the long line of maternal incoordination, the daughter's refusal to take baths to that bullish pinprick midway down the winding Y strand, until eventually their children's entire repertoire of mannerisms were conveniently done away with, checked off like items on a grocery list. Ruth had adored Audrey with the kind of fascination borne of bewilderment. Even as her fear for Audrey's vulnerability grew, Ruth couldn't fail to be stirred by the beauty her daughter so weakly, so skeptically grasped. Although her meeting awaited, she had continued to stand by the tree, her stomach in knots, after Audrey was lost within the spirited mob.

The staff room was a large rectangular room at the front of the school with two tall bay windows that overlooked the long driveway leading up to the school's entrance. Larissa McAllister had wanted the room to feel like a luxurious library, so she had furnished it with several deep red leather wingback chairs and two matching couches, as well as two heavy rectangular oak tables, at which teachers could eat their lunches or mark papers. The walls were mahogany panelled and unadorned—not for Larissa the jovial inanity of educational posters of students partaking in school activities like soccer, reading, and cooperation, colourful photographs of spirited staff events, a bulletin board bursting with outdated messages. She deplored overly personal spaces, so she had allotted one cupboard, beneath the microwave, to teacher's mugs from home and other personal kitchen effects. The refrigerator, which she reluctantly conceded as necessary, though it undermined the library effect, was tucked away in a corner where it would least interfere with the desired atmosphere.

Most of the teachers had already arrived and were criss-crossing the grid of the staff room, brightly conducting loud-voiced, far-reaching conversations about their summers. Ruth headed straight for the coffee pot. It was not yet eight o'clock, an hour she hadn't witnessed in over two months. She reached for her mug and found that the handle had broken off and a large crack zigzagged down the side. She crouched at the cupboard, at a loss for how to proceed. Years ago, Larissa had complained about the teachers bringing their own mugs from home and then showing unabashed possessiveness of them: how could her colleagues, people she admired, not understand that such attachments were infantile? Ruth had voted against Larissa's suggestion that they stock the staff room with sensible brown mugs like her own, and now she regretted it. She scanned the shelves of mugs and settled on the plainest one, poured herself a cup of coffee, then shielded the mug with her hand as she moved to the sitting area.

Ruth sat in an armchair, slightly removed, feeling herself come back to life at the taste of coffee. Sunlight streamed through the freshly washed windows. The chatter around her was lively enough to be pleasantly indistinct. Several teachers nodded to her affably but no one seemed to expect anything of her. Ruth had known most of these colleagues for years, and their familiarity, though sometimes irksome, was a comfort on mornings like this. The feeling of being alone in company was a pleasure as timeless and unexceptional as a warm breeze across the face.

She was nearing the end of her coffee and contemplating another cup when Michael Curtis, who taught biology, stepped grandly into the seating circle, sipping water from a glass bottle. "It's so good to be back!" she exclaimed, throwing her arms out. "I had a beastly holiday!" She sank dramatically into one of the couches and began regaling her audience with stories of a horrific August cottage rental.

Michael was the most striking woman on staff, tall and regal, with long, poker-straight, enviably Asiatic hair and unfortunately low-slung breasts. She dressed in layers of black and silky jewel-toned scarves wound in voluptuous piles around her neck. Ruth had never quite recovered from the idiocy of her first words to Michael. "Oh, I always wished to have a man's name! How fashionable!" Ruth had exclaimed, a patently false and bizarrely flirtatious comment, made worse when Michael icily informed her that she had been named after a would-be older brother who had died shortly after his birth. In the intervening decade, Ruth had done her best to make Michael like her—it was a compulsion, really, nothing to do with her feelings about Michael's own likeability—and had never gotten past her disappointment in the failure of her early endeavours.

Michael was the mother of six children, three of whom were adopted, and when people asked her which (yes, rudely), she liked to say that she couldn't remember. In spite of Michael's endless stories about family horseplay and cheerful chaos, Ruth had difficulty seeing Michael as the archetypal mother. She was too bony and ungainly, too stiffly magnificent. Her main mode of social interaction was to discredit how glamorous she looked as a paradoxical way of underscoring that glamour. "Oh, our kids think we're the biggest dorks on the planet," she was always saying. "We spend our days in the mud digging for worms and looking for treasure." When she was in the room, Ruth's eyes were drawn to her, sometimes much against her will.

"Flies everywhere!" Michael was saying now. "I'm as much a friend to the winged creatures as anyone, but it was bloody ridiculous."

Michael's fondness for British vernacular when she had lived all her life in Canada had once been lambasted in a staff meeting by Larissa, who declared that she hadn't moved to Canada and dedicated her life to pedagogical scholarship to be surrounded by the vulgar slang of the Cockney proletariat.

"Did you have a good summer, Ruth?" asked Sheila Smith, the grade three teacher. She was sitting to Ruth's left, flipping through an old *Chatelaine* from the collection of ancient magazines piled in a wicker basket by the coffee table. Larissa also disapproved of the trivial content of such magazines, not to mention the grade-eight-level writing, but, in an environmentally conscious nod to the principle of reusing, she permitted their presence.

"Yes, thanks, Sheila," Ruth said. "You?"

Sheila nodded vigorously. "But I'm happy to be back."

"Of course."

"You've got to read this article, Ruth," Sheila said emphatically. "It may save your life." She signalled to what she had been reading, a piece about breast cancer. Sheila always went straight for the disease articles and, when she was finished, left them in Ruth's mailbox.

Grey was the word Ruth would have used to describe Sheila (grey hair, grey skin, even grey lips), who in a meeting during the early days of Eliot had used the word *phantasmagoric* to describe herself, prompting one of Larissa's forays into the twenty-pound dictionary installed like a hallowed, gleaming monument on a pedestal by the windows. ("Yes, our aim is to encourage lateral thinking," Larissa had said before reading aloud the definition of phantasmagoric, "but let us honour, too, the strictest accuracy. Imagination, of course, but never at the expense of meticulousness.")

It was partly because of the Sheilas of the world that Ruth had a tendency to let her hair grow too long, why she swept it up crudely into a rumpled chignon, even though she knew that such a look wasn't necessarily appropriate for work. During meetings that went long, Ruth often fell into a daze, looking around at the other teachers, and daydreamed that she had gone to the salon, fallen for the hairdresser's long-winded ramblings about a new mature look, and emerged an hour later with an overgrown bowl cut that was a page straight out of Sheila's style book. Awakening from these reveries with a jolt, she was ashamed, not by her wandering attention during work hours, but by the absurd superficiality of her imaginings. Didn't she have anything more substantial to daydream about?

As Sheila thrust the *Chatelaine* at her chest, Ruth nodded vaguely and began to rise for another cup of coffee. Then the door swung creakily open and Larissa McAllister entered the room.

"Oh!" cried Sheila. "We're on!"

Larissa shut the door firmly behind her. She felt that a teachers' staff room should be kept hidden from prying student eyes, much as a men's washroom should remain a zone of mystery to women. (She had never seen a urinal until the construction of the school had required her last-minute, on-site approval of a bathroom tile.) She offered a monarchic wave and stalked to one side of the room, her sensible, clunky pumps tapping out a marching beat that was distinctly hers. A white board draped in a black cloth was set up on the centre of the wall, and she stood next to it in her speech-giving stance. The air around her was charged with her severe ardour for Eliot generally and for meetings specifically, and with the stamina of her unchanging beliefs about the education of girls. Her presence was magnetized, it seemed, and Ruth found her own gaze locked on Larissa, paralyzed almost, as though she'd been hypnotized without her consent.

Had Larissa been a different kind of woman, Ruth would have said that she was atwitter. But unlike most people, her agitation manifested itself in a robotically rigid bearing of body and head. Ruth's own hands flitted and flapped uncontrollably when she was nervous or energized, flew upwards to her hair to fix straying strands or to her forehead and cheeks to brush away imaginary irritants. Her entire body loosened, threatening to trip her, and she dropped pens, paper, even coffee mugs, for no reason. Larissa, on the other hand, became superlatively controlled, as if all her physical expressions had to be stilled, sublimated to the elaborate, leaping demands of her mind. It might have been a performance, Ruth thought, Larissa's way of capturing notice, like turning off the lights to get rowdy students' attention or lowering your voice by barely perceptible decibels until it was nearly a whisper as a response to shouting, tactics they had all been taught in teachers' college.

Larissa was dressed in an adapted version of the school uniform. This outfit was an annual first-day tradition, and Ruth couldn't help noticing that not just the idea but the clothes themselves had been carried through the decade. Larissa wore the uniform only on special occasions—the first day of school, the closing ceremonies, the rousing final performance at the Independent Schools' Music Festival—and Ruth didn't doubt that she kept it safely ensconced in plastic for the rest of the year, but still the clothes showed their age. Certainly, she had done a better job of pushing the clothes past their expiry date than Ruth could have managed: the pleats on the narrow navy kilt were expertly pressed, and the long silver kilt pin shone as if she had sat at her kitchen table the night before with an emptying bottle of silver polish at her right hand. Unfortunately, the kilt also had a sheen to it, of cheap material too long loved. The tailored grey blazer fit her as neatly as it ever had, but the school crest on a pocket over her heart needed to be re-sewn at the bottom, and the hems of the sleeves were thinning, ever so slightly, much like the great leader's hairline.

In Larissa McAllister's view, her wearing of the uniform did not diminish her authority, but heighten it. She was proud to be associated with this company of brilliant girls, not simply as their devoted leader, but as their creator. She felt that she and her pupils, attired identically, made a beautiful spectacle of democracy—leader (she sometimes wondered whether *icon* was too strong a word) and followers as one. But she felt that she was more than their creator, God-like and distant. She had brought these girls, the hundreds of them, into the world—they were here because of her vision, because she'd seen, as a child attending a grubby grammar school on the Isle of Wight, that there could be more, should be more—through her craving for something too exceptional to articulate, through an almost maternal swell of desire—although what she felt was at once grimmer and more passionate than animalistic procreative instincts could ever be. (And maternal longings were something she counted herself blessed never to have experienced.)

Larissa was nearing sixty, yet she had not aged noticeably since Ruth first met her over ten years before, probably in part because back then she had looked much older than her years, as though she had always aspired to be an ageless, sexless grande dame and had only to get past the obstruction of youth to realize her truest incarnation. The name Larissa did not suit her, was far too flowery for the shrewd, hawkish face, with its jutting chin, the slender, pointed nose, and the tight lips over which she applied a daily slash of cranberry lipstick. Ruth tended to think of Larissa in terms of her full name, but when she considered the first name alone, she felt a fleeting tenderness for the woman—the name was proof that Larissa

McAllister had once belonged to someone else, that a mother had aspired to beauty on her behalf. Even as she squirmed under that critical gaze, Ruth couldn't help acknowledging that Larissa was magnificent, in her way.

"More," Larissa declared, breaking the waiting silence of the room.

"More what?" Sheila piped up.

"That is the question, Sheila," replied Larissa, pointing at Sheila with approval. "More what?"

The high voltage in the room was making Ruth sleepy, and she yawned loudly, attracting Larissa's glare.

"'More' is to be our motto for this year, colleagues. More. More from the girls. More from ourselves. As exceptional as George Eliot Academy already is, excellence lies in constant evolution, constant pushing against predetermined boundaries. Today, I'd like us all to put our heads together to come up with innovative ideas for the coming year. You'll see in just a moment that on one half of the white board, I've compiled a list of last year's most exciting events. On the other half, I've anticipated two suggestions minimum from each staff member, and jointly we'll—"

There was a stirring then by the door, and even though she was about to whip away the black cloth, Larissa lost the attention of the room. Unaccustomed to such lapses, she looked startled and immediately stopped speaking. A man came in, shoulders hunched, dipping his head low, as though he thought he could shrink himself and enter unnoticed. An unlikely prospect, considering that he was, including the groundskeeper, one of only four male staff members. Ruth had never seen him before, not at the June cocktail party introducing the new hires, or at the widely resented, day-long summer meeting at the end of July (which Larissa referred to as "the summit"). She had heard, however, through Moira Loughlin, the art teacher, that there was talk of a late hire, a man who'd taught at the University of Toronto. But every now and then such rumours sprang up—the result of too many women in one place at one time.

And there he was, the rumour wished into reality. His attempts to minimize his presence were useless. His long lean body did not fold easily in on itself and his gangly weaving around the outstretched legs of the women on the armchairs and couches by the door only made him more conspicuous. Although he made little noise himself, a bright nebula of sound followed him as he manoeuvred: the women roused from their torpor, moving their legs to grant him a pathway, shifting nervously in their seats, whispering questions to each other or murmuring low hellos to him.

Ruth waited for the stern rebuff from Larissa, the short lecture on tardiness and example setting. She had been on the receiving end of Larissa's castigating arrows more than once and had found herself blushing like a teenager, a burning blotchy red from forehead to collarbone. Surely Larissa would be especially irritated by his timing, his interruption of the zenith of her presentation, the moment of high drama when she would unveil the white board. Better for him to halt the brainstorming, which was harder to control anyway, than the flourish of her revelation. But Larissa brightened visibly, letting her hand drop from the black cloth as she stepped away from the board.

"Henry!" she said. "You're with us at last. I hoped you would make it, but we all know how trying first days can be."

She was smiling warmly. (Could Larissa McAllister smile warmly? Ruth had seen her smile politely, had seen her smile proudly, contentedly, conceitedly, reluctantly, tightly, angrily, but never, not once, warmly.) The cranberry lipstick had faded in the middle of her dry lips, leaving only an outline around them. She advanced on Henry, shook his hand heartily, and led him to the front of the room, where he tried to shrink even more.

"Some of you know, and some of you may not, about our dear Ms. Davidson's sudden personal decision to opt for early retirement. Those reasons, of course, are highly confidential. Ms. Davidson, naturally, was extremely concerned about the terrible inconvenience caused by her change of plans. However, as luck would have it, one of our Eliot parents, Clayton Quincy, heard of our conundrum and pointed us towards her very own husband, the talented man standing at my left. I present your new English teacher, Dr. Henry Winter. We're very fortunate to get him."

Larissa was unable to stop smiling as she went on to recount at length Henry Winter's professional biography, all the way back to the academic awards he had won as a PhD candidate at Columbia University. Drawing particular radiance were his five years as a tenured professor at the University of Toronto. This was the first Eliot rumour Ruth had heard that turned out to be entirely true.

From across the room, Moira caught Ruth's eye and looked sideways towards Henry Winter, raising an eyebrow in mock lasciviousness. Henry Winter's appearance suffered from an odd duality. From the neck up, with his groomed face and freshly cut silver hair, he resembled a newscaster, but the rest of him was every bit the rumpled professor. He wore a tattered tweed blazer that looked as though it would smell musty, and beige corduroys, slightly worn at the knees. At his feet, the preppy re-emerged with a pair of well-worn Top-Siders. As Larissa rhymed off the long list of his published papers, he looked mortified, though he had surely supplied Larissa with the publications list in the first place.

Ruth wondered why anyone not ruled by some kind of perversion—self-destructiveness at best and sexual predation at worst—would leave a tenured university position for a job at an all-girls school. He looked benign enough, but wasn't that the insidiousness of such predators, their disguise of harmlessness? Ruth could imagine the author's photo on one of his tomes on literary theory (though she had always stayed well away from those books and guessed that their authors abjured the physical vanity signified by such likenesses): the wall of thick books behind him, the light from a window across one side of his face, his pensive gaze at the camera, through the camera, and the arm of his reading glasses like a piece of hay in his mouth. His eyes alone seemed to rebel against this image, as if showing up its pretensions: large and thickly lashed, baby blue.

"As remarkable as these intellectual achievements are," Larissa was saying, "what impresses me the most, as a lifelong passionate educator of young women, are Dr. Winter's reasons for leaving the University of Toronto. He grew disaffected by the university's focus on research, the pressure on professors to publish or perish, often at the expense of the blossoming minds they are there to expand. Dr. Winter seeks direct contact with the young mind. Dr. Winter wants to teach!" Here she brandished her fist as if inciting a rallying cry.

When Larissa finished speaking, several teachers immediately approached Henry to introduce themselves. Ruth could feel Sheila looking at her, waiting for her to look up so that they could share their excited reactions to the new hire. But Ruth felt an inexplicable resistance to taking part in the enthusiasm. Although lively curiosity about a new teacher was typical, the atmosphere today was notably different. The teachers were standing in small groups talking in low voices, stealing nervous glances at Henry Winter. A few tried to catch his eye, offering coy, falsely casual smiles. They reminded Ruth of the girls during school dances, trying to elicit invitations during the slow songs. Even Larissa, with her dry lips and owl glasses, her concerted attempts to seem too high-minded to care about appearance, was not immune to his maleness and treated it as an accomplishment rather than a chromosomal coincidence. The PhD heightened her exhilaration but was not the cause. Two other teachers had PhDs, and Larissa never capitulated to them or made reference to their accomplishments; in fact, she sometimes appeared to consider their extra years in academia a red flag, betraying an ugly truth: that George Eliot, rather than being the realization of their lifelong aspirations, was a comedown of sorts. Yet Larissa McAllister held Henry Winter possessively by the elbow as Michael Curtis and several others crowded in on him.

Pretending not to notice, Ruth got up and wandered over to the kitchenette for more coffee. Through the fragmented blur of her peripheral vision, she gleaned what information she could about the intruder. Larissa was shepherding him around the room, facilitating introductions, a courtesy Ruth had never seen her extend to another teacher. Larissa had also never been so accommodating of a teacher's lateness, new or not. In fact, she often unleashed her most scathing reprimands on new teachers, like an army sergeant trying to weed out the weak. Ruth didn't understand why everyone was getting all worked up. She, at least, would not be swept away by the regressive, boy crazy inanity to which the other teachers had so easily succumbed. What was all the fuss about, anyway? He had fallen from grace, clearly. Why else would his next career move have been a placement at a girls' school? Yet he was bound to think he was better than they. It wouldn't be long before he was mentioning authors they had never heard of. As far as Ruth was concerned, his presence had stolen the morning from her, from all of them. She had no wish to meet him.

"Oh, well! Six children! How about that," he was saying. He was quite tall, her sideways glance registered, and stooping slightly, as though at pains to appear understanding.

After several minutes, Larissa moved with him over to Lorna Massie-Turnbull, the music teacher, and the two male math teachers, Chuck Marostica, who was drinking from a small carton of chocolate milk, and Chip Moore, whose pointy ears and queerly sculpted goatee gave him a vaguely Mephistophelean cast. Ruth had a kind of sad affection for these men. Years ago, after hearing her mention her fondness for Toni Morrison, Chuck Marostica had given her an autographed first edition of *Beloved* for her birthday. (He had bought the book for himself when it was originally published because he loved ghost stories, but this one hadn't been quite what he bargained for.) Although Chip and Chuck had been the only males on staff for years, they tended to attract the opposite of the fevered admiration with which most staff members were now blasting Henry Winter and ate most of their lunches in a corner of the staff room while grading papers.

Not far from that group, Sheila was telling her favourite story, about how her heart had stopped once during a routine operation she'd had two years earlier. Wincing compassionately, Chandra Howard had an arm around her shoulder. Larissa and Henry swooped in at the tail end, and Larissa listened with a sour expression as Sheila circled back to the beginning for Henry's benefit.

Michael Curtis brushed past Ruth to the sink and refilled her bottle with water.

"Goodness, someone ingested a touch too much vino last night, methinks!" she said, a hand on her forehead.

"Oh, no!" Ruth replied.

"I saw Audrey earlier. Doesn't she look just darling."

Ruth smiled.

"Poor girl was like a deer caught in headlights. I am so glad she stuck with it and powered through all those entrance tests. A great lesson for her in how hard work pays off, *n'est-ce pas?*"

Ruth nodded. "That's what Richard and I were hoping. She's a bit nervous, though."

"*Bien sûr!* Henceforth begins the real work! Now, have you thought about getting her a tutor, Ruth?"

"Oh. I'm not sure."

Michael drew Ruth into the refuge of her long arm. "Make sure you keep a lookout and stay ahead of problems. I always do some sessions on study habits near the start of the year, and the girls rave about how useful they are."

Ruth tried to nod with confidence. Getting Audrey into Eliot had consumed so much of her attention that she'd spared little worry for how Audrey would fare academically once in. As Michael sailed back to the group, Ruth busied herself with pointless tasks, wiping down the counters and rearranging cleaned mugs in the dish drainer. She was rinsing out her borrowed mug when Henry Winter moved in next to her at the sink, waiting his turn to fill a mug with water.

"Hello," he said.

Ruth looked up. "Oh."

His voice was clean and deep, a 1940s radio voice that made everything he said sound more incisive than it really was. She glanced out at Sheila and her group, who were reorganizing themselves sombrely in the wake of his departure. Ruth and Henry stood uncomfortably for some moments, Henry smiling with detached affability, sipping water from the Far Side mug Sheila had lent him. He didn't introduce himself or inquire her name, and she was pondering how to extricate herself from their impasse when Michael cried from across the room, "Henry! Let me see you down to assembly!"

So he had been claimed already, it seemed. He nodded a good-bye and retreated, his hands tunnelling deep into his pockets. Tittering, the women encircled him, their laughter borne up on the air like birdsong.

Chapter Four

THE FIRST ASSEMBLY OF the year was reliably a stirring event, mobilizing the school spirit in old girls and new, but Ruth spent the length of it fidgeting, looking around the chapel for Audrey. Her own class of girls sat along the pew beside her, but she paid them little attention. Wide eyed, respectfully inhibited on this first morning of school, the girls required no management anyway, none of the shushing and stern glances, the behaviour management she so disliked, that made her feel prissy and alien to herself. It wasn't until the assembly let out, when she was on her way back across the quad, distractedly correcting the disarray of her class's line, that she saw Audrey emerging from the shadows of the chapel.

In an instant, the jittery tenderness she had been feeling for her daughter evaporated. Audrey walked alone, unmistakably apart from the girls heading in the same direction. She seemed not even to be trying to talk to anyone. In fact, her expression was vividly grumpy. Ruth stared at her, suppressing the urge to go over and say something. As though sensing herself studied, Audrey looked up and met Ruth's eyes. Ruth smiled, a small smile—it could have been meant for anyone—but Audrey's face went dead, and she hurried away as quickly as if Ruth had been reaching for her.

The trace of irritation Ruth had felt that morning in the car erupted into full being. What cause did Audrey have to be so morose? How could she expect anyone to speak to her when she had taken cover under such sulkiness? A sensation of something, guilt almost, brushed against Ruth, but she had no time to make sense of it before the head girl, Kate Gibson, sailed past with a friendly wave.

"Good summer, Ms. Brindle?"

As if to banish the cloud released by Audrey, Kate stood in the middle of the quad, glowing with the pleasure of the new year, her new position. Ruth could not help smiling widely in response. "Lovely, Kate, thank you," she said. Kate represented everything most exemplary about Eliot. In grade nine, she had arrived at Eliot with a greater disadvantage than most girls her age could fathom, yet her triumphs formed the kind of inspirational success story everyone loved. At twelve, Kate had been in a car accident that resulted in the amputation of her left arm above the elbow, but if she had ever felt frustrated by her disability, ever experienced self-pity, she had never allowed a second of bad humour to surface on her sunny, freckled countenance. Ruth watched Audrey walk away, both arms intact, and felt the urge to yank her back. *Look!* she imagined saying to her daughter. *Only one full arm!* What complaint of her own could Audrey put up against a prosthetic limb? What a lesson Kate was in patience and victory, in indestructible spirit. Moreover, she was proof that Eliot was the seat of higher minds. The girls had not ostracized Kate, they had voted for her, they had made her their leader.

Hours later, Ruth was still raw with disappointment. The drive home to the Beach was long, and she had trouble keeping her eyes on the road, though she knew the route so well she followed it mindlessly. It had been the same house on Silverbirch all these years, however little it resembled its original self. When she and Richard bought it during her pregnancy, it had been a small semi-detached at the top of a steep hill. For years, they had made only small improvements; then the old woman next door died and her errant children descended, appraising the neighbourhood and counting their money. Richard suggested that he and Ruth buy the house and make one large detached home out of the two. A trendy architect was deployed to replaced every existing wall, every known corner, with a better wall, a superior corner, yet every time she faced it, Ruth was frustrated by the lack of finesse that had gone into its design. The house looked exactly like what it was: two houses that had been joined awkwardly into one.

Closing the door behind her, she dropped her briefcase and tossed her keys onto the console table in the front hall. The keys clanged as they hit the ornate porcelain dish that served as the table's centrepiece. The disruptive noise was satisfying, a splash of cold water on the face, and Ruth had a flash of a different outcome: the compote toppled like a bowling pin. An act of carelessness so easily avoided might have been perversely gratifying. A kind of wicked fulfillment would be found in kneeling on the floor amid the jagged shards—the physical defeat of the maid-like posture, the clink as she dropped each broken piece into a garbage bag, the satisfaction of wallowing in her stupidity. The day's pleasures had fallen short of her forecast, and disillusionment brought out the anarchist in her.

The dish had been Richard's first gift to her. There had been no occasion for the offering, a fact that ought to have doubled the sweetness of the gesture but had only ever added to Ruth's bewilderment. It was an antique English compote (a term she'd never heard until he offered it), a delicate, fanciful thing. The first part was a scalloped cream bowl with intricately carved cactus lilies and vines winding around its outer wall. This bowl sat atop a similarly garlanded pedestal, around which stood three winged cupids involved in the work of making gilt arrows, each at a station supplied with tools, also gilt. When Richard had presented it, in a box wrapped in pink tissue paper, she looked to him for some sign of ironic intent, though she knew there was none. The compote was rare and expensive. That much was clear.

Over the years, Ruth's perception of the compote had changed. Still it clashed embarrassingly with her cooler antiques and still she was bored by such sincere, fastidious craftsmanship. Still she was puzzled over the wrongness of the gift, but no longer did she see this wrongness as a failing. She pictured Richard puttering around a musty antique store and picking this present in a wave of foolish bliss about their future. To be so smitten that his sense deserted him, to try so hard and be so wide of the mark—there was something endearing about the misstep. Ruth found that to imagine his innocence was to imagine her own, to conceive of herself as a gentler person than she was truly becoming.

It was out of such surprises that their life together had been born. The ordinary ways people ended up together had always needled Ruth's conviction that true love must grow out of inflammatory circumstances. She and Richard had met at a vet clinic, where Ruth was working part-time as an assistant for the summer before she started teachers' college. Their relationship had been companionable enough—in her view sorely lacking in the tempestuous ill will she associated with passion. Dinners followed by polite kisses followed by dinners followed by impolite kisses: she was certain that love ought not to develop so functionally. Their first visit to her mother's house became their true beginning, in spite of—indeed because of—the fact that it was almost the end of them.

Ruth's parents had bought one of the Playter estates in Greektown before they were fashionable and before they were called estates. Although widowed, Ruth's mother, Antonia, had continued to rattle around in the roomy three-storey Edwardian house. Ruth and Richard were removing their shoes in the octagon of the entryway when Antonia, a slim and elegant woman who still managed to look like she could beat Richard at an arm wrestle, materialized in the doorway to the kitchen, running her hands upwards through her short white hair like a child waking from a nap. "So sorry," she said. "I was just outside watching the dust in the sunlight." So began a monologue that ranged in subject from the lawyers across the street who wanted to buy her latest series of photographs (in which the conflict between Apollo and Dionysus was variously depicted in nighttime scenes from her recent trip to Brazil) to the cat across the street who had a crush on her golden retriever, and that included no one in particular, least of all Richard, who, by the time the roast chicken was served, sat in the stifling heat of the dining room dabbing at his forehead with a monogrammed handkerchief, staring blankly at his wine glass.

If Ruth had thought nothing could ruin an evening more than her mother's determination to prove how delightful she was, that was because she hadn't yet experienced Richard countering Antonia's posturing with humourlessness so impossibly extreme that Ruth wondered if it were a form of deep irony too sophisticated for her to understand. She gave him chances to prove that he was just being rebellious. She repeatedly let her leg fall against his under the table, offering opportunities for stealthy groping, but Richard kept his hands well ordered on his lap or occupied with his utensils. She went into the kitchen to fill the glass pitcher with fresh water and lemon slices, hoping that he would follow her in and accost her at the refrigerator, or at least touch her breast. To Antonia's story about moving into the neighbourhood long before gentrification was even a consideration, Richard replied that it must have been the last thing the architects had in mind, Greek immigrants right off the boat buying these grand houses. As Antonia used her fork to feed the dogs chicken scraps, Richard volunteered that his advice, as a veterinarian, was never to feed animals from the table, particularly when the dogs are already overweight.

Ruth excused herself immediately after dinner and went upstairs to her mother's room to consider how to break up with him. A short time later, she heard Richard closing the door to the bathroom across the hall. Minutes later, he appeared in the doorway and cleared his throat.

"Was this your room?" he asked. "I don't see you in it."

"It's my mother's. Well, my parents'. But my mother hasn't slept in here since my father died."

An ornately engraved Louis xv walnut bedstead with a pristine white quilt draped tidily over its high mattress took centre stage on the long wall opposite the windows. Ruth sat on the edge while Richard took in the room in long, respectful strides. She wanted to be angry at him, as she had been earlier, for being so much himself at every moment, but the sweat-moistened creases in his shirt pulled her back to sadness. She wished he weren't so correct, so conservative. She knew he was the kind of man she ought to love. Just before meeting him, she'd had a short-lived relationship with a boring man whose casual cruelty had briefly made him seem exciting. Near the end of their first date, he'd leaned over the dwindling candle on their restaurant table and told her that he loved her sexiness, the daring of it, because the horsey edge in her looks prevented her from being truly beautiful. She couldn't think that was what she wanted from Richard, but his appropriateness, his consideration, his geniality— his obese, immovable respect—were killing her.

He stopped at a Group of Seven calendar fixed at April 1985, two years earlier. "This calendar is outdated," he said instructively.

"I realize that," Ruth replied. "My father died that April. My mother won't change the calendar."

He moved towards the bed. Now he would offer the tedious apology. Now he would hover above her, reverently skirting the dead man's bed. Now he would take her hand.

"How very Miss Havisham of her," he said.

For all her notions about passion as an unruly, uninvited guest who stumbled drunkenly through the house and smashed all her best antiques, it had been a long time since Ruth had been surprised by anything, least of all her own feelings.

Then Richard leaned over her.

"I want to rape you," he whispered.

Ruth remembered lying back on the quilt, thinking, *At last*.

Through the tall windows that ran along the back of the house, she now saw Richard in the backyard throwing a ball for the dogs. Stevie and McGill raced in tandem while Marlow lay panting at Richard's feet, casting worshipful eyes upwards each time Richard stooped to pat him.

In spite of their first meeting, it had been Antonia who observed that Richard would age well. This prediction had immediately made Ruth value him more highly, for what was the use of good looks if they were just a flare, a dying sparkle? Richard had certainly been attractive as a young man, though what prevented him from being notably handsome was unclear. Perhaps he was too generic, too vague a version of the dark and handsome prototype. Or perhaps he was simply too apologetic to be striking. The problems of aging had only served him well. As a young man, his height had had an edge of lankiness that could make him look weak, but the added bulk of middle age had made him more elegant, more at ease in his frame. His extra weight was not a softness—regular morning jogs along the boardwalk kept him fit—but rather the physical solidity that suggests an inner solidity. The dashes of grey in his brown hair had the same effect of conferring dignity. He was certainly no longer the man who had given her a compote.

Outside, the late afternoon air was still heavy with the heat of the day. Richard's cheeks were flushed, his T-shirt damp at its underarms. Marlow still lay at his feet.

"Where's Audrey?" Ruth asked, pushing open the screen door.

"Upstairs. Door closed. I wouldn't dare."

Sighing, Ruth sat on a deck chair. Marlow ambled over for a pat, but the greeting he received in return was distracted. After a moment, she launched into her version of the day's events. Within seconds, Richard was shaking his head.

"What? What is it?" Ruth said

"Kate Gibson has no bearing here."

"But—"

"She's pretty and confident, and that prosthetic—"

Ruth rolled her eyes. This was not the first time Richard had been keen to point out that Kate's prosthetic was a decent double for the real thing and that, in any case, the adjustments in deportment she had to make to compensate for her missing limb lent her an against-the-odds magnificence, a worldly confidence that made her popularity inevitable—never mind the fact that, on top of Kate's own obvious charms, Eliot liked what a one-armed head girl said about its values. No matter what he said, Richard could not make Ruth accept his sour interpretation, and she was determined that her view was the one Audrey would share.

At the end of a long day, she wanted to find an ally in her husband, but behind Richard's every word trailed the history of all the disagreements they'd ever had about whether she should give up on getting Audrey into Eliot. "Let's not fight about Eliot anymore," she said.

"I don't want to fight about Eliot."

"You know I just want what's best for her. I still remember my friend Mary leaving Leaside to go to Havergal."

Richard sighed.

"And she loved telling me about how her IQ was 120. Like that was good!"

"Yes, yes."

"If my mother had let me—"

"Ruth, we've been through this."

Ruth could still conjure the outrage she felt almost thirty years earlier as Antonia, opposed to private education, tore up Ruth's acceptance letter and let it flutter into the garbage, after all the trouble Ruth had gone to, gathering brochures, taking the entrance exam, the IQ test (of which she never received the results). But she knew that the more forcefully she advanced her point of view, the more Richard would withdraw. He had already resumed throwing the ball for the dogs, a reminder that his patience was limited.

"All right, then," she said. "How was your day? What happened with the pit?"

There was some anger behind the forceful pitch that followed. The fluorescent orb went sailing over the fence into their rear neighbour's yard.

"I bought some time. Managed to convince the owner to let me board him temporarily."

"Good for you."

"It's not a solution. But he's promised to think it through."

"What I can't understand is why he wouldn't be happy just to let you find the dog a new home."

"He insists he could never forgive himself if the dog hurt someone. I think we're dealing with more of a control issue, though."

"Well, stand your ground. You're the expert."

Stevie and McGill scrabbled at the back of the yard, whimpering at the sight of their inaccessible toy, but Richard abandoned the game. Stepping up to the deck, he stood over Ruth for a moment, his head blocking the descending sun. Then he pulled her out of the chair and put his arms around her, pressing his scratchy cheek against hers. Ruth had a weird urge to laugh. She could hear it inside her head, a lunatic cackle. Her skin prickled with sensitivity at his closeness. They had not made love in a long time. Weeks, she thought. Maybe a month. She cast a backward glance at August, and then July. She could not remember sex in as long as the weather had been hot. That couldn't be right. The fact that she couldn't even remember seemed more distressing than the prospect that it had really been since spring.

He took her hand in his and regarded it contemplatively. "Your hands look just the same as when we first met."

In the dimming light, he, too, resembled his younger self. For a second, Ruth blinked out of the moment, and when she returned, it seemed no longer to be Richard who was there. Another face flickered, threatening to materialize. Flustered, she looked away, now inexplicably embarrassed to be standing so close to him.

ÀUDREY LAY ON HER back across the width of her bed, her legs dangling over the side. There was homework already, so there was procrastination already. *Oedipus rex* lay next to her on the pillow. She had opened it with the ambitious intent to read the first half by bedtime, but the pressure of that unrealistic goal caused fatigue to overtake her at the first line, and she had fallen into a dream of nothingness. She was dressed for apathy, in an old denim shirt with badly frayed elbows and the loose grey sweatpants she jogged in sporadically, when sudden disgust at her own laziness upended her in the middle of a quiet morning. The pants were a size too large, with a hole in the bottom big enough to give anyone a clear view of her underwear when she bent over. Across the rear were the patchy words "Camp Oconto," the middle and final Os of Oconto long since rubbed away. In spite of this endorsement of a hated camp, Audrey had formed a strong attachment to the ratty garment, and she had sought the pants upon arriving home from school as a repudiation of the uniform she'd been wearing all day.

Audrey's bedroom always made her feel at least a little bit like a fraud. Ruth had initiated a redesign of the room earlier that year, with the aim of obliterating all vestiges of childishness, and for six months Audrey had inhabited this superior space without ever feeling at ease. Rather than reflecting what she liked, the room reflected what she ought to like. The decor was a work-in-progress. The idea was that it would always be a work-in-progress until she left for university and set about visiting her personality on her drab residence room. Every few months, Ruth would drag her to a flea market or an antique show and urge her to take delight in the quirky treasures on display, and wasn't content to leave until Audrey had pointed out at least two items upon which her heart was set. Audrey had never actually set her heart on anything, but she learned that by watching Ruth, she could figure out which things Ruth hoped she would set her heart on. Most recently, Ruth had come upon her in a trance near a headless 1950s female mannequin and exclaimed, "I was thinking exactly the same thing!" The mannequin now posed in the corner, uncostumed, her wrists lifted demurely, and at night Audrey draped a blanket over her and tried to forget she was there.

If Audrey's new bedroom was an expression of the teenager she should have been, her old bedroom had been a reflection of the childhood she had hoped to have, with pink walls and a white canopy bed, a ballet theme throughout, even though she had never actually been interested in ballet. It was, she had to admit, an embarrassing room for a teenager, but she missed it. The high canopy bed had been replaced with an austere metal bed frame from IKEA. The walls were painted white, with the idea that they would simply be a backdrop to the collection of hangings Audrey would cull from visits to various flea markets. Above her bed hung a cracking green vintage sign that read "Fred's General Store," and on another wall a deck of 1940s vintage tarot cards were tacked up in messy rows. Ruth, on Audrey's behalf, had fallen in love with a rose-coloured 1950s Arborite kitchen table, used now as a desk, and a wall of acid-green vintage lockers, repurposed as a clothes armoire. On Audrey's behalf she had also replaced the flowery duvet with a lime-green comforter patterned with white zigzags. The bed itself, a queen also aspired to on Audrey's behalf, felt far too large to Audrey, and often at night when she stretched out her feet, she discovered cold planes of sheet, unfriendly regions where dark things might find her: spiders, or the hard, grabbing hands of the mannequin, come alive.

What a day it had been. In her classes, although little material was actually covered, it was clear from the teachers' introductions alone how far behind she was. Her mother had warned her that

Eliot was two grade levels ahead of the average public high school. Audrey couldn't even understand Mr. Marostica's simplified over-view of what they would cover in math over the coming weeks. In one particularly atrocious episode, she was forced to sing aloud by herself in music class so that Ms. Massie-Turnbull could determine whether she was an alto or a soprano. She ate lunch at her desk as quickly as she could, then fled to the library, the only place she could be alone without embarrassment, where she wandered the stacks until the bell rang.

That morning, Audrey had felt lost when she and Ruth went their separate ways at the car. A part of her had wished things could be different, that her mother could shepherd her through the day, as she had when Audrey began kindergarten. But when she got inside the school and the minutes began to pass so painfully, she began to think that she could feel Ruth everywhere, watching, pitilessly judging her performance. In the quad after assembly, the instant she had stepped out of the chapel she was jarred to spot Ruth standing in the sunlight, looking like the first Eliot girl that ever was. The red of her skirt made a striking contrast with her crisp white blouse, and her hair, freed of its ugly tortoiseshell restraint, now sheltered her face as though consciously arranged to conceal it until the perfect moment. Ruth had no need to bark out orders at her straying pu-pils or to corral them with singsong commands. Her elegant pres-ence alone seemed to draw them into her orbit. Audrey had cast her head down and tried to get by unnoticed. She had hoped to evade that gaze, so composed, so entitled. Stupidly, she had looked up too soon and been caught.

With the end of the school day came relief, but also the need for a new kind of evasion. The prospect of dissecting her day with Ruth was demoralizing. Now that they shared the common ground of Eliot, communication seemed more, not less, complex. Audrey sensed a protocol she was failing to follow. Luckily, a series of interruptions at dinner had delayed the looming discussion. Stevie had jumped up on the kitchen counter to steal some raw broccoli from where it lay cut up on the bread board, knocking a plate onto the floor in the process. Then Richard had received a call from the clinic about the care of a post-surgical dog boarding overnight. Although Ruth kept trying to find a way into the conversation, between the racket of Richard's rebuke of Stevie, the subsequent vacuuming of the mess, and the ringing phone, she had finally given up and said they would talk after dinner.

The yellow task lamp on Audrey's bedside table cast a defined circle of light on the first page of *Oedipus rex*, and Audrey turned onto her stomach in a half-hearted attempt to corral the words swimming beneath her sleepy gaze into a string of meaning. A knock came at her door. Before she had a chance to answer, Ruth entered.

"Off to a good start, I see," Ruth said.

"I can't believe there's already homework on the first day."

"This is Eliot."

"I know. But still."

"You'll get used to the rhythm of things." Ruth went over to the window seat and sat down, looking out the window. Leaning against the wall, she stretched her legs out across the length of the window like a sunbather. The languor seemed phony, though, part of a plan to present herself as unintimidating. Her purpose was evident.

"So, tell me everything," Ruth finally said with a smile.

"There's nothing to tell."

"That's impossible!" Ruth's long hair was still wet from the shower, and she was combing it with her fingers to work out the tangles. She wore a plain white T-shirt and the faded Levi's she claimed to have bought in 1985, and around her neck was the necklace she always wore, a sapphire necklace from her mother, the most ornate thing she owned and the only jewellery she ever wore aside from her slim platinum wedding band.

Audrey's disquiet shifted into a clearer shape. Like most little girls, she had always wanted to look like her mother. Lately, though, an unsettling awareness had begun to encircle this once-innocent desire. The sight of Ruth that morning in the quad had roused it. Now she was hit again. Ruth and Audrey had never much felt the imbalance of being adult and child—their relationship had always been one of conscientious equality—but Audrey was starting to perceive another force sabotaging their fragile parity. She was unable to ignore the hierarchy that attended the presence of beauty. How could they continue to talk openly when one was a beautiful woman and the other was, clearly, not on her way to becoming beautiful? And when each of them was so aware of this difference?

Ruth leaned forward brightly, waiting for the confidence she had always considered her due. But Audrey couldn't bring herself to divulge the dispiriting particulars of her day. Certainly, she longed for the catharsis that might come from confessing everything, from her vast disappointment to her fear of failure—her certainty of failure—but when she studied Ruth's face, it no longer seemed a face that welcomed confession, too much did it want for her what seemed out of reach. Confronted by Ruth's curiosity, Audrey felt a fresh rush of the burden of being the only child. People didn't realize, when they lamented the lot of such a child, that the main difficulty wasn't the lack of a sibling; it was the exposure. In the flurry of a bigger family, there would be countless places to conceal one's failures. Here, there was always Ruth, wanting too much.

Ruth rose from the window seat and got into bed next to Audrey, curling up her legs under the duvet. "Come on. It can't have been that bad."

There was no easy way of explaining how bad it had been. The truth was that nothing much had happened at all, and in that nothingness lay a bleakness impossible to evoke. In the days leading up to school, Audrey had imagined so many scenarios of failure that she had grown accustomed to waking in the morning under a cloud of ill-defined alarm. But she was learning now that disaster wasn't necessarily acute and conclusive. It didn't have to be a fall over a cliff. It could stretch over a long and twisty scenic road, with a landscape of unexpected hills and turnoffs, but a desert's interminability.

Audrey knew that her despair was out of all proportion. It was just one day. It need not represent all the ones that would follow. But for so long she had believed that Eliot would launch her real life. How could she square herself to the lunacy of her prodigious expectations? She had longed for nothing short of a baptism.

Never had she understood how hostile indifference could feel. Except for Seeta Prasad and the laughing girls in the bathroom, no one had talked to her. From assembly in the morning, through lunchtime, to that final bell: not a word. At her old school, she'd had friends to eat with and sit next to in class, a small cluster of girls inside which she was sheltered from the hurtling noise in the hallways. How she now regretted the meagre investment she'd made in those friendships, so certain had she been that a more dynamic life lay ahead of her at Eliot. Stripped of that social buffer, she was astounded by how everything could get at her. The laughter was almost unbearable. It hadn't been directed towards her yet, not that she knew, but the sound of it, the suddenness, knocked the air right out of her. In moments, she had felt she might go crazy as it closed in, engulfing her without including her, the dissonant frenzy of it.

"I can't explain," she said.

"What's to explain?" Ruth asked. "Just tell me what happened."

Audrey let her eyes go in and out of focus on the page of *Oedipus rex*. "No one talked to me," she said at last.

"Not one person?"

"I guess the other new girl."

"Well, that's not no one."

"You haven't seen her."

"Is she ugly?"

"No, not exactly. It's hard to explain."

"Well, don't be so picky! You're making up your mind too quickly. About everything. More people will talk to you. That I can guarantee."

The optimism in Ruth's face only made Audrey feel more glum. She wanted to be happy, to retain her faith in that future whose details were so hazy as to constitute little more than a romantic vapour, but she supposed that she had also always seen her unhappiness as essential, even protective. To exist in a mild state of gloom was to stave off a deeper melancholia. How awful it was to hope for too much.

"Arriving in grade ten, I think it's just … it's too late for me," Audrey said.

Ruth took a handful of Audrey's hair and shook her head playfully. "Listen to your mother! Kate Gibson didn't start until grade nine. Would I have sent you to Eliot if it hadn't been the best thing for you?"

Audrey stared intently at the diagonals on her duvet, willing the tears away. Over the blanket, Ruth put a hand on Audrey's knee and looked away, as though reluctant to witness such a moment. "I promise you," Ruth said. "You're going to love Eliot so much, you'll forget you ever felt this way."

But for the first time, Audrey's future was not a pretty delusion, not a utopia peopled according to her brightest thoughts, but rather a reality standing darkly in front of her. And it no longer mattered what Ruth had to say about it.

Chapter Five

THE FOLLOWING WEEKS AT Eliot unfolded for Audrey in much the same way as the first day. Like a dying watch, she kept falling out of time: lagging imperceptibly, then noticeably. All of a sudden, like a watch reset, she would land back in the present, dazed by the sudden travel, but within minutes she was lagging again, the battery still failing. Normalcy was descending—the perpetual excitement of the girls had softened, the rigours of study asserted themselves—but for Audrey there was little pleasure in the warm tedium of routine. Each day was a locked vault. She could find no way to get inside.

Life at Eliot demanded a new language. It was this, perhaps, more than anything, that made Audrey certain her exile would be an unchanging condition. Sometimes she could barely understand what was being said around her. This defiant new syntax—built on inside jokes and scornful hyperbole, the unrelenting rhythms of mockery—was so puzzling that she thought it must be no less hard to decipher than Mandarin. Audrey tried to smile good-naturedly as the words flew past her. She hoped to give the impression of a kind of den mother affection, as though her exclusion were a choice she had made, stemming from maturity rather than cluelessness. At the most basic level were the popular words—*la toilette* for bathroom;

danke schön for thank you; "rad," used ironically, as a throwback to the eighties; "scruff," invented by the most popular girl in the class, Arabella Quincy, to convey a messy, unattractive feeling.

Even more mystifying than the vogue words was everything that wasn't expressed directly, the cryptic outcries and varieties of laughter. Audrey was often certain, when she heard a muffled snicker coming from behind her, that she was the subject of mockery —perhaps there was something in her hair, or she had mispronounced a word when called on by a teacher, or she had offended in some way far more abstract and therefore beyond the bounds of correction.

On a rainy Monday morning, the first in October, Audrey half-ran across the quad and took her seat in the chapel. As she squeezed the droplets of water from the ends of her hair, all the talk around her was of the second period math quiz, the first test of the year. Most of the girls claimed to be certain they would fail and were desperately quizzing each other in the hopes of gleaning some key piece of last-minute information. A girl named Vanessa Blair had been brought to the verge of weeping by her faith in her own inadequacy. The girls sitting on either side of her put their arms around her and murmured assurance, but she was inconsolable.

Audrey was trying to ignore all of it. She knew she would do abominably on the test—there was no doubt, no encouraging margin of uncertainty. Every week, she fell further behind. All she wanted now was quiet. The chapel was her favourite part of the school. Although its uses were mainly secular—the Anglican prayers and hymns during assembly were ceremonial flourishes rather than expressions of religious feeling—it resembled a miniature Gothic church and felt to her like the most sacred place she had ever been. During assembly, she was as relaxed as she ever got at Eliot. She was free, finally, to be just a spectator. Observation had never struck her as a particularly debasing activity until recently. Everywhere the class went, she watched from the fringes, feeling like a salivating voyeur peering into a bedroom window. In chapel, though, nothing was expected of her. There were no conversations she should be having, no answers she should know. It was the only place where she was able to recapture her old reverence for Eliot, the memory of the magic it had once held.

When the chapel was nearly full, everyone seated, there were some moments of waiting during which something seemed to be happening offstage, and then the person who bounded out was not Ms. McAllister, but Ms. Massie-Turnbull. For some minutes she fussed with the microphone until finally, unable to adjust it adequately, she withdrew to the darkened side of the chapel, then reappeared carrying a stool, which she clambered onto and kneeled atop, finally at the microphone's height. Ruth had told Audrey that Ms. Massie-Turnbull had been a gifted jazz singer in her youth, a story that summoned a vixenish sophisticate difficult to reconcile with the woman who perched before the assembly now, so tiny she might have been mistaken from behind for a child, dressed in a pink sweater emblazoned with a needlepoint white cat, one of whose button eyes dangled from a loose thread.

Ms. Massie-Turnbull now clasped her hands in delight and embarked on her yearly explanation of the morning music program. She was so happy to see everyone, she said. When she looked at the Eliot girls, she couldn't help seeing not just their faces, but the multitude of beautiful voices. Summertime was lovely but left her at a bit of a loose end. Being a choir mistress with no choir to direct, she submitted, was a bit like being a prime minister without a country, a policeman without criminals, a chauffeur with no passengers, forced to drive the limo around and around in aimless circles in a parking lot. A single voice was all well and good—she hoped they had kept their voices exercised during the humid summer months—but a choir? A choir was a testament to unity and individualism, to formality and collaboration. True fellowship was found through the process of harmonizing, the soprano melody ("But we don't let them get all the glory," she laughed) strengthened by the complementary alto.

As everyone knew, she continued, a key part of the school's music program was the musical prelude performed by a student as everyone arrived in the chapel for assembly. Every year, she made it her business to ferret out the students who took private piano lessons and recruit them to perform a piece before chapel each morning. This was not, Ruth had already warned Audrey, a job with status. Performances tended to consist of Royal Conservatory minuets and sonatinas played stiffly, with all the joy of detention attendance. The extracurricular obligation was strong, however, and performers were rewarded with points for their school houses if they played several times a month. There were four houses in all—Balmoral, Chiswick, Harewood, and Leighton—and the one that had amassed the most points by the end of the year won the house cup. At Eliot, the pressure to serve the collective was fierce, stronger than the warring impulse to serve the self, and in convincing Ms. McAllister to allot three points per performance, Ms. Massie-Turnbull revealed in herself a streak of savvy that belied her seemingly childlike enthusiasm.

Her fingers fluttered nervously as she announced that this year, there was to be an exciting addition to Eliot's musical landscape. She didn't want to say too much—she would let the music speak for itself—but she knew that the students would be as enraptured as she was by what they were about to witness.

It was then that Seeta Prasad strode out onto the platform, carrying a guitar case. When she reached Ms. Massie-Turnbull, she set the case, which was covered in peace symbols and stickers bearing political messages such as "My Canada Includes Quebec," on the ground and hiked up her knee socks, while Ms. Massie-Turnbull placed the stool in front of her. As Seeta climbed onto the stool and tuned her guitar, Ms. Massie-Turnbull retreated to the side of the platform, where she stood wringing her hands like a mother at a child's piano recital. In her face was an illumination like none the students had ever quite seen: it was hope allowed finally to admit its imagined zenith, the seizing of potential, fantasies of a quest undertaken and followed to its golden climax. A guitar act on the chapel platform. Instead of stilted classical notes, a fevered, though tasteful, rock performance. An unprecedented rejuvenation of the morning musical scene.

Seeta smiled fondly at her audience and said that before she began, she'd like to offer a few words about what the guitar had meant to her life.

"I think Jimmy Page summed it up as only he could," she said. "He said, 'I always thought the good thing about the guitar was that they didn't teach it in school.'" She winked in the direction of the teachers. "No offence, Ms. McAllister."

Audrey felt a bolt of terror bound through her. Indeed, if all in the grade ten class were not initially appalled by the sight of Seeta onstage, even the most open-minded among them felt their goodwill falter when Seeta began to discuss her spiritual journey with her guitar. A physical tension spread along the row, a shift towards the vigilance of perfect posture, as Seeta bowed her head in a private smile and went on to describe her soul's awakening to the paradise that lay in the strings of an instrument, her soul's belief in the heaven-bound supremacy of guitar music, her soul's search for the musical destiny that was a world unto itself, the generally unshakable marriage of guitar to soul.

She told of how her father presented her with her first guitar on her twelfth birthday, how he had said, "Never abuse it, Seeta. It will be your friend in good times and bad." And when she described how her father left her alone, then, in her bedroom, the speech enveloped the entire class in her shame, as she recounted in luxurious detail her fingers' exploration of her first, very own guitar.

"My fingers were shaking because I couldn't believe what was finally happening to me. I wanted to go slowly, but another part of me just wanted to go ahead and do it, to pick it up and give it all I had. But I didn't know what I was doing, so I just traced my finger along the neck. I was so nervous, touching the nut, it was like I was afraid I was going to press too hard and break it, but then I gained courage because it felt so right. I got to know every ridge and crease as I moved down to the body and held its curves in my hands. It was like nothing I had ever experienced. My father came back half an hour later and I was still running my fingers all over the neck and the body, and he said, 'What are you waiting for? It's not going to hurt.'"

Recalling this, she laughed.

"And it didn't hurt either, once I got going. Well, actually, it did hurt my fingers a little. But practice made it easier, until I finally felt I knew what I was doing. I want to share some of that with you, my new friends."

Her selection of song—Simon and Garfunkel's "Feelin' Groovy"—did not help matters. Nor did it help matters that she was highly musical to the point of becoming oblivious to her surroundings. Hers wasn't a voice that sought to impress with power. It seemed almost to be a natural extension of her speaking voice. In its higher registers, rather than becoming shrill, it opened up, pure and pretty. With earnest ardour and a lighthearted tossing of her head, Seeta made her way through "Feelin' Groovy." Every now and then, she would stop strumming so that she could snap her fingers and jiggle her head amiably. At one point during the song, she stopped playing altogether and incited her schoolmates to *Get up and feel it, feel the music,* as she clapped a beat with both arms above her head. When she came to the line "I'm dappled and drowsy and ready to sleep," she enacted with lilting eyelids and a coy smile what it might look like to be dappled and drowsy. And when she sang, "Life, I love you," she looked choked with happiness. The problem was that Seeta did seem to be feeling groovy, far too groovy for anyone of sound mind to admit.

When she finished, she held her hand to her heart and mouthed, "Thank you, thank you," as if answering to a standing ovation rather than to a smattering of applause and Ms. Massie-Turnbull's clear, measured claps.

As Ms. McAllister took to the platform to read a prayer, Seeta, flushed with delight, took a seat at the far end of Audrey's row. There was a slight, reluctant shift in bodies to accommodate her. She balanced on the edge of her seat, looking restlessly around, as if waiting for the deluge of congratulations. When she caught Audrey's eye, Audrey looked quickly away. Audrey was as mortified as if she had been singing herself. The misfortune of ending up seated next to Seeta struck her as freshly catastrophic.

After the final hymn had been sung—with even less feeling than usual, a possible compensation for Seeta's ardour—Seeta stood and held her guitar to her chest as students began to file outdoors.

Arabella and her best friends, Whitney Oke and Katie Douglas, spilled out into the aisle behind her.

"Hey, Seeta," Arabella said. "Are you going to Scarborough Fair this weekend?"

"Oh," Seeta replied, stopping. "Um. I'm not sure."

"I'm definitely going!" Whitney exclaimed in a singsong voice. "So awesome. You can get all these cool things. Like parsley, sage, rosemary, thyme."

Katie Douglas was giggling too convulsively to speak.

"Okay, good, well, have fun." Seeta was frowning slightly.

What Audrey felt then was not compassion for Seeta or dislike of Arabella—she knew that she might well have wished for some waiting fund of morality, but she was too busy worrying about herself, and besides, you couldn't rage, not really, against the inevitability of this—but what she did feel was a longing for escape. Not to the far past or the distant future, or to somewhere else entirely, but back to the time when she had simply wanted to be an Eliot girl. How curiously pleasurable it had been, to see and hear things so indistinctly.

THAT SAME AFTERNOON, RUTH was getting ready to head outside for playground duty when word came that Ms. McAllister had called an emergency after-school meeting.

"Do you know what's going on?" she said to Sheila in the hall.

Sheila was fussing with the placement of the black beret on her head. "Haven't heard!" she said.

"Well, I'm not sure I can make it. It's such short notice."

"Yikes," Sheila replied with a wince. "Larissa said it's essential that all staff be present. If you're a no-show, you better have a darn good reason."

Ruth did not have a good reason. But she was sure that Larissa owed the teachers reasonable notice if she wanted them to stay past the workday. She was tired. In her first years at Eliot, she had drifted through weeks, months, in a haze of giddy idealism, barely aware of work as work, barely aware even of the passage of time. The Christmas holidays would arrive when it seemed autumn had just begun. Back then she had walked home from work every day so that she could work off the skittish energy that was the after-effect of her enthusiasm. Now she felt panicky at the thought of having to make it through the evening at home without the post-work catnap she'd been promising herself all afternoon.

Most of the teachers were already waiting when Ruth arrived with a tea from the café around the corner. She took a seat by the windows, away from the main sitting area, next to a cluster of glazed-looking Senior School teachers, though it was probably wiser to stand. During last period, she had felt her eyes drooping while her students completed a math worksheet. Sheila was sitting on one of the couches talking chirpily to Lorna Massie-Turnbull, as though greatly invigorated by the prospect of a meeting. When she saw Ruth, she beckoned with her head, but Ruth gestured to the heavy briefcase on her lap with a helpless shrug, to indicate that its weight had her somehow pinioned to the chair.

Chuck Marostica slid into the chair next to Ruth's and offered a kind of smile-grimace combination. "Ruth."

"Hi, Chuck."

"Long day."

Ruth nodded.

"I hear that…" Speaking slowly, he broke off to rub his knees firmly with both hands. "So—Audrey…"

Chuck Marostica's nervous half sentences were sometimes endearing, but not now.

"Audrey?" Ruth smiled impatiently.

"I'm concerned about the results of her first quiz. She has a really weak grasp of trigonometric ratios."

"Oh."

"Have you thought about getting her a tutor?"

"I was hoping she wouldn't need one."

Chandra Howard, who sat on Ruth's other side, looked over with a sympathetic smile.

Chuck scratched his head. "It's probably best to...I'm sure Audrey could benefit. Get on the need sooner rather than later."

Ruth tried to look appreciative of the advice. "I'll look into it."

"How long will this meeting last, do you guys think?" asked Chandra. "I need to pump."

Chandra Howard, a Senior School biology teacher whose maternity leave had ended over a year ago, was the mother of two children, aged two and four. It was said that she was still breastfeeding both of them. Ruth knew little of her but often heard her bragging about how sleep-deprived she was. And she did, indeed, look perpetually bedraggled and virtuous, with her canvas Big Carrot bags and her unkempt hair, which was overrun with coarse and kinky grey strands.

"Not long, I'm sure," replied Elaine Sykes, a young chemistry teacher who was sitting on Chandra's other side, patting Chandra's knee.

"I only got three hours of sleep last night," Chandra said.

"Insomnia?"

"Wouldn't that be a luxury! No, if it wasn't Sienna wanting to eat, it was India. Just one of those nights."

Elaine stuck out her bottom lip. "What if Gus gave them a bottle of milk so you could sleep longer?"

Chandra fixed her with an appalled stare. "Would you feed kangaroo milk to a baby elephant?"

"Well," said Elaine, looking confused. "No."

"It's all worth it, though. Isn't breastfeeding the greatest thing in the world, Ruth?"

Ruth had barely been listening to the conversation, so busy was she worrying that Audrey would refuse more tutoring, but she snapped to attention at the sound of her name.

"Oh. Yeah!" Ruth paused. "Actually, I only breastfed for a few months."

"Ohh," said Chandra, her voice falling. "Breastfeeding can be really hard for some people. You have to really keep at it."

Elaine nodded in agreement.

"I know this mom who had so much trouble breastfeeding her first child that she just gave up, and of course she was devastated. And then her second came along a year later, and nothing could have been easier. So the older kid, who's no fool, says, 'Hey, I want some.' And Sue said it was just like a light bulb went off for her. She said, 'What the hell,' latched her toddler back on, and breastfed both kids for another two years. I thought that was such an inspirational story."

"Did you know that breastfed children have higher IQs?" said Elaine. "Isn't that something?"

Ruth let out a clumsy, honking laugh. "Well, then, I suppose I have only myself to blame that Audrey's doing so poorly in math!"

There was an awkward silence, and Chandra and Elaine looked uncomfortably at each other. Ruth turned to Chuck Marostica and sheepishly muttered, "A tutor is a really good idea, Chuck. Thanks."

Some minutes later, Ruth was thankful to hear Larissa's approach. She stalked into the room, flicked the lights on and off, and promptly announced, "The flasher is back."

The response Larissa was hoping for—a collective gasp, the stirrings of shock and concern—was diluted by the way the teachers were spread out across the room. Several guiltily muffled snickers issued from various corners. Larissa's habit—a consequence of what Ruth thought of as the theatricality of the severe—was to follow such major announcements with silence, in which she basked until someone asked for more information. She finally got the response she wanted from Michael Curtis, who raised her hand and asked in a stricken voice whether the police had been alerted.

"Of course," said Larissa. "As soon as I heard of the incident from a parent this morning."

"When I think of my own wee ones ..." Michael said, staring despondently into the middle distance.

"The police," Larissa said, "are taking this very seriously."

Few others, however, seemed to be. No one was genuinely afraid of the flasher, except Larissa, who carried pepper spray in her purse. (Ruth said to Audrey and Richard later, at dinner, "Of course she's petrified. She's never laid eyes on a penis. Which, of course, she can only bring herself to refer to as a 'member.'" "As in, an upstanding member of the community?" Richard responded, making them groan.) The flasher was said to be in his mid-forties, grey haired and balding, pudgy. He wore a tan trench coat (with a poppy, apparently, around Remembrance Day), and he kept a respectful distance, so that in the end no one had ever gotten a good view of what he was so compelled to show off. Ruth felt that he was harmless, ultimately. There almost seemed an element of play about it, though she knew that thinking such a thing was naive, that this exhibitionism had something much darker at its core. There was a true danger of these displays escalating.

The students also found the flasher funny and considered it a badge of honour to be selected as his victim. Those who had actually been flashed basked in fame for weeks afterward. "Watch out for the flasher!" the girls called to each other when they set out in the direction where he was known to loiter, on the pathway that ran beside the fence on the school's western border. Ruth understood their perverse fascination, the warped pride of the chosen ones. Larissa, however, was furious when she got wind of the flasher's actions being taken lightly.

"So the question is, what can we do to keep our girls safe?" Larissa said, passing around handouts summarizing the flasher protocol. The teachers were to alert their classes to the threat and make clear the importance of notifying an adult if the flasher struck. Girls walking home must be always in pairs. Portable music devices, an impediment to hearing, were to be banned. It was essential that the students understand that the flasher was not a joke.

Sheila nodded vigorously as she reviewed the handout. "Pairs, I like that. That could be a truly impactful solution."

Ms. McAllister stopped moving suddenly, as though someone had unplugged her internal wiring. Then she marched over to the dictionary and read aloud the definition of *impact*, and the list of its legitimate derivations. "This is the second time I have heard you employ the word 'impactful,' Sheila," said Larissa. "'*Cuiusvis hominis est errare, nullius nisi insipientis in errore perseverare.*' 'Anyone can err, but only the fool persists in his fault.'"

Sheila nodded again, this time in perplexed shame, studying her handout.

"If I may ask," said Michael, raising her hand. "Who was the victim?"

"Deborah Fields."

Michael shook her head. "That poor, darling girl." Always quick to appoint herself the mouthpiece for thwarted female justice in the world beyond the Eliot enclave, Michael stood now and gathered the teachers to her with an embracing, outraged stare. "Imagine simply being on your way home from school in broad daylight and being accosted by the sight of a stranger's dangling phallus. Although God knows dangling is certainly preferable to the alternative."

Henry Winter, Ruth noticed now, was sitting near Michael, listening with apparent interest as she spoke. Ruth had hardly seen him since his introduction in the staff room, though she had nearly crossed paths with him just the other day in the parking lot. She had been applying lipstick in her rear-view mirror when he pulled in next to her in his car, a beaten-up old black Saab with a dented door and red duct tape where the glass was missing from one of the brake lights. Through her peripheral vision, Ruth saw him register her presence, and after he locked his door he paused for a moment between the cars, possibly waiting for her to get out and accompany him into the school. Wanting to avoid early morning small talk, she had pretended to rummage around for something in her briefcase until he disappeared. On her way into the school, she noticed on his car a bumper sticker that said, "My other car is a bicycle." She was surprised, having failed to detect in him any environmental zeal.

"How dare men use their genitalia as a threat. A weapon of intimidation." Michael's voice had fallen to a haunted, impassioned hush. "It's sickening. I remember back in my single days how awful it was never having a moment's peace when I was out with my girlfriends. Men constantly interrupting. Pushing themselves into our conversations. Insisting upon buying me drinks. Sitting on bar stools with their legs spread wide, thrusting their groins at the world."

Demoralized at the recollection, she sank to her seat and Lorna Massie-Turnbull patted her shoulder.

"Don't worry," said Larissa. "We'll get this bastard."

A delighted, nervous titter rose up from her audience. Larissa was known for reviling curse words as the lazy man's mode of self-expression.

"Let's see how brave he is then," put in Chandra Howard.

Larissa made a lengthy note on her clipboard, then looked sharply in Ruth's direction.

"May I ask why you are smiling, Ruth?"

Ruth's gaze had been fixed on the handout in her lap. The more she had tried to tell herself that the situation was not humorous, the sillier it had seemed. She had tried to imagine Audrey being a victim, how upset she would be, but all she could think of was how they would laugh about it together. She was sure that teenagers weren't permanently scarred by that kind of thing.

"Was I?" Ruth answered. "I'm very sorry, Larissa. Something else entered my mind."

"I'm sorry this news fails to hold your attention."

All the teachers had turned around in their seats to look at her.

"I'm sorry, Larissa. It was a momentary lapse. I assure you that I'm just as concerned about the flasher as you are." Ruth bowed her head to convey her shame, and as the meeting drew to a close she remained in her chair, unmoving, as though held down by the lingering weight of the reprimand.

As Larissa withdrew to the side of the room to discuss the morning's musical program with Lorna Massie-Turnbull, some teachers rose from their seats, stretching with a somewhat post-coital contentment. Chandra and Elaine began conversing in hushed tones, making Ruth suspicious that they were talking about her. In the centre of the seating area, Michael, flanked by Henry and Sheila, was animatedly describing her methods for training her children not to speak to strangers. After a year or so of what she called total intimidation ("and we spare them no gruesome details!"), she and her husband arranged to have an acquaintance attempt an abduction in a crowded mall or grocery store. So far, only one of her children had failed this test, a lapse that, given the number of children involved, struck her as an acceptable record of success.

Others joined their cluster, and the conversation turned back to the flasher. Ruth couldn't hear them well now, but she thought she heard someone say, "Apparently not small at all!" She decided she must have been mistaken—Larissa was still in the room, after all— but then she noticed that Henry was laughing, though the sound could barely be classified as a laugh. It was very contained, almost reluctant, a rustle in his throat: an acknowledgment of humour more than a release of mirth.

For the past month, rumours about Henry had been vigorously circulating. Some people claimed that he had left his University of Toronto job after a nervous breakdown. Others guessed that he'd had an affair with a student. What was known was that he had recently married Clayton Quincy, the mother of Arabella. Out of this lone fact, the teachers spun a simple but epic tale. Clayton Quincy was perhaps the only single mother in the Eliot world. And although the fact that she could well afford to send her daughter to the school separated her from the truly disadvantaged, that she had been widowed in Arabella's infancy was compensation enough. Ruth herself had no concrete recollection of the woman from Arabella's time in grade four, but someone recalled that she had once been a cellist. Sheila had extracted the nugget that they had been engaged on top of a mountain. That Henry held himself apart, offering scant information, only inflamed their interest; speculation was more arousing than knowledge anyway. A Byronic hero had happened into their own little school.

Ruth tried to stay out of these conversations, not because she disliked gossip as a rule, but because she disapproved of the subject, resenting Henry's unearned renown.

Secretly, she preferred to dwell on the probable disgrace that had ejected him from the University of Toronto. This projection of the noble romance, love after widowhood, hit a nerve. She didn't care whether he'd proposed on a mountaintop or the car ride home after a night in jail. There was nothing in his story that merited such fervour. Wasn't there something a little weird about a fortyish bachelor anyway?

People were beginning to wander away now. Conversation had turned to talk of dinner plans. The heavy door opened and closed, opened and closed, as one person after another left. Michael and Henry were still standing in the circle, alone now, and Michael was speaking in an intense whisper. Henry had leaned in and his head was cocked slightly, his ear bent towards her mouth. When Michael finished, with a troubled nod, Henry put a hand on her upper arm and left it there. Of course, Ruth thought. How tedious of him.

The clock was moving towards five o'clock. Ruth closed her eyes for a moment of repose, and when she came to, everyone had left.

Chapter Six

WHEN AUDREY ROSE EARLY the next morning, she noticed her parents' bedroom door ajar. No stirrings were audible in the darkness beyond the door, other than the measured rise and fall of Stevie's snores. Although they didn't speak of the practice, Audrey knew that Ruth sometimes left her door open in case Audrey became scared in the night, and Audrey always felt somewhat irritated when she encountered the sight in the morning, that portal flung wide, the invitation she had outgrown yet her mother persisted in believing she needed. Her parents' realm was one she now preferred they keep private. No longer did she desire the barrier torn down, certain she was safer between them. She tiptoed over and closed the door noiselessly, then headed downstairs, grateful to have even a minor fraction of the morning to herself.

Outside, the wind was blowing hard, with a hollow, haunted sound she found comforting. In the dusky hall, she paused before the mirror, detecting the outline of her reflection, but not the thing itself. She liked herself better this way, scarcely visible. As a girl, she had often pretended that she was the main character in certain of her favourite books: Sara in *A Little Princess*, Pauline Fossil in *Ballet Shoes*, Anne Frank, even. Now, she required something more than imagination to help her effect this transfiguration, and here in the dimness, it was easier to impose on her image a quality that was not otherwise there. The sensation was romantic, a fleeting escape, and she lingered before the mirror, letting her gaze drift in and out. Then she glanced down and remembered herself. Her biology textbook was peeking out of the top of her knapsack. There was a test that afternoon, and she had risen early to do some last-minute studying.

In the kitchen, Audrey turned on only the pendant light over the kitchen table, and under its interrogation-room spotlight, she attempted to focus. Ploddingly, she took notes and made an effort to memorize key definitions. She had done poorly on several recent tests—not just math, but French and geography—and the pressure to perform decently this time, combined with the dullness of the material, made concentration a challenge. Valiantly, she tried to commit the chapters to memory, but how hard it was to do any of the real work related to Eliot.

She began each day with the intent to study harder, better. But at the first sight of a textbook, her purpose wilted. Although Eliot was forever on her mind—she thought about it constantly, with the kind of possessed anger, the fluctuating love and hatred, of a romantic infatuation—she found it impossible to direct those musings along more productive channels. The academic angle of school felt secondary to everything else. Certainly, getting back tests and essays on which she'd received marks in the sixties and seventies was humiliating, not to mention alarming—Ruth told of girls expelled for too many of such shoddy grades—but still she struggled to engage in the lessons themselves. The tumult of Eliot's social realm seized all her attention. She felt unspeakably privileged to be at Eliot, so privileged, in fact, that the question of whether or not she actually liked the school was immaterial. Eliot was her chance to craft a new identity, but what was it that she wanted? To be athletic? Brainy? Popular? Yes, she knew that popularity was what she wanted, as impotently and potently as some people desired fame. It was a shameful ambition, for the embarrassingly low-minded. This was popularity in an abstract, amorphous sense. She thought only of the result, the golden glow of happiness and success. How she might get there was a mystery.

The obstacle, she sensed, was nothing more terrible and specific —nothing less surmountable—than the very core of her. Did she even have what people thought of as a self? She intuited, from time to time, some obscure nucleus, but it was so elusive and mutable as to be totally useless. All her life, her desires had been Ruth's desires for her. Her mother was like a trespasser in her fantasies, and when she imagined herself trying to achieve something, all she could picture was Ruth pushing her from behind, like a certain kind of parent willing her child up onstage at a beauty pageant. For so long, she had believed that she and her mother were on the same side. They had walked up that driveway and shared the sublime surge of admiration, that desire to be part of something remarkable. They had felt it together. Or so she had thought. Now she began to wonder whether the things she felt had ever really been her idea. How could she even know the difference between her mother's wishes and her own? How was she to achieve anything at Eliot when she was confounded by so basic a notion as personal identity?

The kitchen had grown light by now, and Audrey had robotically amassed three pages of notes, but she was more certain than ever that she was completely unprepared for the test. The sound of dog feet prancing across the hardwood, followed by the rushing of water in the bathroom, signalled the true start to the morning. And after a time, Ruth appeared on the stairs, dressed for school, but looking as though she had just staggered out of bed.

"Hello, love child," she said.

At this allusion to their old joke, Audrey smiled in spite of herself. Upon first hearing the term as a child, Audrey, attracted to the euphony of it, had expressed disappointment that there was no similar magic around planned conceptions such as her own. "Well," Ruth had replied, "I'll pretend that your beginning was scandalous and accidental if it will make you feel better."

"Studying?" Ruth asked, pouring water into the coffee maker.

"Biology."

"Good luck. Do you like Chandra?"

"She's okay. But bio's not really my thing."

"It's not mine either."

With a gulp of water, Ruth swallowed a vitamin and made a face, then leaned back against the counter as the dogs came stampeding through the kitchen to the back door. Ruth let them into the yard, then sat at one of the high stools by the island and watched Audrey for a moment. Finally, she said, "So, how do you feel about the idea of getting a math tutor?"

Audrey sighed. She knew this was coming. A tutor should have appealed to her, she knew. Wouldn't it be better not to be so confused as Mr. Marostica's rapid scribbles traversed the blackboard? Wasn't academic success the most important kind? But the thought of trudging to the homely grey-lit studio of Miriam Jarvis after school to review math for yet another hour was discouraging. The hard part was supposed to be getting into Eliot. She was reluctant to accept that she was just at the beginning of a gruelling odyssey. "Do I have to?" she said.

Ruth was silent for a moment. "Well, no, of course you don't *have* to."

"Because I'm just catching up now. I'm sure I'll do better."

"There's no shame in it. It's not like anyone will know. Lots of Eliot girls go for tutoring so they can stay ahead."

"I don't want to talk about it right now," Audrey said.

"Well, give it some thought." Ruth clapped her hands on Audrey's shoulders and planted a kiss on the top of her head. "So, who are you hanging out with these days?"

Audrey shrugged away Ruth's hands and stood up. "I'm trying to study," she said peevishly. "Why do you have to bug me with all this first thing in the morning?"

A blush spread over Ruth's face. "It was an innocent question. I'm just making conversation."

Audrey roughly crammed her binder and notebook into her knapsack. "Well, I don't have time to give you constant reports on my progress. I have things to do."

Ruth was too flustered to respond, and Audrey was glad. It was a strange pleasure, starting the day on such an antagonistic note. Just the sight of Ruth, in her immaculately ironed white blouse and tweed skirt, looking so smugly concerned, annoyed Audrey. How good it felt, for a change, to be the one whose mood determined the atmosphere of the house. The feeling rocketed her into the day. "I'm leaving," she said.

"Now?"

Audrey had no intention of revealing the real reason for her departure—her math homework was incomplete, and she'd forgotten her textbook at school the prior afternoon. She grabbed her knapsack and headed for the front door.

"But don't you want a ride?" Ruth called out. "I'm leaving soon."

It only added to Audrey's satisfaction that Ruth's last words, as Audrey pulled the front door shut behind her, were, "Aren't you even going to say goodbye?"

THE MINUTE AUDREY ENTERED the classroom, she could feel that it was not empty. No one was initially visible, but after a second, she noticed a trio of heads in the back corner.

Arabella Quincy could change the configuration of a room. She altered the composition of its oxygen. Her loose curls tied carelessly into a messy bun, she was a Pre-Raphaelite muse fallen from grace, the vacant gaze and welcoming suppleness replaced by a wicked glint and a shrewd smirk. The illusory innocence of Arabella's looks was the source of their brutality. The temptation to watch her was inescapable, as was the fatal urge to speak to her unbidden. Once, a lock of her hair had fluttered against Audrey's cheek as they stood next to each other in line, and Audrey had still felt its fragrant brush an hour later. Even when Arabella was out of the room, she seemed not to be entirely absent. The void left by her departure only made her presence more keenly felt. Although gone, she would return, and the anticipation of that return created an intoxicating tension.

Arabella's latest coup had been to liberate the entire class's dislike of Seeta. Every time Seeta entered a room, from the back corner predictably came a series of breathy gasps and shrieks—a reference, Audrey suspected, to Whitney's observation that when Seeta sang "Feelin' Groovy," she had looked like she was having an orgasm—followed by satirically operatic voices singing "Kumbaya." The word *groovy* fluttered up, softly and furtively, in the air around her when she made her way through the classroom. Although Seeta herself seemed staunchly oblivious—two days after her first performance came a second, followed by a third, a fourth, a fifth—Audrey was not. As Seeta's deskmate, she felt perilously close to the whole mess.

Just as Audrey had suspected from the first words she spoke, Seeta had proven hard to shake. There she was in music class, singing in Audrey's ear. There she was in pre-calculus, primly opening her binder and setting her supplies at her desk's northern tip. There she was in the French room, copying out conjugations of irregular verbs to kill time before class started. There she was in the gym, limbering up like a runner before a race. There she was at lunchtime, eating pungently spiced foods out of giant Tupperware containers. One day, she had just taken out her meal when Arabella walked past, sniffing the air in dramatic disgust. "God, what died in here?" she wailed. Audrey had been waiting tensely for the trouble to light on her.

Arabella and her best friends, Whitney Oke and Katie Douglas, whom everyone called Dougie, now sat in a tight circle on the floor, strangely silent, as though they were holding their breath to avoid detection. On the closest desk, partially obscuring them, was Arabella's knapsack, unmistakably hers, covered in buttons—one with a likeness of Alan Thicke, others bearing messages such as "Jesus loves you but he loves me a little more" and "Proud grandmother"—their obscure messages a testament to her superior sophistication, to the fact that she had acquired her place in the class through some genetic destiny, a monarchical inevitability that made her unchallengeable. Upon hearing Audrey's footsteps, Arabella peered around the side of the bag, cocking her head slightly like a dog hearing a suspicious noise. Audrey's instinct was to turn and leave immediately, but she knew that to do so would be a declaration of fear, the end of a moment but the start of something much longer.

"I'm just getting a textbook," she muttered.

Arabella watched her, saying nothing.

The mess of loose papers inside her desk fluttered onto the floor as Audrey rummaged around for the book. "Oh, shoot," she mumbled as she crouched to gather them. "Oh, shoot," came a small echo. Audrey looked up and saw Arabella examining her with Buddhic inexpressiveness. Her lips were closed and her expression was unusually flat, a parody of a poker face. Whitney and Dougie glanced from Audrey to Arabella, and then settled on Audrey. Audrey felt her face growing red under their united appraisal. Stuffing the papers back into the desk had become an absurdly complicated endeavour. Like hair that wouldn't lie flat, they refused to be tamed, and continued to peek out every time Audrey tried to close the desktop. She gave a little laugh, which was, in another small feat of ventriloquism, invisibly mimicked. The thought occurred to her as she pressed her hand on the chaos that she had never loathed herself more.

At last she turned to leave. She was almost at the door when Arabella called out, "Hey, new girl. Come back here for a second."

Right away Audrey knew that this was one of those random moments of adjustment in life. A minor and accidental revolution. It was Arabella's voice. Even as Audrey's heart leapt in alarm, she heard something that strengthened her: the note of curiosity, an opening.

She turned around. "Me?"

"Me?" mimicked Whitney.

"Is there another new girl here?" asked Arabella. "Have a seat." She gestured to the floor next to Dougie and smiled sweetly.

Audrey tried not to think about the math homework that wouldn't get done as she wedged herself into the one clear spot of floor in the back corner.

"Make yourself comfortable, dahling," said Dougie.

She wondered for a second if they had invited her over expressly to enjoy the spectacle of her attempt to fit her body into a space that was clearly too small for it. They made no shifts to accommodate her but watched with aloof half smiles as she tried to make room for herself. She had never been so close to them before, and it had seemed only right that this distance remain intact. She saw them now with too much clarity. Normally, Whitney and Dougie commanded little attention of their own. Too much were they simply a facet of Arabella's aura. Now Audrey understood the symbiosis among them. Their near constant presence with Arabella enhanced her power, and they, in turn, received the contagion of her beauty. Audrey supposed that Whitney might have been intimidating in her way, with her striking pale skin and her impenetrable coldness, but Dougie was all freckles and giggling, utterly ordinary without Arabella's neighbouring splendour.

"So," Arabella said. "We were just talking about that gross handout Ms. Crispe gave out the other day in gym."

The previous day, Ms. Crispe, the gym teacher, had given the class a detailed lecture about personal hygiene on gym days. Accompanying this talk was a handout upon which she had listed the five cardinal rules of gym attendance, and although the majority of girls had appreciated her insistence upon the use of antiperspirant, less welcome was her legislation on menstruation. The first rule was introduced by the title, "To Pad or To 'Pon? That is the Question." Only tampons, Ms. Crispe instructed, were to be used on gym days, since girls wearing sanitary pads were unable to give the games their all. In the locker room before the bell rang, the girls had fumed about the handout while forming countless theories about what they deemed a homoerotic interest in their vaginal proclivities.

During lunch, Whitney had suggested that they all wear pads to the next gym class as a matter of principle.

"We've all agreed that we have to do something," Arabella said. "It's not enough just to complain about it. Or wear pads, since she might not even notice that anyway."

"She's totally violating our privacy!" exclaimed Dougie.

"And our civil liberties," added Whitney.

"And, like, why is she so obsessed with our menstrual blood?" Arabella said. "Don't you find that really disturbing?"

Audrey nodded.

"So, listen. Whit came up with the most hilarious plan." Arabella fizzed with excitement, her hands fluttering in her lap as her hair fell across the aristocratic slope of her long neck. On her chin was a pimple, small but clearly still at the beginning of its life. Audrey glanced away, hoping Arabella hadn't seen her notice it.

The idea was to leave a pad, smeared with ketchup, in the middle of the locker room floor. When Ms. Crispe came in, clipboard in hand, whistle around neck, to badger the class to hurry up, she would spot it. From there on, the plan grew more formless, its goal somewhat unclear. It wasn't even about the rules anymore, Whitney insisted. But there was a point, and it seemed to them an important one. It was a matter of honour, almost, to humiliate Ms. Crispe for talking about their periods so openly, for forming her beliefs into a list of regulations and then detailing them on a handout. A lesson had to be taught. The girls looked at each other and aimed squalls of hyena-like laughter at the ceiling.

"Isn't it an awesome idea?" giggled Dougie.

Audrey had to agree that the plan was, in its sheer pettiness, rather formidable. The amount of energy and passion they poured into these trivial injustices astounded her. There was no precedent for it in her life. At her old school, all any of the girls had cared about was boys. And the size of the school had prevented any single event from having such resonance. She wondered what Ruth would say if she knew that such things went on.

Arabella looked slyly at Audrey. "Do you want to do it?" she asked, as though offering an opportunity she might not grant.

"I want to do it," Dougie whined.

Arabella ignored Dougie and fixed Audrey with her magnetic stare.

"Now?" Audrey said.

"Well, we have gym first period."

Audrey glanced at her math book and then at the clock. It was almost 8:30. If there had been morning soccer or basketball practice, the locker room would soon be full of girls changing into their school uniforms. But refusal was not an option. She nodded her consent. They clapped their hands in glee as Arabella stuffed a wrapped sanitary pad and a restaurant packet of ketchup into Audrey's knapsack.

The locker room was in the basement, and when Audrey swung open the door, she discovered it empty. Her instructions were simple enough. She unwrapped and unfolded the pad, smoothing out the creases and twisting it up roughly in her hands in an attempt to make it look used. Then she opened the ketchup and smeared it down the middle, rubbing the surface with her fingers to make it look more natural, like blood that had been collecting for hours. It wouldn't absorb, though, and lay glistening and congealed on the top, quite obviously ketchup. It smelled obviously of ketchup, too. It was at this point that Audrey realized she had nothing with which to clean her fingers, so she picked up the pad's crinkly paper wrapper and wiped her fingers as best she could, then buried it under a mound of used Kleenexes, a dirty, torn gym sock, and an empty carton of skim milk in the big rubber garbage can.

She set the pad conspicuously in the centre of the floor and stepped back to get a view of her handiwork. The plan suddenly seemed less a subversive and witty comment on a teacher's over-stepping than a prank by twelve-year-olds. Outside the door, a herd of footsteps might have been headed towards her or away, so she grabbed her knapsack and headed for the bathroom, where she washed her hands, then sat in a cubicle until the bell rang, breathing deeply to calm her galloping pulse.

When she returned to the locker room after chapel, much of the class was already there. She took a spot in the corner, pushed her bag into the cubbyhole overhead, and started undressing. The pad was already garnering much attention. Upon entering the locker room, most girls sidestepped it deferentially, giggling. Rebecca Knowles called out, "Is that real blood?" To which Dougie answered, "Yeah, that's my big bloody pad. Sorry, I'm just human." Audrey's face was burning. A part of her thought that she should have been proud of her part in it, flattered and exhilarated to have been taken into one of Arabella's plots, but the prevailing part of her was still afraid of getting into trouble. Ms. Crispe was due to arrive at any moment, and Arabella kept glancing knowingly in Audrey's direction.

A hush fell over the room as the door swung open and Ms. Crispe, wearing khaki walking shorts and a white-collared polo shirt, a pencil behind her ear, walked in and planted herself stockily by the garbage can, hands on her hips. Like everyone else who'd come in, her eyes immediately went to the crimson pad, but unlike everyone else, she offered the pad no deference. She said nothing, her very body the antithesis of a girlish squeal. Then she took one step over to the pad, squatted, and picked it up by its corner, holding it aloft under the fluorescent lighting.

"What is the meaning of this?" she asked calmly.

Half-dressed, the girls stared at her, unanswering.

"To whom does this belong?"

The girls remained silent for some seconds. Then Arabella raised her hand.

"Maybe it belongs to someone who has her period?" she said in a querying, helpful tone.

"Thank you, Arabella," said Ms. Crispe. "What is this doing on the floor?"

"I'm not sure what it's doing on the floor, Ms. Crispe," Whitney said innocently, "but remember you said we're not allowed to wear pads in gym class? I guess maybe someone just remembered that and was trying to respect your rules, but didn't have time to go to the bathroom before the bell?"

Ms. Crispe turned around and flung the pad face down into the garbage, where it landed with a squelching wetness.

"You have one minute to finish getting dressed," she said.

When the door swung shut behind her, muffled laughter issued from all corners of the room, but the joy was gone, not so much because the incident was over as because of Ms. Crispe's deflating reaction, her refusal to get particularly angry or to acknowledge the ketchup, to seem at all ruffled, or the least bit aware that her rules had been shown up by the grade tens. Arabella and Whitney, lacing up their shoes in the opposite corner, were conferring.

"Just ask for a tampon next time, Seeta," called out Dougie.

Seeta was pulling on her gym shorts, and she looked up, startled to hear her name.

"What? I didn't—"

Arabella burst into laughter, relieving Seeta of the need to finish her sentence.

Seeta sat on the long wooden bench and concentrated on tying up her running shoes. Whitney whispered to Arabella something Audrey couldn't hear. Seeta seemed to be moving very slowly— whether in an effort to calm herself or to resist intimidation, Audrey couldn't tell. She looked up from her shoes and gave Audrey a small smile, then finally stood to leave. When the door swung shut behind her, Arabella exclaimed, "That was classic!"

"Did you see Ms. Crispe's dykey face, like, salivating over that pad?" exclaimed Dougie.

Audrey wasn't sure that was what she had seen, but she smiled as if in agreement. She got up to leave before their approval was withdrawn, turned skilfully by Arabella's sleight of hand into its inevitable contrary. Just as she was crossing the room, Dougie jumped off the bench and shrieked that her bladder was going to burst. As she sprang forward, she fell theatrically into Audrey, knocking her to the floor. Writhing in some combination of pain and hysteria, she howled that she had twisted her ankle. Audrey lay trapped beneath her as she squirmed, laughing uncontrollably. "Who's the lesbo now?" Whitney said, poking Dougie's stomach with her foot as she walked past.

"Oh my God, I'm going to wet my pants!" Dougie screamed.

"Not on me!" Audrey said, trying to wriggle free. She didn't want to laugh. She wanted to hang on to her guard, but something was releasing, almost without her consent.

Whitney and Arabella piled onto Dougie, tickling her to see if she would wet her pants. Giddiness had infected them all by now. On the other side of the door, the school day was starting.

So this was how it felt, Audrey thought, to be on the inside of the noise. This was the sound of your own resurrected laughter.

RUTH WAS STILL MOVING through the smog of sleep-deprivation when she reached for the staff room door and Larissa McAllister nearly opened it into her face.

"Ruth!" she cried. "Good morning to you."

"Hello!" Ruth returned with inexplicable conviviality.

Even when she'd fallen asleep the night before, Ruth had been merely dozing, and her dreams had been light and misleadingly realistic—negotiating shower times, finding the milk carton empty—so that only upon waking did she realize they were dreams. Being poorly rested had initially made her feel heady and buoyant, weirdly energized. But after teaching two classes, math and science, her least favourite, she had been able to think of little other than coffee, the smell of which wafted out from the staff room behind Larissa.

Sipping from her steaming mug, Larissa cast her eyes over Ruth's outfit. "Ruth," she said, "perhaps your educational agenda would be better served if you fastened one more button on your blouse."

Ruth looked down in surprise. Only one button below the top was undone, and even from her prime view, only a small, flat patch of chest was visible. "Oh, I didn't realize. Of course." With her free hand, she fastened the pearly button above her collarbone, eliciting a nod of approval.

"To show too much skin strikes one as a touch bourgeois, no?" Larissa peered down at Ruth's hand. "So, what is that weighty tome you're brandishing?"

"Oh, it's, um, Flannery O'Connor." Ruth had taken the book from her briefcase with the intention of retreating to a corner of the staff room for a bit of reading while her class was in gym. "It's part of an idea I'm working out for an English assignment for the kids. Not the book itself, but—" She stopped. It was implausible that she'd be using Flannery O'Connor with grade fours.

But Larissa nodded, seemingly intrigued, and Ruth felt a forgiving rush of warmth and gratitude that Larissa was, in fact, as forward thinking in her academic objectives as she purported to be. Lying could be easy under such circumstances.

"I'll leave you to it, then," said Larissa, turning from Ruth to issue a sharp rebuke to a pair of grade sevens who were running in the hall. Ruth slipped into the staff room and made straight for the coffee machine, hoping that the right dose of caffeine would disarm the irritability that was building inside her. She had never thought of her mental state as something that required diligent maintenance, but for several days now, she had felt frustratingly volatile—one moment skittish with energy she didn't know how to channel, the next moment lazy and discouraged. Her disconnection from Audrey was part of it. The more helpful Ruth tried to be—she had offered to sit with Audrey, in case she had any questions, while Audrey was doing her French homework—the more Audrey treated her presence as a bother. Ruth had done her best to keep her own moodiness in check. She continually reminded herself that Audrey was adjusting. But she was more than a little disheartened that Audrey's acceptance to Eliot, the move that ought to have brought them closer, had begotten only estrangement.

Lorna Massie-Turnbull was standing by the counter, humming as she prepared a cup of herbal tea. As Ruth rooted around in the fridge for the cream, she set a loaf of bread on the counter, and Lorna tapped her back, saying, "Ahem, um. Sorry to be a pest, Ruth, but the bread…" She grimaced apologetically and gestured at the counter.

"Oops, sorry," Ruth said contritely, removing the offending loaf.

Lorna had been diagnosed with celiac disease the year before and had since isolated one corner of the kitchenette—the stretch where Ruth had placed the loaf—for her food preparation. There sat a deluxe avocado-green KitchenAid toaster, as far away as it could get from the ancient dented toaster designated for communal use, several bread boards personalized in permanent marker with the initials L.M.-T., and a glass jar full of utensils. On this bit of counter also sat a white wicker basket loaded with homeopathic remedies. These also belonged to Lorna, but she was happy to share them with anyone in need. Once, when Ruth had been complaining about a headache and asking around for Advil, Lorna had intercepted Sheila's tablets and insisted she take several drops of gingko biloba in a glass of water instead.

Ruth generally preferred to eat away from Lorna, whose lentil and quinoa salads made her feel obscurely guilty about her own food choices, especially after she observed Lorna regarding her peanut butter and jam sandwiches with a mixture of disapproval, pity, and fear. Although Ruth didn't doubt the legitimacy of Lorna's diagnosis, she couldn't help viewing Lorna's dietary restrictions as a feature of her general hypersensitivity. In response to a recent remark of Ruth's that she was craving chocolate, Lorna had exclaimed, "Then my naturopath would say that it's the last thing you should be eating! Have these soy nuts instead."

Looking around for a snack, Ruth took some Bran Buds down from the cupboard and poured them into her raspberry yogurt. Sheila approached and surveyed the contents of their bowls. "Look at the two of you, showing off with your health food! Well, I'm just going to eat my blueberry muffin and enjoy every bite! No matter what you say!"

"I can assure you I won't say anything," Ruth replied icily.

"Ruth," said Lorna, blowing on her tea. "Audrey is only mouthing the words in music class. Tell her to sing! I want to hear her beautiful voice."

Sheila turned in curiosity. "Whyever would Audrey just pretend to sing?"

"Her voice is perfectly adequate," Lorna said.

"I'm sorry," Ruth replied. Whereas Chuck Marostica had been concerned about Audrey's mathematical aptitude as a key intellectual skill, Lorna seemed personally wounded by Audrey's apathy.

"Why would anybody not want to sing?" asked Sheila.

"Is she terribly self-conscious?" asked Lorna.

Backed into a corner of the small kitchenette, Ruth smiled in discomfort as Lorna and Sheila beamed their concern into her. "Aren't all teenagers self-conscious?"

"Has the adjustment been very challenging for her?" Lorna asked.

Ruth was taken aback by the question. The fact that Audrey wasn't particularly liking Eliot seemed like a dirty secret to her, one she barely wanted to admit to herself. "It's early yet. I think..." But she didn't know what response might appease them, whether she should defend Audrey's emerging mediocrity or confess her worries.

The door swung open then and in walked Michael Curtis. She headed straight for the now-crowded kitchenette and transferred her lunch from a Lululemon bag into the fridge.

"Ooh, cute bag!" said Sheila. "I'm not sure I've got the bum for yoga pants anymore, but I've just got to get one of those. Don't you love it, Ruth?"

Ruth nodded vaguely. Although she liked Lululemon clothes,

she found the aphorisms covering the bags irritating and moralistic, not to mention simplistic—New Age tripe about doing something every day that scares you and children being the orgasm of life. The only one of these prosaisms she could wholeheartedly agree with was that one should floss daily.

As the women discussed the relative merits of Lululemon and Roots, Ruth took the opportunity to escape to a wingback chair at the side of the circle. In addition to Lorna, Michael, and Sheila, the circle held Janet McLeod, the Latin teacher, who was marking on her lap, and Pat Bernstein, an English teacher with a bosomy warmth. Ruth cast a longing glance at the Flannery O'Connor in her lap but supposed the scene was manageable. Then she heard a rustling behind her and saw Henry Winter by the window, fiddling with the blinds. She sighed.

"What's that book you have there, Ruth?" asked Sheila.

Ruth held it up.

"Mm. Only one I've read is *A Good Man Is Hard to Find*. Don't I wish I didn't know how true that is!"

Sheila was recently divorced from her husband of twenty-five years, and she claimed to have an active, if amusingly disastrous, dating life.

A shadow fell over the surface of Ruth's book. "There we go," said Henry, stationing the blind halfway down the window.

"Thank you for that, Henry," Michael said as Henry stepped into the circle. "That glare was blinding."

The room now seemed divided into two weather systems: on the far side a sunny day and on the sitting area side the gloom of rain. The last thing Ruth wanted was to read in the dark, but everyone else seemed to be in agreement that they were best off without the distraction of sun. Henry took a seat in the chair next to Ruth, his legs crossed effeminately as he sipped from a mug full of steaming water with lemon. Sheila leaned forward with her chin in her hand. "How about you, Henry? Did your lengthy studies bring you into much contact with Flannery O'Connor?"

He shook his head as though not much interested in the question. "I'm not excessively familiar with O'Connor's work."

"What *should* we be reading?"

"Ah, in reading, there are no shoulds, Sheila."

"Well, who is your favourite author?" asked Sheila, unwilling to give up.

Ruth took a long sip of her coffee. Now he would name some obscure Brazilian writer no one had ever heard of, someone whose forbiddingly dense prose no normal person could enjoy, an unappreciated genius whose aesthetic of inscrutability would attest to the incomparability of his intellect. And his rapt audience would swoon over how well informed he was, how impressive was the mind that had conquered its lowdown and facile need for entertainment.

"I'm not generally given to favourites," he said, "but in this category, my loyalty is unwavering. Jane Austen has no close competition in my mind."

"Oh!" Sheila exclaimed. "Great minds think alike!"

"And who's up and coming?" asked Michael, uncrossing and recrossing her legs grandly. "Who are the young geniuses bursting onto the scene, revolutionizing everything?"

"Oh, I don't know about that," Henry said. "My tastes are decidedly antediluvian."

"Mine too," said Sheila cozily.

"I can think of nothing better than an evening in front of the fire with *Pride and Prejudice* and Angela Hewitt playing the Goldberg Variations," said Michael. "After the kids get to bed, of course!"

Lorna released a noisy sigh of longing. "I have searched high and low for a student who can play Bach," she said. She was sitting on the couch next to Pat Bernstein, with her legs tucked up under her. The effect was of a bird perched on a branch.

"Lorna," said Sheila, "speaking of music, what a wonderful job you've done with Seeta Prasad. She's brought the fun back to assembly. I find myself looking forward to chapel each morning. When she played 'Fast Car' the other day, boy, did I get chills."

"She is an extraordinary talent," nodded Michael austerely. "What a breath of fresh air."

Pat Bernstein gathered her layers of skirts and shifted heavily, transferring her marking to the coffee table. Around her neck were tiers of bulky, beaded South American–flavour necklaces, which knocked and rustled like a percussionist symphony as she moved. In some ways Ruth envied Pat and wanted to be like her (although, of course, she didn't want to be like her at all)—the throaty voice that clearly belonged to someone of ample body and spirit, her clipped white hair, her loose, monochromatic blouses and skirts, and the jewellery collected on her extensive travels. She seemed unconcerned about her appearance, not aggressively or defensively so, and not as though she had given up, but in a way that called into question whether stereotypical beauty was of any value at all.

"I've heard," Pat said, "that Seeta is not having an easy time of it in her own class. Peers aren't always the most receptive audience."

"I heard the same," said Lorna, nodding vigorously. "I asked Seeta about it, and she was wonderfully courageous. She looked me in the eye and said, 'The voices of one or two dissenters won't keep me from entertaining all the others.' Did that ever give me the shivers. I felt I was in the presence of a great, great human being. What kind of kid has that perspective?"

"Have you heard anything, Ruth?" asked Pat. "Isn't Audrey in Seeta's class?"

Ruth had been staring at the cover of her book, wondering whether it would be rude to crack it open. Even just a couple of pages, like two sips of red wine, would do to restore her. "Audrey hasn't mentioned anything," she said. "She's probably too busy getting used to things to notice."

"Mm." Pat nodded sympathetically. "And you know how secretive kids can be with their parents."

"Well, no, Audrey's not..." Ruth didn't know the end of this sentence—Audrey wasn't secretive? Was that claim still true?

"I was speaking to Claire Wright the other day," said Michael. "As you may know, I've always been a bit of a mentor to her, and since her mother passed, she and I have become extremely close. Well, we were gabbing, and she told me all about it. A slew of highly unimaginative comments. 'Anyone up for a round of "Kumbaya"?' 'Hey there, Garfunkel'—that sort of thing."

"Claire's always been such a lovely person," said Sheila.

"True," replied Michael. "I had to do a bit of work redirecting her to the high road, however. She thinks it's all somewhat inane, but she also holds the typically unsympathetic teenage opinion that in so flamboyantly showcasing her considerable talent, Seeta is 'asking for it.'"

Looking around the circle, Ruth felt something welling up in her. She didn't think before speaking. "In addition to being lovely, Claire is astute."

All heads whipped around as rapidly as if she had just upended the coffee table.

"Ruth, what on earth could you be suggesting?" asked Michael. Although usually quick to commit herself to indignation, Michael was frowning with concerned confusion, as though Ruth had just barged drunkenly into the staff room and she wanted to intervene for Ruth's own safety but wasn't sure how to do so diplomatically.

Sheila cocked her head and looked to Henry as though he could provide the clarification Ruth could not.

Ruth's hands quivered slightly as she set down her coffee. "I just…yes, the music is excellent…but…I don't know how anyone can deny that a student who plays an acoustic version of—what was it yesterday?—"Sympathy for the Devil" is asking for it, no matter how talented she is."

"So you're saying she should conform just to fit in? Pretend to be mediocre?" Henry asked. He paused with the aplomb of someone who knew everyone was willing to watch him and wait to hear what he would say next. "I thought going beyond the mediocre was what Eliot stood for."

Was there a sarcastic edge to his voice?

In a move that was simultaneously sprightly and angry, Lorna untucked her legs and landed on the edge of the cushion, leaning forward rigidly. She clutched her hands so tightly in her lap that her knuckles whitened, and when she spoke, her voice was quivering. "Seeta Prasad is the most talented student musician I've ever met. Without close competition. But then, clearly, not everyone can be musical."

Lorna's narrow chest moved quickly up and down as she squared herself challengingly. There was something personal, queerly taunting, in Lorna's expression, as though her comment had been intended as a piercing coup, and Ruth was puzzled, unable to account for Lorna's bright-eyed defiance. Was she referencing Audrey's musical inhibition? Ruth took a deep breath. She was supposed to be enjoying her book. Its promise of escape had gotten her through the morning. Why had she opened her big mouth? Why was she speaking as if she cared about these things? She didn't care about any of it, least of all Lorna's ridiculously subtle jab at Audrey. As if she would have wanted her daughter making that spectacle of herself. As if she wouldn't have sooner seen Audrey with two mob-style broken wrists than up in front of that audience belting out "I Guess That's Why They Call It the Blues."

Ruth held up her hands. "Please, it's not that I disagree with you. I'm not saying that Seeta deserves harassment. I know she's talented. I know that. It's just, I think you're misunderstanding what I'm saying."

"Does the problem lie in our understanding or in your expression?" said Michael, settling comfortably into her usual mode.

"What *do* you mean, Ruth?" asked Sheila slowly and gently, the way she spoke to children made incoherent by distress.

Ruth wasn't sure what she meant. She had barely paid attention to Seeta's playing in chapel, and she certainly didn't feel strongly enough about it to be taking on a team united by the belief in one's right to play amateur guitar in public. A part of her wished she were standing up so she could escape, taking backward appeasing steps, claiming she was late for a meeting somewhere. But another part of her, the part that was morally weaker but vocally stronger, found that the stridence of the opposition was making her form a strong opinion she hadn't previously held.

"Look," she said. "Teenagers are brutal. Is this a surprise to anyone?"

"I think we have all tried very hard here," Lorna said, "in fact, it's been our life's work, to create a welcoming learning environment where gifted people are safe from assaults on their spirit."

"I don't disagree."

"Bollocks!" said Michael. "For someone who doesn't disagree, you're doing a lot of disagreeing."

"So her classmates are being mean!" Ruth exclaimed. "That's not exactly unusual. They're teenage girls! It's not as if Seeta is the first loser ever to darken Eliot's door. She just may be the first one oblivious to it."

A hush travelled across the room like an electric current.

Michael closed her eyes and shook her head. "Ruth, let's not resort to the name-calling we discourage in our students. But perhaps more seriously, please refrain from using racist terminology, at least in my presence."

"What? What did I say?" Ruth was stunned. She looked around searchingly for an ally, but even Sheila, whose alliance she had always been quick to reject, had lowered her head in consternation. What had she said? She could barely remember now. Some kind of amnesia overtook her mind when she was arguing, and the memory of what she had said evaporated the moment the words left her lips.

"I don't think anyone is comfortable repeating it," said Michael.

Sheila glanced up furtively from her lap and mouthed something Ruth couldn't make out. Then it hit her: darken the door.

"That's not what I meant! That's a common expression!" Ruth cried. "I'm not being racist. You know I'm not racist."

"I don't know what I know," offered Lorna.

She would have to find a way to leave the room, naturally or not. The impossibility of remaining was obvious.

Perhaps part of the problem had been the edge in her voice. She had heard it without understanding why it was there, and the mystery of its origins rendered her unable to control it. Even as she had wanted to go unseen, to make a getaway into her book, when she heard the teachers talking she had felt eager to disagree. Ruth had to acknowledge that to herself, even as the heat of their ire suffocated her. She had wanted to show herself to be more honest and perceptive than they. If only she had Larissa's air of moral authority, she could express ideas in a dispassionate way that would make people believe her.

"Let's all take a deep breath," said Henry, sitting forward. "The verb 'darken' here does in fact refer to the casting of one's shadow across the threshold. I'm a great believer in the healthiness of lively debate. But let's make sure we get our facts straight."

"Nevertheless, the name-calling is unacceptable," said Michael.

"I have to go," Ruth said.

She stood and left, not backing out tentatively as she had in her mind, but moving in a quick series of motions that came much closer to flouncing. In her clumsy desperation for escape, she nearly slammed the door behind her. Her heart was beating erratically as she made for the side stairwell, afraid that before she could get away, one of the teachers would be dispatched, in a parental capacity, to chase her down and strong-arm her into apologizing.

She was almost at the stairwell door when she heard footsteps behind her. She turned around, and indeed, there was Henry, clearly heading straight for her. Although he usually moved restlessly, with a kind of distracted poise, as though the present bored him but his mind was full of amusing diversions, he approached now with resolve. Unwilling to be seen as running away, she stopped outside a classroom to let him catch up. She realized that she had left her half-empty coffee mug on the table, but she couldn't, she absolutely couldn't, go back to tend to it. No doubt she would find a memo in her mailbox later reminding her that all teachers are responsible for cleaning up after themselves.

When he reached her, Henry stopped and plunged his hands deep into his pockets. "I'm sorry for that," he said.

Ruth said nothing.

"It got out of hand," he said.

"Mm," Ruth replied, looking down at her shoes. She was afraid to speak for what her voice might sound like. She knew she should be angry, that she had every right to be angry, and a ferocious sense of righteousness had certainly flooded her as she fled from the room. She wished she were angry: it would be easier to speak, dispassion be damned, if indeed she were. The difficulty was that she was no longer feeling any reassuring fury. Her throat was tight and her knees were wobbly, and she knew that if she spoke, the unmistakable warble in her voice would betray this weakness, this mortifying upset. She couldn't allow anyone—certainly not Henry, with his infuriating calm—to see her in this pitiable state. She knew that he hadn't done anything to start the fight, but she blamed him for it. His mere presence brought the women to a pitch.

Avoiding his gaze, she glanced at the window in the door to the classroom, and she saw Audrey sitting in the front row, next to Seeta. She realized that she had never asked Audrey whom she sat beside. Chuck Marostica was standing at the blackboard, scribbling out the barely legible numbers and letters of a math equation with dizzying speed, and Audrey was watching with that look of concentration and wonder that reminded Ruth of the little girl she had been, poring over the pictures as she read on Richard's lap. That expression: Ruth knew it so well. It always made her feel penitent, and wracked with painful love.

Henry's eyes followed hers.

"I'm going to try to get Audrey involved in the play," he said. "She has a real talent for delivery."

But it was all too much. She walked away without looking at him again, letting the swinging door be her reply.

THAT EVENING, RUTH HAD to stay late at work. At lunchtime, Larissa had summoned Ruth to her office—initially Ruth had expected a scolding for the staff room argument—but what Larissa really wanted was to reveal that she had selected Ruth to be the chief editor of that year's Junior School literary journal, *The Pomegranate*. Early in their relationship, the women had shared certain literary sensibilities. In addition to enthusiastic assaults on what they perceived to be the misogyny of certain male writers—Larissa said that she sometimes wished Hemingway were still alive so that she could trounce him in a hearty debate—some of their earliest conversations had been in praise of writers no one else Ruth knew seemed to care about: Elizabeth Bowen, Elizabeth Taylor, Muriel Spark (though Larissa admitted that she had found it difficult not to read *The Prime of Miss Jean Brodie* from the perspective of an educator). Those had been the days when Ruth was excited about almost everything Eliot stood for. She had sometimes come to work early expressly for the purpose of having tea with Larissa, to sit in the office overlooking the green fields, talking of books. In time, however, their tastes diverged, and after a testy conversation about the relevance of a reader's morality—Ruth said that to be encumbered by one's own moral framework was to be a weak reader, Larissa strenuously disagreed—their literary talks were reduced to Larissa commenting patronizingly on whatever book Ruth was carrying.

Larissa now evoked those early days of fond agreement. "Though we might disagree on some matters, I have the utmost faith in your taste," she said. She produced from her desk a copy of last year's *Pomegranate*, edited by Candace McClelland, the grade six teacher, and leaned across the desk confidingly. She had had reservations about allowing Candace to edit, she said, given the botched villanelle she had penned for Eliot's fifth anniversary, and so she had only herself to blame for several wasted mornings of self-recrimination after she saw the cover photograph Candace had come up with, a decidedly blurry image of an open pomegranate, purchased at IKEA.

Ruth had to admire Larissa's artfulness, casting the extra work as a privilege. She did indeed feel flattered. Such was the difficulty of her relationship with Larissa McAllister. Ruth could not help wanting her approval, no matter how little she enjoyed the woman, as though in that affirmation lay some objective assessment of her worth.

After the school emptied out, Ruth settled herself on the staff room couch with a folder of submissions. There was a time when she had loved being at Eliot after hours. Alone in the dark, she had never been scared; she had felt the enormity of purpose in the space around her. There had been peace in having her life decided.

Her mother, Antonia, had opposed Ruth's decision to become a primary school teacher. How unimaginative, she bemoaned. How unambitious. Was Ruth under the impression, she asked, that because women had been schoolteachers at a time when they were allowed to be little else, Ruth would be showing some useless female solidarity in becoming a teacher by choice, that precisely because "the schoolteacher" was an archaic profession, it was daring, or transgressive somehow, to seek it as a modern woman? Did she believe that in reclaiming the terms of oppression, Ruth would find true freedom? Antonia's ideas were immovable behemoths: the arguments went on for months.

It wasn't until she met Larissa McAllister at an acquaintance's dinner party that Antonia gave up the fight. Larissa had spoken of her nascent school all evening, and although Antonia had not found her exactly interesting, she had been transfixed by Larissa's intensity, her ideological fervour. One of Ruth's greatest weaknesses, Antonia felt, was that her ideas were muddy and inconsistent, always changing. She was all inspiration, and inspiration was formless, undependable. Larissa's ideology would give Ruth structure. Not long after, Ruth met Larissa and knew instantly that her mother was right, that being a teacher at this school was exactly what she ought to do. (How could it be that someone who readily saw the worst in you still fundamentally understood you?)

It all seemed so very long ago. Before Ruth now was a folder with nearly two hundred submissions, often multiple submissions from the same ambitious girl, and as much as she wanted to be invigorated, her interest in the project was already waning. After flipping through last year's *Pomegranate,* she was confident that with barely an ounce of effort she could do a far better job than Candace, who had commissioned poems on subjects such as "My Favourite Summer Holiday" and "My Favourite Christmas (or Chanukah) Tradition" and had bookended those sections with inspirational aphorisms such as "Everyone smiles in the same language." Larissa had encouraged students to submit plentifully. She didn't mind that many girls' work wouldn't make it into the published version. It was never too early to begin teaching the lesson that at the core of life was a basic hierarchy of superior and inferior and that hard work resulted not only in private satisfaction but in public approbation. This meant that Ruth now had to endure fifty poems about the exact shade of green in the summer grass. It was on her to judge the relative merits of rhyming couplets about rainbows and similes about happiness. Her heart sank as she realized she probably wouldn't make it home before nine o'clock.

She read dutifully until seven o'clock, when she fell asleep for fifteen minutes and woke up disoriented. Her sense of time had gone askew, and she was sure it must be ten or eleven o'clock. The windows were dark, slick with rain, and on the street below the sound of cars had subsided. When she looked at her watch she was frustrated to see that it was still quite early. She had to put in another hour before she could justify stopping. She got up to make a pot of peppermint tea and rooted through the fridge for something to eat. There was little on offer: half a carton of peach yogurt with Michael's name on masking tape across the top, and ham and cheese on a greasy croissant, no label. Ruth grabbed the sandwich and ate it at the counter, staring at the wall in a daze, until her kettle whistled. She was briefly revived, but when she returned to the couch, the urge to take another nap washed over her. She decided to go home.

She packed her briefcase, grabbed her keys to the school, and let herself out the back door to the parking lot. She was almost at her car, on the far side of the lot by the fence, when she realized she had left her purse, with her car keys, inside. Sighing, she set her briefcase on the hood of the car and doubled back.

Glancing towards the pathway on the far side of the school grounds, Ruth thought of the flasher. She felt like her girlhood self, half hoping for a sighting. The threat level was low. He had probably long since gone home—it was disconcerting to think of the flasher having a home, a stodgy, overheated apartment somewhere—and even if he were around, she was too old for him. She imagined looking up to see him standing under a street lamp, a quirky smile on his chubby, red-cheeked face. He would open his trench coat penitently, as if he just kept getting the better of himself.

She was jingling her keys in her hands, almost at the door, when she felt something from behind. For a second, she thought it was just a strong gust of wind, but then she was tripping forward, dropping her keys, and there was no doubt that she felt something now, a brawny grip on her arm and a force shoving her into the brick wall of the school. She heard the blunt force of her head hitting the wall, but she felt nothing.

A man's face was close to hers, but not the face she was expecting. He was blond, with near-white eyelashes and eyebrows, young. She could see him plainly under the parking lot lights. He was not dressed to hide himself, no black hood enshrouding his face, no toque, neither the disguise nor the demeanour of a criminal. He couldn't have been much more than sixteen years old, and his hair was like a baby's, fine enough to show his pink scalp. His face was forgettable. Already she knew that she would never be able to evoke it if called upon to describe him to the police. Only his bulk was remarkable, obliterating all the strength she thought she had, reducing her to a flimsy, insubstantial thing as it pinioned her to the wall. He demanded her wallet.

"I don't have it," she said, out of breath. "I swear. Just my briefcase full of work."

She gestured towards the car. Her school keys lay on the ground beside her. Would he now follow her into the school? She must prevent that above all else. She didn't think he was going to kill her —wouldn't he already have shown her a weapon if he had one?— but she knew that you were never supposed to let yourself be transferred to a second location. If he were going to rape her, he would have to do it right there. It surprised her that she was able to think about whether he would rape her so lucidly, even dispassionately. She could see what would be the right choices to make, as if she were watching a character in a movie. If he demanded to follow her in, she could tell him there were people inside. But wouldn't the empty parking lot betray the truth?

"Please don't hurt me," she said.

"Give me your fucking jewellery," he said, giving her a push.

At first she thought she had none, but then she realized she was wearing the sapphire necklace from Antonia, as well as her wedding ring, thin and platinum, engraved with her wedding date. She did not want to give these things up. She was amazed by how she resisted inside, how her mind leapt frantically to find a way around it, especially given how often she had hammered into Audrey's head that if she were ever robbed, she must relinquish everything without hesitation. They were just things, she told herself, as she unhooked her necklace and pulled off her ring, just objects onto which she had imposed meaning. She placed them in his upturned palm, dry and rough and bizarrely patient. Anyone looking on might have thought the transaction was without coercion.

"Your earrings too," he said.

Only then did she remember that she was wearing diamond solitaire earrings. How he must loathe her.

She handed them over.

"Thanks, cunt," he said in a singsong voice, as though it had all been a game. Then he released her arm and fled.

She remained pressed to the wall, still feeling his powerful hand on her arm. A streetlight flickered and she snapped to attention, as if someone had slapped her. She picked up the keys and unlocked the door, fumbling. She checked to make sure the door was locked behind her at least five times before running back up to the staff room.

The light was still on inside. She thought that she must have forgotten to turn it off when she left, an instance of the kind of carelessness that Larissa was always correcting. The urge to dwell on the alternate reality was powerful. If she had only remembered her purse in the first place, she would be in her car now on the way home. She pictured herself driving home through the wet streets, listening to CBC, and then at home in the kitchen, eating the leftover lemon pound cake Richard had brought home the day before from a work party. Shaking and out of breath, she stood, perplexed, in the middle of the room. Her purpose—to call Richard to come get her—had been so clear as she'd run up the stairs, but her mind was now blank. She couldn't remember whether she had double-checked the rear door to make sure it was locked. Should she go back down and lock it or barricade herself in the staff room and get on the phone? Should she call Richard or the police? Even as she began to catch her breath, her hands continued to shake uncontrollably.

The door to the staff room creaked open, and a scream began to rise in her (though screaming would have been pointless), until she saw that it was Henry Winter, holding a pile of brown file folders.

"Ruth," he said. "I didn't know anyone else was here."

"I was just mugged," she said, astounded by how normal her voice sounded. She wondered whether he would think she was lying for attention. As she spoke, she started to shake more strongly, and her teeth chattered, though she was not cold. The purely physical reaction of her body puzzled her. She didn't at all feel like crying.

Henry advanced on her quickly. He seized her shoulders firmly.

"Are you hurt?" he asked.

"No, I'm fine," she said. "I don't know why I can't stop shaking. It's stupid."

"You were assaulted," he said.

"Nothing really happened. I only had some jewellery. I'd forgotten my wallet in here."

"Ruth," he said, with an edge of impatience. His grip on her shoulders seemed almost to be holding her up. She had never been so close to him; she was too close, really, to see him at all. She sensed that he had come out of the shower not long before—his silver hair was dark with damp, though it was no longer raining, and he smelled of soap. End-of-day stubble shadowed his cheeks and chin, some of the hairs a stark white shining in the expanse of grey.

"He called me a 'cunt,'" she said wonderingly. "I don't...I was so compliant. Why would he say that?" She found it odd that the name the man—the boy?—had called her felt like the true violence, more than his theft, more than his brutal hand on her arm.

"That kind of hatred is like an ideology," Henry said. "It has nothing to do with you."

He spoke with effortless authority, and for some reason—perhaps because they had no relationship—she believed him in a way that she would not have if Richard said the same thing. She still had the sense that his hands were keeping her upright, and though a part of her felt deeply foolish, she thought that her numbness must be protective in some way, that without it she would be feeling too much: the burgeoning bruise on her upper arm, the soreness of her head where it had hit the brick.

The lights, so reassuring when she had first burst into the room, now seemed excruciatingly radiant. She knew what a wreck she must look—her hair disheveled from a post-school dash to Starbucks for a coffee, her eyes red and swollen and stinging as though she had been weeping. All the things she usually ignored about her face—the wrinkles around her eyes and mouth, the violet circles under her eyes, the occasional spots of sun damage—she became freshly conscious of through Henry's first sighting of them.

"It's over, Ruth," he said. "You're fine now."

She wanted to tell him what had happened, in detail, but speaking felt frivolous. She was afraid of boring him, of being histrionic, of making more out of the incident than was appropriate. When he loosened his hands, she retreated to the sink for a glass of water. He took a step forward as if to follow her, then stopped. Looking at him from the sink, she could see him more clearly. As perplexed as he looked, as aimless, standing in the middle of the room with his arms hanging loosely at his sides, the light served him better than it did her. She felt watched by her former self, who thought Henry an ass, and was embarrassed by her antipathy towards him, which she had taken no efforts to disguise.

"My mother gave me that necklace for my birthday," she said. "It was the last thing she ever bought for me."

"I'm sorry."

"How long have you been here?" she asked. "I didn't see your car. I mean, there were no cars but mine in the lot."

"I'm parked in the driveway out front. I was only hurrying in to pick up some essays I forgot earlier."

This reference to essays brought the room back to her. Her legs were wobbly, and she leaned against the counter, pressing her hand to her forehead.

"It's really the necklace," she said. "That's all it is."

He reached her in two long strides and grabbed her shoulders again. "What do you need?" he asked.

"I don't know," she said, faltering. She had a sense of herself as an old woman, lost in a fog of senility.

"Ruth," he said.

He looked very serious, and she had a flash that he was going to slap her, as people in shock were slapped in movies. But instead of the crisp thwack of his palm on her hot cheek came his lips. He seemed to be giving himself over completely to her, reserving nothing in the event of rejection. "What are you doing?" she wanted to say, but she was embarrassed, overcome by the need to be polite. How could she reject him and still face him the following day? To object would be to expose her own lack of sophistication, a defect that struck her as pathetic in a way that the absence of family loyalty, of basic morality, was somehow not.

Henry's warm hands were gripping the back of her neck almost roughly, and it was only on instinct, she was sure, that her hands travelled under his shirt to his back, to the small patch of hair just above his belt. She wanted to laugh at the silliness of it. Shouldn't some honourable outrage have come surging up from the core of her? But no such fount released. And as the seconds passed, the question of rectitude evaporated. She was not herself. She was not in the place where she walked every day, in all its practical familiarity, in the place where she and Henry Winter were people to whom this had not happened, where they were virtual strangers. What she might think of this on a different day, from a different vantage point, was irrelevant. The room faded from the periphery of her consciousness, and they were suspended in a small space that enclosed only their two bodies. Henry was holding her face now, and she kept her eyes closed, sensing that his were open.

How could something that had never occurred to her have such a feeling of inevitability? She was aware of how strange it was that the possibility of this happening—with Henry or anyone—had never entered her mind. Yet it was happening. She didn't know how, or why, but that was part of the pleasure, that was part of the painful, rapturous clenching in her stomach. It seemed more right this way than if she'd been anticipating and hoping all along. Had she ever felt this way before? This falling inside? His hands were under her shirt, pushing it up in front, then travelling the length of her torso up to her chest, under her bra. She heard herself utter a faint moan, and was embarrassed.

He told her afterwards that he had never been in such a state. From the second he had seen her in the middle of the staff room, her streaked face and tangled hair, her disoriented helplessness, he had known that what he was feeling was no longer deniable. When she told him what had happened outside, he had wanted to kill the mugger. His first instinct had been to tear out of the building and see if he could find him, though he had never been in a physical fight in his life and suspected he would be outmatched if it came to that. But he had realized that the mugger would be long gone, and that, even if he wasn't, Ruth needed him. He could smell the rain on her hair. And then another feeling, a feeling he shouldn't have had, began to rise in him. He was envious of the mugger. He wanted to kill the mugger, and he wanted to be the mugger, to be the man who had been so close to her, who had seen her so raw, so vulnerable, in a way no one else had. He wanted to be the man who pressed her up against a brick wall and felt her force recede under his power. He wanted to feel her against him, under him, locked with him in a moment from which there was no return to normal.

For the time, though, he said nothing. And she needed him to say no more than he already had, when he murmured her name with new understanding, as if its meaning had finally become clear to him.

Chapter Seven

IT WAS SEVERAL WEEKS after Ms. McAllister's announcement about the resurfacing of the flasher, and the happy furor the news had created was dying down. Although the Eliot girls' appetite for scandal was endless, the power of any single crisis to captivate long-term interest was weak. There was always a new outrage, and mass histrionics tended to recede as rapidly as they had arisen in the first place. In the eight weeks that had passed since the start of school, Audrey had watched this ebb and flow with a kind of seasick fascination. First had been the outcry when Tara Dinnick, one of the best basketball players, had decided not to go out for the team because her free time was being eaten up by her attendance at her new boyfriend's soccer games. Then the soccer team had suffered a blow when an unreasonable referee with an obvious bias for Branksome had caused the loss of the first game of the season. The drama department proved no luckier when Laura Willis strained one of her vocal chords and had to give up her lead role in *Man of La Mancha*. The school-wide wail inspired by these events had stunned Audrey at first—dire predictions were made, conspiracy theories were hatched, a curse was spoken of—but she was finally figuring out that the intensity of reaction was unmatched by depth. Ferocity of opinion was just another way in which Eliot girls were bound together, sealed from the outside world.

One morning, Audrey was sitting in her usual spot in the chapel when a small commotion started up in the aisle. The entire row of girls seated in front of Audrey stood in a fluttery panic and fled the pew. A spider, it seemed. Ms. Glover pushed unceremoniously past the crowd, flicked the spider off the bench, and ground its carcass brusquely into the floor with the toe of her running shoe. "Enough silliness," she barked. She then tried, without success, to herd the girls into the pew as they fought over who would sit nearest the squished body. "Bravo, Ms. Glover. You're a hero," said Henry Winter, standing just behind the congestion. He glanced over at Arabella and nodded with a vague smile. Arabella returned a little wave.

"You're *my* hero, Mr. W.," said Whitney.

"That's Dr. W. to you," Arabella replied. "He didn't spend, like, twenty-five years in school for bitches like you to call him mister."

"Language, girls," Henry said.

Whitney's mouth fell open. "Girls?" she exclaimed. "Girls? What did *I* say? Dr. W., watch the favouritism."

He laughed softly and left to find a seat, his posture slightly slumped as though it were the end of a long day.

Audrey listened to the exchange with interest. It was widely known in the class that Arabella's father had died when she was a baby; the tragedy significantly enhanced her celebrity. Occasionally, when another girl in the class mentioned her own father, Arabella withdrew to her desk to place her head sorrowfully in her arms, a posture that reliably drew to her a crowd of girls offering solace. Henry Winter was her new stepfather. Unlike Audrey, though, who continued to be troubled by the complexity of having her mother in her daily world, Arabella seemed not to feel her stepfather's presence as any kind of hindrance. Sometimes Arabella referred to him sarcastically as her "pappy"; otherwise, the exchanges Audrey had witnessed betrayed no personal relationship between them.

Arabella's disdain for teachers was so significant that it was difficult to imagine her living with one. She was, however, a master of an atypical breed of self-control. While she made it known to everyone that Ms. Glover's breast shelf desperately required more support, that Ms. Massie-Turnbull should buy a bottle of Head & Shoulders (and while she was at the drugstore, she could get some dental floss for Mr. Marostica), she was never anything but entirely sweet, almost doting, during her interactions with them, and indeed it added to her contempt that their affection was so easily procured. Seeing Arabella and Henry interact outside of class was mildly rattling to Audrey. The significance of this proof that Arabella existed outside of Eliot did not escape her.

Arabella turned to Whitney and said, "Dude was in the bathroom for like twenty minutes this morning. I kid you not."

When the chapel had filled up, Larissa took to the platform with a brisk energy that, though not dissimilar to her usual vigour, seemed to contain an edge of anger. She gripped the sides of the podium, frowning at a cue card in her hand. The girls around Audrey shifted with nervous excitement and whispered their speculation that there would be imminently unleashed a mass reprimand over one person's wrongdoing. Larissa McAllister's blanket rebukes were not entirely unwelcome. Hilarity blossomed in direct proportion to her fury. The terror and shame she believed she produced, and enjoyed witnessing—the girls rendered silent, studying their laps in stunned humility—were in fact the effects of amusement suppressed. No one could be truly repentant that an unnamed grade twelve student had been spotted eating McDonald's in her school uniform, an act of bad taste strictly against the rules. Upon hearing that a grade nine student had failed to offer up her seat for an elderly woman on the bus, few could feel the level of intense personal guilt Ms. McAllister considered appropriate. No one agreed that public gum-chewing was an offence that brought down the reputation of the entire school. The lectures these gaffes inspired were an enlivening diversion from the ordinary routine. They were imitated for days.

Tapping her cue cards, Ms. McAllister brought everyone to attention. Even before she opened her mouth, Arabella Quincy was stifling giggles. But what Ms. McAllister ended up saying was not what anyone had expected. She had been informed that morning of a death in the extended Eliot family. Martha McKirk, a former member of the grade eleven class, had died in a car accident over the weekend. It would be boorish to get into the particulars, she said— here she cleared her throat and pursed her lips, perhaps stifling a smirk, for there were few things she enjoyed more than withholding particulars—but a memorial assembly would be held the following morning, and although she trusted that the girls would not allow the news to distract them from their studies, they were permitted to avail themselves of the therapeutic support of Ms. Loveland, the guidance counsellor. A regular assembly followed, though no one was able to pay attention, and Ms. McAllister spent the duration peevishly shushing the spreading chatter.

Later, Ruth told Audrey that if Larissa seemed angry, it's because she was. That morning, she had been planning to unveil her plan for a new inter-school event that would be part educational and part fun. An amalgam of math, literature, and obscure trivia, it would be like an Olympics for the brain. The idea seemed so inevitable, so teeming with social and academic possibilities, Larissa was amazed that no one had conceived it sooner, and she was happily plotting the wording of her announcement when she received the sombre call.

Ms. McAllister and Martha McKirk had a tempestuous history. Martha McKirk had started at Eliot in grade one as a submissive, bucktoothed girl with math skills far exceeding her grade level, but somewhere along her way to what Ms. McAllister hoped would be MIT, she got derailed—perhaps, the theory went, because her mother had left her law career to pursue life as a yoga instructor— and she could no longer commit to Eliot's vision of excellence. Dying her blonde hair black was the first sign of what was to follow. The nadir of her contributions to Eliot was showing up drunk to the carol service at Christmas and singing loudly off-key all through Nikki Sanderson's solo during "Once in Royal David's City," and then disrupting Ms. McAllister's reading from the Gospel of Luke with a noisy release of false flatulence every time Ms. McAllister said the word *Lord*. It was agreed during a subsequent conference with Martha McKirk's parents that it would be best for Martha's class, and for Martha herself, if she were withdrawn from Eliot.

After the phone call, Larissa had deliberated for fifteen minutes about whether to delay the announcement of Martha's death and proceed with her original plan. In the end, though, she knew that she could not. So if she seemed angry in assembly, it was not at the tragedy that had stolen a young life, it was at Martha McKirk, for upstaging her once again.

Nowhere, however, were Ms. McAllister's true feelings in evidence the following morning in the chapel as students gathered for the memorial assembly. An ambience of forced solemnity had overtaken Eliot's corridors. The gleeful gossip had abated, and all were united in understanding the importance of projecting the spirit of grief. The students filed quietly into the chapel, which was furnished with poster-sized, sepia-toned pictures of Martha engaging in a variety of Eliot activities. The sepia tint had made Martha's image timeless and, in removing her coarser modern edge, had conferred upon her a comforting lack of nuance. She was a pigtailed first grader, beaming a guileless smile full of missing teeth. She was a head-geared seventh grader, reading *The Velveteen Rabbit* to the Junior School. She played soccer. She spiked volleyballs. She studied a Bunsen burner. Thus contained, Martha was the very incarnation of the ideal Eliot girl. Conspicuously absent were images of Martha post tar-black hair, save one, where she was bundled in winter gear and a wool toque. Audrey was amazed by the sheer number of photographs (and by the appearance of Ruth in one, looking much older than her age in a dated outfit, her hair feathered and sprayed in place, her neck swallowed by mountainous shoulder pads, as she helped Martha, dressed as a bunch of grapes, carve a pumpkin for a Halloween party). The gallery gave the impression that Martha's entire life had been spent in Eliot. The rest was an ellipsis.

The service began with a hymn, "The Lord's My Shepherd." Ms. Massie-Turnbull accompanied on the piano, leaning into the chords soulfully. She had dressed in black for the occasion, but because she favoured happy colours, the only black items she had been able to locate in her closet were a faded black sweatshirt, black cords worn grey at the knees, and a black plastic headband. When the singing ended, Ms. McAllister ruffled the pages before her and surveyed the room disapprovingly, unwilling to begin until the motion had subsided and all eyes were dutifully transfixed on her.

"'It is not death that a man should fear, but he should fear never beginning to live,'" she said with an unnatural calm, as though practising her radio voice. "So said Marcus Aelius Aurelius, and when I think of the short life and tragic death of Martha McKirk, no words seem more appropriate. Although Martha's life was cut short, we can take solace in the fact that she must have met her end peaceful in the knowledge that the charge of never beginning to live could not be laid against her. All of us who knew Martha could not fail to be touched by her powerful presence, her refusal to be complacent, her courageous resolve to live each moment of her life fully—values, I dare say, she learned right here at George Eliot Academy."

She went on to give a speech about Martha's time at Eliot, or more precisely, the positive effect of Eliot on Martha's life. She spoke fondly of Martha's math skills and lamented the fact that they would never reach their full potential. At one point, she lost herself in an extended digression about the qualities of the ideal Eliot girl and ventured that such a person knows the value of words and uses them wisely, as in the instance of asking for tape. This was a personal pet peeve of hers and came up regularly in her lectures. The ideal girl, she said, understood the meaning of the word *borrow*, which means a temporary loan with the implication of a speedy return. Students too often came to her office saying, "May I borrow some tape?" These girls, of course, didn't mean "borrow" at all. They were asking if they could *have* some tape. Here Ms. McAllister paused and cleared her throat. She was heartened to recall a time not long past when Martha McKirk appeared in her office, asking if she could have some tape. Such memories could not be overvalued. She concluded with an invocation of Gandhi, transforming his philosophical observation "Live as if you were to die tomorrow. Learn as if you were to live forever" into a firm injunction to all girls to study hard "for Martha's sake." Then she stepped away from the lectern, saluting a photograph of Martha presenting a tray of brownies at a bake sale.

Girls from Martha's class hugged each other in the back rows. Elsewhere, students sniffled discreetly, dabbing their eyes with damp, balled-up Kleenex. A strangled whoop sounded behind Audrey, and she turned to find Arabella Quincy shuddering in a display of full-bodied sorrow that seemed somehow disproportionate to the actual number of tears being produced.

Ms. McAllister now invited up to the front any teachers and students who wished to express some concise thoughts about Martha. This portion of the service was seen as an opportunity to delay first period for as long as possible, and girls clutching scraps of paper flooded the platform, crowding the centre in whispery disorder until Ms. McAllister, with the instructive hand gestures of a traffic cop, directed them into an orderly line. The microphone underwent many adjustments and screeches as girl after girl came forward to seize her moment. Plentiful were stories about childhood experiences with Martha, roller coaster rides at Canada's Wonderland, slumber parties, horror movies. Kate Gibson told a long story about a Saturday spent volunteering at the Daily Bread Food Bank, allegedly Martha's favourite charity. A full twenty minutes later, Ms. Loveland took to the microphone and offered a short summation of Martha, submitting that she was an "open spirit." The mawkish New Age ring of this label seemed to please everyone. "We always lose our open spirits too soon," she said, sniffling.

As the press of girls departed to return to their seats, an insignificant figure hidden by the shadows at the back of the platform moved. A stool, being dragged, scraped the wood floor. It seemed to Audrey later that a full minute must have passed before the obvious became clear to her. Not until the chords had begun their tribute, not until the words "I have no doubt Martha is smiling down on us now" had been spoken, did she actually understand that Seeta Prasad was performing "Candle in the Wind." Seeta made the most of her moment, playing the song at a funereal tempo, glancing occasionally at Martha's pictures with a compassionate smile. Bowing her head, she seemed satisfied, as well, by the response of the student body—she could not claim responsibility for the tears, to be sure, but they must have struck her as stirring confirmation of her power.

Audrey was relieved that for once she wouldn't have to staunch the rise of her own tears. She'd felt the sadness building in her from the first words of the service, intensifying with each reverent display, but she'd expected her own shame to beat it back. It wasn't even fair, really, to classify such feelings as sadness, given how exclusively they were roused not by distress over the dead girl, but by pity for herself. To watch the whole school rally in mourning for Martha McKirk only made Audrey more aware of how remotely she still stood from Eliot's innermost gate. She ought to have known Martha McKirk. She ought to have been a part of all this history. But she had been shut out, then, as she was shut out now.

As Seeta finished her song and retreated to the wings, the sound of a choir started up in the shadows at the back of the chapel, where Martha McKirk's former class was beginning a procession down the aisle. The girls were all holding yellow roses and singing "Be Thou My Vision." As each girl arrived at the front of the chapel, she laid her yellow rose at the base of Martha's grade eight class portrait before withdrawing. Some bowed their heads solemnly; some crossed themselves; many blew Martha a kiss.

They were all so wonderfully sad for Martha, so moved by the spectacle of themselves grieving her, but Audrey was entitled to none of it. How was it that even Seeta believed herself connected to all this feeling? Seeta, whose playing, not a week before, had been universally reviled? The injustice of it confounded her. And even though she knew the real story of Martha and Eliot, even though she knew that Ms. McAllister couldn't stand the girl, the only thing she could truly see was her own seclusion. If there was something profane in meeting a young person's death with such dishonesty, she didn't care. She envied Martha McKirk. The smallest part of her wanted to be Martha McKirk. Martha was no longer an Eliot girl, but still the Eliot girls considered her one of their own. They wanted to be part of the grief at her death. Did the quotient of sincerity matter, in the end? If there was one benefit of dying young, it was surely this: to be misremembered so beautifully. The sun shone through the high stained-glass windows, casting regions of multicoloured light around the chapel with seemingly strategic flair—over Martha's flower-bearing classmates, over Martha's unknowing smile.

Ms. McAllister stepped forward to lead the congregation in the prayer of St. Francis of Assisi, and Ms. Massie-Turnbull took to the piano to play a final hymn, "God Be with You till We Meet Again," which Ms. McAllister, not requiring a hymn book, sang bullyingly into the microphone.

And it was over. Someone had propped open the heavy oak doors at the back of the chapel, and people were already leaving, laughing and calling to each other as they made their way out into the sun.

AUDREY WAS CROSSING THE quad on her way back to Devon Hall when she felt a warm, moist hand over her eyes.

"Guess who?" sang Seeta's voice.

Audrey pried the hand away and kept walking. "Hi."

Audrey's unfriendliness did nothing to deter Seeta. Whether she was needy or unaware, Audrey couldn't tell. Even when Audrey blatantly tried to escape her, taking a seat at the back of the room one recent morning in music class, Seeta took no notice, waving to Audrey with the full force of her arm, as though Audrey were trying to spot her in a dense crowd. In the hallways, in the classrooms, her eyes chased Audrey down with their bright, uncompromising stare.

"That was a really beautiful ceremony," Seeta said, falling into step next to Audrey on the quad, raising her face to the sky in contentment.

Audrey shrugged.

"Didn't you think so?"

"It was nice, I guess."

"It made me wish I'd known Martha. I've heard some things about her, but I don't think they can be true, given everything Ms. McAllister just said."

Audrey gave Seeta a mystified look. She was incredulous that Seeta had been on the inside track of even the smallest bit of gossip. "What have you heard?"

"On the bus home yesterday, Laura Chang was telling me that Martha McKirk was, um…" Here Seeta coughed prudishly and looked around. "I probably shouldn't repeat it."

"You've got to tell me now," Audrey said. "You can't start then just stop."

"But it's not really appropriate, especially now that she's passed away."

"Why did you bring it up then?"

Seeta made a worried face. "I tried to get Laura not to tell me, but she was determined. You're right, I shouldn't have brought it up."

Audrey sighed. "Fine, then." She started walking again.

Seeta quickened her pace to keep up. "Okay. But you have to promise not to tell anyone else."

Audrey nodded.

Seeta leaned in and spoke in a voice just above a whisper. "She and her boyfriend were caught, um, you know, in the bathroom at the St. George's semi-formal."

"What?" Audrey said. "They were having sex at the semi?"

"Shhh," Seeta replied, her eyes wide.

Arabella, Whitney, and Dougie were just then passing, and they stopped beside Audrey and Seeta.

"You don't say," Arabella said in a British accent. "Sexual relations? Really? How scandalous!"

Whitney and Dougie laughed.

"Poor Larissa must have been jealous," said Whitney.

"It can't be easy being a ninety-year-old virgin," offered Dougie.

"Actually," said Seeta, raising her chin defiantly, "it's an inspired life choice. Ms. McAllister's chosen to make a really sophisticated assertion of her feminist values."

"Ms. McAllister's a virgin?" asked Audrey. "How do you know?"

"How do you *not* know? She tells all her religion classes," said Whitney coldly. She turned to Seeta. "That's the first time I've heard someone call being a dried-up old bitch a feminist statement."

"She's standing up for what she believes in," replied Seeta.

"It's not feminist," Arabella said. "It's religious and reactionary. But hey, it's a good thing you admire it. I'm sure one day you'll be just like her." She gave Audrey a queenly look. "We'll let you girls get going. I'm sure you don't want to be late for math." And with a laugh that drew her friends to her, she turned away. Within seconds, they were lost in the crowd congesting the open doorway.

"Well, I'm always up for a debate," Seeta said happily, "but of course it's better when everyone plays fair."

She took Audrey by the elbow and pulled her gently towards the door. "Come on, pal. It's true. I don't want to be late for math. Mr. Marostica promised to give me some harder problems for extra credit."

Chapter Eight

WHEN MIDTERM REPORT CARDS arrived in early November, Audrey spent the day feeling as though she might throw up. There were rumours that Larissa McAllister kicked out students who got more than two marks below seventy percent, and although Ruth said this wasn't true, the fact of the matter was that very few girls regularly received grades in the sixties. In Audrey's class, many girls considered even seventy-five a calamity. Sarah-Jane Day had once required a paper bag to breathe into when she got seventy-one on a math test.

The report cards came during English class. Henry Winter was lecturing on "A Rose for Emily" when Ms. Moss, the secretary, knocked with foreboding quiet. Henry Winter started in surprise, then crossed to the door and engaged her in a whispery conference before returning with the pile and placing it next to his briefcase. He then resumed his lecture as though nothing had happened, seemingly oblivious to the anxiety coursing through his audience. Finally Whitney called out, "Please, show some noblesse oblige, Dr. W. Put us out of our misery!" He looked up, as though confused to hear a voice other than his own.

"Oh, are you interested in these?" he asked, gesturing towards the envelopes with a crooked half smile, suggesting that perhaps he hadn't been in a cerebral daze all along.

Audrey couldn't quite get a handle on Henry Winter. The other teachers fit various expectations of what teachers should be: the popular ones who were approachable and funny and tried to meet the students as equals; the older ones who were kind but out of touch; the strict ones who could barely be believed to exist outside of school. Henry Winter did not fit any of these types, a fact that made him infinitely less approachable. During class, he often paced at the front of the room, jangling coins in his pocket. He glanced at the clock frequently. His mind seemed not to be entirely with the class. It was as though he were performing in a pageant written by grade schoolers, and although bound to indulge the children and recite the lines, he couldn't hide that he found the dialogue atrocious and utterly lacking in credibility. At other times, he was charming and dropped sudden jokes into the middle of lectures, and when the girls laughed, he was clearly gratified. His own laughter would swell up, then just as quickly subside, as if he had lost himself for a moment before remembering where he was.

He walked the aisles now with a slowness that might have been real or a torturous tease. The report cards were in alphabetical order, so Audrey received hers quickly, but unlike everyone else, she felt no temptation to rip it open right away. As Henry Winter had handed it to her, their eyes met, and she tried to read what she saw there. But he offered no clue—no sympathy, no consternation—nothing that foreshadowed what he might have seen inside.

When Seeta opened her report card, she made a noisy intake of breath, then whispered, "Yippee!" to herself. All around Audrey, the rustling and tearing of paper, the nervous silence, gave way to sighs and mumbles, the occasional groan or shriek of relief. Audrey's results were worse than she thought. Of eight subjects, she'd received seventies in only three. Three others were in the high sixties, and two—math and French—were a nausea-inducing fifty-eight. Most of the teachers had made prim comments about the meeting of her potential. Mme. Moreau had written, "I keep hoping for some improvement," as though Audrey's performance had been a terrible blow to her personal sense of expectation. Henry Winter's comment was illegible, a scrawl that didn't want to fit into the small rectangle provided, though Audrey thought she made out the word *adequate*. She knew that she shouldn't have been surprised, but some tests were yet to be returned, and somehow she had thought there could be a disparity between the marks she had received along the way and the final result. She was about to stuff the report back into the envelope when she noticed a note at the bottom: "Please be in my office at four o'clock sharp. Ms. McAllister."

Audrey glanced around the room. No one appeared as pale and troubled as she was. Most people were showing their report cards to their friends. Vanessa Blair had lain her head, face down, in her arms on her desk. (Audrey overheard later that this was because she had received a seventy-eight in math.) Arabella was loudly bemoaning, so that everyone was sure to hear, that she had done horribly, absolutely horribly, in French. "Eighty-three," she wailed. "It's so bad." Seeta had placed her report card flat against her desk, as if to appreciate it, like a work of art, from a different angle, and Audrey noticed no mark below ninety.

Audrey knew that she would not look at hers ever again, unless she was forced to by her parents. Having foreseen exactly this outcome, she didn't understand why she felt so jarred. There was something in the nature of a formal document, she supposed. As individual marks, sixties and seventies had been easy enough to ignore—they had seemed somehow temporary, the possibility of change, of improvement, still existed. But here before her was the power of compilation, accumulation; there was the bleakness of authority, of irrevocability. Particularly galling had been all the comments about how she needed to try harder. She felt she had tried, though perhaps not in the way her teachers meant. She didn't even know how to try in the way they meant. She had sat at her desk many school evenings and Saturday mornings, in her black ergonomic chair, bought by Ruth in the hope that by facilitating the appearance of scholarly aptitude, she could engender the proper inner feeling. But no matter how Ruth designed the exterior, the interior would not follow. Audrey simply had not been able to keep her mind trained on her work. She considered the image of herself, bent over her books in a useless show of academic piety, and was overcome with self-pity.

Audrey stayed in her seat while the classroom emptied, then packed her bag and headed down to Ruth's classroom to report the news. They had planned to go shopping for new jeans and were due to meet at 3:45.

"I can't bear the thought of going to a mall," Ruth said when she saw Audrey. "I was thinking Bloor Street and then dinner at Spring Rolls."

Audrey shook her head dolefully. "I can't go."

Ruth cocked her head in query.

"I have to meet Ms. McAllister in ten minutes." Audrey cast her eyes down.

Ruth's face fell. "Oh, come on," she said, holding out her hand. "Give it here."

Audrey produced the wrinkled report. For several silent moments, Ruth stared at it, looking as disgusted as if it were a particularly vulgar piece of pornography. Then she shut her eyes. The struggle that played out over the course of a millisecond was almost visible. Ruth wrested her natural response—anger, and the impulse to punish—into something more suitably delicate. When she looked at Audrey again, she was a model of vivacity. "Well, it's just the first report! Things will change," she said.

"That's it?"

"What more should there be? It's just a midterm report. It's not that significant."

Audrey shook her head. She had thought that she feared Ruth's passionate dismay, but this reaction was far more disorienting. It was clear that Ruth was being circumspect, and in that tact was a quality Audrey found dishonest. Concern about Audrey's academic fate had always been a key feature of Ruth's life. Audrey had felt almost debilitated at times by the weight of her mother's hopes for her. A decade-old image of Ruth, standing on the front walk in the twilight, under the specific light of the iron lantern, still haunted her. In Ruth's hand, a white envelope: Audrey's first rejection from Eliot. It was Audrey's chore to bring in the mail, but she had forgotten that day. Hearing Ruth's car pull into the driveway, she had run to the window to greet her mother, but Ruth had stopped in her tracks. A sickness flooded Audrey's gut. Never had she seen her mother's face so bereft. Minutes later, she discovered the contents of the letter, and felt worse still, not at the retreating promise of the Eliot life, but at the woe in her mother's face. In that moment came Audrey's first confrontation with her own power, a glimpse of the responsibility she would consciously bear for the rest of her life.

She knew that she should be thankful that they were not now embroiled in a heated argument, fighting to keep their voices down so no one would overhear. But she was not. Her mother's artifice felt like yet another way she had been cast out of the familiar world.

Ruth sat on the edge of the desk and glanced at the report again. "It's my fault anyway. I should never have let this happen."

But this absolution was no more welcome. "How is it exactly that *you* made it happen?"

"You need a tutor, Audrey. We'll get someone really great. Please agree." Ruth leaned forward and kissed Audrey on the head just as footsteps sounded out in the hall. Ruth and Audrey looked up tensely and saw Henry Winter approaching at a leisurely amble. As he continued around the corner, he gave them a little nod.

When he was out of sight, Ruth handed the report card back to Audrey. Then she stood, and as she pulled on her own coat, she gave Audrey an impatient shove in the direction of the door. "Look, you should go. The last thing you need now is to be late for Larissa."

IN THE OFFICE, AUDREY waited for ten minutes before Larissa McAllister was ready to see her. Ms. Moss sat at her desk, alternately typing and filing papers. In what seemed an ostentatious show of avoidance, she scarcely acknowledged Audrey's presence. No sounds emerged from within the chamber, but when the door finally opened, a grade seven girl exited, looking red-eyed and chastened.

In stately silence, Ms. McAllister ushered Audrey inside and gestured for her to sit in the ladder-backed chair. For some moments, she relished the hush her office produced. The last of the day's sunlight poured in through her pristine windows, slanting across her tidy desk. Audrey had last been in this room for her entrance interview, and she was no more at home now than she had been then. Still, this was the room in which all her deficiencies were brought to unsparing analysis. Still, this was the room in which her most graceless self came tripping out into the spotlight.

"I have always been loath to make exceptions," Larissa McAllister said at last. "Second-guessing is for the halting mind. In life, as in an examination, my approach is confident. Never have I changed an answer on a test paper."

Audrey studied her hands, waiting for more.

"I was not," she continued, "under the impression that you would be one of our star pupils. Our entrance examinations serve the very important purpose of helping us to assess a potential student's intellectual promise. Your results on these tests were telling. And I fear that I predicted you and I would end up exactly here."

She primly adjusted her glasses and leaned forward, hands folded, a pose that might have seemed confiding had it not been for the sparkling hostility in her face. Audrey's own face burned. Larissa gently tapped the tiny gold cross that lay just below her jutting collarbone, as if calling on divine sustenance.

"In what has been proven to be a regrettable error," she said, "I set aside my own sizeable misgivings because of your mother. She had high hopes for you."

Audrey noted the past tense.

In spite of Ms. McAllister's repeated allusions to her displeasure, there was nothing in her demeanour to suggest upset. On the contrary, exhilaration coursed visibly through her. Her face was bright and hard, her dry cheeks flushed. The battle against academic apathy was a terrifying one, she declared. They were in the trenches, all of them, fighting for a mandate on which the whole world seemed to depend. And could there be a more critical mission? Could there be a nobler cause? Audrey knew that her desolation must only remind Ms. McAllister of the passionless masses, that it must make her angrier, hungrier, but she couldn't speak. She had no self-defence.

"I'm sure you realize that your mother's position as a teacher makes your results even more distressing," continued Ms. McAllister. "Do you understand how badly it reflects on George Eliot Academy for the daughter of a teacher to produce such substandard results? Have you anything to say for yourself?"

"I'm going to get a tutor," Audrey answered. "I know I should do better."

"It goes without saying that you *should* do better. The question, I suppose, is whether you *can* do better." Here she swung her chair around to face the window, leaving Audrey to stare at its tall leather back. After a moment, she circled back to Audrey, her hands folded in her lap in a prayer pose. "Tell me. Why did you want to come to George Eliot?"

Audrey considered this question. In truth, she no longer knew why she had wanted to come to George Eliot. It had something to do with a memory she scarcely understood. A floating red balloon wending its way over the clock tower of Devon Hall, that murmur of magic in the place. From earliest childhood, her desire for Eliot had an inevitability she never thought to probe. She had championed Eliot's progressive feminist agenda. She had trained for the entrance exams and engaged in practice interview sessions with Ruth. She had visited the school and roamed its wide corridors in aspirational wonder. Never had it occurred to her to analyze why she might want to go there, any more than she could now explain why she wanted to stay there. Before that final round of entrance exams, trudging to tutoring every day after school, she had never considered opposing her mother's wishes, so indistinguishable from her own. Even now, as daily life involved no satisfaction greater than mere survival, the Eliot dream was not an easy one to relinquish.

"It's the best school there is," Audrey said feebly.

"Indeed," replied Ms. McAllister. "The question now is what will *you* do to be the best *you* can be?" She rose from her chair and crossed to the door. "You have much fodder for thought. Introspection is to be the order of the day."

As Ms. McAllister opened the door, Audrey saw Kelly Stiles, a grade twelve who had reputedly once been paid a hundred dollars by a UCC boy for a blow job, waiting her turn, looking pre-emptively chastised. Ms. McAllister gripped Audrey's upper arm firmly with her bony hand and said, *"Per studia mens nova."*

Out of the burnished library light of the office, Audrey shrank in the exposure of the wide corridor. Head down, she hurried to her classroom. All she wanted was to get out of the building. She felt watched, overheard. There seemed no privacy to her failure. Surely everyone knew. A stronger person, she thought, would have been motivated, determined to prove herself, but all she felt was a sinking inside. She wanted to cry, not so much in embarrassment as in regret. If only she had refused to take that last entrance test. If only she had summoned all her strength, corralled every rebellious impulse she had never acted on, for just one moment, a millisecond, really, to say no. How could she have neglected to foresee this mess? In a haze of humiliation, she made straight for her desk and began throwing binders and pencils into her bag.

She became aware of the sound of quiet music only after it stopped. Looking up, she saw Seeta lounging in a window seat, strumming her guitar.

"Hey," Seeta said, jumping down. "Just practising a new tune for tomorrow."

Audrey returned a thin smile.

Seeta set her guitar down and let out a sigh heavy with the troubles of the world. "So, I'm glad you're here, actually. I've been wanting to talk to you."

The first thought that entered Audrey's mind was that Seeta was going to make a direct plea for friendship. Maybe invite her to her house. Audrey was stricken with panic at the prospect of this confrontation. She could bear going on as they were, but the thought of formalizing their association, intensifying it, making a public declaration of sorts, was unthinkable.

"This is difficult," Seeta said, sighing again. "Look, yesterday, we had that math test. I think you know where I'm going with this. I thought of telling Mr. Marostica, but that didn't seem like the honourable thing to do if we could sort it out ourselves."

Audrey looked at her in confusion.

"Are you going to pretend you don't know what I'm saying?" Seeta asked.

The hesitance in Seeta's face was retreating and in its place grew something harder and more formed. Audrey searched her mind for a clue. "There's no pretending. I have no idea what you're talking about," she said.

"The math test," Seeta said emphatically.

"The math test?"

"You cheated. You were looking at my paper. I saw you. If you're going to deny it, I might as well just tell Mr. Marostica."

Audrey was astounded. She and Seeta sat in the front row, right under Mr. Marostica's nose, and even if it had occurred to her to cheat, she would never have dared.

"I didn't cheat," Audrey said. "I didn't look at your test."

"I saw you."

"Don't flatter yourself."

"I see your marks when you get tests back," Seeta said. "I know you need help. I saw your report card, no matter how you tried to hide it."

"My report card is none of your business!" Audrey exclaimed.

"It is if you're cheating off me."

Audrey turned her back and Seeta came around so that they were again standing face to face. "I have rights here!" Seeta said. "My work is private, and just because I got stuck sitting next to someone who can't calculate the value of x doesn't mean I should pay—"

"Just fuck off, would you?" Audrey burst out.

Seeta blinked at Audrey as though she had never before heard the word *fuck*. She looked almost dizzy with shock, her eyes wandering, her face washed of all expression. For a second, she teetered on the spot, then lurched forward, grabbed her guitar, and fled from the room. Audrey sat at her desk and pressed her forehead with the heels of her hands. Now Seeta would tell on her. Swearing was an infraction that incurred demerits, but given her academic performance, the punishment might be worse. Detention? Such a penalty seemed so crude. Did detention even exist at Eliot?

She sat in worried silence for some minutes, half-expecting a teacher to thunder through the door any second. Finally, she gathered her things and made her exit into the early evening.

This was how so many days ended now, in an orchid dusk whose descent she had scarcely noticed. The streetlights had come on in the quiet avenue beyond the tall Eliot gate, and it was there that she wanted to be, on the roads that streamed in every direction away from here. For the first time in her remembered life, she longed to be on the other side of the enclave. But it was the ultimate escape she desired, not just a departure, but a purging: her mind capsized, emptied of all its knowledge of the place. She couldn't leave, though, not now. It was too late.

A few girls milled around on the front steps, waiting for late rides, but no one noticed her. No one said goodbye. Down the long driveway she started, under the spartan coverage of the winter-ready trees. She walked quickly, paying little attention to the dirty black SUV pulling up alongside her. On its passenger side door, someone had traced "xoxo" in the thick dust, and when it screeched to a stop, the rear window opened. Low hoots and soprano shrieks of male and female laughter flooded the air like a gale of smoke. Audrey looked up to find Arabella sitting in the back, packed in tightly with five other people.

"Yo, yo!" called out a Crescent boy in a mocking tone.

Whitney was sitting on a boy's lap, nuzzling his neck, at the far end of the back seat.

"The walk of shame?" Arabella said with an imperious lack of sympathy.

"I guess," Audrey replied.

"Larissa's probably up there smoking a cigarette as we speak."

Audrey forced a little laugh. For a second, she wondered if they were going to offer her a ride, but then the driver revved the engine, and Arabella let her hand flop out of the window in a throwaway wave. "Well, ta-ta!" she cried. The window rose, and she became again an unidentifiable silhouette behind the tinted glass. A spurt of exhaust clouded the air, and the SUV was off, speeding towards the front gate and screeching out onto the road, leaving too much silence in its wake.

Chapter Nine

RUTH OFTEN HAD FLASHES where she felt that she had been transported to an alternate reality. She would tune out for no more than seconds, and when she returned to herself, everything looked just a little different, in no way clear enough to articulate. She might be sitting at a red light, the stream of pedestrians drawing her into a meaningless daze, a welcome moment of emptiness, and when her senses reawakened, there was a film between her and the world. It was as though she had been hit by a temporary, mild myopia. The trees and the sky seemed to have withdrawn slightly, and all the objects in her vision were vaguely hazy. Her sense of unreality was so strong that she would wonder if something terrible had happened, if she had been catapulted out of the known world and was suspended in some liminal psychic space, that maybe she was not sitting, as it seemed, at the red light, watching all the pedestrians walk past, that in fact she had ploughed straight through them all and simply didn't know it yet, that she was caught in a chasm between before and after and it would take some time for her mind to catch up to what her body already knew. She'd had such flashes often when Audrey was a baby. She would be walking down the stairs, baby in her arms, and her sleeve would catch the top of the banister, or she would lose her footing and almost trip, and when she reached the bottom of the stairs, she would wonder if she really had fallen, if now in reality she was screaming over the broken body of her baby while her mind remained in the protective realm of what was supposed to be.

So did she feel as she walked into George Eliot the morning after Henry came to her in the staff room. Nothing looked quite as she remembered it, and nothing looked altered. She could see the school from the road, through the newly leafless trees. In every definable way Eliot looked as it always had, but the clear day allowed the sun to fall unobstructed across the buildings in such a way that she felt alert to them for the first time in years. There was an unworldly precision to the buildings' outlines that gave her the sense of a sophisticated film set, as though she were looking at mere façades that would topple in a strong wind.

All day she had seemed to be on the verge of seeing him. She looked for his little Saab in the parking lot when she arrived and didn't see it, but minutes after she settled in her classroom, she heard his voice in the hallway. On Wednesday mornings, Junior and Senior school assemblies were separate, and when her class was filing into the gym, she saw the back of his head as he ushered the grade elevens out the side door to the chapel. She was irritated that each time they nearly collided, it was she who had heard him, she who had seen him, while to him she remained unobserved.

The night of the kiss she had not slept. She had lain in bed on her back, eyes closed. She was not exactly replaying the kiss, for she could not have replayed the scene even with great effort—she was living, still, too much inside it to confer on it such objective study. It reverberated inside her with its obscure sensory power, and she relived it as miniature explosions in her consciousness. Now and then, a punctuating snore from Richard startled her out of her reverie, but when all was quiet again, she resettled in the absorbing private regions of her mind.

In the pale grey clarity of the morning, however, she found that she was no longer able to summon the sensations of Henry Winter's insistent lips, his long fingers on her skin, the aftertaste of apple in his mouth. The more she thought about the kiss, the more she was taken away from a conviction in its reality—the less plausibly it seemed to be anything but a construct of her hyperactively wishful mind. It could not have been Henry Winter—Henry Winter, who had coolly informed Larissa McAllister in front of a staff room full of teachers that he preferred not to overuse the word *brilliant* when she had just applied it to an award-winning grade twelve English essay—it could not have been that man who embraced her with such crushing warmth. His advance on her conflicted with every impression she'd ever had of him. The change was incomprehensible and destabilizing.

And then there were her lies to Richard. As soon as she got home, before he could notice its absence on his own, she told him that her wedding ring had rolled down a sewer. She described, without suspiciously excessive detail, how she had placed the ring on the hood of her car while she applied hand cream, then accidentally knocked it off when she reached for it, how it had rolled neatly, as if along a track, and then through the grate before she knew what was happening. The story made very little sense, but Richard wasn't prone to doubt and analysis. The earrings and the necklace he would never even notice.

The reason she had lied to him about the mugging was not particularly clear to her. It had something to do with the attention he would heap on her if she told him the truth. She didn't want the plans and solutions and rehashing, the concerned awe, the husbandly indignation and the overprotection that might follow, the whispery comfort he would offer in bed. She just wanted to be left alone with her thoughts of Henry. Richard had given her a short lecture about carelessness, while she sat at the table with her head bowed, not listening to a word, and then he left her alone because he was irritated. He thought she was quiet because she felt guilty about losing the ring.

But she felt guilty about nothing.

She was as aware of guilt as she might be of any obligation that was a drag. The unwashed dishes piled in the kitchen sink when all she wanted was to sit down with a book. The plate of broccoli, the snow needing to be shovelled, the yard full of dog shit. Her compassion for Richard and her marriage was crowded out by her desire to see Henry again. Guilt was nothing more than a principle, honourable and valid in the abstract but sterile and useless in application to her specific needs.

On the day of Henry's and her shared break, she nearly avoided going to the staff room because she didn't want to appear to be seeking him out. The prospect that he would apologize terrified her. If he showed remorse, if he were cautious with her, she didn't think she could bear it.

He entered while she was preparing a cup of coffee, and when she heard him laugh at a remark made by Michael Curtis, she became so agitated that she upset her mug on Lorna's loaf of gluten-free bread. Muttering to no particular audience that she'd forgotten something in her classroom, she mopped up her mess and made a bashful exit.

Several minutes later came a knock on her classroom door.

"Are you always so clumsy?" he said.

He came inside and closed the door, and at his touch, she went floppy and yielding, as though someone had removed all her joints. He pushed her into the corner behind the door and pressed himself against her, so that anyone looking for her would have opened the door right into them. He held his mouth near hers for a moment, then kissed her with reserve, as though his lips were determined to be more polite than his urgent body, its persuasive weight pinning her to the wall.

At first, she was aware only of his lips and his hands, but then she heard a knocking, distantly, at the margins of her consciousness. For a moment, the sound seemed to be coming from inside her until she realized that it was footsteps in the hall. She jerked in shock, and they came apart.

Trembling—whether with fear or reverberating desire she was not sure—she went back to her desk and sat down, a red pen and an open folder of papers before her. Henry opened the door and leaned against the frame, slightly out of breath. They watched each other in silence until the footsteps receded.

"Were you all right getting home on your own last night?" he asked in a low voice.

"Yes. Uneventful."

"I was concerned about the after-effects of an event like that."

She dismissed the comment with a wave of her hand.

"Is there any chance of your belongings being recovered?"

"I wouldn't think so," she answered. "I never called the police."

When Henry left, Ruth got up and went to the bathroom. A dying fluorescent bulb over the cubicles hissed and flickered for several minutes before it went out. Facing her reflection in the cold grey light, she started to giggle. Laughter was burbling up, from a place deep in her gut, a place that was raw like the skin under a fingernail. She put her hand over her mouth instinctively, like a child trying to contain laughter in church, but it was beyond her. She took several deep breaths, calmed herself, then regressed, and finally managed to gain control.

She studied her face. She wouldn't have said that she looked exactly good that day—she had rejected the self-abasement implicit in prettying herself, and she was wary of any actions Henry might interpret as special effort for him—but she was comforted by what she saw. Of course she was aging, but she could still look at herself and see the teenager she had been. One day, she knew that she would look in the mirror and find an unrecognizable old woman. But for now she still looked like the girl who had not yet conceived of a husband or a child, the girl who smiled sweetly in old pictures of high school dances, who was only just beginning to intuit the exhilarating scope of her own power.

THE FOLLOWING AFTERNOON, HENRY approached her in the hallway at the beginning of the lunch hour.

"Shall we take lunch outside?" he asked.

She stared at him, clutching a brown paper bag containing leftover pasta and an apple. They were standing in the crowded hallway, people swirling around them. The possibility of conversing openly had never occurred to her.

"When I was walking the other day, I noticed a little park not far away," he said. "I could use some air. You?"

Ruth glanced towards the staff room. She was just as glad to avoid it. Lately, it had been a social minefield. Since the argument about Seeta, she had found even the most minor communications excruciating. Every time she stepped into the room, someone was at her, wanting to share a word of support or concern about Audrey's adjustment. It seemed that everyone considered Audrey perilously shy. Ruth despised being constantly confronted by this new view of her daughter—for her part, she couldn't tell whether Audrey cared too much about being liked or too little, whether she suffered from intensity or apathy—and she couldn't help being annoyed at Audrey for putting her, however unwittingly, in such an uncomfortable position.

Ruth looked around nervously. "Okay," she replied. She didn't know whether to be reassured or disappointed by the lack of flirtatious subterfuge in his voice.

She followed him out and around the corner in silence, uneasily affecting the cavalier attitude he seemed interested in establishing.

"I can't believe we made it out without anyone seeing us!" she said once they were out of sight of the school. She wanted to grab his hand and bask together in the delightfully subversive purpose of this trek. Henry, however, didn't seem interested in viewing their exit as an escape, or this excursion as a rebellious romantic stroll. His sense of justification ought to have been encouraging—they were consenting adults, colleagues, walking in broad daylight on a public sidewalk—but it was more than a little dispiriting. Her heart had pounded as they descended the side stairwell of Eliot. She had felt young and insane. But now there seemed no need for her enlivening adrenaline. Again, she feared that he might be leading her to a private place so that he could apologize for the liberties he had taken with her and put a civil end to the madness.

His strides were long and purposeful, as though he were trying to get them somewhere on time, and she found herself scurrying in a rather undignified way to keep pace. They talked idly about the unseasonably cold November weather, and Ruth made some mindless remarks about colleagues already planning their Christmas shopping. Then a silence fell upon them.

They continued for several blocks. What was his point in bringing her out? If he had no desire to connect, why not let her stay inside? He had chased her, she reminded herself. It was not her job to make a case for the survival of his attraction. They passed a noisy construction site and had to walk onto the dusty road to get around a backhoe. From a distance came the shouting commands of the workers, though little was visible beyond the temporary plywood fence, covered in images of the sophisticated urban life on offer to buyers of the condos being erected. In black and white, smiling men and women gathered with wine glasses on balconies. Lovers embraced. Across a male model's chin was scrawled, in black marker, "My nose looks like a dick."

"Really?" Ruth barked awkwardly. "That nose doesn't look like any dick I've ever seen."

She looked to Henry, laughing gruffly. He returned a mild smile.

Silence fell upon them again, and Ruth contemplated what an idiot she was.

When at last they came to the park, she was ready to return to the school. Already exhausted by her nerves, her ungloved fingers red with cold, she flopped down onto a park bench and sat on her hands. She really would not talk first now, no matter how much quiet he made her endure. She had always despised people who controlled others with silence. He sat next to her, pulled an unappetizing, slightly squished cheese sandwich out of his pocket, and began to eat. She fished out her apple and regarded its many bruises with distaste.

The park was bordered with neat lines of fledgling trees, and as the wind gusted up, quite suddenly, from the west, they arched in the wind. A golden retriever chased a tennis ball while its owner, a white-haired man in a McCarthy Tétrault baseball cap, talked furiously into his cellphone. A young mother had spread a picnic on a patchwork quilt, her stroller parked lopsidedly beside it on the uneven ground. Her newly walking son, undeterred by frequent falls, toddled along with poorly controlled speed, as if his motion were propelled by gravity. From an enormous canvas bag she unloaded Tupperware containers full of small cubes of cheese and banana, a bag of Goldfish crackers, a bottle of water, and a pile of children's books. The baby staggered over to the books, sat heavily in a kind of free fall, and immediately started tearing pages out of one.

Ruth glanced towards Henry and was faintly repelled by the sight of his teeth sinking into the bland wad of his lukewarm sandwich. The very fact that he was eating seemed improbable. There were so few real things she knew about him. Nearly everything had come from the inter-staff chatter. As when he had first arrived, she tried to hold herself apart from these stories. Of no concern to her was Sheila's report that he never drank coffee, only tap water, out of his University of Toronto mug because he refused to let anything have that much control over him, having at one time been so fiercely addicted to coffee that if he didn't have time to drink some before a morning meeting, he would spend the entire time in a fever of distraction, thinking of nothing else. Irrelevant was Michael Curtis's intelligence that he loved baseball but had been teased terribly as a young boy for his lack of coordination, and although forever causing his own black eyes—getting in the direct path of a hurled ball, standing too close to a swinging batter—he trumped up schoolyard fights to gain some masculine credibility with his parents. The only thing he had ever told Ruth directly about himself was that his favourite tome to read from was a Norton anthology, because he loved being able to sink into each dense thousand-word page. But she felt no lack in her ignorance. She preferred to feel the quiver of mystery.

The wind whipped ribbons of hair across her face. Henry reached over and brushed a hair from her lips. She sighed more audibly than she would have liked.

"Are you not hungry?" he said, gesturing to her uneaten apple.

She shrugged. "I guess not. I had a big breakfast."

"Are you cold?"

"Not really."

"Because we could go back."

She shook her head and insisted that she was fine. He wrapped up his sandwich and stuffed it back into his pocket.

"It's not an environment I'm used to, in the school" he said. "The activity is unending. The noise can be..."

"You may never get used to it. It's a far cry from the libraries at U of T," she replied. "Finding your own space there can be a challenge. Some people, like Michael..." Her voice trailed off. Trying to bait him into negative pronouncements about their colleagues would only make her look bad: predictably catty, too desperate for conspiratorial talk.

"Let's not talk about work," he said.

She nodded in agreement. What would they talk about, then? She waited for him to introduce a new topic, but he seemed quite comfortable saying nothing. Finally, he lifted her hand, cupped it in both of his own, and blew his warm breath on it. "You're freezing," he murmured. She started to shake her head again in protest, but he began to kiss her fingertips one at a time. A teenage boy was approaching farther down the sidewalk. He had the look of an evolving thug, like he had been working on his walk and had to concentrate to get the half limp just right. As he passed, he stared at them defiantly.

Henry released her hand, and they watched the boy's back as he walked away. Even after he had disappeared around the corner, his presence lingered in the air. Their earlier self-consciousness descended again.

"I trust that he looked in no way familiar," Henry said.

Ruth was briefly confused and thought he was asking whether she knew the boy, whether they had been spotted, and she felt a flush of annoyance—*he* had suggested the walk, *he* had taken her hand; how cowardly it was to initiate risks and then fret over the possible consequences. Then she noticed the worry in his face and it dawned on her that he was referring to the mugging.

"Oh, no," she replied. "Funny, I'd all but forgotten about that." She looked down at her new wedding ring, a plain white-gold band that Richard had bought her as a temporary replacement. Perhaps, he had said, they could consider an eternity band for their next anniversary. She disliked the new ring—it was thick and boring and looked as though it may have been purchased at the mall—but Richard had been so proud of his purchase, so solicitous, that she pretended it was exactly what she wanted as he slid it on.

They watched the park in silence for some minutes more. The mother was now settling her baby back into the stroller, burying him beneath layers of fleece blankets. A border collie mix trotted across her crumpled quilt, grabbing the sheaf of napkins and tearing away with them.

"My dog Marlow used to—" she began, then stopped, seeing Henry check his watch. "I guess we should head back."

He gave her a long, almost sleepy look and nodded his agreement.

When they were nearing the school, Henry halted in the middle of the sidewalk. At the stop sign ahead of them was Chandra Howard, holding the handlebars of her bicycle and fussing with the contents of its wicker basket (which she referred to, affectionately, as her pannier).

"We have to meet elsewhere," he said, looking straight ahead.

Eliot was just now in sight, the top of the ornamental bell tower emerging with imperial self-importance, cresting the heads of the trees like a crown. What had happened between them had seemed possible only there, within those walls, and she couldn't imagine their encounters in another venue.

"I want to hold your hand so badly it's killing me," he said.

"How about my house?" she replied quickly. She didn't let herself look at him too closely as he mumbled his assent and crossed the street to return to school on his own.

AUDREY SAT IN THE library at a long table by the window. It was Friday afternoon, and Monday was to bring yet another test, this time history. Ruth was in a meeting but had left a note on Audrey's locker offering a drive home. Audrey's former school had been nearly deserted so late in the day, but the Eliot library was bustling. Although exams were weeks away, most of the grade tens were already fretting. Every morning when Julie Michaels arrived at school, she claimed to have been up until two o'clock the previous night, and every morning she loudly predicted that between basketball practice, debating, and school work, she was well on her way to an early coronary.

Outside, the soccer team was practising in the last light of the day. Even from a distance, Audrey could make out Ms. Crispe's irritation, the unmistakable pose of whistle-blowing. On the other side of the field, Ms. Sampson, the elementary geography teacher, sat under a tree observing the practice, bundled prematurely into a puffy down coat with a fake fur–lined hood. Because they lived in the same apartment building, though apparently in separate units, Ms. Crispe and Ms. Sampson were rumoured to be having an affair. Dougie claimed to have once come upon Ms. Crispe addressing Ms. Sampson in an ardent whisper as "Peaches." Audrey watched them, trying to detect some invisible chemistry, a girlish devotion in Ms. Sampson's sensible demeanour, a corresponding boastful competence in Ms. Crispe's coaching, but she was too far away to impose any specifics.

At a table not far away from Audrey's sat Arabella and Whitney in whispery conference, their heads close together. They looked up and caught Audrey staring at them. Blushing, she picked up her pen and started taking notes. A few minutes later, she heard rustling behind her. She looked back, expecting Ruth, but found Arabella emerging from the stacks.

"So," she said, plopping into the chair next to Audrey. "I just figured something out. Audrey Brindle. Ruth Brindle."

Audrey looked over to where Whitney had been sitting and saw that she had disappeared.

"Fuck!" Arabella said delightedly. "I can't believe I missed that!"

Audrey shrugged sheepishly in consent.

"Dude, there's nothing to be ashamed of," Arabella said. "Your mom is awesome."

Audrey wasn't exactly ashamed of Ruth, but she still wasn't sure how to handle having a mother who was also a teacher. She smiled, fighting down the panic that was always rising in her when Arabella was around.

"So, this morning," Arabella said. "What the fuck, huh?"

That morning, Seeta had given another performance. She was, by now, performing at least twice a week. Her repertoire was seemingly endless, tending towards the upbeat ("Feelin' Groovy" had become her signature piece, and she had played it several times as an unsolicited encore, always with a sly grin of assumption that this was what everyone had been waiting for). She favoured the classics, declaring that no one could be anything but happy while listening to the Beach Boys, and offering a small speech about her personal environmental initiatives before "Big Yellow Taxi." Every now and then, she grew eager to show off her range, and she opened the morning with a selection from AC/DC or Jimi Hendrix, "You Shook Me All Night Long" and "Castles Made of Sand" transformed into mellow, heartbroken ballads by her sweet voice pushing its gritty edges.

For the first several weeks, the grade tens had reacted to her performances with pointed boredom: long yawns staggered as if perfectly timed along the pews, explosive coughs throughout, and a lazy smattering of applause at the end. But at some point along the way, Arabella and Whitney had instigated a change in strategy. Now people leaned forward in the pews in a parody of rapt attention. They squealed in delight when she played the opening chords of "Let It Be" and let out whelping cheers when she finished. Arabella had once stood, applauding forcefully, saying "Bravo" in a projecting, manly voice. Whether or not Seeta perceived the fraudulence in this enthusiasm was impossible to tell. There was no reduction in her visibility. She went about as she always had, taking her bow, humming in the halls and strumming her guitar at lunchtime, raising her hand at every question.

What had distinguished this morning from other mornings was that after singing "Peace Train," Seeta had announced that her brother, Ravi, a student at St. George's, was joining her for a special duet. When he took to the stage, a murmur had spread through the chapel. Holding a guitar of his own, he perched on a stool, and together they tuned their instruments. Their impeccable harmonization during "Don't Let the Sun Go Down on Me" won them little respect, and their unsolicited encore of "Time After Time," during which Ravi played a harmonica to oddly mournful effect, inspired even less. During the long morning that followed, every time Seeta was out of the room, Whitney and Dougie had twisted their hair into buns at the front of their heads and held hands, gazing into each other's eyes as they sang "I've Had the Time of My Life."

Audrey nodded nervously. "It was brutal."

"I want to show you something," Arabella said with a private smile. She looked around to make sure they were alone, then reached into her knapsack, pulled out a piece of cardboard, and set it gingerly before Audrey, as though revealing a rare piece of stolen artwork.

"Whit and I made this. You like?"

Before Audrey lay a note whose intended recipient needed no illumination. In letters cut out of a magazine and placed crookedly together were the words, "No good can come of your songs. Stop while you're still ahead." As Audrey studied the note, Arabella bobbed in her seat, as though her giggling had been trapped inside her body, where it fluttered around madly. Audrey couldn't tell whether the note was funny or genuinely creepy. There was something gleeful about its campiness, its ironic horror-film quality.

Audrey felt herself awaken, as to a granted wish. "What are you going to do with it?"

"What are *we* going to do with it?" Arabella replied.

There was a plan. With Arabella, there was always a plan. The appearance of spontaneity was paramount but in reality far too dicey a proposition. Someone would put the note in Seeta's locker, where it would sit like a love letter gone wrong, a jeering hallucination. In Arabella's imaginings, she would come upon it first thing in the morning, guitar in hand, a Beatles tune tingling at the tips of her fingers, at the highest pitch of her morning perkiness. Would she gasp, as though confronted by the flasher himself? Would she rip it up and hurl the shreds to the floor? Might they hope for tears?

As Arabella described this scenario, her usual poise crumpled and she became nervously jubilant, giddily whispering to Audrey. In her excitement, she kept forgetting herself, and her voice would rise until a sound in the stacks brought her back to herself. Then she would pause and look around edgily before resuming in a whisper. Audrey listened in a daze of disbelief. No matter how close to her Arabella murmured, no matter how seemingly dismantled her guard, Audrey couldn't see her from anything other than an intimidated distance. It was amazing, really, the lust Arabella could pour into such schemes. Held up in comparison, love was ordinary. But this derision? This spellbinding hatred? It was visionary.

"Dougie really wanted to be the one to do it," she said. "But she's so bad at that kind of thing. She's like a magnet for witnesses. She always gets caught. Last year, she was putting orange wedges inside the music room piano, and she didn't even get two pieces in before Ms. Massie-Turnbull came in. So I said no way this time."

Arabella regarded the note with admiration. The magazine letters were laid out strategically, with intentional crookedness, the letters ripped from headlines, clearly chosen for their bold fonts and strong colours. There was a stiffness to the paper, a result of all the glue applied, and when she passed it to Audrey, it crinkled like a child's arts and crafts project. "Do you want to do it?" she asked, as though doubtful of Audrey's fitness.

Audrey knew instantly that she would not say no. She had known even before the question was formed, perhaps even before Arabella herself knew that she would ask. And it was unnecessary for Arabella to heap compliments upon her, to praise how well she had executed the ketchup plan, to say things like "masterful touch." It was unnecessary for her to pause for a minute before releasing the note to Audrey's care, as though she were agreeing to something Audrey had suggested. Beyond the fear of getting caught, beyond the fear of Arabella's recrimination, of trying too hard and disappointing, beyond the sweeping fear that had so commanded her life for months, there was desire.

As Audrey opened her knapsack, Arabella was already standing to leave. "By the way," she said. "Your hair looks really good that way."

Audrey fought to keep the smile off her face.

AUDREY HAD NEVER BEFORE known the thrill of rebellion, of real secrets that could get her into trouble. Her body had gone unexpectedly quiet, but her mind leapt and blazed, a flashing mess of wordless impressions that couldn't properly be called thoughts. Later, it occurred to her that this was her body's way of letting her do something risky. If her body had been in the same state as her mind, all tingling, turbulent disorientation, she would barely have been able to walk. But her legs were dependably solid, carrying her to her purpose.

It was Monday morning, and Audrey was hurrying down the hall. She had reached the point where physical and mental determination were unified. Transiently, transcendently, she was nearly able to obliterate all awareness of the outside. She registered the classroom as she passed it, registered even the figure of Seeta, standing by the window, but she averted her eyes and kept her pace. It was like diving into a cold lake. An immersion.

She was unzipping her knapsack as she rounded the corner to the lockers, pulling out her binder even as she hastily surveyed the scene, noting just one person in sight giggling into a cellphone at the far end of the hall. Circumstances were as close to ideal as they were going to get. Seeta's locker was second from the end. Wasting not a second, she dropped her bag and, barely glancing at the note, slid it through the crack.

And it was done.

Two strides took her to her own locker, where she exhaled heavily, feeling as though she were breathing for the first time in minutes. Now her body came back to life. Her fingers trembled as she fiddled with her lock. Her heart began to race violently. The sensations of her body were so commanding that it took her a moment to account for her emotions. And when she did, she realized that what she felt was not the expected guilt, flaring uneasily in her gut, not panicky regret. No urge to reach in with tweezers and reclaim the message. No, she was overcome by elation, thorough and unconflicted. Her nerves only fed the rapture, intensifying its novel countenance. She wanted only to stand where she was, letting it wash over her.

As she stood there, she understood that this feeling was the only necessary end. That all along, the note had been about this, just this. The act itself. The heady, resolute journey down the hallway. Her too-known fingers set to a purpose never foreseen. Her awkward body, in a moment of utter clarity.

IT WASN'T UNTIL NEARLY the end of the day that Ruth knew it would happen. With Richard late at work and Audrey at a French tutorial, she had been frantically determined to take her proposal to Henry, but she hadn't been able to locate him until lunch. His reply had been that he had to check his schedule, as if she were booking him for a dental appointment. It wasn't until just before the final period of the day that he snagged her in the hall and confirmed that he could make it. The lack of resolution had made her testy and restless—how easily she shifted from adoring him to hating him and then back again—but she realized as she rushed home from school that not knowing sooner had preserved her sanity.

Once in the door, she fussed about the house. She had only fifteen minutes to get ready for his arrival. She let the dogs into the yard, stifled the impulse to hop in the shower, and focused on the appalling amount of dog hair in the front hall. She dragged the vacuum up from the basement and went aggressively to work. She worried about how her house would represent her. Looking around, she saw all the antiques, the pieces she had loved when she bought them, and was somehow embarrassed by them, by the values they revealed her to have. She should seem to care less about things.

Ruth had just stashed the vacuum back in the basement and was becoming convinced that Henry would not show up when his knock broke the silence.

Approaching the door, she saw his tall figure perfectly framed by the long, oval window. He was looking downwards and to the side. When he glanced up and saw her, she gave an awkward wave. Stevie and McGill, spotting the visitor, howled and paddled at the back door. She held up a hand to Henry to indicate that she'd be with him in a moment, then let the dogs back in and was almost knocked over as they made for the front door, wagging uncontrollably. Marlow took a seat at the base of the stairs, panting heavily, his tongue hanging out the side of his mouth. He had recently had several decaying teeth pulled, and the gaps were well displayed now; the rank odour of his breath filled the hallway. Embarrassed, Ruth gave him an ineffective shove in the direction of the kitchen.

When she finally opened the door, the barrier remained. She and Henry stood on opposite sides of the threshold, and they neither moved nor spoke, at a loss for how to go ahead. It wasn't until this moment that she stopped wondering whether he would go through with it. Her own follow-through she had never questioned. Such thoughts, she felt, were rarely anything more than a disingenuous, rather cowardly nod to morality for people who wanted to believe they were better than they were. At least she would be honest with herself.

She pulled him inside—fear of the neighbours masquerading as an assertion of desire—but once she had him in the hallway, she had no idea how to behave. Even though they were in her house, she wanted him to take the lead. She couldn't figure out either how to be with him in her home or how to be in her home with him. Where was all the consoling busywork of the hostess? The prospect of offering him a drink made her feel like the aging fifties housewife in her pink satin bathrobe, clanking the ice in her glass of Scotch, trying to seduce the young mailman. The fear of getting caught was present, but only abstractly. She was conscious of her stupidity, her recklessness, but was unable to take their full measure. More immediate was the mystifying stress of having him in her space, among the things that reflected her so inaccurately.

"Would you like a glass of water?" she finally asked.

He shook his head.

The dogs were skittering around them, sniffing his pant legs, their noses aspiring upwards towards his groin. He patted their heads dismissively and tried to ignore them, but they persisted.

"I'm sorry," she said. "Strangers excite them."

Henry nodded with a tolerant smile.

When she had finally managed to bribe the dogs away from him and settle them on the couches, using cookies from the pockets of her winter coat, she returned to the hall and dropped her head defeatedly. "Listen," she said.

"Must I?" He stepped towards her and grabbed the front of her shirt.

As she led him upstairs, she offered a cursory nod to all the thoughts she knew she should be having. She knew how it was supposed to go. You think of the fact that you shouldn't be doing this. You think of what can go wrong. You think of the minutes, the seconds that remain for you to change your mind. You do not lead a man who is not your husband into the master bedroom, the bed still unmade from last night's sleep, certainly not when there's a perfectly impersonal guest room across the hall, with a barely used queen bed dressed with barely used sheets, with freshly dusted night tables and tastefully generic botanical prints on the walls, with the airy nowhere smell of a place no one has fought in, no one has spent a wakeful night in, no one has made love in. You do not breeze past that place of indifferent welcome and fall back on the rumpled sheets that smell, just slightly, of your husband's hair. You do not let yourself go so completely without a thought for the consequences.

Ruth's hair was in Henry's hand, being pulled somewhat uncomfortably, but she had no time to adjust his grip, to consider the improvement of this choreography, so grateful was she to find herself here, with him. A button popped off her blouse and went skittering across the wood floor. As if in repudiation of the comic potential of this gaffe, Henry roughly pulled her skirt off, followed by her underwear. Then his clothes were gone, and his kiss was pushing her head into the pillow. It was not like her to be so submissive, so ecstatically trapped, but dominance suddenly felt like passion, submergence like flight. She could do nothing but yield as his hands pushed her thighs apart. Yet for all this force, it was the lightness of his body upon hers that confirmed how far she'd strayed from everything she knew.

Afterwards, Henry lay on his back on her side of the bed, his arms folded behind his head and her pillow bunched under his neck. His body was as lean and athletic, as taut and insignificantly muscled as a teenager's, and his grey hair was damp along the temples, his brow dewy. Though his long body was open and languid, laid out with an almost feminine looseness, his left hand grasped her inner thigh tightly, as if it alone were still caught in the transports of several minutes ago.

Then he began to shake his head and laugh, a real laugh erupting from his belly. Abruptly he rolled onto her and lifted himself up on his elbows. His face hovered over hers.

"You should know this," he said. "Some vaginas are like tomatoes. Some are like apples. Tomatoes and apples are both good. But yours? Yours is most definitely an apple."

Ruth giggled. Held up against his usual reserve, the absurdity of this made her delirious. She had never thought him capable of madness.

"It's going to be very hard to leave this bed." He spoke in a low voice, as always, a boyhood habit he'd developed as a method of fighting his stutter.

When he kissed her neck, his breath formed a moist fog in the hollow of her collarbone. A noise from downstairs startled her, but it was only a dog digging at the carpet. Ruth tried to lose herself again, but the world was barrelling towards them: the car door slamming on the street outside, Stevie and McGill play-fighting in the living room, the loud whirr of some massive electrical tool in a house being renovated nearby. There had been an elemental innocence about the physical predictability of sex. It was far more difficult now to dispatch her mind into oblivion and the brief deliverance it offered. Dogs barked. Cars slowed and sped. Water dripped from the bathroom faucet. (Could she really be hearing that?)

He turned onto his back. "This I like very much," he said, gesturing to a minimalist etching of a nude woman framed above her bedside lamp.

"It was my mother's," she replied. "She met the artist once, I think."

From the etching, her eyes cast down to the nightstand, to the framed photograph of Audrey and her taken a decade earlier. With her index finger, she tipped it down, then turned back to see if Henry had noticed.

"I like the way the artist doesn't try to make her beautiful," he said, still looking upwards.

One of her long hairs lay across his forehead. Ashamed of her shedding, she reached over and pulled it away. "What I always liked about it is the way she's looking at something we can't see. There's all that subservience in the way she's sitting. When I was a kid, I liked to think she'd been captured and whisked away to some remote beautiful place. I thought she was looking into the distance for her saviour. Of course I don't see it that way at all now."

"How do you see it?"

"I suppose I see less depth in it now. I assume the artist told her to look that way. It's his vision of how the picture should look, not hers."

Henry sat upright and repositioned the pillow behind his head. "When I was young, I thought all women looked like this, that beauty was just their natural state. I never much noticed women who weren't beautiful. They simply didn't exist. My mother was the first woman I ever saw naked, as is true for most people, and of course, I didn't recognize her as beautiful. I just thought that was the way women looked. She was tall and slender, and entirely comfortable being naked. Publicly, she was quite severe, and indeed privately severe in most ways, but she used to walk around the apartment naked after a bath or a shower, rubbing her hair with a towel. I never thought anything of it. But when I saw an unclothed woman sexually for the first time, I was probably fifteen or sixteen, and I was unbelievably disappointed in her body. I didn't quite realize what she would look like naked, based on how she looked in clothes. She was about 160 pounds, not a particularly tall woman, so obviously I knew she would be thicker, but I was floored, absolutely floored, by how dowdy and flabby her body was. It didn't at all fit my idea of the female form."

"Don't say that! It's terrible," Ruth said, secretly delighted. "How callous of you."

"I felt bad about it. I was still attracted to her. You know, I was a sixteen-year-old male, she was willing. I liked her fine, but I always had to make adjustments when I saw her body. I always took a moment out. I stayed with her for nearly three years. Didn't want to be superficial. But towards the end of our relationship, I would look at her body during sex and wonder how much longer I could carry on." He paused. "Now that I think of it, I suppose that consciously resisting superficiality was solid proof of what a bastard I was in the first place."

"I'd say so."

He traced his knuckles down the side of her body, from her shoulder all the way to her knee. "But you," he said, "you require no adjustments."

"To be compared unfavourably to a lover's mother," she said. "Not a desirable position to be in."

"Think of all the scintillating hours of psychoanalysis I've contributed to." He coughed into his arm. "I could use a little water."

Before she could offer to get him a glass, he jumped up and headed for the bathroom. He slurped noisily from the faucet, then urinated, the door still open. She felt a rush of affection for him. The light was fading in the windows, but she couldn't bring herself to feel worried. Audrey was meeting Richard at the clinic after her tutorial, and he had said that he wouldn't be home until at least 6:30. Something could always happen to change that, of course, but she wouldn't let herself consider that possibility. The toilet flushed, and Henry returned, wiping water from his mouth as he crossed the room.

He glanced around. "How long have you been married?"

She thought for a second. "Fifteen years. No, sixteen."

"You were quite young."

"Not really. Not for the times."

His stare dissected her, as though he was about to challenge her. She shifted uncomfortably, nervous but revelling. Then the light splintered his iris and his attention bounded away again.

She was tempted to turn the question around on him but afraid that if she mentioned his wife, he would remember that he shouldn't be there. One of the things she had heard at school was that he and Clayton Quincy had been married for under a year, a fact that further foiled her attempts to read him. This was the inequity she was always fighting—the thirst to know about him when he seemed uninterested in knowing much about her other than the way her neck tasted. Even at work, this essential detachment was there. She had been so certain that he would be a show-off, that he would be perpetually hammering her and the other teachers with his superior knowledge, but in time she came to realize that a more typical boastfulness might have been a relief. His intelligence seemed to be something he protected, as though they weren't worth displaying it for. Where were the theatrical verbosity and rhetorical pyrotechnics that had so dazzled her in her university professors? But this disengagement had its appeal, too. He was a stranger to her, as she was to him.

"Well, it's a good marriage," she said. "It's not a bad marriage anyway."

The room was growing dark around them, the thin light in the windows replaced with deep indigo. The days had been getting shorter for a long time now, but Ruth felt she was noticing the season change all at once, for the first time. She was surprised, as always, by the hasty end to the day. She turned on the lamp at Richard's bedside, and the room filled with a warm light. A private glow of home and hearth, domestic interiors.

"It's odd seeing someone's room when it's so different from how you pictured it," he said, lying down again.

"You pictured my room?"

"Of course."

"How?"

He looked around. "I don't know. I can't quite put my finger on it. I wouldn't have anticipated a print like that, for instance. It doesn't quite fit with the nude, does it?"

He gestured towards a large picture on the far wall, of white horses in a field. She had bought it early in her marriage at an overheated print shop on Wellington Street. It was a decidedly dated print, no longer remotely to her taste. Against the backdrop of a watery teal sky, three white horses grazed on a meadow's long grasses, which swayed dreamily in implied wind, while at a distance the rest of the herd loitered angelically, also grazing. Richard had initially refused to hang the picture, mistaking the horses for unicorns. Now it was so sentimental a relic of her past that Ruth had never considered removing it.

"A long ago purchase," she said, looking away in embarrassment. "Look, it's getting late. The clock wants me to notice it."

"It's a lovely room," he said, reaching out his hand. "Far better than anything I've ever lived in."

"It's just a room."

"I'm tempted to fall asleep here."

"Don't," she replied. She sat up and buttoned her shirt crookedly, then tossed his underwear and socks to the foot of the bed.

He rose slowly and gathered his clothes like a child being ordered to pick up toys. She averted her eyes while he dressed. This nakedness seemed entirely unconnected to his earlier nakedness. Where his eroticized body had been an argument, an assertion of itself, a demand to be followed, this body sought invisibility, was benign and defenceless, asking to be shielded. He stood in front of the window and stooped to pull on his old grey underwear, which had a small rip at the hem of the right leg. He pulled his black socks up lopsidedly, balancing precariously on one long, pale leg, then the other. When he reached for his pants, she felt his eyes seek hers, and a torrent of feeling came over her, more similar to what she felt for her daughter than anything she'd ever felt for a man: a throbbing protectiveness, an affection far more raw, more fierce, than sexual desire.

She knew that soon he would be gone from her bedroom. She knew that they would have to negotiate their way back downstairs, and that the descent would be delicate and tense, as perilous as the ascent was mindless. She knew that the dogs would bombard him and he would drive away too quickly. She knew that she would tear the sheets off the bed and stuff them into the bottom of the laundry hamper, and she knew that her house would return to her, then, in all its uncompromising inevitability.

But for some moments yet she had him there, in her bedroom, mutely unrepentant, in the heady convolution of foolishness and bravery, and she joined him in acknowledgment of what they had just done.

Chapter Ten

IN THE WEEKS THAT followed, the insomnia that crept up on Ruth periodically in her life became a fixture. It seemed that she had entirely forgotten how to fall asleep. What had once seemed so simple was now as elusive and tortuous a process as trying to find her glasses when they were sitting on top of her head. She thought of other nights longingly, as if recalling a perfect long-ago kiss. What had she done on those good nights?

Could she really hear, or was she just imagining, that someone had been turning over a coughing car engine for the past fifteen minutes? When Audrey was a baby, Ruth had often lain in bed, thinking, even though everyone was fast asleep, that she could hear her crying in the distance. She would evoke, with disturbing verisimilitude, behind the house's ticking and heaving, the radiator's irregular thumps and the creaky exhalations of the old pipes, the exact rhythm of Audrey's wails, the choking rise and wearied pauses, the splutters of frustration and need. What was real, and what was in her head? A heavy bass beat—presumably from a teenager's car parked not far enough away—invaded the dark. The throaty squeals of fighting raccoons erupted undeniably. She was glad to have her unwilling vigil disturbed by these sounds. They were real. Richard's uneven breathing was real. The stifling heat of his body.

Finally she got up, wrapped the chenille throw around her shoulders, and went downstairs, noting the time—1:13—on the greenish light of the oven clock. In the living room, Stevie greeted her as if it were one o'clock in the afternoon, then climbed back into her spot on the couch and fell asleep, as promptly as if she were rubbing Ruth's nose in it. Could it really be that simple?

Of course, it was no wonder wakefulness plagued her. Her head was stuck at Eliot, in the final moments of her afternoon. She had returned to her classroom after stealing a package of paper for her home printer and found Henry sitting in a shadowed corner, his hands folded tidily in his lap, watching her. His voice started out of nowhere. "Touch your breast," he said. It was by now the last week of school before Christmas break, and the fact that they would not see each other for over two weeks hovered in the air between them. When he said, "Come with me," she didn't stifle her ready consent, nodding with complete, though hidden, happiness, smothered by the scratchy embrace of his winter coat.

All her feelings for Henry were headily regressive. Something about being in love seemed essentially girlish, an inciting of emotions and activities she ought to have outgrown—she hadn't been so desperate for approval in years, so unreasonably hopeful, so wracked by pleasurable despair—but she was doing all those trite and tired things, holding hands, kissing in the rain, necking in cramped back seats, and for once her feelings were spinning in a maelstrom of incautious superlatives, for once her mind wasn't spoiling it all with cynical commentary. Could she be in love in this way as a woman with lines on her face, a woman whose body was aging noticeably, a woman with a teenage daughter? All this gasping excitement, this scatterbrained unrest, was unseemly somehow: it made her both young and old, acutely aware of her age and forgetful of it. She should be interested in politics. She should be reading historical non-fiction.

People often said that what destroyed them most about an affair, what ultimately made them end it, was the secrecy. Ruth had thought that she would feel that way—after the first night in the staff room, she had worried that she couldn't go ahead with it—she had thought that she would feel revulsion for herself, for the lies she was blithely offering Richard, for her callous bliss. She had thought that every joy would be cancelled out by guilt, by concern for her family, by a reliable moral pulse. But the secrecy was a dizzying liberation. A revelation. She felt that she could never again live without the energy her secret breathed into her. She wanted to fight this thing with Henry—a fight that was not just the fight against infidelity itself but the fight against failure, against the collapse of decency, against being a certain kind of person—but to complicate this fight, the proper fight, was the competing fact that she also didn't want to be another kind of person: a person who wouldn't do this. The strongest part of her didn't just want to have an affair. It wanted to be someone who could be blindsided by an impossible love, or a love that might not even be love at all, but merely an extravagant infatuation.

Beside her, Stevie twitched and yelped softly, dreaming. The floorboards creaked upstairs. She thought Richard was getting up to use the bathroom, but his figure appeared on the stairs, naked. He didn't speak until he was in the doorway.

"Come back to bed," he said.

His voice had none of the husky tremble of sleep about it, and he didn't look at all cold, but his face did look tired, unready for lucid interactions. He half-squinted at her as though even the moonlight was too harsh. There was nothing he could do for her, but she stood and accepted his outstretched hand, followed him back to bed.

Under the covers, she lay on her back, stiffly alert, like a child assuming the posture of sleep but not the spirit, and Richard lay on his side, his head on his bent arm, sleepily stroking her arm. Marlow snored on the floor.

"I can't sleep either," he said. "I'm coming up on that awful deadline. Max the pit."

"He's still boarding, no?"

"I'm being pushed."

"Well, it's long enough for the poor dog. There are lots of people who would want him. It's time for you to bring an end to this standoff."

"I know. I keep putting the owner off. He won't agree to an adoption."

This picture of Richard at work, ineptly trying to stave off his clients' most ignorant demands, was not the one she had cleaved to over the course of their marriage, not the one she needed when she suffered a loss of faith in her union. As he spoke of the dilemma, which ought not to be a dilemma at all, she was overcome by a terrible sense of defeat.

"You've got to do something, Richard," she said, her urgent voice hardly conducive to the tone his hand, still stroking her arm, was trying to create. "The dog needs you. Don't let some fool make all the wrong decisions."

She thought of the pit bull, shut in its crate at the clinic, lucky in its ignorance alone, booted from the family it loved while its fate was feebly debated by two men who claimed to love dogs. Richard ought to have been its protector, but some intangible weakness was preventing him from embracing this role. An urge to hit him stole over her. She sat up in bed and pressed his arm hard. "Richard, are you listening to me? Richard?"

"I'll figure it out," he said at last.

How could she convey to him the importance of this particular moment, this particular animal? The view of Richard that had sustained her—it was not just a memory, but a living stream that carried her past the petty disturbances of every day—was of a man in total control. A man who was the guardian of the most uncomplicated, and sometimes the most exemplary, love people experienced, a warden, indeed, of life itself.

It was with him that she had first seen an animal euthanized. They had been working together for several months when he had asked her one afternoon in June to assist in the euthanizing of an old ginger cat; she had just watched in sympathetic misery as its elderly owners had left, shaking, unable to stay through the procedure. Every part of her wanted to bolt, but she scooped up the cat gently but definitively and followed Richard into the upstairs exam room. In silent complicity they readied themselves. She was careful not to betray how wobbly she was feeling. She didn't sing to the cat in that irritating voice so many assistants used or look mournfully at Richard as if to say, *Must we do it? Is there a way around it?* She rubbed behind the cat's ear and said in a common sense voice, "You've had a good life, haven't you?"

Until this moment, she had never paid much attention to Richard. The things about him that left her sexually indifferent—his conservatism and diffidence, his inviolable professionalism—now rendered him a steadying presence. He presided over the event both calmly and compassionately, and his witnessing of this death, of this moment before death, aroused such gratitude in her that she discovered it was possible to feel utterly adult and utterly girlish at the same time. And she knew that she ought not to be noticing his deep brown eyes (she had looked around them or over them or next to them before, but never at them), or the shadows beneath (always present, she realized), and if she knew that she ought not to be noticing his eyes as the cat lay between them, then she knew that she certainly ought not to be noticing his lips, the way he pressed them together in concentration. But she was feeling somewhat unhinged, dreamily sad, and she couldn't stop herself from thinking that she would like to end just like that, histrionics banished, a sacred silence all through the room, and at her side one who understood the respectability of death.

Richard administered the two needles promptly, and it was over.

Months later, Richard confessed that he had felt anaesthetized himself that day—by the proximity of recent death, he initially thought, but he knew that no past euthanizing had cast a similar spell over him. As a vet, he'd had to put many animals to sleep, and because there was no way he could square himself with being an administrator of death, he'd come to see the needle as the one with the will, himself as the necessary mechanics behind it. No, it was a proximity of a different kind that had disarmed all his physical capabilities, that both troubled and soothed him: every warm rising breath of the body that had never been so close to him. He had never before noticed Ruth's hands. One lay on the metal table at the cat's head and the other rested on the cat's stomach. Her fingers were slender and straight, but the nails were rough and unmanicured, and he hadn't expected the effect this observation had on him.

Richard had once received a birthday card with a photograph of a woman cupping a brimming handful of red currants. The card was not to his taste, but he found himself drawn again and again to the image. In a gesture of sentimentality that wasn't at all his style, he tore off the photograph and saved it in his desk drawer. In the foreground of the photograph were the woman's plain hands and the glistening currants, linked by a network of green stems, and in the blurry background was the woman's blue gingham apron. For a time, Richard had thought that he would have to find something worthwhile in the composition of the photograph to justify his attraction to it. Did he detect an unusual vibrancy in the blue of the gingham? Was there sexual imagery in the bursting red currants? Or perhaps, more compellingly, the photographer was presenting a feminist argument about the relationship between sexuality (the currants in the foreground—why?) and domesticity (the long-suffering apron). He finally gave up theorizing and allowed himself, after a humbling assessment of his taste in art, simply to be content with the feeling the photograph gave him. He knew that it was shamefully womanly to store a card photograph in his desk and to approach that desk every so often with the sole intention of pulling out the photograph to stare at it in the dusty light of the window, to seek entrancement and find it so easily, and to estimate conscientiously how often he could refer to that picture without diluting its impact (once a week, he settled on), to go against his self-respect and pride in his taste all because of the warm, obscure feeling that washed over him every time he glimpsed the currants, the gingham, those hands.

In Ruth, as the cat lay between them, he saw some suggestion of that picture he had saved for so many years. The connection lay in the hands: those slender, athletic fingers with the masculine nails. He understood, finally, his vision of the feminine. Ruth was not the kind of woman behind that apron. But it didn't matter. As she and Richard looked at each other over the cat's body, both were conscious that nothing more intimate could have passed between them. Death had come into the room, and along with it, the wonder they'd been missing.

In the years that followed, Ruth sometimes worried that they had bungled all the quintessentially sublime moments of a life: the engagement, the wedding, the new baby. No one would ever tell stories about them; they were too boring. She had told Richard that she was pregnant on an answering machine message, as an aside to her main reason for calling, a request that he bring home soda crackers. In the minutes after giving birth, her first words had been, "I can't believe I wanted to do this." Richard's proposal had been equally a mess. In her shared house on Howland Avenue, her roommates squabbling in the kitchen, he had produced a blue velvet ring box from his knapsack, where it lay next to an extra pair of briefs and half a tuna sandwich, and asked her if she would like to get married. Even in the midst of these moments, a part of her had known that such blunders had consequences beyond the immediate, transient disappointment. She and Richard had failed to form a compelling account of their life together, a narrative that referenced all the amazing collisions of time and space that delivered them into each other's worlds, a myth that was poignant and self-reverential and sustaining.

Yet there was this: a cat's heart had ceased beating under her hand, but Richard's eyes had assured her that everything would be okay.

"WE NEED TO TALK about Marlow" were Richard's first words to her the following morning.

Ruth was standing in the corner of the kitchen in cotton underwear and a T-shirt, holding a skirt to be ironed, and Audrey sat at the table picking at a bowl of Cheerios. Alert to the sound of his name, Marlow thumped his tail against the tile floor. "You there, old man," said Richard, crouching down to box his ears gently. "Ruth, I got an email from Jess this morning. She can't walk the dogs today. She's got stomach flu."

"It's just one day," Ruth replied. "They can go without."

"Marlow can't hold his bladder all day. Can you come home today at lunch to let him out? I've got a surgery at noon."

Ruth bolted to attention. She was unfolding the ironing board, and she lost her grip, dropping it to the floor. Richard turned to her. "Since when do you iron skirts first thing in the morning?"

"I have nothing to wear," Ruth replied tersely. "Look, I can't come home at lunch. I have things to do."

"Things," said Audrey ominously.

"I have a job!"

"You don't say."

Ruth's and Audrey's eyes met, and they regarded each other with the suggestion of hostility. Ruth was sick of trying to deflect Audrey's general unpleasantness. Every day was a battle for optimism. She had begun to worry that she had made a terrible mistake by pushing Eliot so hard on Audrey. Yes, of course she thought Eliot was an excellent school. She had dedicated a decade of her own life to it, and she had considered it only natural that Audrey should share the experience with her. But a darker perspective had started to insinuate itself into her reflections. Why had she been unable to accept the repeated rejections, to take them as a sign that Eliot was not meant for her daughter? Had she only needed an obsession? Had she wanted something she couldn't have? Violently, she had tried to refute this interpretation of the matter—how could she accept that selfishness had been lurking at the bottom of every decision she had made for her child?—but her disquiet had been awakened now, and like a deluge of acrid smoke, could not be contained.

Each change she noticed in Audrey only added to her frustration. Even physically, Audrey was different. Lack of sleep, along with the disappearance of her summer tan, had made her skin more pale. She was leaner, too. The overall effect was of added fragility, though in her manner with Ruth, Audrey had never shown less vulnerability. It was an odd feeling, Ruth thought, noticing someone so familiar who seemed somehow indefinably different. And the truth of the matter was that she didn't even want to think about Audrey. She didn't want to be noticing and scrutinizing and worrying. For the first time in years, within her grasp was the pleasure of total self-involvement, and she wanted to be swallowed.

"Why are you staring at me?" Audrey said.

"Why are *you* staring at me?"

Audrey stood up and dumped the soggy remnants of her cereal into the sink, then turned to leave the room.

"Excuse me," said Ruth sharply. "What did your last servant die of?"

Richard turned to her. "Can we focus please?"

"Can't we find someone else to do it today?" Ruth said.

"How do you propose we do that on such short notice?"

"Well, I don't have time to come home at lunch!" she cried. "And I don't have time to talk about this now."

Marlow sat in the doorway to the kitchen, watching Ruth with jolly eyes as he awaited the verdict.

"We've got to do something about his breath," Ruth said.

"Christ, Ruth! Do you hear yourself?"

Ruth pressed the iron hard into her skirt and furiously went at a wrinkle. What was wrong with her? Marlow had always been her favourite dog. He was everyone's favourite dog. Strangers stopped them on the street to ask what breeder he had come from and were shocked to hear that he had been found as a stray eating garbage in the street. "I guess I could try to do it," she said. "It's just Larissa. She's so on me right now."

"We don't believe in trying, do we?" Audrey said. "What is it Ms. McAllister always says? Either you do it or you don't."

Although Audrey was ostensibly joking, in her voice was a sour edge, and Ruth wondered whether Richard had noticed it.

"Audrey's got a point," Richard said. "I need your commitment."

Ruth sighed. "Yes, fine, I'll do it."

Richard gave her a wet kiss on the cheek. "That's all I wanted to hear."

When she went upstairs to brush her teeth some time later, Ruth ran into Audrey loitering pointlessly in the hall. "Is that a new blouse?" Audrey said.

Ruth looked down at her shirt in artificial surprise. "This? No, it's not new," she said. "I guess you've just never noticed it before."

AS SOON AS AUDREY entered the classroom, she could feel that something had happened. Nearly all the girls had congregated in the back corner in a circle, forming a barricade that eclipsed whatever lay at its nexus.

"What's going on?" Audrey said to Elise Smith, a quiet girl whose diminutive stature rendered her approachable even to Audrey. She was one of the few people who hadn't been drawn to the crowd, and she sat at her desk sketching a horse on a piece of lined paper. She looked up inattentively and shrugged. "I think Arabella got flashed or something."

That this was truly what had happened struck Audrey as impossible until the crowd parted slightly and she caught a glimpse of the victim herself, sniffling implausibly. Whitney's arm was coiled protectively around Arabella's shoulders, and she was sipping listlessly from a Styrofoam cup. In her reduced state, she attracted even more deference than usual, and as the girls crowded in, they spoke gently, as though fearful that too much volume might undo her. In its rarity, the hush expressed greater urgency than the usual racket, and Audrey couldn't tell whether Arabella was genuinely upset or basking in the drama of her condition.

The strike had apparently taken place shortly after eight o'clock, not long after Arabella's mother had delivered her safely to the front door of the school. Arabella had gone around back—to accomplish what, no one explicitly asked, but a secluded pocket at the side of the school was known by everyone but the teachers to be an illicit smoking station. She hadn't been there for long when she heard a rustling in the shadows not far away, a movement that might have been nothing more than a pile of leaves. When she looked up, there he was. The wrought-iron fence separated them, but her view had been as clear as anyone's ever had. (Arabella's competitive spirit was such that even victimization was something she had to do better than everyone else.) His face had been decidedly neutral, neither sneering nor grinning, neither sinister nor jovial, not the red-eyed pallor of a porn-obsessed shut-in, or the flush of the irrepressible adventurer. His coat opened, and then he was gone, before she had a chance to get her mind in order and run away.

On her way into the school, the first person Arabella had seen, conveniently, was Michael Curtis, who'd immediately shepherded her into Ms. McAllister's office, where she delivered a cool-headed précis of the incident and was roundly praised for her presence of mind. "We've got to nab this guy," Michael Curtis had said. "This can't go on." Ms. McAllister, absorbed in copious note taking, offered a severe "Agreed."

Possibly more distraught than Arabella herself, Michael Curtis had then immersed herself in the comfort of motherly ministrations. Whisking her ward possessively into the staff room, Michael prepared for Arabella a cup of chamomile tea and then, carrying her knapsack, accompanied her to the classroom, where she hovered, assuring Arabella that she need not tell anyone unless she was up for it. When students began to arrive, Michael Curtis reluctantly withdrew, but not before stroking Arabella's hair and saying, "If your description helps us catch this sicko, you can consider yourself a hero."

And it seemed, as Arabella relayed her story with excessive dignity, that she did indeed consider herself a hero. "I don't know if I even believe her," whispered Shannon Worth uncertainly, as though compelled against her better judgment to raise the spectre of doubt. If anyone else shared her hesitation, there was no sign of it. Questions were beginning to flow, though haltingly. The consensus seemed to be that showing too much curiosity was in bad taste, but the obvious desire for information outweighed all propriety.

"Did he say anything?" asked Emma Walter.

Arabella bowed her head for a moment's contemplation before offering a shake of her head.

"According to Beth Jensen, when he flashed her, he said, 'You like?'"

"Ugh, that's such a load of crap."

Julie Michaels, who was known for her impression of Chuck Marostica, had pushed her way to the front of the crowd and now sat, without the appropriate reverence, on the desk in front of Arabella. "Suzy W. said that he wasn't even wearing shoes. And that he smelled like garbage." Her upbeat voice inspired a glare from Whitney.

"Suzy W. wouldn't remember to put on her own bra if her boobs didn't hang down to her waist. He's not some homeless guy. He just..." Arabella glanced up with a recognizable sparkle in her eye. "He looks like Vanessa's dad."

Vanessa returned a subdued sneer. She was clutching her French notebook to her chest, torn between the current fuss and her desire to cram in some last-minute studying for a quiz that afternoon.

From her usual spot on the window seat, Seeta began strumming her guitar. Twenty heads turned to her accusingly. Feeling the gaze upon her, Seeta clapped a hand over the strings and giggled. "Oops, sorry, I'll keep it down!"

"Don't keep it down," Whitney said frostily. "Shut it off."

Seeta caught Audrey's eye and looked quickly away. Since she had accused Audrey of cheating, they'd dodged each other as much as they were able, given their forced proximity. In their mutual animosity, they were almost as intimately bound as lovers in a new blush of passion. Each time Seeta sat down next to her, Audrey sighed noisily. They kept furtive track of each other, rising to immediate awareness when the other entered the room. Stuck next to each other in nearly every class, they sat as far apart as their seats would allow, each girl keeping mutely combative guard of her personal space. Other than her discomfort with Audrey, however, little about Seeta seemed to have changed from that first day at Eliot three months earlier.

"Hey, Seeta," called Dougie. "You've got some spinach in your teeth. Might want to check out a mirror. Too much chicken saag for breakfast?"

Seeta frowned and made a face. "Oh," she said, dismounting the window seat. "Um, thanks."

She was halfway across the room to the door when Dougie laughed. "Just kidding!"

Frustrated that the attention had been diverted from her, Arabella let out a loud cough and rested her head in her hands.

"Poor Belle," said Whitney.

"Are you, like, totally scarred forever?" asked Dougie.

"God," said Julie Michaels. "He wasn't hard, was he?"

"As a matter of fact, yes, Julie," Arabella said crossly. "He totally had a hard-on."

A sharp intake of breath signalled the presence in the room of an adult. Ms. Glover swept through the crowd. "Watch your tongue, Ms. Quincy."

Arabella looked duly chastened. The duality of reputation Arabella had managed to create was possibly the most impressive thing about her. She was a favourite among the teachers. She was unfailingly polite, punctual, in their presence masterfully channelling her brassiness into good-natured warmth. Unable to staunch the wellspring of her giggles, it was Dougie who predictably became the scapegoat, bearing the brunt of the blame for the spirit of insurgence galvanized by Arabella.

"I'm sorry, Ms. Glover. Yes, Julie, in response to your concerned question, he was, um, suffering from an erection."

"Now I really do think she's lying," whispered Shannon.

The bell rang, and the girls disbanded. It wasn't until several minutes later, as she was crossing the quad to the chapel, that Audrey saw Arabella again. From behind her fired Dougie's laugh. She couldn't quite hear their conversation, but she thought she caught the word *penis*. Audrey crouched to tie her shoe, and as they were passing, they stopped.

"It's fucking freezing out here," said Whitney.

"Can you get, like, hypothermia of the dick?" asked Dougie.

They were looking down at Audrey as though they were waiting for her and expected her to say something.

"Did you really see it?" Audrey said, standing up.

There must have been something in her voice that gave offence, perhaps the shrillness of excitement, or a babyish captivation at talk of a penis, but the girls' collective demeanour changed almost instantly. The aura of invitation withered. For the first time, Audrey noticed a slight redness around Arabella's eyes.

"What do you want, Audrey? A sketch of his cock?" she said.

Whitney took a half step in front of Arabella, as though shielding her from an imminent blow. "God, how insensitive can you be?"

They pushed past and joined the swarm of students entering the chapel, leaving Audrey alone to negotiate her way inside.

AT LUNCHTIME, THE BAKERY around the corner was overrun by Eliot girls. The crowd of students pressed in, gathering around the glass display case to compare the wilted salads and crusty scones. The heavily steamed windows and the low ceiling, with its copper pendant lights, made for a stark contrast with outside, and every time someone opened the door a rush of gritty street air swept in. Every day the same girls staked out the five small bistro tables, racing over the minute the bell rang. Their position was so entrenched that on a day when two tables remained empty fifteen minutes into the lunch hour, the girls in line looked disapprovingly at a quartet of grade nines who sat down with their donuts and Diet Cokes. The owner, a man named Al with a bushy grey beard and, in spite of his bald crown, a long thin ponytail with a curl at the end, had long since reconciled himself to the fact that his main customer base comprised shrieking teenage girls, and he stood behind the counter with a crooked, easygoing smirk, ladling minestrone into Styrofoam tubs and doling out change with fingers rough as sandpaper. The girls liked to squeal, back at school, that they had found an Al hair in their soup. Arabella once swore that she had encountered a pubic hair afloat in her chicken noodle.

Audrey usually avoided the bakery, painfully aware of her outsider status, but she had forgotten her lunch at home. She considered going without food, but the prospect of her stomach growling noisily during the afternoon periods was more humiliating than venturing out alone. She pushed open the door and was swallowed by a bubble of heat. At the front of the line, Arabella, Whitney, and Dougie were flirting with Al. He chuckled bashfully at everything they said, as though unaware of the irony in their compliments. ("Have you been working out, dude? You look strong enough to snap Dougie's neck with your baby finger." "Al, can you teach me how to say 'I love sausages' in Ukrainian?") The line began backing up to the door, and Kate Gibson called out, "Yo, Al. There are some other lovelies back here who want some of your time."

"Al and I have a special relationship," replied Arabella. "Don't be jealous." She turned back to Al and blew him a kiss.

When her turn came, Audrey bought a plain bun and left, gasping as she opened the door into the biting wind. She hurried back to the school and collected her French textbook from her locker, then made her way to the drafty emergency stairwell near the classroom.

She had taken to eating there lately as a way of hiding her solitude and dissociating herself from Seeta. As she rounded the corner, though, she saw that her spot had already been claimed.

"May we help you?" Arabella asked.

"Your fly is down," said Dougie.

Audrey looked down at her skirt, confused.

"Just kidding!"

She was just about to leave when she thought of the afternoon Arabella showed her the note, that moment when the contours of a tangible possibility began to materialize. She fumbled with her bun. "Is it all right if I sit?"

The girls looked at each other.

"Password," said Arabella.

Audrey covered her panic with a smile. "Groovy?"

They parted to make room for her, and she stepped tentatively over their legs and took a seat several steps down. Arabella, apparently recovered from her ordeal with the flasher, sat at the top with her usual arch smile.

"Did I tell you guys that Audrey is Ms. Brindle's daughter?" Arabella said. "Isn't that wild?"

"You don't really look like her," Whitney said.

Audrey put her bun in her knapsack, knowing she would never willingly eat in front of Arabella. "I guess I look more like my father."

Dougie took a long drink from a water bottle and passed it back to Arabella. "You better not have mono," Arabella said.

"Or herpes," added Whitney.

Textbooks were spread out on the stairs around them. Audrey was relieved to be able to focus on a task as benign as studying, and the thudding of her heart began to abate. Her request to join them counted as perhaps the only expression of true nerve in her life.

Now she had to be equal to that boldness, but she was clueless. She pulled her math book and a pencil out of her bag and was about to ask a question about a polynomial function when Dougie passed a piece of paper to Whitney.

Whitney cast a skeptical glance over the page, then said, "I think you've been generous. I'd give Julie a five point five at most."

When Audrey thought about it later, what amazed her was how she had understood the nature of the discussion at once. Yes, the paper had been somewhat visible over the partial shield of Whitney's arm, but she had not needed to decipher the pencil scribbles, to see each name printed down the left-hand column, or the crudely executed accompanying cartoon faces, to know that their classmates were being rated. Female cattiness was a knowledge into which women were born, like the formation of language, the thousands of words saturating infant brains, lodging there with growing meaning until they are ready to emerge, allusive and unquestioning labels on an already known world. The surprise lay in how much it thrilled her, how its heat enfolded her: the unifying sensation of scorn, the closeness of it almost indistinguishable from love. Even more intimate, perhaps, than love.

At the bottom corner of Whitney's paper was a figure with a red dot between the eyebrows, a guitar in hand, and a large number three next to it. Audrey felt an impulse take flight within her. "I think three is generous," she said. "Don't you think Seeta is more of a two?"

A kind of darkness fell, clarifying everything. Audrey could see the constellation of expectations realigning themselves.

Arabella drew a pencil out of her bun and cocked her head. "Give the new girl the paper, Whit. You're being too PC."

From around the corner came the sound of humming, and before Audrey had a chance to meet Whitney's glacial half smile, Arabella's cheeks flushed. She put a finger over her lips, then reached into her knapsack and pulled out a sheet of orange construction paper. "Behold," she whispered. With ironic demureness, she held up what was clearly another note to Seeta. The message was again made up of magazine letters pasted messily together: "The sweetest songs have the saddest endings. Parsley, sage, rosemary, and turmeric..." She smiled at the note fondly, with a mother's soft affection for her child's handiwork.

"Awesome!" squealed Dougie.

Whitney shushed her angrily.

Arabella looked around to make sure no one had heard. "A little discretion, Ms. Douglas?" she said, lowering the note face down into her lap. She held out a gallant hand to Audrey. "Luckily, we have the master of discretion with us today."

The bell rang, and Arabella held out the note. Audrey made no pretense of contemplation. Alongside her habitual fear had lit something much more alive. In Arabella's smile was the perverse resurrection of all the things Eliot had once meant to her.

As Audrey slid the note into her knapsack, Dougie sprinted to the top of the stairwell, where she let out a muffled whoop. Seeta was standing outside the classroom door, ukulele in hand. "Fuck me, it's music now," Whitney said.

Arabella strode towards the classroom. "So tell me, Seeta," she said. "Is it true, what they say about a man with perfect pitch?"

Seeta looked puzzled.

"'Cause I was going to ask your bro to the semi, but, you know, you seem to have a pretty special bond."

"She wouldn't want to get in the way," Whitney added.

But before Seeta had a chance to respond, they galloped off down the hallway, leaving Audrey behind them, as they laughed with deranged delight.

"WHERE HAVE YOU BEEN?" said Richard, advancing on Ruth from the kitchen before she'd even closed the front door.

"What do you mean?" she said, looking studiously away as she hung her coat.

Her cheeks were flushed from the attacking wind outside, the redness conveniently masking the burn left by Henry's stubble. There had been no question in her mind, until that second, that she had been safe. Henry had been to the house just once, and she was certain they hadn't been sighted. Even if a neighbour had seen him coming or going, there would have been no cause for suspicion. Yet as carefree as she had been when she left Eliot with Henry that afternoon (for the parking lot of a nearby Shoppers Drug Mart, as it turned out), as insulated in her certainty that there had been no fractures in the shell of her protectiveness, all the way home she had worried that she had made a mistake.

With artificial gaiety, she rubbed her numb hands together and faced Richard. "What's up?" she asked.

"Well, gee. Think about it for a minute, Ruth."

She frowned in reflection.

"Where were you at lunch?"

"I was at work, of course. Where else might I be?"

Richard's words were clipped. "Well, you were supposed to be here, if you'll recall. I came home at six o'clock, thinking I had made a very clear arrangement with my wife that she would come home at lunch and let the dogs out, and what did I find but Marlow lying by the back door next to a pool of his own urine. Wagging his tail apologetically, might I add."

"Oh!" Ruth clapped a hand over her mouth.

"Oops," said Richard.

"I totally forgot. I'm sorry. I am. You know I am. I have all this extra work, the lit mag Larissa is making me do, end of term marking. It's been crazy."

Richard withdrew to the kitchen. "I don't want to hear it," he said.

"Richard, give me a break. I made a mistake," she said. But her protest was feeble; she didn't truly want to come home at lunch.

She noticed Marlow, lying in the middle of the living room, thumping his tail ardently. His molten brown eyes were locked on her, unreservedly welcoming. She crumpled beside him, patting his ear and resting her cheek against the top of his head. The steady thudding of his tail accelerated.

"I'm so sorry," she said. "I'm so sorry, my boy."

With effort, he rolled onto his back, his tail still oscillating with undiminished happiness between his hind legs, where the feathers were still damp with what she assumed was urine.

"I'm so sorry," she said.

She rubbed his belly for several minutes, until she heard Richard collecting cutlery to set the table. "I'm not hungry," she called out, heading up the stairs. "You and Audrey go ahead and eat without me."

Richard's voice, returning from the dining room, was too far away for her to make out his reply.

Upstairs, Ruth ran a hot bath and tried to set the scene for relaxation. She lit freesia candles and put on a meditation CD playing music that wasn't really music, but birdsong and trickling water set against a bland tune played by an echoing electronic flute. Once she was immersed, her unease grew. The water was too hot, and within minutes she was sweating. The candles, too far away to blow out, produced a sickeningly sweet smell, and the music—how could people listen to this stuff? She had not listened to meditation music in fifteen years, not since Richard had played it for her during thirty-five hours of labour, and now she remembered why, shocked by how viscerally her body recalled the connection. But she felt too lazy to get out of the water and correct any of these blunders. The bath was irrelevant.

What she was really doing was avoiding the disapproving gaze of her family. Cloistered in the bathroom, she had stopped time, in a sense, removed herself from its passage, thereby securing a respite from the consequences of her actions, and her equally odious in-action. She was doing everything poorly—being a wife, a mother, a dog owner. Yet on top of her unrest still floated that guiltless high, an unfaltering selfishness. (In self-forgiving moments, she hoped that admitting her own selfishness somewhat mitigated the vile-ness of its presence.) She felt far worse about what she had done to Marlow than anything she had done to Richard. But she knew how despicable she was. Nobody, hearing the things she'd done over the past months, would deny that she was a terrible person.

With her toe, she rubbed at the water spots on the faucet. The fix-tures had been a mistake, the result of overreaching: brushed nickel, easily stained, intolerant of regular cleaner. She had been warned away from them by the man in the store. The marble countertop of the bathroom vanity was also covered in subtle stains. Why had she bought so many expensive things for the bathroom? She had been so sure they would make her happy. On the floor was the bath mat, white and plush, she had bought for Marlow, so that he could lie by her while she took baths. But it had been some time since Marlow had kept her company by the tub. His hips were too weak to propel him up the stairs; at night, he waited in the front hall for Richard to carry him up to the bedroom.

She pushed these thoughts from her head. Before her lay the Christmas holidays, a stretch of Henry-less time. How would she conjure the requisite festive spirit? Ruth had always placed a great onus on Richard and herself to generate unparalleled levels of merriment. She bought so many presents for Audrey that she often felt embarrassed by the abundance as she descended the stairs in the morning. She dressed the dogs in Santa hats and presented them with a special cake made of carob. In the week leading up to the day, they baked enough cookies for a family of ten. Richard had sometimes resisted the extravagance, but Ruth had insisted upon it. Without this vaguely offensive level of decadence, it was too easy to be aware of certain absences.

There came a knock on the door, and Richard entered before she had a chance to deter him. He lowered the toilet seat and sat down.

"We missed you at dinner," he said. "Couldn't you have taken your bath after eating?"

"I've had a long day."

"Why don't you tell me about it?"

"Later."

"You may have missed your one chance to see Audrey in a good mood," he said.

She attempted to smile, but there was no levity to be found in that subject. Audrey moved on the margins of her consciousness, always, like a nagging and imperative task that needed to be addressed, that could not be delegated, and yet that she continued to procrastinate with a fluttering anxiety in her stomach. "That's nice."

"Listen," he said. "We need to talk about Marlow. You know that."

"Can't I just take a bath?" she moaned.

"His health is not an issue that can be avoided indefinitely."

"No! I'm not talking about that. Not yet."

"No decisions need to be made. But we need to review the situation if only so that we know we've reviewed it. Our actions have to be a choice, not an evasion."

"He still loves his food," Ruth said. "He's still happy. End of conversation."

"That's not a conversation at all."

"Richard, it's just stained rugs."

"You think I care about stained rugs?" Richard's voice rose in anger.

She had never liked being naked in front of Richard when they argued, but her sense of vulnerability had evaporated. She was barely aware of her body. She could have stood, naked and dripping, screaming, and it wouldn't have bothered her. "Look, he's happy," she said. "If you could ask him, he would not choose that. You know that. What about that other drug you mentioned? I met a woman in the park who said it took years off her dog."

Richard was quiet for a moment. "I just don't want this to end up like Heathcliff."

Ruth sat forward in a furious whoosh of water. "I am not my mother! I'm not making this decision for my own needs. He's happy!"

Richard studied Ruth as though undecided on the extent of his opposition. "Yes, I think he is," he said finally.

The argument thrummed in the air around them. Already, though, Ruth regretted the spectre of accusation in everything she had said. Even in the throes of anger, she had known how wrong footed she was, how baseless and unfair the implication that Richard treated Marlow as a burden and had a needle at the ready. He loved Marlow, and Marlow adored him. When Marlow was younger, he had followed Richard everywhere, and she had fumed with jealousy at their bond—he was supposed to be her dog. But marriage had taught her that there was no division of ownership. And there was certainly no controlling the tides of affection.

She was about to apologize when Richard pressed the heels of his hands to his temples as though he had a headache. "Look, I've had a hard day, too," he said.

"Oh?"

Richard shook his head. "Max. The pit."

Ruth's heart surged into her throat. "This sentence better not end the way I think it's going to."

"What was I supposed to do? The guy was determined the dog was not adoptable."

"I can't believe you."

"It's his dog, not mine, Ruth."

"I can't believe you."

"What would you have me do?"

"Bring it here!"

"How simple it is for you!" he said angrily. "You don't have to make these decisions. Isn't it all so goddamn clear? Bring them all home. A dog for every room."

Sweat and water streamed off Ruth's forehead. She felt very close to vomiting. "How dare you heap all that guilt about Marlow on me when you killed a dog today for no reason?"

Richard was silent, and for a second, even in her fury, Ruth feared she had gone too far. But there was a part of her that wanted to go even further. She was aching for release, for the pugilistic heat of a certain kind of fight. "You pretend to be so moral, but you're weak. You were too weak to say no. It comes down to that."

Richard began nodding slowly. "Yes, I'm sure my weakness is something you're frequent witness to."

Ruth continued as though he hadn't spoken. "You hold up this claim of professionalism, but you're just hiding behind it."

Richard still nodded, saying nothing more.

"Say what you think!" she cried. "You make these wishy-washy statements. Say what you want to say!"

She waited. But she saw that he would not give her this, could never give her this. He would leave her floundering forever, fighting with herself. She stood and grabbed a towel, threw it carelessly around her chest.

"I just wanted to tell you about my day," he said, retreating to the bedroom, trailing a piece of used dental floss on his black sock.

Chapter Eleven

JANUARY CAME IN WITH an eerie quiet. The weather itself seemed to express the anticlimax of holiday cheer. It was too cold for the softening countenance of new flurries, and the hard banks of old, dirty snow looked like permanent fixtures in the streetscape. The class was still waking up on Monday morning when Ms. McAllister appeared in the doorway of the classroom with a curt rap. Even before she spoke, a murmur rose from the class. Rare were the occasions when Ms. McAllister made use of her autocratic right to commandeer the class in the middle of a lesson. Even Henry Winter, who had just begun a discussion of Frost's "Birches," was startled by her interruption. Offering an obedient nod, he moved to the side of the room and fixed her with a glassy-eyed stare.

"A serious matter has been brought to my attention," she declared, taking up position in front of the blackboard, her hands behind her back. "I wish I were here speaking to you under happier circumstances, but alas, that is not the case."

Up rose a chorus of whispers, which she swiftly terminated with a militaristic raise of the hand.

"It has been brought to my attention that a member of your class has been receiving threatening notes. The particulars shall remain private. It is, however, my duty to inform you of this ha-rassment. I know that most of you are in agreement that this type of anti-social behaviour has no place at our dear school. George Eliot Academy was created as an intellectual haven, and so it shall remain." She paused and looked around with majestic sever-ity, taking the pulse of her audience. The girls returned her gaze, riveted by her restrained fury, afraid to speak. "Perhaps at pub-lic learning institutions, this type of behaviour is met with laxity, but I assure you that here, bullying is considered the lowest form of interaction, and offenders will be punished very severely indeed."

The tiny metronome of alarm in Audrey that had begun to sub-side just before Christmas started up again. Seeta sat stiffly beside her, tracing with her finger a groove someone had carved in the wood. Audrey kept her eyes fixed on Ms. McAllister, careful not to betray her guilt inadvertently. She had never particularly considered the consequences of the notes. She feared getting caught in the act, certainly, but her mind had looked no further into the future than that. Arabella's world demanded a surrender to immediacy. And Seeta had made it so easy. She carried on as she always had, singing in chapel, raising her hand at every question. Her imperviousness was stunning. It granted freedom from accountability.

Yet the notes had gotten to her, clearly. As Ms. McAllister spoke, Seeta stared, wide-eyed and unblinking, at her desk. It was possible that she was holding back tears. Although Audrey was still far from remorseful, she was taken aback by the realization that she might have been wrong in presuming Seeta's sense of self to be so durable that no unkindness could penetrate.

Arabella, Whitney, and Dougie sat at the back of the room, wearing elaborately serious expressions, a dead giveaway that tem-pests of laughter were being suppressed. It was clear from Arabella's dancing eyes how much this outcome was exactly what she had hoped for. They were not in the least afraid of getting caught. This lecture did not, for them, represent the rallying forces of official protection, but the breakdown of Seeta's spirit. The danger of the enterprise, the confrontation with the possibility of exposure and punishment, only added to Arabella's glee.

"I don't need to remind you what a fortunate position you are in, as Eliot girls. I know that most of you wear your uniform with pride, and your teachers and I rely upon you to do it justice. I will need you to be my partners now, my sleuths on the ground, as it were, to honour the uniform that it is your privilege to wear. Together, we will catch this culprit, who is not, at heart, an Eliot girl."

As Ms. McAllister spoke, her eyes moved systematically from girl to girl, as though prolonged eye contact would help her ferret out the offender. Arabella raised her hand.

"Ms. McAllister, how do we know that the 'culprit'"—here she made quotation marks with her fingers—"is in our class?"

"That is a very astute question, Ms. Quincy. The sad and intolerable truth is that we know nothing. No avenue will be left unexplored. Until then, I am speaking to each grade separately in order to circumvent the sensationalist effects of a public announcement."

"Well," replied Arabella, smiling sweetly, "I think I speak on behalf of the entire class when I say that we will do everything in our power to see that justice is served."

THEY RAN DOWN THE long hill to the ravine, tripping on the twig-strewn path, the frosty gravel underfoot. Arabella was out in front, and her run was loose, ungainly, as if she were a bike veering out of control. The wind lifted up her laughter and whisked it away over Audrey's head. Winter made the ravine more approachable, its density thinned by the absence of leaves. The pale sky lay flat on the tops of the bare branches, and the weak ripple of the creek and their own footsteps on the crunchy path were the only nearby sounds. When the girls reached the bottom, they headed into the trees, following the path single file, as if single-mindedly.

The cold air had a deadening effect, and the girls were quiet as they made their way, Arabella out in front, collecting dead leaves into a bouquet. Audrey brought up the rear, and in front of her walked Whitney, whose hair, tied into a high ponytail with a red ribbon, swung back and forth perfectly like a pendulum. The silence had a palpable charge that bound them together in a new way. The enduring terror Audrey felt in their presence fed her gratitude at being with them, made every moment imprecisely exciting, elevated with unreality. The power of group complicity was irresistible.

How she had been drawn into their circle was, as ever, a mystery. Arabella, Whitney, and Dougie had been standing by the lockers after school, imitating Ms. McAllister's lecture. Nothing resembling a plan was forming in her mind, but she was riveted by their impersonations. Catching her eye, Arabella drew another note out of her binder. A simple look was all it had taken to signal her willingness. And then they had left together. Audrey wasn't sure there had even been an invitation.

They had been walking for a time when they came to a widening of the path where a pack of five boys stood huddled around something on the ground, their bikes discarded to the side. The boys took no notice of the girls' approach. They were about ten years old, young enough to be oblivious to the witnessing eye of the world outside. As Audrey drew closer, she was just able to make out what lay in the middle of their circle. It was a dying baby animal, curled into itself, its tiny paws up by its raw pink snout. Did she just imagine a tremble beneath its inadequate dusting of fur?

"Should we move it?" one boy said.

"Nah, don't bug it."

"What if something comes along and eats it after we leave?"

A boy with red hair shrugged. He was holding a long stick, and though he seemed to have no intention of using it, it gave him an air of authority.

Dougie squealed in disgust. "Gross!" she mouthed exaggeratedly.

"You should just put it out of its misery," Arabella said.

They looked at her in horror.

"What do they know?" the red-headed boy said.

"What kind of psychos stand around watching an animal die?" Whitney said, looking around for agreement.

Audrey nodded, though she didn't agree at all. There seemed only to be compassion in their curiosity: an acknowledgment that death, for whomever it came, should be noted. Their bikes, piled carelessly on top of each other, gave Audrey a pang. Their lives seemed so easy, their manners so artless. Arabella strolled haughtily into their circle, as though they had gathered there expressly to observe her procession, and as she passed, affecting regal indifference, she stepped on the animal, producing a crunch, and continued on her way, tossing her leaf bouquet behind her. The boys let out a collective gasp and crowded in on their charge, cautiously assessing what damage had been done.

"Later, gentlemen," Whitney said, blowing them a kiss.

Audrey looked back apologetically, but the boys had already closed themselves against further trespassers. The mood of silence now broken, Dougie chattered about how hilarious the whole thing had been. There ensued a small debate about whether the animal had been dying or dead. Arabella and Dougie maintained that it was clearly already gone, while it seemed important to Whitney that the animal had been merely on the brink before Arabella's foot came down. Audrey wanted to believe that her father would argue that putting a dying animal out of its misery was in fact the more humane choice, but she was finding it hard to get past the cracking of bones, the pleased expression on Arabella's face.

When they came to the crest of a small hill, Arabella led them onto a less travelled path towards a small clearing in the trees. There she threw her knapsack onto the ground and let out a sigh. From her coat pocket, she produced a pack of cigarettes. Scattered amongst the dried pine needles were cigarette stubs from past smoking days. As she handed the pack to Dougie, she looked at Audrey and said, "I guess *you* don't want one." Audrey shook her head, aware that trying to smoke and doing so badly, choking and spluttering, even gagging, would be worse than declining altogether. Whitney and Dougie exchanged sidelong glances. They drew deeply on their cigarettes and exhaled with stagy contentment, as though to emphasize the difficulty of the day's deprivation.

"Did you see that creepy stain on Mr. Marostica's pants today?" Whitney said. "I don't even want to think about what that was."

"Mayo?" said Dougie.

"Or so he claims."

"Ugh," Dougie shuddered. "What would you do if Mr. Marostica came on to you?"

"Oh my God," Arabella shrieked. "You have such a perverted mind."

"What would you do if Ms. Crispe came on to you?" said Whitney.

"Mm," replied Arabella. "Tempting, but I like my dykes a bit more femme."

They drew on their cigarettes in unison, and Whitney exhaled smoke rings. "That's so grade eight," Arabella said.

Through an open space in the trees they saw Samantha Starkey, one of the senior prefects, ambling past with her boyfriend, a Crescent boy. She looked around, then pulled his pants and underwear down and burst out laughing. He clapped a hand over his mouth in faux horror, then began a kind of burlesque stripper dance, shimmying towards her, his penis flapping. She pushed him in the chest so hard that he stumbled back, grabbing her hand so that she fell against him as he backed into a tree.

"The worst thing about Sam Starkey is that she's so predictable," said Arabella, raising one eyebrow and blowing out a thin line of smoke, a gesture surely much practised.

"Ugh, I feel so scruff," Arabella said, shaking out her hair.

Dougie cleared her throat and began talking in her version of a Pakistani accent. "What is this 'scruff'? Is this what happens when your sari needs dry cleaning?"

"Might I trouble you for a razor?" Whitney chimed in. "I believe I forgot to shave my moustache this morning."

Dougie laughed with her mouth wide open, revealing the silver line of the retainer glued on the back of her bottom teeth. Arabella dropped her cigarette and ground it underfoot with a peculiar daintiness, with just the tip of her shoe. "Goodness me," she added. "Your body odour is especially fragrant this morning. Do I detect cumin? Or is it garam masala?"

"Isn't it groovy?" said Dougie.

Sudden barking erupted not far away, and they squinted into the distance.

"Holy fuck, is that Ms. Lee?" whispered Dougie. "She's walking her fucking boxer."

Arabella reached out and pulled Audrey down behind a sparse bush, and Dougie and Whitney snuffed out their cigarettes and crouched behind them. The possibility that this was all a manufactured emergency occurred to Audrey as a nondescript Asian woman, possibly Ms. Lee, the physics teacher, possibly anyone else, walked past, her face half-obscured by a navy-blue baseball cap and a grey scarf wound thickly up to her chin. Dougie quivered on the ground in a fit of staccato giggles. Arabella's hand pressed down on Audrey's shoulder. The firm weight of it immobilized her, summoned all of her senses into awareness of it. She was reluctant to move, to breathe, to do anything that might make it depart.

"My brother says he can get us some goodness this weekend," whispered Whitney, holding an imaginary joint to her lips. She turned to Audrey. "You want in?"

"Maybe."

Arabella stood up and pulled on her fluffy red mitts. "You know what we're talking about, right?"

Audrey was slow to rise. "Of course," she replied, but this area was littered with verbal mines. Better not to say the word at all than to say it wrong, to use an unpopular nickname, to say "pot" when she should say "weed," to say "weed" when she should say "a joint." Julie Michaels had once referred to it as "some doobie," and they had made fun of her for a week.

"Let's walk," said Dougie. "I can't feel my toes."

They set off, quiet again. Audrey could barely feel her fingers as they circled, without any apparent point, around the same loop they had just travelled. The sky was growing dim, and even the dog walkers were deserting. Each time the girls passed someone, they smiled politely, always mindful of the image people expected of the Eliot girls. As they passed the spot where the boys had gathered around the animal, Dougie laughed, though no trace of them remained. At the small bridge they veered to the left until they came to a narrowing of the river. There Arabella stopped and flung her knapsack to the base of a tree. "Someone dare me," she said. "I bet I can jump across."

"You have delusions of grandeur," said Dougie.

"I have ambition."

"Don't worry, lovebug," said Whitney. "If you fall in, I'll get naked with you and bring you back to life."

"The other side is just ice," Dougie said. "You won't even be able to land, you crazy bitch."

"Ah, but yes I will, because Audrey will be over there to catch my hand." Arabella met Audrey's eye and smiled.

Audrey saw it all, in that smile: the challenge glimmering there, like the tiny diamond studs in Arabella's ears. Arabella took off her coat, and Audrey's eyes followed hers across the distance. If there was a moment for refusal, this was it. But Audrey found herself crossing the bridge and finding her footing on the icy slope. Cold water seeped into her shoes as her feet sank into the sludge of wet leaves. "Look alive, Brindle," Arabella called. She rubbed her hands together and blew on them, then took a few steps back and made an arching leap high across the river. The girls on the other side were cheering, but Audrey barely heard them, absorbed as she was in studying Arabella's flight. Even in the air, her face was poised and tranquil, betraying no exertion. Her right foot landed on a bundle of twigs, and a second later her left came down on a patch of ice, then slid an inch, and she teetered, trying to catch her balance. Audrey reached out to grab her right hand, but her own grip on the ground was failing her, and Arabella's weight was pulling her back. As she dug her feet in and yanked, she felt, for a second—although she didn't review this feeling and what it meant until later—as though Arabella was trying to jerk her off balance, back into the river. Arabella started laughing, and with an involuntary grunt that made Audrey wonder if it wouldn't have been preferable to fall in the water, she redoubled her exertion, falling back on her bottom as Arabella landed firmly ashore. She was on her hands and knees, but still laughing.

"That was priceless," Whitney called. "You looked just like Ms. Crispe, trying to heave her up."

Arabella got up, brushing off her knees. Her hair was wild and wind blown, and she had tucked a leaf behind her ear like a flower. "Your turn," she said.

"What?"

"It's. Your. Turn," she said.

Audrey stared at her in disbelief.

"Whit will catch you when you land," she said. "She's got the pipes for it."

The thought crossed Audrey's mind that this was all part of an elaborate game they'd planned beforehand, orchestrated to land her in the freezing river.

"Come on," Arabella said. "Are you waiting for wings?"

Audrey resigned herself to whatever was going to happen. There could be satisfaction in plunging into the freezing water, the grand failure of it, a surrender, finally, to the inescapability of humiliation. The fight was too exhausting. Tiny flakes of wet snow began to fall as Audrey threw off her long navy coat, took a running leap, and landed just at the edge of the shore, one foot in the water. Whitney stood on the bank, hands on her hips, in no way ready to catch her. "Oopsie," she said.

"Guess you won't make the cross-country team," Dougie added.

As Audrey pulled her foot out of the frigid boggy shoreline and tried to shake the excess water out of her shoe, the girls were already on their way to the bridge, where Arabella stood with Audrey's coat and bag. "I'd say nice try, but trying is useless," she said, thrusting Audrey's things at her. "Either you do it or you don't."

"It's going to be dark soon," Dougie said, peering up at the lavender sky.

As Audrey buttoned her coat, Arabella, Whitney, and Dougie started walking away. From the end of the bridge, Arabella pointed in the direction they'd just travelled. "You'll want to go back that way to get to the bus," she said.

"Aren't you guys going?" Audrey asked.

"We're going to Whit's house," Arabella replied. "It's just up there."

"All you have to do is follow the path," Dougie said, her voice wavering with a hint of apology. "It'll only take you about ten minutes."

"Do you need a chaperone?" Whitney asked.

Audrey estimated that she had about fifteen minutes before she would be stumbling through the obscurity of evening. "Of course not," she replied.

Before long, the girls' voices had receded entirely. The walk was longer than they had said, and Audrey's outlook was bleak. The wind ripped through the inadequate wool coat her mother kept promising to replace. The glacial puddle in her shoe swished with her every step, and her wet toes were numb. A glance at her cellphone confirmed her suspicion that the battery was dead; she wasn't sure which bus would take her to the subway. Reaching a fork in the path, she puzzled over which direction led to the parking lot, and as she continued on, she grew certain that she had chosen the wrong way. The sound of her own footsteps, resonating in the sepulchral air, seemed to announce the arrival of some horrible fate.

She vowed this would be the final such mistake she would make. Would she never learn to control her hope? She sat on an ice-encrusted log, took off her shoe, and poured out the water. Yes, she had conceived of a future in which she was truly friends with Arabella, Whitney, and Dougie. She had not extinguished that obstinate wish. But she saw now that there would be no turning point. They were not friends now, nor would they ever be. There would be no victory of mischief, no marvellous iniquity, Audrey could pull off that would change this.

And just like that, a new feeling came over her in a powerful rush. It was a deviant elation, an emotion so unfamiliar that it took her a minute to identify it. Glancing up through the outstretched arms of the winter trees, she felt fearless for the first time in recent memory. What madcap joy, all the more pure for being irrational, and the desolate chill of the valley only fed it. All the sensations that had been so unpleasant just seconds before—the hacking wind, her freezing foot—had morphed into their opposites. It was as though she had sunk deep enough into her sadness to find a rare and mysterious harmony between loneliness and freedom. If only, she thought, she could die in a moment just like this, caring about nothing. The woods around her were dark, but she felt no call to move on, to return to the light-speckled metropolis just visible above her.

It was then that Audrey's deep breaths were joined by the sound of approaching footsteps. Turning, she saw the unmistakable figure of Arabella.

"Why don't you come to my house?" Arabella said, barely breaking her stride. "You can dry off there."

And Audrey was back in the world, just like that.

HENRY PARTED THE SHABBY orange curtains to peer out at the subsiding snowfall, then drew them again across the dirty window. Someone had made a cursory attempt at cleaning the glass, creating a spotless circle like a porthole in the centre while the periphery remained smudged with the grubby accumulation of motel life: mud splatters kicked up by spinning car tires, dust from the gravel parking lot, a cracking splotch of bird shit. A crumpled Kit Kat wrapper lay on the outside windowsill. Henry stood in front of the window for a moment, holding the side of each curtain in his hands, his head bowed. His posture made Ruth think of a priest outside a confessional: humourless and quietly full of his own secrets.

When he had suggested finding a motel room after last period, Ruth had been quick to agree. She was still reeling over the interminable length of the Christmas holidays. She had known that her separation from Henry would feel rotten, but she hadn't anticipated how toxic her own longing would become. Thinking about him was a torment—she was certain the contemplation was one-sided—and she had been barely able to contain her grumpiness, even on Christmas day. When he had come to her classroom after lunch, she hadn't even made a show of mulling over her availability.

"Is it snowing?" she said.

"It's just stopping. We should probably leave extra time for getting back, just in case."

"Of course."

He returned to bed and lay down, his head on her stomach. There was a pain in her gut that his weight was pressing, but she didn't dare ask him to move. Outside, a green minivan with a struggling muffler pulled into the lot. It was visible through the gap where the curtains refused to meet, and beyond its rusting roof, Ruth could see the cars on Lakeshore whipping past. She thought of Richard driving by (he wouldn't, of course, not at this end of the city), how it would never occur to him, if he glanced at the sun-bleached grey sign, the unshovelled sidewalks, the blue glow of the small television in the office, that his wife was inside, that she had ever been, or would ever be, in such a place. The idea of her displacement was exhilarating. She wondered if there had ever been a moment in her life when she felt so free—even when she was a teenager, when being free was the perpetual condition of life, automatic and therefore unnoticed. The feeling had to do with being in an anonymous place, an unappealing place. She wouldn't have felt so exultant in a beautiful room with Henry, with French doors opening onto the wide ocean, a private balcony with a rose bush growing along its wrought-iron railings. Such loveliness would undermine them, render them an ordinary, inauthentic thing, just one more undistinguished facet of a beautiful tableau.

"I think the woman across the street from me may have died," Ruth said, "but I don't know how to check because I don't know her name. The house is for sale."

"That doesn't mean that she's died," he said, handing her the full glass of cloudy water from the night table. On the rim of the glass was a very faint lip print, not lipstick but the memory of lipstick.

"She's nowhere to be seen. The house is dark at all hours. I used to see her light on upstairs in the middle of the night."

Henry reached for a second glass and drained it, then settled under the sheet next to her, closing his eyes.

"I saw her just last week. She seemed fine." She felt, as she often did, that he was barely listening to her. Even at his most ardent, she felt that there was another part of him not fully engaged—that he was not so much surrendering as committing himself to the appearance of surrender, and that she was not so much a participant as a witness—and no matter how much he was next to her, on top of her, no matter how many facts she knew about his life (not many, at that), there would always be this spectral self behind him, ironic and unsentimental, shaking his head wryly, needing nothing. About that Henry she could know nothing at all.

He stifled a yawn.

"Are you going to sleep?" she said, hitting him lightly.

"No, no." He propped himself up on the pillows, still lying more than sitting, but seeming moderately more alert.

"I can't believe I don't know her name," she continued. "She's lived there as long as we have. Audrey's trick-or-treated at her house. Even fifteen years ago, she was the old woman across the street." She put her water down, untouched, on top of a *Reader's Digest* someone had left on the nightstand. "Doesn't that strike you as wrong?"

"Do you have to socialize just because you live near one another?"

"There's socializing, and then there's acknowledgment of your shared humanity. It seems terrible that I don't know her name."

"Terrible might be an overstatement."

She thought of her grandmother's death nearly thirty years before. While she lay dying upstairs, already ghostly behind her oxygen mask, Ruth had taken a trip down to the cafeteria with her grandfather. There she was supposed to be distracting him with cheerful conversation, but of course distraction had been impossible. Halfway through his black coffee, which he had been drinking with painstaking slowness, he broke off, nodding as though he had just remembered something. "We've been married for sixty years," he said. She must have said something in response, offered some kind of inadequate sympathy, but what she recalled was feeling rather blank, discomfited by his sorrow. She had not been an exceptionally callous teenager, but she had been unable to comprehend sixty years with someone coming to an end, being near the end of your own life and knowing that you're going the rest, the worst, most undignified part of it, alone. It was not until the beginning of her own marriage that she had a flash of understanding how he must have felt.

She wanted to ask Henry how one lived at the end of one's life, when there was no expanse left to make corrections, no horizon on which to pin one's hopes, but he was glancing away again, towards the watch on the nightstand. "That poor woman died alone," she said.

He regarded the ceiling with monk-like impassivity. "Most do," he said.

There was always this comedown, as though they had spent too much time together. It wasn't even thirty minutes since they'd arrived. She tried to hold on to his whimper of surrender at the end of sex, but it was a memory she couldn't quite tap into. Her mistake, she understood, had been letting things get here too quickly. She thought of the very beginning, that night in the staff room, and she saw that even though she was always wanting more—even now, as he peeked at his watch for the fifth or sixth time—having less had been infinitely more satisfying. Perhaps all she had really needed was something to anticipate outside her own life. After that first kiss, she should have pulled away, said no, and when he returned, said no again. This failure to prolong anticipation had been a strategic error, an amateur's misstep.

From somewhere came the sound of music, and Ruth realized the radio was on at a low volume. She had noticed the static while they had made love, and she'd been distracted by it, unable to figure out the source of the noise. Henry fiddled with the knob, tuning more precisely into a station, and the song, Led Zeppelin's "Going to California," made her smile.

"That was quite a performance this morning, wasn't it?"

"Hmm?" Henry replied bemusedly.

"Seeta."

"Ah."

"I think she was expecting an encore," Ruth laughed. "The way she wouldn't leave the stage."

"Well, she is quite talented."

"Of course." She sensed that she might be violating an unspoken rule by talking about work. The longer she had known Henry, the less they had talked about school, about anything, really. Yet she pushed on. "But don't you think, really, that Seeta should give it a rest? I mean, she may be good, she may be excellent, but come on."

Henry sat up fully and looked straight at her. "Come on what? She deserves to be harassed?"

"It's just a little bullying. Do we really lead such politically correct lives that we have to pretend to be mortally offended that some ordinary teenagers are sending mean, and frankly stupid, notes to the class loser? Is this really an unprecedented event?"

"I don't think we can reasonably call it 'a little bullying' anymore."

"Henry. The music was fine in the beginning, but now? Come on. It's like watching someone who's morbidly obese inhale a Big Mac. You must agree with me!"

"Why must I agree with such a preposterous—and dare I say mean-spirited—comparison?"

Ruth drew the sheet around her naked body, light-headed with mortified anger. She had always assumed that that they would be kindred spirits in this. She was not a sociopath. Of course she felt some sympathy for Seeta, but over the past month she had also grown sick of all the tiptoeing: the earnest whispers of concern, the virtuous debates. Pretending not to think what everyone knew to be true. Teenagers got bullied. It was the way of life.

"Bullying can kill, Ruth."

"Nobody is murdering anybody!"

"How do you account for the suicides of some of these persecuted kids?"

"Henry, come on! Mentally sound teenagers endure the bullying and move on with their lives."

"How would you feel if Audrey were the one being harassed?"

Ruth was silent. Henry regarded her with a level gaze. She felt, suddenly, as though she wasn't in a fair fight. Of course she would feel awful if Audrey were being bullied, but this wasn't a conversation about how she would react to her daughter's pain. It was flawed argumentation, surely, to broaden the scope to the personal, but she didn't know how to articulate the wrongness of it. What did Henry even know about Eliot?

Swiftly and clumsily, she got out of bed, an exit that unfortunately required her to abandon the coverage of the sheet. Two shaky steps later, she was in the bathroom with the door closed firmly behind her. She took a deep breath, willing her racing heart to settle.

The flimsy door seemed barely any separation between them. She turned the water on full blast and splashed her face, then rubbed it hard with a rough white towel that smelled intensely of bleach. What she was feeling for Henry came very close to hatred, but the real trouble was how little empowered she felt by such loathing. She was careful not to look at herself in the mirror, knowing that the dingy lighting would show her reflection to her in its true light. It would allow no romanticizing of her under-eye circles, the chafed red skin, the untidy hair. Even one glimpse could wreck her. It was imperative that she reclaim the confidence to go back into the room and be seen in the unsparing afternoon light, to make things right, to take his body into her custody with the playful aggression, the barest hint of hovering violence, that drove him crazy.

When she returned, he was dressing by the side of the bed.

"You're leaving already?" she exclaimed.

The spectral Henry was already standing at the door, jangling the keys in his pocket.

"I guess you'd prefer it if I had no opinion," Ruth said. "If I just lay here and shut up. Well, I'll do my best to comply next time."

"It's my dinner night," Henry replied. "Clayton carries every other day."

Ruth nodded vigorously. "Oh yeah, I'll bet she's just a super housekeeper!"

With his back to her, Henry swiftly pulled on his clothes. "You have no call to say anything about her," he said.

Ruth grabbed her blouse and arranged it awkwardly over her top half. "You never say anything bad about her. But you must feel something bad," she said, despising the sound of her own voice. "At least a little bit. You must. You're here with me."

Henry looked at her frankly. "I'm not here with you because of her. It's because of me."

"Of course not because of me."

"Ruth, let's not do this."

Was it really too much to expect the paltry accommodation of an obvious lie, the standard appeasement, however flimsily consoling? *Yes, I'm here because of you. It could only have been you.*

"No, indeed" she said, shaking her head bitterly. "Let's not do any of this."

AUDREY SAT IN ARABELLA's living room, her legs dangling gracelessly off the edge of the high, plush couch. Hushed voices drifted out from the kitchen, where Arabella was in conference with her mother. Audrey stared straight ahead of her, afraid of being caught showing too much curiosity in her surroundings. None of her imaginings had prepared her for the reality of Arabella having a home, a mother cutting vegetables in the kitchen.

The house was a small semi-detached, but the simple flair of the furnishings made the living room seem much larger than it was. With the exception of an enormous vase of sunflowers in the adjoining dining room and a piece of art above the mantel that looked like an elongated red teardrop on a white canvas, everything was black and white. The couch and chairs were white with jet black velvet throw cushions, the wood floors a glossy black, the walls largely bare. In the corner next to one of the armchairs, a cello leaned against the wall.

They had spoken very little on the bus. Audrey hoped for some indication of why Arabella had found her in the ravine. There were few things in the world she expected less than an invitation to Arabella's house. "I can make my way home," Audrey had said with a trace of defiance, but also trying to let Arabella out of whatever atonement she felt obliged to make. Arabella had simply said, "Don't be stupid."

Reappearing now in the hallway, Arabella looked at Audrey as though she didn't know quite what to do with her.

"I'll go get you some dry socks. Shoes I don't think are going to happen." She looked dubiously at Audrey's inelegant feet, noticeably larger than her own, and disappeared.

The mood of liberation that had swept over Audrey in the ravine was retreating all too quickly now that she was at Arabella's. She was bewildered by her purpose, even more uncertain than usual of how to behave. Was she there for a visit or simply to replace her essentials before being sent on her way home? That Arabella was upstairs rummaging for socks was implausible. How disorienting, too, to hear a mother humming in the kitchen, to see a mantel lined with family photographs: Arabella captured in black-and-white profile, staring contemplatively at something in the unobservable distance; a young woman reading a book by a window, her hand resting on top of her pregnant belly. Audrey was startled to see Henry Winter in the lineup. She hadn't exactly forgotten that he was married to Arabella's mother; it was more that there was a realm she associated with Eliot, a universe that, though crammed and chaotic, was essentially one-dimensional. That any of these people were alive outside of Eliot was an abstraction. Maybe it was self-preservation, compensation for the fact that in every moment at school she felt locked out of a massive splendid secret. She worried about everything constantly—Arabella and her friends' mockery, the teachers' disappointment, Ms. McAllister's wrath—but there was a peculiar narcissism at the bottom of it all. They barely existed for her except in relation to what they thought of her. But there stood Henry Winter on a beach some-where with Arabella's mother, before a sunset sky of such a deep blood orange as to give the impression of manufactured scenery, smiling in different directions, as if at separate cameras. And there they were again, in a dingy governmental wedding room, Henry blending in drably in an ill-fitting tweed jacket, the woman lam-bent and ethereal in a silky slip dress and a little pillbox hat with a long blue feather on top, her long, unstyled hair limply blanketing her shoulders.

Arabella shuffled halfway down the stairs in a pair of enormous bunny slippers and leaned out over the banister. "Come on up."

Audrey paused, wondering if Arabella could be talking to her mother.

"Are you waiting for a written invitation?" Arabella threw a pair of black socks at Audrey and trudged back up the stairs.

Up in Arabella's room, the only light came from tiny white Christmas lights strung up around her window, dotting the sump-tuous turquoise drapery reminiscent of a ball gown. Arabella sat cross-legged on the bed, the puffy, heart-speckled duvet drawn up over her legs. She pointed to her computer chair and told Audrey to sit, less an invitation than a command, then smiled uncomfortably, as though wanting to be hospitable but unsure how to surrender her usual persona.

On the wall above the desk were two huge bulletin boards, one covered in pictures of Arabella and her friends, the other with ones of Arabella and the woman from the mantel photographs. "Your mother is so beautiful," Audrey said.

"Clayton? Yeah, she's a hottie."

Audrey gestured to a picture of Arabella, Dougie, and a girl she didn't recognize. "Who's that?"

Arabella broke out laughing. "So you've discovered Whit's secret."

Audrey looked at her in confusion.

"It's Miss Oke herself," Arabella said. "Pre–nose job. Wait. Corrective surgery, I'm supposed to say."

"Are you kidding?" Audrey asked. She didn't understand how she could have missed that in all her ventures through Ruth's old yearbooks. The difference between the Whitney she knew and the Whitney of this photograph was astounding. The former nose dominated Whitney's face, more or less eclipsed her other features.

"She likes to tell people she broke it on the high diving board at the Granite Club, but everyone knows that's bullshit. She claims it grew wrong." Arabella laughed again. "She had her father's nose. Anyone who knew her family knew that. I kinda liked the original, though. It gave her street cred."

Audrey supposed that this story should have made Whitney more human to her. Anyone who concocted such an outlandish story clearly hated herself in some way, but as she thought of Whitney's aquiline new nose, its only flaw perhaps that it was a little small for the rest of her face, she felt no sympathy, no heartening recognition of a kindred spirit. She wanted to tear down the illusion, the delusion, all of these protecting lies, and expose her—but expose her to whom? Everyone accepted the new, perfect Whitney. The old man nose had been excised like a borderline mole, so cleanly that Whitney seemed to have lost all recollection of whatever pain it had caused her. Audrey studied the photograph. How had Whitney managed to bring her inner, imperfect self and her outer, purchased self into such harmonious alignment? What was the trick of it?

"Hey guys, want some veggies and dip?" came a voice from downstairs.

"Dude, I'm starving," called Arabella.

Audrey shadowed Arabella back downstairs, where Clayton stood in the hallway, looking up at them brightly. In the dim light, she resembled a figure in an old sepia-toned photograph, an impression created not simply by the light, but by the fact that the woman herself, with her disproportionately long and slender nose, her large hooded eyes and angular bone structure, looked like a refugee from postwar Europe. She was lanky and shapeless, wearing a blue man's Oxford shirt with a spot of ink on the pocket and jeans lightly splattered with paint. She smiled, revealing a gap between her front teeth that, in detracting from the simplicity of prettiness, made her striking.

"Hey, kiddo," she said, smiling at Audrey. "You should call your mom. She's probably worried about you. I'm Clayton, by the way." She came forward, her hand extended.

Arabella laughed. "Audrey's still reeling from her discovery that Whitney's not quite the man, I mean woman, she used to be."

"Arabella," chided Clayton gently. "Are you staying for dinner, Audrey?"

The sound of keys in the door, heralding the arrival home of Henry, saved Audrey from having to reply. Bursting into the hall in a gust of cold air, he stomped his boots on the seagrass mat and coughed into his glove.

"Look who's decided to grace us!" Clayton exclaimed, reaching out her arms for a hug.

"Sorry, love," he said, giving her a loud kiss on the cheek. "I got held up." He looked into the living room and registered Audrey's presence with clear surprise. Setting down his briefcase, he took off his coat and took several moments arranging it in the closet. He turned back and nodded at Audrey with mock foreboding. "Young lady," he said.

"Pappy," said Arabella.

"My darling," he replied.

"So we're just trying to figure out whether Audrey's staying for dinner," Clayton said. "What did you have planned?"

"Just a simple tomato pasta."

Audrey stood. "Thanks, but I should really call my mom to come get me. I've got tons of math homework."

"Audrey's quite the mathematician," Arabella said.

"Phone's in the kitchen," said Clayton.

Audrey tried to listen to what they might be saying about her in the living room, but she could make out nothing over the whirr of the dishwasher. On the counter were rows of neatly cut vegetables and a bowl of homemade avocado dip, a small pile of skins and pits discarded in the sink. The bulletin board above the phone displayed more family photographs, Arabella in her pyjamas with a plate of pancakes before her, Henry Winter manning the barbeque.

Ruth didn't answer the phone until the fifth ring. "Hello?" she said edgily.

"It's me. I'm sorry I didn't call sooner. My cell was dead."

"Jesus!" she exclaimed in a piercing voice. "Where have you been? I've been sick with worry."

"Sorry. I'm at Arabella Quincy's."

Ruth breathed asthmatically into the receiver. "Hence the number on the phone."

"I need you to come get me."

Ruth was silent. "I can't," she said at last. "I just put pasta on the stove. Call a taxi. I'll pay when you get here."

Audrey whispered urgently into the receiver. "I can't call a taxi! They'll think I'm hinting for a ride."

Again, Audrey was met with silence. "Mother?"

"Fine," Ruth said. "But listen. I am *not* coming up to the door to get you. I will be there at seven sharp. Come out or you're in deep shit. I mean it, if you get distracted and forget the time, and—"

"I'll be there."

Audrey was about to hang up when she saw Henry standing in the hallway. She looked at him inquiringly, and he held his hand up, as if in apology, before returning to the living room as if nothing had happened.

WHEN THEY GOT OFF the phone, Ruth poured the pasta water into the sink with an angry whoosh and paced the kitchen biting her nails. She had just arrived home from the fiasco at the motel. The traffic had been terrible, and her nerves were rattled. She had never had such an unsatisfactory meeting with Henry. All the way home, she had fretted about its consequences. She had tried to say good-bye nicely, so that they wouldn't end on such a bad note, but she'd been unable to re-engage him. After their parting kiss—a stodgy, dry affair—she had tried to get him to commit to meeting again, but he had been uncertain about his schedule.

She couldn't show up at his house, not now. Even with a legitimate reason, it was unthinkable. Her first move was to call Richard, but the secretary told her that he was expected to be in surgery for another hour. For several minutes, she sat on the stainless steel stool by the phone and looked at the notepad where she had scribbled the address of the house, barely legibly, a gesture intended as a comforting show of normalcy. She already knew, and struggled not to know, exactly where Henry lived.

The inexorable fluctuation: although a part of her craved information about him, the better, and so far more successful, part of her clung to her limited knowledge. Ignorance was her ally. It was the only way she could preserve her dwindling dignity. One bleak evening over the Christmas break, she had sat in her car in the descending darkness, preparing to drive to Henry's house and sit outside for as long as it took for her to catch a glimpse of Clayton. But she had pulled herself back from that precipice. Yes, there might have been short-term gratification in seeing a fat, dowdy-haired Clayton panting over a snow shovel, or the couple in the tense posture of argument through the living room window, but in the end, the negative consequences of this information would prove far more crushing than any pleasure she would experience. The only way for her to feel she knew Henry, beyond the facts and distractions, beyond the immaterial matters of public life, was to know very little.

Twenty minutes later, she was sitting outside Clayton's house, the heat roaring in her car, cursing Audrey for not coming out at the appointed time. She had been sitting in the car for nearly ten minutes, eyes searching for some sign of exit. In the front door of the house was an octagonal window encircled by an evergreen and pine cone wreath, and she strained to see past it, searching for some interplay of light and shadow, the suggestion of heads moving inside. She was wondering how, without being rude, she could call the house from her cellphone and request that Audrey come out— there was, of course, no way of doing this without being rude, and equally odious was the prospect of honking—when the front door swung open, and a woman waved her inside.

"Fuck, oh fuck. Fuck you, Audrey," she muttered to herself, opening the car door. As she kicked excess snow off her winter boots, she glanced down at her legs and was visited by horror at the realization that she had not bothered to change out of her red plaid pyjama bottoms.

They waved to her from the door, the image of the perfect family: in the centre, the woman who must be Clayton, to her right, Arabella, to her left, Audrey, and in back of them, Henry, his presence somehow encircling them, the dignified patriarch sheltering his flock. Clayton's arm was around Audrey's shoulder.

"Hello!" Clayton cried. She took Ruth's cold hands into a warm, manly grip. "You have to come in for a minute."

The group parted to grant Ruth entry.

"Oh, I can't stay," Ruth said. "I have a roast on for dinner."

"Five minutes won't burn a roast," Clayton replied, pulling Ruth indoors.

"I apologize for the way I look," Ruth said, as Clayton helped her out of her coat, which was not her coat at all but Richard's red hooded dog-walking coat. After trying unsuccessfully to stuff the mammoth bulk of it into the small closet, Clayton gave up and draped it on the banister, then shepherded everyone into the living room. She directed Ruth to an oversized armchair, just one in a set of furniture that seemed designed to make them feel like miniature versions of themselves. Henry stationed himself in the matching chair and Clayton perched on its arm while Audrey and Arabella sank into the couch. An arrangement of raw vegetables and green dip sat in the middle of the coffee table, and Clayton gestured for Ruth to help herself, smiling in uneasy acknowledgment of how little they had to say.

At last, Clayton said, "So we were just talking about the girls' big math test next week."

"Ah, yes. The math test," Ruth replied, trying to sound as though she cared.

"Whit heard that Mr. Marostica may be leaving for jury duty," said Arabella. "Have you heard anything about that, Ms. Brindle?"

"Not a word. Sorry to disappoint you, Arabella."

"But would you tell us if you knew? Like, would that be a breach of some teachers' etiquette?"

Ruth let out a light laugh. The room was too warm—the undersides of her breasts were already blooming with sweat—amplifying her feeling of suffocation. She kept her eyes studiously trained on the girls across the room. If she tried hard, she could blur her peripheral vision enough to block out Henry and Clayton almost entirely.

"I think the dude is masochistic enough to plant the rumour about jury duty just so that no one studies and we all fail," Arabella said.

"I doubt that," replied Clayton.

Ruth tried to calculate how long minimal civility required them to stay. She looked at Audrey, sitting forward at an awkward angle with her arms crossed, and had the impression that Audrey wanted to leave as much as she did. She had no idea that Audrey and Arabella were even friends. Audrey had never mentioned Arabella, and every time Ruth had seen Audrey around Eliot, she was alone. But then, there was so little she knew about Audrey's life lately. She had always thought that Eliot would bring Audrey and her closer together, but Audrey's blatant unhappiness filled her with such a sense of failing that her latest tactic had been to ignore it.

"Well, extra studying never did anyone any harm," Clayton said.

Ruth turned to Henry with a false smile, trying to transmit her displeasure, but he appeared not to notice. When he had told her that first time in her bedroom that she required no adjustments, she had taken it to mean that Clayton required many. Why had he misled her so? She found it difficult to get beyond her own unease, her frenetically magnifying disbelief, her flustered sense of injustice, and actually *see* Clayton. But when Clayton had stood, she had taken in the full view in an ascending, dissonant scale of fury. The enviable architecture of her face, the man's Rolex watch dangling from her thin wrist, the cellist's erect posture: the effect was of something more penumbral than ordinary prettiness. It was a face that would not grow boring, that would reveal itself slowly, year by year. Ruth stared at her lap. If she wasn't better-looking than Henry's wife, then what was she?

She was so possessed by indignation that it took her a minute to put something else together, something she was surprised she hadn't caught sooner: the shirt Clayton was wearing. Henry's shirt. She knew it from the spot of blue ink on the pocket. That spot of ink for which she claimed credit. Henry had been in her classroom, wrestling her into submission over her desk, and when he had pulled away she had noticed the ink, spreading like a spot of blood. That afternoon had been one of their best. There had been a rough energy about him that made her feel exhilaratingly weak. They had hardly said a word to each other, and she had never felt more sure of her hold on him.

Clayton reached forward to load a piece of red pepper with dip, then with a little laugh delivered it into Henry's waiting mouth.

Looking away in disgust, Ruth found Audrey watching her. She tried to read what she saw in her daughter's face, but lately she couldn't interpret even the most basic of Audrey's expressions. She was surely just being paranoid. There was no suspicion there, no alarming acuity.

"Audrey, we have to go," Ruth said, standing.

"Oh," said Clayton. "Can't I convince you to have a cup of tea?"

"Thanks, but no." Ruth took a dirty Kleenex out of her pocket and blew her nose. Out in the hallway, she had a clear view through the large kitchen window into the snowy garden, which was lit with the bluish glow of small lanterns placed around its perimeter. She pulled on her coat and opened the front door. In her haste to get outside, she nearly tripped on an enormous stone urn filled with levels and varieties of evergreens, slim cranberry-coloured branches, dried pomegranates and rosehips, and in the middle of this pretty jumble, a tiny rustic birdhouse. Yes, in the contest between them, Clayton won, hands down.

"It was nice to meet you," Clayton called as Audrey hurried past her, holding her coat over her arm.

Ruth was already closing the car door, starting the engine.

"CAN I ASK YOU something?" Ruth said.

She and Audrey had been silent in the car through blocks of traffic. Ruth had needed that long to regulate her breathing. None of her forethought had prepared her for the rage she would feel at the sight of Henry and Clayton. As they had pulled away from the house, she had feared what Audrey might say about what had passed inside, but luckily Audrey was no more open to conversation than she was. She had withdrawn as far as she could into the corner and was gazing moodily out the window.

"Why did you never tell me that you sit beside Seeta Prasad?" Ruth asked.

"Why would I tell you?"

"With everything that's gone on, I would have expected it to come up."

"I got stuck with her on the first day of school. It's not like she was my first choice."

In the windshield, Ruth could almost make out Audrey's distorted reflection, its dubious accompaniment to her removed voice. "So do you like Seeta?" she asked.

"Of course not!"

"Do you know who's been bothering her?"

Audrey paused. "I have no idea."

"What were you doing at Arabella's house anyway?" Ruth said. "I didn't know you were friends."

"We're not. Not really."

At a red light, Ruth watched as a woman pushing a red stroller began her journey across the intersection, stopping every two steps to peer at the baby inside. Ruth didn't think she had ever looked that bloated and haggard, but her unreasonable nostalgia for that period of her life distorted everything. Having a young child had been so preoccupying, so consuming. Even when she had felt most frustrated and trapped, there was fulfillment, too, in being so required, in being sapped by a child's demands, that devoted dependence. She thought of a night several months after Audrey's birth when she had gone out alone to meet a friend for dinner on Queen Street. The chaos of the street had dazzled her, the hurrying pedestrians, the speeding cars, the conversations circling like scrounging birds. She felt like a tourist who'd been transported, blindfolded, to a foreign city, then returned her sight and let loose without a guide. How insignificant she was inside all that motion. How naked she felt without her baby. For so long, she had been either pregnant or accompanied by the child; she'd forgotten how to be a solitary woman. Her empty hands, especially, undermined her composure—what to do with them? Forty, then, had seemed so far away, yet she had already been envious of the years that lay ahead for Audrey. To have her own child, she had learned, was not to embrace, finally, her own adulthood, but to long more achingly for childhood.

Audrey was twirling a lock of hair around her index finger. It occurred to Ruth that there would never be a better opportunity to ask her about Eliot. For weeks, she had wanted an update but had been afraid to disturb the tenuous peace. What did Audrey think about her own circumstances? How on earth had she ended up at Arabella's house? Maybe in the dark, travelling sanctuary of the car, neither here nor there, they could be visited by their old candour. But she couldn't get a proper handle on the words. She was too rattled, still, by the hazardous pleasantries of Clayton's living room, by the sight of Henry's fingers on the small of his wife's back.

She sensed Audrey's eyes searching her face. "Who do you think I look like?" Audrey asked.

"What do you mean?"

"Do I look like you or Dad?"

"I don't know. Not like your father."

"Not like you."

"No, I suppose not. But sort of."

"Nobody thinks I look like you," Audrey said.

"Well, why should you want to?"

Audrey looked out the window again. "Because everyone thinks you're pretty."

"But that's all I am," Ruth said, turning onto their narrow street. "One day, you'll be beautiful."

Chapter Twelve

WHEN LARISSA MCALLISTER ASSUMED her usual spot at the chapel lectern on Friday morning, it was evident even before she opened her mouth that her mood was unusually morose. Contrary to Audrey's expectations, however, the source of her gravity was not the recent bullying, but rather certain looming festivities. As principal, Larissa McAllister knew that it was her job to establish a robust morale, but she could not hide her low spirits from her captive audience. She was not altogether against coeducational activities. The blend of tenor and soprano at the Independent Schools' Music Festival was undeniably stirring. And the debate tournament counted as one of the highlights of her year. Indeed, she found her delight difficult to contain when she popped into the back of a classroom during a debate to witness one of her stars trump a male of inferior intellect. Dances, however, were the bane of her administrative agenda, and she was not pleased to be standing before her pupils reviewing the ground rules.

Ruefully, she acknowledged the necessity of dances. In abstaining, her institution would mark itself as an outcast. But insofar as dances brought out the wildness, the immaturity, the sheer inanity of her girls, their brainless appeal struck her as far from harmless.

Assessing the fallout in the days after, she was even compelled to question how effectively her daily lessons on female comportment had penetrated her students' minds. Reports of drunkenness, sexual debauchery, and generally unladylike conduct were far too common. It struck her as offensive that she even had to recap the rules, which should by now be so well internalized. Standing at the lectern before her agitated audience, she was irritated. Would they not all rather be home reading fine books?

No amount of severity could dampen the spirits of the student body, however, for the George Eliot–hosted dance had finally arrived, an event eagerly anticipated in the months leading up to it and fondly recalled in the months following. At Ms. McAllister's first reference to that night's event, cheering erupted. With prim tolerance, she allowed the explosion. She considered cheering a boorish way of expressing one's enthusiasm, but understood it to be part of what she called the integrating discourse of school spirit. When the noise began to die down, she gave a short lecture reviewing the school rules with resentful precision. The most useful guide for behaviour, she advised, was for the girls to think of themselves as figures in history: let them not be waylaid by impulses they wouldn't care to see reported in the biographies of their lives.

Audrey shared Ms. McAllister's displeasure, though for different reasons. There had only been one dance, at UCC, near the beginning of November, and although there had been no question of her going, the social consequences of her absence were few since grade tens commonly opted out of the dances held at the boys' school. Because the boys' schools invited only the girls' schools to their dances, and the girls invited only the boys, gender parity was impossible, and the unspoken rule was that only grade elevens and twelves were welcome. But when Eliot hosted, the ratio was finally to the girls' advantage, and everyone, including grade nines, went. Audrey had been anticipating the event with dismay all week.

On the night of the dance, Audrey expected Eliot to be a magical place, an idealized version of itself, sentimentally made over in the image of a high school from a movie. She had envisioned coloured Japanese lanterns strung across the quad, casting their mellow pastel light over the patches of snow and grass, clusters of balloons tied to the basketball hoops in the gym, artificial trees threaded with tiny white lights in the corners and a dusting of silver sparkle blanketing the gym floor. As soon as she and Ruth, who was a chaperone, turned the corner into the long driveway, however, she was confronted by the silliness of her predictions. An ascetic decorating scheme was the one way Ms. McAllister had managed to assert her tastes. Loath to create an impractical climate of love in the corridors of academics—and believing such decorations to be tacky, misleadingly celebratory, and possibly a little dangerous, nurturing as they did puerile notions of romance—Ms. McAllister had made only two concessions to transforming the place: a sign outdoors, with a slightly deflated helium balloon tied to its top, and a long drinks table in the gym wrapped in leftover red plaid Christmas paper. The girls were to remember they were in their school. Their aspirations ought always to be, first and foremost, scholastic.

But whether Ms. McAllister liked it or not, the atmosphere in the school was utterly changed. Boys were everywhere, and had brought with them a different brand of boisterousness, a physical camaraderie, as if any minute they were about to fall to the ground and start wrestling. Most of them didn't yet seem even to care about the girls. They were messy and unself-conscious, with worn rugby shirts and shaggy hair, and didn't seem embarrassed that they were already growing sweaty in the overheated gym. Immediately noticeable as well was a change in the quality of the noise, which was almost entirely male generated. Their shouted conversation rang out in the hallways and all through the quad. The girls, meanwhile, had fallen quiet, whispery and secretive, huddled in corners and against walls in protective groups. They took little notice of each other now. Absent were scathing looks at what others were wearing, the sarcastic compliments. All their attention was focused on the boys. In this, they were together, their joint sense of daring and delight, the novel intimacy of having males in their gym, the same gym where they played volleyball in their navy-blue shorts and endured Ms. Crispe's graphic lessons on STDS.

The air in the gym was tropical, filled with the hot breath of hundreds of dancing teenagers. A teacher had opened the emergency exit door, but no breeze could diffuse the cloud of humidity. Audrey's class had convened loosely in one corner of the gym, so she made her way there and loitered on the edges. She noted with gratitude that, for once, she was not alone in her tense observation of the busy scene. All the grade tens looked as unsettled as she. For all of them, this was a first dance, and though Ms. McAllister's rules of comportment were clear, their own were not. Where generally the girls ensconced themselves in their usual cliques, tiny, intimate provinces with boundaries as clearly defined as any country's, they had opened their enclosures, spread themselves out, together yet apart, possibly in an effort to welcome any male approach.

A song came on that Audrey didn't recognize, but everyone else seemed to, and while the girls cheered, the boys pumped their fists in the air, jumping. Most of the teachers seemed to have gone out of their way to look just as they did during the school day, though some were dressed even worse, as if heeding Ms. McAllister's caution against the hormonal male threat. Ms. Glover was wearing a pair of old running shoes, a blousy grey sweatshirt, and high-waisted, pleated brown cords, which had a huge bottle of Tylenol sticking out of one pocket. Only Ms. Howe, the youngest teacher on staff, seemed to be having a good time. In an attempt to age her naturally pixieish face, she usually wore untailored suits and her hair in a bun, but now she swayed slightly to the rhythm, her long hair halfway down her back, precisely lined cherry-painted lips lazily mouthing the words of the music, an act of self-forgetfulness that elicited an appalled double-take from the patrolling Ms. Glover.

It was hard not to notice Henry Winter at the drinks table. Tall and unmoving, gazing without focus into the middle distance, he seemed in no way engaged in his surroundings as he took little sips from a bottle of Evian water. Most of the teachers were making an effort to look watchful and concerned, to at least appear to have embraced their humourless watchdog roles. Ms. Glover paced the walls with a small spiral notebook in hand, possibly recording unseemly behaviour for later punishment. Even Ruth, whom Audrey spotted at the far end of the gym, wearing what Ms. McAllister would surely consider an inappropriately clingy white T-shirt, was looking distractedly observant, restless and agitated, as though torn between her desire to look hot and her obligation to supervise untrustworthy minors. Rather than loosening up, the teachers had lost their individuality and had formed, according to Ms. McAllister's decree, a disapproving perimeter around the licentious dance floor. What stood out about Henry was the quality of his boredom, its forbidding force field. He looked at his watch, then at the crowd, and caught Audrey staring at him. Blushing deeply, she turned away and stumbled into Seeta, who was standing directly behind her.

"Hey there," Seeta said, smoothing her ruffled pink blouse.

"Hi."

"Are you having fun?" she asked.

Audrey shrugged.

"Do you like dancing?"

Audrey didn't answer.

Seeta tried again. "This is a good song. Don't you think?"

"It's fine."

"It's one of my favourites," said Seeta.

"Actually, I hate it." It would be preferable to stand alone, Audrey thought, than to align herself with Seeta. She stared despondently out onto the dance floor, where Kate Gibson was making out indelicately with her boyfriend, her prosthetic arm slung protectively around his skinny, pimpled neck. Audrey had seen them together before—he often picked her up from school—but not like this, woozily swaying in each other's arms in a transport that had attracted the notice of Ms. Glover, who hovered nearby, scribbling furiously in her notebook. The rest of the prefects had paired up and were doing the tango across the middle of the dance floor, weaving their way around the song's tentative couples.

"*Excusez-moi,*" Arabella said as she and Whitney coasted onto the dance floor, where they entwined themselves in an ironic slow sway.

Dougie walked past wearing her dangling turquoise earrings and a red Eliot baseball cap, hand in hand with a boy.

"You've got lipstick on your teeth," she said to Seeta, then just before they disappeared into the crowd, turned back and sang out, "Just kidding!"

Near the end of the song, Arabella and Whitney waltzed past, halting when they caught sight of Audrey and Seeta. Arabella smiled crookedly and raised one eyebrow like a soap opera star. "Having a good time, ladies?" she said.

Seeta was tapping her foot to the beat of the song. "It's really good," she said, nodding. "I was hoping to persuade Audrey to come dance with me."

"Aahh," said Arabella indulgently, like a teacher listening to the long, boring story of a hyper child.

"Hardly," Audrey said.

Arabella pivoted and scanned her grandiosely from head to toe. "So Audrey, you a big fan of the Ramones?"

Audrey looked at her shirt. Just before the dance, she had found a puzzling new outfit laid out on her bed: a cut-off denim skirt, black leggings, and a vintage Ramones T-shirt. "I guess," she replied.

"What's your favourite song?" asked Whitney, exchanging glances with Arabella.

"I don't really have one."

"Well, there must be one you like better than the others."

Seeta jumped in. "I always liked 'I Wanna be Sedated.' Maybe I'll start rehearsing it for assembly."

"You do that," Whitney replied.

"You girls make a sweet couple," Arabella said, smiling. "You should go hang out with Ms. Crispe and Ms. Sampson. By the way, Audrey, your mom is over there looking crazy hot. I think one of the UCC prefects asked her to dance."

"Are you sure you're not adopted?" Whitney asked, scrutinizing Audrey's face.

Before she could give good thought to what she was doing, Audrey found herself struggling against the crowd of people cramming into the gym. She burst through the double doors into the hall. The sudden brightness of the fluorescents made her squint, and she looked down the hall to the bathroom, where a long line of girls trailed out into the hall. To her left was a dark stairwell, and although students were forbidden to enter other parts of the school during the dance, she swung open the door and was swallowed by the cool silence.

On the second floor, she was disoriented by the changed aspect of the unlit halls, as though she had stepped through time and ended up in a place that ought to have been familiar, but wasn't. The known world of Eliot was somewhere here, but inaccessible to her. It must be like this, she thought, to be a grown woman returning to your childhood home, to find the rooms intact, the old furniture hidden under dusty sheets.

Night had altered her homeroom, like everything else, into an alien landscape. The slim light of the crescent moon cast a reflective blue film along the lengths of the spotless windows. All the identifying features of the class were absent, the personal clutter stored away. Ms. McAllister had made the announcement that afternoon that classrooms were to be left in states of superlative tidiness since the school was to be host that night. As they roamed the classroom under the supervision of Henry Winter, tucking books into cupboards, Duo-Tangs into desks, and recycling into the bin, Whitney said, "Okay, Dr. W., this is a legitimate English question 'cause I have a thirst for knowledge. Isn't it an oxymoron when Ms. McAllister says to get things extra clean? I mean, something is either clean or it isn't." Arabella popped up from where she was fishing a drink box out from under a desk and said, "You mean redundant, you dimwit. Oxymorons are opposites." To which Henry Winter replied with a curt and weary, "Just do as you're asked. In silence."

Audrey sat now at the teacher's desk and tilted her chair back until it rested against the ledge of the chalkboard. The desk was the only surface that hadn't been properly cleared. A book, *The Rainbow* by D.H. Lawrence, lay in the middle, its back cover bent, as though it had been carelessly flung and forgotten. The distant strain of music drifted up from the gym. A headache pressed in on her.

Minutes later, the noise of laughter in the hall, retreating, brought her back to herself. She rose to follow the sound, not wanting to confront it so much as confirm. Her black ballet flats allowed her to travel light-footed, undetected. She had grown used to carrying herself secretively anyway, slipping here and there on the periphery. The voices drew her to them, like a pinprick of light in the pitch black. She edged forward until she was just close enough to make out the words.

"Didn't you think Julie Michaels looked like a total whore? Actually, she's too fat to look like a whore. Before you got here, she leeched on to me. Literally following me everywhere, smelling like her house."

"I hear she gives good head," came a male voice.

"Ugh. Thank you. I'm literally going to have nightmares with that image in my head."

"Hey, man, fat, thin, a mouth is a mouth."

"Is a mouth is a mouth."

"I'm so going to get one of those hats," said a voice Audrey knew all too well.

"Well, I'm a gentleman. I'd be more than happy to help you out."

"Never going to happen, sweetheart. Grade elevens only."

"Um, ladies. What are we talking about here?" asked a different male voice.

"It's this thing the grade elevens are doing. A contest, sort of."

"SBGG. I'll leave the rest to your imagination."

The voices stopped, as if their owners heard the breath of the intruder, and Audrey hurried off in the opposite direction. She had a dim idea of what they were discussing. Over the past couple of

weeks, more and more grade elevens had been wearing red baseball caps with "George Eliot" on the front and "SBGG" on the back.
It was against the rules to wear hats during the school day, but on
the buses after school, the grade elevens formed a distinctive pack.
Although Audrey had grown accustomed to the perpetual anxiety
that she was missing out on a joke, that feeling opened out into a
sweeping loneliness now that she had a better idea, at least broadly,
of the act to which SBGG alluded. It wasn't simply that she hadn't
conceived of participating in such activities; it hadn't even occurred
to her that others were. She tried to see herself in that pose—
kneeling as if in prayer?—but all she could conjure was a room so
dark that even her mind's eye couldn't penetrate.

She was in front of the double library doors when she heard a
rustling in the side hall, followed by migrating laughter, shushed
into a furtive babble. Not desiring a collision with Arabella, she
darted into the concealment of the library and strayed into the tall
stacks. The darkness here was almost complete. She sank to the
floor and breathed deeply, consoled by the mildewed smell of the
towering books. The hands of her watch glowed, but she looked
away, unwilling to acknowledge the decree of time, its reminder of
what awaited below.

How unlikely it was, she thought, that it should be in the library
that she felt most at home while at Eliot. The volumes enclosed her,
watchful and beneficent. In spite of her academic struggles, she felt
connected to the books; they seemed to represent a superior world
to which she should aspire. Lining the rows at eye level were aging
Penguin paperbacks, their spines worn and peeling. As her eyes adjusted, she squinted at the titles and author names, barely able to
make out the words. McEwan. Morrison. Munro. The final book in
the row was *Who Do You Think You Are?* She pulled it out and tried

to make out the cover image. A tanned girl sat in the grass, her arms and legs bare, knees to her chest, lank, straw-coloured hair falling around her shoulders. The pages let out the warm, musty smell of a book long loved; the words were an inky blur. Audrey felt she had to have it.

Voices surfaced in the stillness. Different voices. So remote did the rest of the Eliot world seem that Audrey wondered whether the murmurs were a figment of her imagination. But there was anger in them—low and restrained, but intelligible nonetheless. She crept to the end of the row and peered out into the open space. There she saw, in a basin of opal moonlight, what she first thought must be a ghost. The figure was pale, clad in white that gleamed in contrast to the pewter shadows, expressing some kind of lament, twisting slightly in an aspect of explanation or pleading. It was a second before Audrey made out a second body; the voice came first, divulging its owner's identity.

"And that," it said, "is a fantastically inappropriate T-shirt."

The first figure turned into profile, the face still hidden by a veil of dark hair, but the voice, when it came, sent Audrey stumbling back into the coverage of the bookshelf.

"Jesus, Henry! Why are you being so hard?"

The exchange that followed was muffled. Then: "I had no choice. As if I wanted to be there."

A mirthless laugh was released.

There was no time for Audrey to consider what she had witnessed. She knew only that she had to escape without detection, and as quickly as she could manage it. She stole back to the exit and, cringing at the noise, pushed open the creaky door and hurried back to her locker. Only once there did she realize that she had forgotten the book, out of sequence on the edge of the Ws. She sat in front of her locker and rested her head on her arms. Tears of disappointment welled up in her eyes. It was just a library book, she told herself, read by many Eliot girls before her. She could get it on Monday. But the sense of a botched destiny left her nauseated, breathless, so certain she had been that it contained a message just for her. An answer to a question she couldn't even formulate. All through the weekend to come, her mind returned to it again and again, there in the library, bearing the invisible imprint of her hand.

ON SATURDAY MORNING, WHILE Ruth was out grocery shopping and Richard was at the clinic, Audrey went into their bedroom and sat down in the middle of the unmade bed. She stared for a time at the horse picture, listening to the quiet house. The smell of Ruth's rosewater cream wafted out from the bathroom, the oddly old-fashioned smell of it recalling Ruth's mother before her. When Audrey was quite young, and her parents had left her with a babysitter for the evening, she had liked to fall asleep in their bed, listening to the raccoons tangle in the pear tree outside. The mattress, long since replaced with a superior model, had sagged in the middle, and she had burrowed in there, hoping they would forget to return her to her own bed. Now she spent very little time in their room. It made her uneasy to think of the private life they carried on away from her. People didn't realize that being an only child wasn't just about lacking a sibling with whom to experience childhood. The biggest problem of a small family was that none of its parts existed independently. There was such exposure, and within that exposure such a resonant loneliness.

She could almost see her reaction to what she'd witnessed in the library—like an object masked by a heavy fog—but she couldn't quite grasp it, bring it close to her and make out its shape. People often said of deceptions that they had known all along. But over the preceding months, she had sensed nothing. Whatever had happened—was happening—had gotten past her.

She caught a glimpse of herself in the mirror above the dresser. She looked like one of those deranged children from the movies, scowling, her bob flipped outwards, a bobby pin securing her hair off her face. A spinning, anaesthetized sensation washed over her. More than anything—more than the treachery against her father, more even than the prospect of her family's dissolution—she was appalled by her own maddening innocence. That stubborn, useless part of her. How could she have failed to sense the change in the air of her house? A titanic untruth had been unfolding right under her nose: Ruth was carrying on a hidden life. All the moments of their shared world, down to each boring word uttered over dinner, had been part of a hollow display, an enactment of something that did not exist.

At home after the dance, she had lain in bed, searching for another interpretation of what she had seen. But then she recalled Henry eavesdropping on her phone conversation at Arabella's house. Very quickly, her disbelief had collapsed catastrophically into belief. And what was she to do with belief? Where did such knowledge leave her? Her family?

Her mother, she'd always thought, was the person she knew best. There was scarcely a memory in Audrey's head that didn't involve her at least peripherally. When she was a little girl, her mother had been everything to her. More than that: she had felt her very self to be embedded within Ruth. A future existed, she knew, in which she would live independently, be married, have her own children, but this outcome hovered as abstractly, as insignificantly, as the stars in the city's night sky. She and her mother had argued sometimes, of course, but even then Audrey had felt only that she was tugging at Ruth's sleeve; no real separation had been possible.

Since she started at Eliot, Audrey's every thought of Ruth had coursed longing and comfort and hatred and alienation, all together. Every good feeling about her mother awakened its opposite. Audrey felt herself straining away, but as poorly as she ran from danger in nightmares, with wobbly legs, tripping over her own feet. Daily, she despised her mother, but still she couldn't help wanting to retreat into what had once been.

On the nightstand rested an old framed photograph of Ruth reading to Audrey in her canopied girlhood bed. There was a time when they had ended every day that way. Sometimes the dogs had joined them, piling onto the bed. Sometimes Richard sat on the floor. It was as though every being in the house had been drawn to that epicentre, pulled in by the sound of Ruth's voice. A perfectly ordinary voice it was, but Audrey had never wanted her to set the book down and leave. The transience of the reading was part of the pleasure—knowing that soon she would have no choice but to be shut alone in the darkness of her room. The future was always intruding, making each moment a glorified version of itself.

To the side of the photograph lay a paperback, face down. Audrey picked it up. *The Rainbow.* She opened the front cover and found Henry Winter's name scribbled inside.

She was still sitting in the bedroom when Ruth returned from the grocery store some time later, but she made no move to leave. From the kitchen came the noise of groceries being put away; minutes later, footsteps on the stairs.

Ruth appeared in the doorway. "Oh, what are you doing in here?" she asked pleasantly.

"Just sitting."

Ruth peeled off her old wool sweater and threw it to the floor, then stepped out of her jeans. One of the curtains was drawn so that light came through only half the window, casting her left side in a pale light. She studied herself in the mirror, one hand on her hip, her feet shoulder width apart, her hips squared forward rather than softly angled, less a model's pose than a critical study.

"Why are you getting changed?" Audrey asked.

"I have to run a few more errands."

"Does that answer my question?"

"That sweater's too itchy." Ruth frowned at her reflection. "The mirror in your room is better. This one makes me want to kill myself." She swung around to face Audrey. "Tell me the truth. How bad is this jiggle?" She slapped her lower stomach and looked down in revulsion.

"What jiggle?"

She rotated towards the mirror again, taking a step back. "Oh, God. I can barely...Ugh." Ruth rotated away from the mirror again and looked over her shoulder at the back of herself. It could have been a child's dance, pirouetting towards the mirror, then away, towards and away. "I wish I didn't have my period. I'm so sick of it. No. I take that back. God, menopause will be awful."

As Ruth adjusted her bra, Audrey closed her eyes, but distorted images of Henry Winter and her mother burst garishly onto her mental screen.

Audrey fixed her eyes on Ruth's reflection in the mirror. "You never told me," she said. "What did you think of Arabella's mother?"

"Clayton?" Ruth wrinkled her nose. "Her skin is so sundamaged."

Chapter Thirteen

ON MONDAY MORNING, RUTH sat outside Larissa McAllister's office, inspecting the loose papers in her briefcase in order to avoid assuming the posture—sitting straight up, staring ahead—of the errant student summoned to face the authority. It was not yet eight o'clock, and the school was disarmingly quiet. No movement was audible behind Larissa's closed door, and Ruth worried that she might have gotten the meeting time wrong, a slip that wouldn't have been surprising given her fractured frame of mind.

A splash of early morning light threw a golden glaze across the deep scratches in the hardwood at the base of the door frame. She thought of her first day at Eliot many years before, that moment of stepping into her pristine classroom, the unused chairs propped upside down on the glossy desktops, the vacuumed floors, the spotless blackboard, the long sticks of chalk in a line along its tray. Flushed from her walk, contentedly aware of her own glow, she had breathed in the air that seemed never to have been breathed by anyone but her. She had thrown open the windows and looked out at the blanket of undisturbed green stretching to the houses beyond. She could not believe that Eliot had not always been there. Its presence seemed almost organic, a necessary feature of the landscape.

Out of sight a groundskeeper had been humming, and the purity of his tenor, its artless flight through the air, had seemed a perfect expression of her own emotional state. The moment demanded nothing of her but that she allow it, that she suspend herself in its nothingness, that she not think ahead to the day's schedules and tasks, to her first meeting with her students, to the grocery shopping that awaited after work, to the pizza she would make as a dinner treat, or to the vaster responsibility of being not just at a personal beginning but the school's beginning, the first official day of an institution that would, over time, affect the lives of thousands of girls. The weeks leading up to this day had been some of the busiest of her life, filled with formal two-hour meetings that lingered over information she estimated could have been delivered concisely in ten minutes, as well as nightly, long-windedly therapeutic telephone conversations with Larissa about the quality and accuracy of the media attention on Eliot, the barrage of inquiries she was fielding from parents, the appallingly countless lists of all the things that had yet to be accomplished in order for school to start smoothly. All this activity had drained out of her as she listened to the groundskeeper's tune. Fancifully, she had thought that his disembodied song might not, after all, be an expression of her joy but an answer to it, an element of the intuited connection between them, two people sharing, separately, the same sliver of morning.

Ruth was still recalling that long-ago hum when it was overlaid by another melody, a strident, discordant rendering of "And Did Those Feet in Ancient Times." Jolted back into the present, her heart sank.

"Ruth! *Quelle surprise!*" bellowed Michael at a volume better suited to a later hour.

"Good morning, Michael."

"Awaiting your demerits?" Michael chuckled as she skipped around Ruth's briefcase to the photocopier next to the secretary's desk. She set down a canary yellow folder and began what looked alarmingly like a marathon copying session. "Staff room copier is on the fritz again. I think Larissa is going to have to bite the bullet and get a replacement." She sighed contentedly as the copier spat out her handouts. She picked up a worksheet on Virginia Woolf's "Shakespeare's Sister" and held it to the light, gazing at it with beatific satisfaction. Then she turned to Ruth and cocked her head. "So, how's Ruth?"

Ruth forced a smile. "Pretty well. You know, busy, of course. But well."

"Busy, busy, busy... aren't we all? I'm just amazed by how quickly the year is flying by. Before we know it, March break will be here! I'm counting down the days already."

"Big plans?"

Michael bit her bottom lip, smiling flirtatiously through the contortion of her mouth. "You're going to hate me!" she sang out.

Ruth looked at her in bewilderment.

"My girlfriends and I are taking off on a cruise in the Caribbean. No hubbies! No kids! Just us gals and a tray full o' margaritas!" She jiggled her head in delight.

"Oh, that sounds fun," Ruth replied doubtfully.

"Did someone say Caribbean cruise?" called out Sheila accusingly from the hallway. She popped her head into the office and thrust out her bottom lip. "No fair!"

Michael threw her head back in a noiseless laugh. "It's my first time away from the kids for more than a weekend. They're devastated. But they'll have a grand time with their dad. Of course, Graham is already puttering around the house trying to keep track of where everything goes. He actually asked for a refresher on how to work the washing machine! Poor bloke! He's going to be lost."

"Well, if I know you, you'll leave them well provided for," returned Sheila.

Michael nodded a demure concession. "I've been cooking like a madwoman for a fortnight."

"Make sure you take along as much sunscreen as you can pack into your suitcase," advised Sheila. "I just finished reading this gut-wrenching article about this beautiful young woman, just the world at her feet, who died of melanoma. And you, with that beautiful porcelain skin of yours..."

"I have bottles of SPF 60 lined up in my lavatory. I was telling our lad Henri L'Hiver that I can't comprehend how these people come back from vacations so burned to a crisp that you can barely recognize them. Don't they think of their skin, not to mention their health?" She smiled broadly and gestured towards her lack of crow's feet. "Never you worry, Sheila, I shun the sun."

"I hope you protect your skin, Ruth," said Sheila.

"Of course. I have better things to do than lie out."

"It's not just sunbathing, though. It's everyday things like just being outside. This poor, beautiful girl had never had a sunburn a day in her life..."

Ruth rummaged around in her briefcase in an effort to look busy. She was desperate, now, for them to leave. Although she was doing her best to look casually distracted, she was fuming. Who did Michael think she was? She was insufferable, positively repellent in her presumption. Henri L'Hiver? Of course, what else should she have expected of a woman who, in announcing her third pregnancy, circulated her ultrasound picture with the caption, "Oops, we did it again!"?

Michael and Sheila chatted on amiably about the pros and cons of cruises and resort vacations, showing no inclination to take their conversation elsewhere. Ruth considered telling them she had work to do in advance of her meeting but knew that would only invite prying questions.

"Ruth," said Sheila, spinning around, "is it true that at the dance a UCC prefect asked for your hand?"

Ruth waved her hand. "Not seriously."

"I'm not surprised," said Michael, her smile weakening. "I could barely tell you apart from the students. You always look so youthful, Ruth."

Ruth was saved, then, by Kate Gibson poking her head into the office. "Hey, ladies!" she said sunnily. "Ms. Curtis, would you be willing to come watch our sketch for this morning's assembly? We're, like, kind of locked in this disagreement. We need another opinion."

"My pleasure!" Michael crowed.

"Oh, and I guess my opinion isn't worth two cents," said Sheila, mock-petulantly.

Kate's face fell.

"I'm just giving you a hard time!" Sheila laughed, shooing them away. "I've got a million things to do. And I like to be surprised by the skits you kids come up with. They're so creative!"

When they were all gone, Ruth exhaled deeply. Her hands were trembling slightly with leftover fury. But just as she closed her eyes to compose herself, Larissa's door opened and a throat clear projected its familiar censure into her ear. "Come in and take a seat."

With arthritic ceremony, Larissa strode to the other side of the desk and sat in her wingback chair. This chair, Larissa's first purchase for her office, was a regal, deep crimson leather, bordered with polished brass nailheads, and seemed itself to preside, to demand, to disapprove, to exemplify the spirit of Larissa's pedagogical goals, her philosophy, her aspirations. Her hands locked in a tense prayer pose in front of her, Larissa studied the surface of her desk. Prominent veins crossed her thin, spotted hands. Ruth had never seen Larissa's desk so messy, strewn with piles of papers and open textbooks jammed with Kleenex bookmarks. The phone peeked out from under a brown folder. One closed book sat by Larissa's elbow: the Bible.

Ruth was rigid in the wooden ladderback chair, a seat that had no comfortable nook, that seemed designed, in fact, to prohibit relaxation, to force the sitter to perch, unwillingly erect, awaiting condemnation. How Larissa expressed so much with such economy of movement and expression was a matter of continual amazement to Ruth, who perceived something hazier than simple exasperation emanating from her clasped hands, her rigid mouth. In her physical reserve, Ruth saw the control, the inscrutable complexity, of a leaping mind. She breathed loudly—only there, in her slow inhalations and quicker exhalations, betraying the strain of trying to be patient, imposing yet benevolent, with a tiresome underling. A car horn sounded abruptly outside, followed by nothing.

"So, bring me up to date," Larissa said at last, wearily, as though the literary journal were a pet project of Ruth's to which she had graciously agreed.

"Well," says Ruth, pulling out her folders and holding them awkwardly, unsure of where to set them on the cluttered desk. "I've been having a lot of fun reading these submissions! You were right on the money giving me this project. So much great work here. The real challenge will be whittling it down to the very best and figuring out the right format for showcasing it. You know how it goes, I'm mulling over an assortment of different ideas and I haven't yet made up my mind. There are so many possibilities and I know what a responsibility I have to these girls and their work. They deserve..." She noticed that Larissa was looking away, towards her bookcases. She had thought she was rather convincingly enthusiastic.

As Larissa stood and passed behind her, Ruth caught a whiff of lilac perfume, a scent that made her unaccountably sad, reminding her that Larissa was not as young and vigorous as she strove to appear. She was standing by the rows of books, some literature, some pedagogical theory, in a pocket of shadow outside the sphere of strong yellow cast by a pot light, and the half light exposed the fatigue on her face, the bags she had attempted to cover with the wrong shade of concealer, the rouge in the fine lines of her sagging cheeks.

A virgin, she claimed. It was a source of pride, an educative tool. She never lectured about the immorality of sex before marriage, but simply offered this personal information to her religion classes, letting her choices serve as inspiration. Surely this choice, though, was about more than morality, more than her Christianity, which struck Ruth more as a token, a nod to tradition, than true religiosity. Ruth had always assumed that Larissa wanted nothing from the world of men. Still, she used perfume. Was her virginity a necessity reframed as a choice? Did she ever wonder where her life had gone, as she sprayed her collarbone after dressing?

Restlessly, Larissa crossed back to her desk, and the burgeoning sunlight through the window behind her shone through her thin hair, teased slightly upwards to give the appearance of fullness, creating the effect, almost, of a halo. She clasped her hands again, then reached down to the bottom drawer of her desk, withdrew a piece of orange construction paper, and set it on the desk in front of her. Ruth could not see past the disorder to make out what it was. At first she thought it was a special submission, something that had tickled and impressed Larissa so much that she wanted to present it to Ruth personally, not only to ensure that Ruth afforded it the proper respect, to shepherd Ruth through her own response to it, but also to seize a rare moment of connection, to bond with Ruth over their appreciation of a gifted student's creativity. Then she noticed that Larissa's gaze upon the paper was far from pleased, and far from proud.

"I don't know what to do," Larissa said, handing the paper across the desk to Ruth.

A full thirty seconds passed before Ruth understood that they were no longer talking about the journal, or Ruth's responsibilities to the school, that the paper was not a submission that exposed the flimsy charade of her coloured folders, not a dazzling piece of student work to be lauded and displayed, and not—the possibility had hit her at the last second—an incriminating piece of evidence linking her to Henry Winter. It was a note to Seeta Prasad. She knew that the notes had not ended—Lorna Massie-Turnbull had reported the news to several teachers, including Sheila, in a hush—but because there had been no official staff meeting to discuss the situation, she had assumed that the harassment of Seeta had evolved into nothing more than an occasional nuisance, half-hearted pestering, the obligatory, lacklustre mocking of the class loser. Instantly, she saw how wrong she was and why Larissa was working so hard to keep the situation quiet. She needed to make no effort, as she had thought she would have, to muster the expected indignation, for she was genuinely shocked and, indeed, repelled at the sight of the note. No words taunted the victim, only an image. On the construction paper was glued a cut-out from a magazine, a still shot from the movie *Carrie*, the moment just before Sissy Spacek is doused in pig's blood.

Ruth shook her head. "I had no idea things were so bad."

"I cannot understand," Larissa said, "the pathology of the brain that seeks to make itself heard with this kind of abuse."

"It's a little sinister."

"Ruth, I think we've gone far beyond diminutives such as 'a little.' When Ms. Loveland delivered this to me yesterday evening, I knew that we had crossed into new territory. What exactly are we dealing with?" Now that she was speaking at greater length, Larissa's voice grew smoother, more lubricated, had lost its unnervingly geriatric crackle and regained its usual braying heft. "I apologize. Here you are to discuss this inspiring project, and I'm utterly preoccupied. I had every intention of reviewing your progress."

"Larissa, it's fine." Ruth reached a sympathetic hand across the table, as if to take Larissa's in her own, but unable to follow through, let it rest on the papers between them, an unexpressed thought.

Ruth had come to George Eliot after two years of teaching at a public school in an area of downtown Toronto where gentrification was much discussed but scarcely in evidence. As it turned out, she had glorified not only her ability to change things, but also the extent of her own idealism. Every morning as she rode the streetcar along Queen Street, she had a queasiness in her gut that barely abated as her day got underway. The rooms were bathed in inhospitable fluorescent light, the long bulbs dotted with black spots, the shrivelling carcasses of the dead flies inside. The linoleum was always gritty underfoot, the hallways littered with empty pop cans and Wagon Wheel wrappers. Her third graders knew what oral sex was and used it alternately as a promise and a threat. Even among the girls, bullying was blatantly physical. The teachers were of the opinion that you did what you could to ignore it.

There were bright moments too, inklings of promise, but every instance of hope was undercut by the shadow of its implied inverse. After a parent-teacher interview where a mother on welfare told Ruth that she had taken a parenting course, with the result that she now read to her son every night for an hour so that his life would be better than hers, Ruth had sat in a bathroom cubicle with her head in her hands, tears dripping onto her grey skirt, until someone had knocked to see if she was okay. She couldn't accept the paltriness of a little hope, a little light. And then there were just the plain old low moments. Eight-year-olds unable to identify basic vegetables. She wasn't cut out for that kind of reform.

But Larissa's reform—that she could get behind. Here was a school where parents requested summer reading lists before the doors had even opened for the first time. Here was a school where students fought over a hardcover edition of *The Lion, the Witch, and the Wardrobe* with coloured illustrations and gold-edged pages. Even Larissa's office, the first time she saw it, had inspired her and restored her belief in her own passion. With its nine-foot ceilings and grand mouldings, the immovable mahogany furniture, the green banker's lamp on the desk, the crimson fabrics, the office seemed an emblem of intellectual prosperity, the consummate merging of tradition with Larissa's robust idealism. Indeed she did believe that new paradigms could be formed here. Ruth felt stirringly diminutive, both insignificant and powerful, as she sat in the shadow of the towering bookcases. How could she feel anything but reassured by the poised permanence of them, as if they were part of the stabilizing architecture of the school, the very syntax of its doctrine? How could she fail to marvel at her own luck in ending up there?

She loved this office as much as she feared it, for the same reasons she feared it: because its ability to terrify her was inextricable from its ability to exhilarate her. The things that filled her with dread and performance anxiety, the things that made her feel like a wayward child, were the same things that made her believe in the power of George Eliot. Sitting in this unyielding chair, she was never able to defy the room's grave, silent command that she be better.

"We can't let this go on," Ruth said.

The light fell in a diagonal block across Larissa's desk, across the offending note, blanching the glossy image of Carrie at the prom. "I've wracked my brain. I've prayed for insight. I simply can't see our way out of this, short of catching the perpetrator. And how do we accomplish that?"

"Eventually, it has to happen. She, or they, is bound to make a mistake."

"My primary concern thus far has been protecting the majority of students. Obviously, I've had to engage the senior classes, separately, in discreet discussions about this matter. But I've balked at the thought of making a more serious, potentially frightening, announcement. We've created within these walls a world of great privilege. Why make our girls feel unsafe? Moreover, why give the act the fame its architects were undoubtedly seeking? But now I'm wondering if I'm going to be forced to go more public. To get the whole school in on the hunt, as it were. The prospect is anathema to me." A burst of laughter from outdoors pierced the seal of the closed windows and Larissa lifted her chin slightly, as though heartened by it. "I've seen the best and worst of our girls in these past months. The delicacy and dignity with which they've handled moral danger have given me renewed faith in the inevitable triumph of the Eliot spirit. I suppose I must cling to that."

"There must be something we're not seeing," Ruth said. "I can't believe that we're harbouring a girl with some evil streak in her. Surely it's just teenage stupidity gone too far."

"Much too far." Larissa stood and again walked to her bookcases. She stood before them, her face upturned, supplicating. Ruth waited patiently. She knew that while Larissa's distress was sincere, her affection for a theatrical silence was incorrigible. "Who could want to harm us?" she said at last.

Ruth picked up the note and studied it again. She was wary of sounding dismissive but sincerely wanted to help Larissa navigate this difficulty, to help her decipher this complex new topography of adolescent venom—not new at all, of course, but new, somehow, to Larissa, who was an innocent, really, blinded by her impractical idealism. "I doubt the girl is thinking of it this way. It's bullying. It's terrible, but I truly believe it just comes back to that."

"This is more than that. This is far beyond the norm."

"Agreed. Not normal. Have you thought about asking Seeta not to play? At least to take a break, let things settle?"

"I did think about that," Larissa replied. "But she—we—cannot capitulate in that way. Not here, of all places. We have a duty, Ruth, not to permit the triumph of bullying. Of mediocrity. I have parents to explain myself to, parents who sent their children here on the best faith in our ability to make their lives better." She paused and pushed her heavy glasses up her nose, then strode to the window and planted herself there with a defiant sobriety, looking out, arms crossed. "Personally, I dislike Seeta's routine," she added. "I would rather start my day with an earnestly attempted, if imperfect, performance of Mozart or Debussy. Give me a mistake-studded 'Clair de lune' over 'Good Vibrations' any day. But to encourage creativity is the most important thing."

The sounds of lively life outside were intensifying. The rush hour of arrivals: the unbroken stream of cars on the salt-strewn icy driveway, doors slammed, greetings shouted. Ruth knew the school so well that she could flesh out the entire scene, theorize whole conversations, from the most muted bursts of sound.

"I don't know how to say this," Larissa said. "I'm not sure if I *can* say it."

Ruth frowned.

"I've heard the tittering over Mr. Prasad's turban."

"Yes, but that's just foolishness. It's harmless ignorance."

"Is ignorance ever harmless?" Larissa asked. "We prize nothing here more than the love of learning. How could such poison reside in our midst?"

Ruth considered this. Had they really prized nothing more than the love of learning? The tests, IQ and otherwise, on which Larissa affixed so much meaning—what did they prove? She thought of Audrey staring out the kitchen window as her homework lay piled beside her, and she couldn't help feeling that there was something they were getting wrong.

"Besides," Larissa continued, "whatever has caused it...does it even matter in the end? There will be gossip. And then all the work we've done here is for naught."

"Oh, Larissa. That's—"

"The whispers are out, Ruth. And now that the spectre has been raised, does it even matter whether the allegation has substance? The speculation is just as damaging. Can't you see that?" She turned heatedly from the window. "I've worked tirelessly, for all my career, at exploding all those damn hierarchies of old. At instituting a new value system. But it seems there's no fruition, just the constant labour."

Ruth was startled by Larissa's strident despair and knew it was her responsibility to pull Larissa back, but she couldn't see how. She was so weak, Larissa so strong. She had no ideas of her own. "There *is* fruition. We've guided girls through the most formative time in their lives. Many have gone on to great things after their educations here."

Larissa picked up the note, appraised it, and let it fall from her hand. "All these years, hadn't we thought we were getting some-where?"

There came now a knock on Larissa's door, and instantly Larissa snapped out of her troubled contemplation, performed an invis-ible, acrobatic leap from the reaches of self-recrimination. Though subtle, the change in her was unmistakable, her gaze refocused, her spine lengthened, her lips already forming her stiffly smiling greet-ing as she called out, "Come in." There were some hierarchies Laris-sa supported unequivocally, and the divide between principal and secretary was one of them.

As Erica Moss entered with a cup of coffee, Larissa turned to Ruth to indicate that the meeting was over, smiling like a tolerant host tactfully dismissing a guest who has overstayed her welcome. Ruth, having run out of things to say, was glad to go.

She was passing the massive window on the second floor land-ing when she noticed a silver Honda turning into the round drive-way. Right away, she recognized the head in the passenger seat, and before she could be stabilized by rationality, she rushed down the stairs and out the front door. Arabella was just emerging from the back seat.

"Hey, Ms. Brindle," she said with a little wave.

Henry, in the passenger seat, leaned across the car to give Clayton a kiss. As he opened the door, he was laughing. A chill descended over his face when he spotted Ruth.

Clayton emerged from the driver's side and leaned with her arms crossed against the roof of the car. "Hey there," she said, without a trace of the animosity for which Ruth had rather hoped.

"Morning!" replied Ruth cheerfully, as though their recent meeting had been the start of an incomparable affinity.

"Enjoying the cold?"

"Just getting a breath of air."

"Big day ahead?"

"Isn't it always..."

They smiled at each other blandly, bolstered by their platitudes.

"Car trouble?" Ruth asked, turning to Henry.

"Trouble is the understatement of all time," said Clayton. "It's like watching those people who just refuse to put their ailing pet to sleep."

"Is that what it's like?" Ruth said.

"I keep telling him he needs a new car," Clayton went on. "You tell him. Maybe he'll listen to someone impartial."

Ruth glanced at Henry. "I doubt very much he'll listen to me."

"I'll get to it," he said.

"Henry's leaving tomorrow for a long weekend in Montreal," Clayton said. "He's planning to take the train anyway. His thesis adviser, who now lives in Russia, has flown in for a conference at McGill. They haven't seen each other in a decade."

Ruth had never heard a word about a beloved thesis adviser. "Oh?"

"Train aside, why fix your own car when you can be chauffeured every day by your loving wife?" She winked at him.

Ruth smiled tightly.

"I best be getting in, my love," Henry said, reaching his hand across the roof of the car to clasp her fingers.

"Yes, yes. Go. Drink coffee." She blew him a kiss and then waved to Ruth grandly, as though she were standing on the deck of an ocean liner pulling out of port.

As Henry watched the car retreat, Ruth slipped into the vestibule. She was waiting in the shadows when Henry swung open the door, admitting a narrow shaft of light.

"So I just had the craziest meeting with Larissa," she said. "It's like she's on the brink of a breakdown or something! I think for the first time in all the years I've known her, I actually felt sorry for her." She felt cheap for offering this information so flippantly, with such gossipy gusto, but was eager to get back in his good graces.

"That's unfortunate."

"Things are bad with Seeta. Worse than I ever imagined. Larissa is at her wit's end."

"Am I supposed to pity her?"

"What are you saying?"

"Larissa is the principal. Is it her job to handle the situation or to worry about her reputation?"

"That's not fair. These things are complicated. Larissa is handling things. Isn't she?"

Henry sighed. "Ruth, I don't really give a fuck. I won't even be here next year."

Ruth's breath seemed to fall out the bottom of her stomach. "Where are you going?"

"York. Part-time position. I'm going to work on my book, at last."

"Your book?"

"Look," he said, glancing at his watch, beginning to move away. "I don't really want to discuss this right now. I've got photocopying. I need coffee. Later."

"Why are you acting—" she halted. Because Henry was turned away from her, she was leaning forward, pursuant, reaching out her hand as if to grab him, and her words formed an unfortunate hiss.

"What's that you said?" He cocked his head, unbothered.

Did he fail to notice the hiss or was ignorance his defence against it? Did he notice anything at all but the sound of his retreating footsteps?

THE FAMILIAR SNICKER FLICKERED somewhere behind Audrey. Seeta was warming her fingers by strumming some random chords. She hadn't performed in two weeks, and speculation about the cause of her abstinence was rampant in the class. As the music began to resolve into a specific song, Audrey knew immediately what it was: Neil Young's "Old Man," Richard's favourite song. Seeta's voice cracked a bit with the first words, but her playing was flawless, and her voice grew steadier with each line. The song seemed made for her voice, its pure, slightly melancholic lilt. Audrey stared hard into her lap, welling up. No song could have exposed her more freshly to that laugh's jagged edges, its sly hush. It made you listen for it: that was its power. It was too refined, too clever, to thrust itself upon you. No, you'd hear something that made the skin on your back prickle. Then, nothing. You'd wonder if your paranoid imagination had concocted it. Then the sound would come again. And this time you were sure. Its potency lay not in its output of noise, but in what it held back, how it used silence to influence and command.

When Seeta reached the chorus, a whelp darted from the shadowy side of the chapel. In answer, from the other side, came another. Mid-chord, Seeta looked up with a perplexed smile. She sang on for a second, then coughed. She frowned at her guitar as though she had lost her place, then coughed again.

"I'm so sorry," she said. "My voice is giving out on me. I've had a cold for the past few days."

She started to strum again, but her fingers fumbled, and she lost hold of the instrument. It clattered to the ground, its strings vibrating. Seeta got up and swiftly exited the stage. For a minute, she conferred with Ms. Massie-Turnbull at the side of the stage, Ms. Massie-Turnbull nodding vehemently. Seeta was shaking her head. "Oh my God, this is hilarious," whispered Dougie. "Do you think she's going to have a nervous breakdown?" She began a round of spirited rhythmic clapping, and after a second, others joined in. Seeta looked up, on her face a mixture of brightness and confusion, clearly uncertain of how to interpret the claps. Ms. Massie-Turnbull seemed more positive that the audience was asking for more and, beaming, she gestured for Seeta to take in her fans. She gave Seeta a nudge towards the stage and pushed up the corners of her mouth with her fingers, her favourite reminder to smile. Seeta trudged compliantly back to centre stage, began the song again, and dutifully followed it through, but all the energy had leaked out of her.

After the performance, Seeta disappeared out the side of the chapel. Audrey looked for her during the prefects' announcements and during the singing of "All Things Bright and Beautiful," which she had often declared to be her favourite hymn. Usually, Seeta's voice could be heard soaring above the listless harmonies of the senior students. She had been known to supply spontaneous descants. Audrey felt faintly worried, though she couldn't have said exactly why. Or for whom—Seeta or herself? Depositing the notes in Seeta's locker had become a ritual. As such, the act required little forethought, and even less post-mortem analysis. But all morning she had been feeling a little sick. Seeta's hair was greasy, and under her eyes were slate-coloured circles. The Neil Young had only heightened Audrey's discomfort. She couldn't deny its beauty.

"Looking for your lover?" Dougie said, as Audrey glanced again towards the back of the chapel.

First period was gym, and Audrey hurried to the locker room to steady her mind. She was sitting on the bench, preparing to change, when Arabella entered alone. It was rare for Audrey to encounter Arabella without her entourage, and solitude only highlighted the artistry of her face. Quiet as she was, the effect was not of serenity, of slow-moving harmlessness, but of finely tuned alertness, a leopard's imminent pounce. As she sank to the bench, her hair tumbled from its bun, obscuring her expression as she pulled her knapsack onto her lap and unzipped it. Removing a piece of paper from inside, she handed it to Audrey, setting her knapsack on her legs as a shield. "*Voilà*," she said. "We wrote it before chapel. Perfect timing, as it turns out."

It was, of course, another note to Seeta. She hadn't used the cut-out magazine letters, as she usually did, but had written her message in block capitals with a thick black marker. Without the colour and campiness of the cut-outs, the effect was far starker. There was just one half sentence: "The day the music died…" Audrey frowned at the paper, her heart sinking. The message managed to be obscure, almost nonsensical, and threatening at the same time—not less threatening, but more, for being so obscure.

"We were thinking that you should do it after school today," she said.

Audrey paused. "I don't know."

"You don't know what?"

"I just…It's so…"

"It's nothing. It doesn't even say anything specific."

"I know, but…"

"Oh, don't tell me," Arabella said with a maudlin sigh. "You and Seeta became friends. Are you going to do a duet with her? Oh my God, that's so sweet. I knew you guys would bond, after all that time sitting together."

"Don't be ridiculous." Audrey slipped the note into the back of her binder, laughing to disguise the pang she felt at the thought of Seeta coming upon the note. The feeling was more bewildering than pity. She envied Seeta, in a way, for caring so much about her music, for refusing to be deterred. What must it be like, to care about something so much?

The previous night, sitting in her room while Ruth and Richard sat in the living room reading by the fire, she had taken out Ruth's old yearbooks and sat on her bed flipping through them the way she had done as a young girl. Briefly, she forgot what Eliot was really like as she studied the pictures of all the girls posing with their arms over each other's shoulders, forming people pyramids, poring over textbooks in library study groups, dressing backstage in makeshift costumes for the school play, sunbathing on the front lawn, toppling over during potato sack races, playing soccer and basketball and tennis, cheering and cheering. In the section devoted to her class, pictures of Arabella, Dougie, and Whitney dominated. They posed, at least some of the time, with what she guessed must be sincere affection, their arms slung around each other's shoulders.

More often, they modelled self-consciously. In one, Arabella stood next to Ms. Glover, frowning satirically, wearing Ms. Glover's glasses on the tip of her nose.

This happy Eliot, the Eliot of the yearbooks, was the place where she had seen herself—not her, of course, but an improved incarnation of her—striding into her spot in Eliot's venerated history. Even in her most desolate moments, she had managed to cling to this vision, this unyielding conviction in the possibility of metamorphosis: the change would come, with mad, magical volatility, and her only responsibility was to be ready. It didn't matter that she now understood that the yearbook was a false document, a choreographed representation of life as it should be. How hard it was not to mourn that vanished Eliot.

The locker room door swung open and the class began to file in. Arabella swiftly departed for the other side of the room, and a minute later Seeta came in and tossed her bag onto the bench beside Audrey and began changing, her movements slow and heavy. She pulled a school T-shirt over her head and unbuttoned her blouse beneath it, then pulled on her shorts before removing her kilt. Across the room, the girls formed distinct factions according to their modesty. Some people dressed with desperate discretion, determined not to reveal any unnecessary skin, while others, like Arabella, stood around in pretty bras intended for display.

A girl named Megan Dunn stood half-dressed by the sink, studying her forehead in dismay. "I'm so getting the mother of all breakouts."

"Must be all the chemicals," Arabella said, smirking at Whitney.

"Arabella," Megan said, turning around with a sigh. "What fucking chemicals? Would you get over it?"

"I used to have a doctor, if you can believe this," said Dougie, "who pronounced the 'ch' in *chemical* like the 'ch' in *chuck*. He was like, 'Stay away from nail polishes that have ch-emicals like formaldehyde.'"

"Whatever," Megan said, shaking her head.

About a week before, she had come to school with her hair curly for the first time. Changes like this rarely passed unremarked at Eliot and were generally met with contemptuous skepticism. It was as though the girls were all perpetually on their guards against being made fools of—being a sucker for the scam, falling for the false image—and Audrey had come to understand it as just another feature of their constant fault-finding. When Megan had entered the classroom with curly hair, the entire class stopped talking and stared at her, and the scrutiny had only intensified when she denied, in response to innumerable, nagging queries, that she'd gotten a perm. She insisted that her hair was naturally curly, that she had previously blow-dried it straight.

"It's just so obvious you had your hair permed," Whitney said, "and for, like, some reason you feel you need to lie about it. Incidentally, perms are so eighties."

"And really damaging to your hair," added Dougie.

The door opened a crack and Ms. Crispe called in a warning of tardiness demerits. "It's an outdoor run this morning," she reminded. "Wear your sweatshirts."

"Perfect," said Arabella, "It's raining out, so now we'll know the truth. If Megan's hair is naturally curly, it'll dry curly. And if it's a perm, her hair will dry straight."

Julie Michaels pulled her T-shirt over her head and smoothed her hair into a ponytail. "That's ridiculous," she said. "Her hair will dry curly whether it's natural or permed. You think some magic happens when you blow dry? Anyway, who cares?"

"I don't care," Arabella said defensively. "Why would I care about her pube-like hair? It's just the way she lies about it." She turned to Dougie imperiously. "Dougie, your breath smells like dog crap."

Audrey sat on the bench, drained, suddenly unsure of whether she'd be able to run a block, let alone a mile. The week ahead seemed an insurmountable obstacle. Even in its inanity—perhaps because of its inanity—the conversation had a baffling, almost hallucinogenic, force about it, and Audrey sensed that she would never forget it. And indeed, much later, weeks, even months, it did remain for her the linchpin, as though once it passed, everything else was inevitable, the embryonic choices of the coming days already irretrievable.

Chapter Fourteen

THE BISTRO WAS THE kind of place Ruth had prodded Richard to try for years: black-and-white chequered floors, crimson walls, dimly lit, cramped, and slightly shabby in a deliberate way that constituted a mission statement of sorts: in the devotion to food, a repudiation of slickness. Richard had long favoured more conservative places, but the choice was out of his hands. Perhaps Ruth wasn't being quite fair: it was his birthday, after all. She had heard Henry speak of this restaurant at work, and she had made the reservation before Richard could protest. When she told him where they were going, he looked disappointed. If she wanted French food, he said, how about that place just north of the lake, a mere five-minute drive from home? Ruth returned the observation that surely the last thing he wanted as he got older was to get set in his ways.

Over the preceding weeks, the household had descended into a morbid mood. Richard was working longer hours at the clinic, often eating dinner there. When he was home, Ruth tried to be busy marking student assignments or working on *The Pomegranate*. She was surprised by how easy it was to get around talking about anything of significance, to pretend that the pit bull argument had never happened. Richard had once been unable to let any acrimony between them pass without redress, but now he appeared as happy as she to dwell within discomfort, to accept it as a condition without easy alteration. He kissed her limply before work each morning, and limply upon his return, then retired to bed, where he slept heavily beside her.

Audrey, for her part, found freedom in the tension. Little was being asked of her. Since the dance, Ruth had been sullen in a way that released Audrey from conversation. Often, Ruth prepared dinner for Audrey, then proclaimed herself not hungry, or too busy to eat. Audrey sat at the kitchen island, picking at reheated chicken fingers or grilled cheese sandwiches and canned soup while Ruth took Marlow for long, slow walks around the block. When their paths crossed in hallways, at home and at Eliot, they glanced away, like acquaintances trying not to notice each other in the grocery store. Audrey wanted her anger at her mother to remain alight, but every sighting of Ruth in her old fisherman's sweater and pyjama bottoms, folders spread across her lap, dampened it. Ruth looked undeniably sad, sipping herbal tea from her lumpy old pottery mug. Better for Audrey to keep to her room, to stare down the homework that could occupy her for hours, that dependably kept aflame her sense of injustice.

She had hoped to be left out of the birthday meal, but Ruth had rounded her up, not even bothering with a phony display of cheerfulness. In the term "family dinner" was an undisguised edict. She was even expected to dress well.

At the restaurant, they sat by a drafty window looking onto the street. Slouching, Ruth kept her wool coat wrapped around her like a blanket too thin to keep her warm. She was wearing heels and a pencil skirt, but her hair, in a lopsided ponytail, betrayed her true attitude. Her blunt nails, usually naked, were painted red. Such a small thing, yet it made her look less like herself. Audrey stared at her mother's hands, willing Ruth to sense how pointedly she was being observed. She liked the idea that there had been a power shift between them. Even in the marginalized light, Audrey could see in Ruth's downcast face that she felt it. The opacity of the conflict only added to its power. Ruth despised any lack of clarity. She glanced at Audrey as though seeking an invitation to smile. Under her blue cardigan, she wore the white T-shirt she had been wearing on the night of the Eliot dance. Audrey cast her eyes slowly over Ruth's torso, daring her to wonder why.

Richard seemed determined to notice nothing amiss. Amid declarations of excessive hunger, he read the entrées aloud, pausing in delight at the description of the mixed grill.

"You're not going to eat horse," Audrey said, aghast.

"I just might," he replied, laughing.

Ruth was smiling down at the menu like it was a baby she wasn't much interested in.

"Will you be joining me, Ruth?'

"You've got to be kidding."

"It's quite well regarded, the *cheval* here."

"That doesn't mean that *we* eat it."

"It's inhumane," Audrey said. "It's disgusting."

"You eat pig," he replied.

"Richard, come on," Ruth said. "Now's not the time."

"Yes, by all means, let's banish culinary curiosity," he said, not yet willing to abandon lightheartedness.

"It's horse, Dad. Horse!"

"Then let's call it *cheval*."

"I'm not even sure I can eat anything," Ruth said. "I feel kind of queasy, I think from this deli meat I ate yesterday at work."

"Oh, for Christ's sake." Richard said, tossing the menu onto the table in annoyance.

The appearance of the waiter brought temporary relief. Audrey took an immediate dislike to him: his affected French accent as he recounted the specials, his beady eyes, calculating their deficit of hipness. With his every glance in her direction, her irritation with Ruth mounted. Why had her mother chosen such a restaurant? As if dining out with parents wasn't bad enough. A waitress circled the room demurely, mindful not to disturb the murmuring couples, touching a match to the tea lights at the centre of each table.

"So, Audrey," Richard began, once they were alone again. "How's school these days?"

Audrey responded the way she always did to this question, with a beleaguered sigh and a half roll of her eyes. "God," she moaned. "Is that why we're here? To bug me about school?"

Richard looked startled. "It's a fairly normal question."

"If I'd known how you people were going to harass me every day of my life if I got into Eliot, I'd never—"

"Whoa." Richard said. "I haven't—"

"Let's just get along," Ruth said pleadingly.

Audrey took a long drink of her water.

"Audrey has totally improved in math," Ruth said. "Isn't that great? Chuck was just telling me that he thinks you're turning the corner."

"Turning the corner," Audrey replied. "How impressive."

"We always knew that Eliot would be tough academically. Your father and I aren't at all displeased with your results," Ruth said. "Right, Richard?"

"It's goddamn ridiculous they're doing grade twelve level math," Richard said.

"It'll be great for her!" Ruth said brightly. "In the end, anyway."

"In what way is it great for her to spend four hours every night doing homework?"

Audrey looked to her father in question. She knew that her parents had differed at times in the degree of their belief in Eliot, but she had never heard her father speak so strongly in opposition to it. Richard had always let Ruth set the agenda, so intense had she been about school matters, and Audrey had interpreted his reserve as indifference, his understanding of the nature of Eliot minimal. Now, as her father studiously redirected his attention to his wine, as if to back away from his overt contradiction of Ruth, a bolt of gratitude went through Audrey. He was on her side, after all.

The waiter appeared with their meals and deposited them on the table, then offered pepper to taste.

"You see, this is always interesting to me," Richard said. "Let me ask you a question. Does the chef recommend extra pepper? Hasn't he seasoned the food as he sees fit?"

The waiter returned a standoffish nod.

"And so wouldn't I be undermining his skill, or suggesting my lack of confidence in his expertise, by choosing to impose more pepper than he found advisable?"

"All right, Richard," Ruth said, blushing. "If you don't want pepper, don't have it."

Richard held up his hands in surrender. "I've just always been curious."

"We don't want any extra pepper, thank you," Ruth said to the waiter.

Unbothered by the exchange, Richard dug into his mixed grill and descended into a minor food ecstasy. "Oh boy, it's a shame you won't try this."

Audrey had never given much thought to her father, such was the stability he provided. Richard was a traditional sort of man, not so much in his values as in the nature of his presence. He left Audrey to her meanderings, to her joys, her tempers; her sense had always been that he didn't know her well. And she had felt no distressing lack therein. Intimacy was Ruth's territory—that nauseating term *daddy's girl* was a joke between them, Ruth seeming bleakly terrified of the family dynamic to which it alluded. Richard's remove had been liberating. He was her father. What more did she need to know of him?

But his pleasure in the meat moved her inexplicably: it was a glimpse into his vulnerability, his humanity, and she felt some defence in her buckle. She had never particularly believed in the myth of her parents' perfection. Their happiness had been irrelevant, of such exclusive concern to her was her own happiness. On a recent morning at school, Dougie had sat in the back of the classroom proclaiming how traumatized she was by hearing her mother behind the closed door of the master bedroom declaring that she had sperm on her leg. Audrey had been grateful that her own life supplied no such anecdotes. Her parents' love had been tactfully concealed; she'd had no cause to consider it.

Since seeing her mother and Henry Winter in the library, though, she had not been able to stop imagining scenarios of her father finding out about the affair. In the most basic, he picked up the phone and unwittingly found himself in the midst of a heated conversation between Henry and Ruth. In another, he came home, feeling sick, on his lunch hour and was greeted by the sight of them half-dressed in the kitchen, kissing up against the fridge, magnets scattered on the floor around them. In the most convoluted, and the most unlikely, she herself was injured at school, and because

Ruth couldn't be located, Richard was summoned, and ran smack into Ruth and Henry in the back stairwell, fully clothed but in a less than platonic embrace. Fantasizing about Ruth's exposure gave her a perverse thrill, not because she wanted her father to know, but because there was something electrifying in the contemplation of something so terrible. This was a secret with the power to reconfigure everything, to dismantle, detonate, her life, to render the family identity instantly useless.

She thought of a decade earlier, when her father had gone into the hospital for an emergency appendectomy. On a visit after the surgery, she'd keenly felt the dire possibilities throbbing in the air around them. The chance that catastrophe could strike made her feel important, improbably excited. The nurses had given her lollipops and made her their pet; in the elevator, a doctor had lifted her up to push the buttons. She had been sitting in her mother's lap in the corner of the pale pink room when her father was brought down from recovery. He'd opened his eyes to smile drowsily at them before drifting back to sleep. This was a different kind of sleep than she had witnessed before, trying to peel her father's eyes open at dawn on a Saturday. Her father wore a hospital gown; an IV bag dripped clear fluid into a tube that snaked into his bare arm. She had started to cry. "Your father is fine!" Ruth had exclaimed, wiping the tears away. "He'll take care of us forever, I promise!" His misfortune suddenly seemed to be her fault. Too much had she been seduced by the dramatic flair of it all, by the attention of so many men and women in scrubs. Alone in bed at night, she had too often daydreamed of being an orphan, made magnificent by tragedy, like so many of her favourite storybook characters. What if her imagination were powerful enough to bring that fantasy into reality?

Now here she was, ten years on, still just beginning to grasp her own impotence. She looked from Richard, contentedly deconstructing his meal, to Ruth, picking at her fish, and was overcome by a wayward impulse.

"Speaking of Eliot," she said, "the dance was pretty interesting."

"Oh?" Richard said, his eyebrows raised.

Ruth's face sparkled in either excitement or alarm.

"Did you meet a boy?" he asked.

Audrey blushed. "Actually, I left for a while. I went upstairs. It was so hot in the gym." She took a sip of her water. "I went into the library. I found a book."

"I'm sure Larissa McAllister would be proud of you for resisting the temptation of male flesh," Richard said. "What was the book?"

Audrey looked squarely at her mother. "*Who Do You Think You Are?*"

Ruth's hand, laying down her fork, betrayed a tremble.

"Ah," said Richard. "How fitting. Did you know that *The Lives of Girls and Women* was the first book your mother ever gave me?"

Audrey shook her head, still levelling her gaze at Ruth.

"I never read it, though, I'm ashamed to say. But think about it. *Lives of Girls and Women*? I was closed-minded. It was a first edition, too. Your mother said she searched the city for it."

Ruth watched Audrey as she spoke. "I did. It's a shame you never bothered to read it."

Richard dipped his head. "I'm sorry."

Audrey dropped her fork with a clang onto her plate. "Well, I guess we all do things we're sorry for."

A fresh blast of icy air heralded a new set of diners, a man and woman, red-cheeked from the wind, clearly regulars. Chattering with the wait staff about a recent trip to Belgium, they stopped to kiss on the way to the table. Audrey turned from her parents, entranced by the woman's waifish elegance. (It is the nature of fascination, isn't it, to most admire those who are nothing like you?) But it was soon clear how much the woman was misrepresented by her entrance. At a distance, her curtain of glossy blonde hair hid all the ways in which she had striven to make herself hard: her thin lips were coated with matte black lipstick, her eyes messily lined with kohl; on the side of her neck was a black tattoo of a dragon with a long, forked tongue, on her ring finger a disturbingly lifelike black widow spider. She was already a little drunk, teetering flirtatiously, laughing too loudly, her head thrown back.

Like Audrey, Ruth watched the couple, dreaming of escape. The woman's hopefulness was riveting, the aura of freedom around her. Ruth felt almost distraught with envy.

She had known a family meal was a terrible idea. But how to get around it on Richard's birthday? She hadn't been sure she could eat a thing. Fish had seemed the most innocuous thing to order, but when the Lake Huron yellow perch arrived, and was sitting before her in its watery juices, she had struggled to push away all thoughts of the texture of fish, the smell by the fish counter in Loblaws.

She had tried to go along with the conversation, but she worried that she hadn't played her part well enough. She had been jumpy, testy: it simply wasn't in her to cast a benevolent maternal ray over the proceedings. Was Audrey driving at something? Or did knowledge of her own sin cause her to interpret every statement as innuendo?

Yes, she and Henry had met briefly in the library on the night of the dance, for no more than ten minutes. What were the chances that her daughter had happened into the room during that narrow period? Her early abdication of guilt had begotten a belief in her immunity. Naturally, she had understood that she and Henry could get caught; that was the inebriating truth, the undercurrent of every encounter. But as with all givens, it had remained an abstraction.

Occasionally, she had wondered what would happen if Audrey did find out. It wasn't impossible. Most of Henry's and her encounters had been inside Eliot's walls. Flashes of running smack into Audrey had come to her while they hunted for secluded spots. The idea had been weirdly exhilarating. Would Audrey lie for her? Even abet future meetings by providing alibis? Might her loyalty to her mother transcend the dull haze of morality? Or would such discovery be the thing to catapult Ruth out of her life? The thought of leaving Richard, of exploding their marriage, had only ever been fanciful, an illogical midnight reverie, floating free of any context of divorce proceedings, custody arrangements, house selling. She simply saw herself in a darkened kitchen somewhere, her head against Henry's lank chest. She had gone no further. Part of the affair's pleasure had been its eternal present. Yet something would happen, inevitably. There was only so long that such a tremulous balance could be held.

Having scraped all the sauce off her chicken and eaten perhaps two bites, Audrey was now regarding Ruth's hands again. Ruth glanced down at her scarlet nails and blushed. She had painted them in a flight of fancy she had quickly regretted. This overreaching —grasping for an image ill-suited to her—was a failure that exposed her worst self. She removed her hands to her lap and smiled uncomfortably.

Audrey stood.

"Where are you going?" asked Ruth tensely.

"Um, to the bathroom?" Audrey replied.

When she was out of sight, Richard put his hand on Ruth's arm.

"I really am sorry I never read that book," he said.

"It's nothing."

"It mattered to you."

Ruth waved her hand. "I got it wrong. It happens."

She glanced at the neighbouring table, where the drunken couple was conversing in forceful low voices. The woman's tongue stud flashed as she licked her lips.

"Do you think I'm boring?" Ruth said.

"Hardly."

"I've been with you for so long, I think I've lost the knack of being interesting." She turned away, half-disgusted with him, either for failing to recognize how boring she was, or for making her so in the first place. "It's too late for me."

"Life doesn't give us many chances to go diving naked into lakes. That doesn't mean you're boring."

Ruth laughed in spite of herself. Their first trip away together had been to Richard's family cottage, a rustic cabin on an island with only two other properties, at the end of miles of dirt road and a short boat ride. Though it was early June, the temperature evoked autumn, and they had spent the week wrapped in sweaters and blankets, reading in the red Adirondack chairs on the screened-in porch, trying to stretch their provisions so they wouldn't have to make the inconvenient trek to the grocery store. They tried to take hikes but were swarmed by deer flies. On the final morning, Ruth ripped off her clothes, ran down the steep stone path to the water's edge, and threw herself off the dock headfirst before Richard had even removed his shoes. She was treading water thirty strokes from shore as he cannonballed into the lake, yowling as he surfaced. She swam in to give him a quick kiss, her lips already turning an opalescent purple, then flipped on her back and glided over the rippling water away from him again.

Richard hated swimming in frigid temperatures, and he climbed back up onto the dock and ran to the cottage to get towels and a camera. By the time he returned, she was a white flare in the middle of the dark lake, an uncertain reflection, disappearing and appearing amidst the insignificant waves. On the car ride home, wearing Richard's cable-knit fisherman's sweater, she had drunk coffee until her stomach burned. They had pulled off the highway and lain in the back seat together. He rubbed her arms vigorously as if to get the blood back into them. He told her that she was a mad-woman. He said that she was the love of his life, that there could be no other, and she knew that this was a noble overstatement, a romantic boast, but she burrowed her face in his warm neck and let him believe it.

The difficulty she kept coming up against now was something more confusing than the betrayal of the marriage: Richard was her oldest friend. She had never kept any of her girlfriends. Her mother was gone. Who else had known her for nearly twenty years, through the discrete portions of her life—from her directionless twenties to the approach of middle age, through the wrangling of that capri-cious girl into a wife and mother—and not just in her lowest mo-ments but in the most banal, the most trifling, in the inconsequen-tial minutes where the heart of their life lay? To whom else could she have said, in the dismal early days of parenthood, that she had to put down their screaming daughter and walk away or risk harm-ing her gravely?

Sometimes Ruth wondered if that was exactly the problem, if she and Richard were burdened by excessive intimacy. Maybe she knew him too well, or simply thought she knew him too well. Was she blind to his possibilities, his capacity to change, to be things she didn't predict? And had being with him for such a long time made her equally fixed, frozen in his image of her, incapable of adaptation, of challenging her notions of what she could be, of what they could be? Often, when she came across him on the street, in the millisecond that he was just a man in the distance, she saw him with a stranger's clemency and found herself admiring his handsomeness, his elegant height and sure gait. He looked like a man from another time. In these moments, she wanted to run to him.

She knew how lucky she was to have Richard. She did. But gratitude was like her youth: it seemed always to be slipping away from her.

"How much longer do we have to stay?" Audrey was back, standing over them, a hand on the back of her chair.

"Give in, kid," Richard reached out and grabbed her playfully. "Let's go wild and get something sweet."

Ruth and Audrey looked at each other. They both wanted to leave, but it was Richard's birthday. The least they could do was say yes to dessert.

LATE THAT NIGHT, LONG after Richard had gone to sleep, Ruth put the house to bed. She let the dogs out and stood at the back window looking out at the wintry yard, the startlingly lucid green of the pine tree in moonlight. When she went to turn out the lamp by the family room couch, she noticed a hardcover, missing its book jacket, on the coffee table. *The Lives of Girls and Women.* Opening the book to glance at the first sentence, she discovered an inscription on the title page.

To Richard, on your birthday, February 1988
In memory of all childhoods,
some forgotten (but to be found one day)
and some deeply remembered.
Ruth

She had no memory of having written the words, but beyond this minor failure of memory was something more disorienting: she could not remember ever having been a woman who would have written something so lovely. She knew the writing to be hers, but it was like looking at the dedication of a dead person, elusive yet enduring, hauntingly bridging the distance between the present and a time scarcely remembered.

A shuffling sound behind her brought her back to herself. Audrey was standing at the threshold of the room in her pyjamas. The only lit lamp now was the small one by the back window, and Ruth was grateful for the diminished light. She and Audrey had become to each other little more than a presence, the known figure of an intimate, seen from the distance only in outline. For a second, she felt as though she had a grip on an important thought, but then it dissolved, leaving her head as dim as the room around her.

"Your thing broke," Audrey said. She held up Ruth's antique compote, its scalloped bowl broken at the joining place.

"You broke my compote?" Ruth was incredulous, angry.

"No, I didn't break it. I guess the dogs bumped the table."

Ruth's voice dropped. "Is there something you want to say to me, Audrey?"

Audrey looked down at her feet, which she was rubbing together in her thick wool socks. "No."

Ruth reached for the compote, and Audrey handed over the broken pieces. Even at close range, Audrey's face was provokingly unreadable. "What a shame," Ruth said.

"You never really liked it anyway."

"That's not true!"

"Then I guess you changed your mind." Audrey turned away. "I'm going to bed."

Ruth turned out the last lamp but stayed in the family room after Audrey left. She felt paralyzed, like a child afraid of the midnight change in a landscape made so benign by daylight. She still held the compote in her hand, and it was several minutes before she was pulled back to herself by the sensation of a hand on her back. She braced herself, calmly certain that she was about to see the ghost of her mother, but when she turned around, there was only the empty darkness.

Chapter Fifteen

THE WEATHER WAS UNSEASONABLY warm for February, and the cluster of boys who awaited the Eliot girls after school stood around in the circular driveway with their coats open, their ties loose around their necks. Audrey, pausing by the landing window, watched the rapturous reunions. Kate Gibson's boyfriend stood in the centre of the group, wearing only his school blazer to keep him warm. Instead of talking to the boys around him, he stared at the ground, a posture that gave the impression not of brooding, as he may have intended, but of a thin neck that couldn't support the weight of his disproportionately large head, his mop of thick, wavy hair. When Kate spotted him, she rushed over and embraced him, her melodramatic enthusiasm unabated by the daily predictability of his presence—it was the custom of the most sought-after girls to pretend to be surprised every time they discovered their congregated admirers—and as they walked away, he clasped her hand in both of his, walked a bit in front of her, smiling backwards, as if leading her to a mystery location.

Audrey circulated the school at an amble until the crowds dispersed. The afternoon was quiet, with no scheduled sports practices, no choir rehearsal. For two days, the note Arabella had given her in the locker room had been buried in her math binder, and she wanted to get the mission done with, the note out of her bag, out of her mind.

She was making her way, head down, through a first floor corridor when she heard the sound of guitar music drifting out of the third grade room. Inside, Seeta and Ms. Massie-Turnbull sat on desktops facing each other, tuning their guitars. Ms. Massie-Turnbull, sensing someone's presence, looked up, smiling when she saw Audrey in the doorway.

"Hey, kiddo," she said. "Come on in and give us an audience. I'm trying to convince Seeta to have a run at this with me in chapel tomorrow."

Unable to come up with a reason to escape, Audrey went in and took a seat near the door. Ms. Massie-Turnbull locked eyes with Seeta, who then glanced uncomfortably at Audrey before looking determinedly down at her guitar. As in assembly that morning, Audrey knew the song right away—more Neil Young, this time "Long May You Run." Audrey was amazed by the power of Seeta's thin fingers as she started to strum. They looked so fragile, yet they glided through the chords with utter assurance. Audrey remembered herself, back in the days when she had played the piano, always stumbling and cursing, her fingers too little practised ever to make their way effortlessly. In the classroom, away from the acoustics of the chapel and the disapproval of the audience, the singing was even more affecting. Seeta lost herself completely, as though she were not quite singing but allowing herself to be a conduit. The warm, confidential sound of it overpowered Audrey, engulfed her in its sonic shelter, and for a moment she forgot herself in a way she never had inside Eliot's walls.

It wasn't just that she no longer hated Seeta's playing; she no longer wanted to hate it.

When they finished, it took a second for her to return to herself. Then she stood to leave. "That was really nice. Thank you."

Ms. Massie-Turnbull pointed to Seeta. "It's all her. This is one talented kid."

Seeta smiled at Ms. Massie-Turnbull but kept her gaze studiously averted from Audrey. For the first time, Audrey wondered if Seeta suspected Audrey's part in the notes. She had always assumed that the widespread understanding held that such an enterprise could only have been spearheaded by Arabella. But Seeta's steely disregard seemed to stem from something that went deeper than their petty friction. In it was a stoicism and loathing, a maturity, that made Audrey's stomach somersault.

"Yes, she is talented," Audrey said. "I wish I were that talented."

On her way up to the second floor, she had to sit on the stairs. There was no reason to call off the plan, she thought, no barrier compelling enough to make her oppose Arabella. You couldn't change a place like Eliot. There was no point in trying.

Upstairs, the hallway was empty, and Audrey knew she could be done with the whole mess, perhaps permanently, in seconds. On the outside of her locker, Seeta had placed a single sticker, a musical note. The sight of it made Audrey unspeakably sad. How innocent it seemed, this emblem of Seeta's passion, marking her small territory at school.

Maybe it was the music, or maybe it was just this—her own fatigue, the dissipation of the intoxicating panic of the early days— more than anything resembling guilt, that made her pause by Seeta's locker. Maybe it was this total physical quiet—her hands weren't shaking and her heart wasn't racing—that made her pay attention to what she was doing in a way she never quite had before. The act had acquired a kind of banality: there was no rebellion here. She had never been more obedient. It was not her own audaciousness she was discovering, but Arabella's master plan, her inscrutable rules. And for what? The pleasure one took in Arabella bore no relation to actual pleasure. Audrey couldn't have explained, even to herself, the compulsion involved. Was this what all her anticipation had come down to? Was this the riotous display of freedom? Her reason for coming to Eliot?

She leaned exhaustedly on the locker next to Seeta's, the note dangling in her hand. She didn't know what she would say to Arabella, and for the moment, she didn't care. She crouched down and pulled a pad of pink Post-it notes from inside her knapsack. "I can't do it," she wrote, then pressed the note onto the words Arabella had written and, before letting a second thought undermine her decision, slid the construction paper into Arabella's locker. All at once she became aware of a sound moving towards her, a shuffling step, feet dragging a bit on the carpet in late day fatigue. She turned her back to the lockers just as Henry Winter rounded the corner. He smiled faintly, without warmth, and glanced down at her knapsack, which was gaping open.

"Hi there, sir," she said.

He nodded. "Audrey."

Since she had found out about Henry, English class had presented her with a conflict unlike the one she'd expected. She could make no connection between the Henry known to Ruth and the Henry who stood before her as English teacher, jadedly lecturing about F. Scott Fitzgerald. She studied him for signs, half-expecting him to grant her some special attention that would constitute a loving, coded message to her mother. But she detected nothing. His attitude towards her was as indecipherable as ever.

She reached down and casually zipped up her knapsack.

"Friday afternoon and still here," Henry said.

"Lots of homework. Just packing everything in."

If anything, he seemed more restless than usual, his hands thrust into his pockets, looking not at Audrey but at the locker next to her head. She pictured him on an incomparably verdant expanse of lawn, mindlessly remarking on the monotony of the ocean, martini in hand.

"*Gatsby* quiz tomorrow," he said. "You'll want to make sure you're prepared."

"It's a hard one?"

He smiled thinly. "Well, it's best always to be prepared, isn't it? This is your education, after all."

She returned an uneasy smile as he continued on his way, at a frustrating amble, glancing back once to give her a final nod.

RUTH STOOD IN THE doorway, waiting to speak. She had been waiting all day. Her class had been gone for an hour, and each moment that passed had confirmed her condition: he was not coming. So, beating back her pride, she had gone to him.

The classroom was lit, but at first there appeared to be no one inside. The smell was stale, of a place long since vacated: no lingering breath of humanity. She cursed Sheila for delaying her downstairs with an explanation of the importance of nut-, gluten-, and dairy-free treats for an upcoming bake sale. Then came the sound of a heavy book falling in the corner. Henry rose, holding an encyclopedia.

"What's up? You working?" she said. Her words aimed for breeziness, but a tight perkiness of tone betrayed her. "An encyclopedia? Aren't you supposed to know everything already?" She laughed.

"I thought I saw a mouse."

"Christ!" she exclaimed, looking around her feet before she could stop herself. "And you plan to kill it with the encyclopedia?"

He shrugged. "Killing a mouse with a book may be ultimately less painful than dealing with a horde of screaming girls on Monday. But now I'm not certain I saw anything at all."

He had gotten a haircut. For all the time Ruth spent summoning him in her mind, she found it difficult to look straight at him, to note the minutiae of his appearance, to absorb what he actually looked like, there in that moment. The freshly cut tips of hair glinted even more brightly with silver. At the back of his neck, in the centre of his hairline, was a little point, like an arrow. She had always wondered why barbers did that, and she didn't want to notice it on Henry. There was a vulnerability she associated with it, and as embarrassed and unwanted as she felt, she didn't care for the defencelessness of his naked expanse of shaven neck, the prissiness of that tiny V.

He walked briskly to the desk and set the encyclopedia down with a resolute thud. Ruth reached behind her and closed the door, then stepped forward, grabbed his hand, and pulled him towards her. With her strained execution, the move was not so much lightheartedly seductive as petulant and demanding, and his body was far less compliant, less flexible, than she anticipated. He stumbled a little, his body tautly resisting the momentum she was trying to create, but she ignored this and grabbed the lapels of his blazer, looking up into his face.

"It's been too long," she said, pulling his face into alignment with hers. When he didn't respond by kissing her, she kissed him hard, her annoyance masked as passion.

He pulled back decisively. "Christ, Ruth," he said, his eyes shooting towards the door.

"You said you liked spontaneity."

"Spontaneity, not stupidity."

"Forgive me," she replied. "I didn't realize we'd never behaved stupidly before."

"Clayton is picking me up today at 4:15. My train leaves at six."

Ruth looked back at the clock and saw that it was not yet four. "There's still time," she said.

He reached out and ruffled the back of her hair, smiling absently with a big brother tameness she was terrified to interpret as pity. He turned back to his desk, where he transferred several folders from the desk to his briefcase.

The previous day, at the end of lunch, there had been a staff room meeting about improper use of staff computers. (Larissa had been appalled to boot up a computer one morning when her office computer was down, only to discover that the most recently browsed website was not the *New York Times,* or the *Globe and Mail*—she could even have abided the *Toronto Star*—but *People* magazine. A further search revealed that celebrity pictures, entitled "Star Tracks," had been perused.) Henry had been sitting directly across from Ruth at the long table, leaning back in his chair with his arms crossed mid-chest. Before her was a mug of tea that she was clutching so hard she felt everyone must notice the telling whiteness of her knuckles. (Did she not want him to detect her tension and feel moved to reassure her with a foot nudge, a hand on her knee?) But he seemed entirely at ease—his posture relaxed, his eyes twinkling in amusement. Was that a message he was scribbling to Michael Curtis on the notepad in front of him? A subversively cavalier comment that made her throw back her head and elbow his arm? Even if the note's content were inconsequential, the revelation was rude: he could enjoy himself in the company of others, with her in plain sight; he could forget her for the world outside them, the mindless pageantry of daily life. Was it so easy to get bored of her? If Ruth had been inclined to think moralistically, she would have theorized that this was the requisite flip side of an affair's early rewards, that the narcotic excitement, the blissful resurrection of self, were merely a bluff, concealing the awaiting punishment: your metamorphosis into this contemptible thing, this grasping, loathsome creature.

Ruth had left the meeting as soon as Larissa stopped talking, and she had deliberately gone all the way around the table so that she could pass behind him on her way out. She looked for a change in posture, a deep intake of breath, even a forced attitude of relaxation, anything that would indicate that he felt her presence at his back, that his apparent indifference was only typically male compartmentalization, or better yet, a chivalrous, loving shield designed to protect them both from the ravenous scrutiny of their colleagues. She noticed that the collar of his blue shirt was up at the back, and she had to resist the urge to reach out and turn it down, not just because they were in public, but because she knew that he would disapprove, even if they were alone, that he would consider the gesture a misguided assertion of ownership: unsettlingly proprietary, repellently sentimental.

When she was at the door, she glanced back as Larissa was barking out a final reminder about the United Way fundraiser, and Henry's eyes met hers; he looked immediately away. That was all she had needed, as satisfying, in its way, as the opposite would have been. How perversely grateful she had been, as she entered the fresh air of the hallway, for this sign that he was troubled by her, that she was not, after all, like everyone else.

On the desk beside his briefcase now lay a dog-eared copy of the Coles Notes for *The Great Gatsby*. He wedged it inside, next to a folder bursting with essays.

"Looking for teaching tips?" Ruth laughed, a breaking into the liquor cabinet kind of cackle. How she hated everything she said.

"Weeding out plagiarism. I had to give them quite a lecture today about what constituted plagiarism. Most seemed to be under the impression that if the ideas came from Coles Notes, they were doing nothing wrong. They seemed genuinely shocked that borrowing from that tripe was dishonest, and not a little unintelligent."

The noise of loud laughter in the hallway burst through the closed door. Someone called out, "We're going to be late," with a kind of wicked glee, as if the speaker very much hoped to be late, followed by the sound of galloping down the hall.

He looked at the clock. "Ruth, I can't have you here."

"Oh, is this not my workplace too?"

"Clayton could walk in at any minute."

"Something tells me that Clayton is impeccably punctual."

"Don't be obtuse. You know that I can't have you following me around when Clayton is due to arrive."

"Following you?" she exclaimed. "I deserve some credit. I've never followed you!" She knew that, at this point, to say less was the judicious choice, but she thought of the hair point at the back of his head and was filled with loathing. Her voice dropped several decibels. "You know, I think you want me to be that kind of lover. You hate that woman but you need me to be her at the same time."

He shook his head dolefully, as if saddened by how wrong she had gotten everything.

Wind gasped at the window. Purple-grey shades tinged the rattling glass, offering even clearer warning of the time than the noisy tick of the clock. Someone slammed a nearby locker, the sound ricocheted off the rows of abandoned lockers in the empty hallway. At the far end of the hallway, a vacuum cleaner started up, the cleaners already beginning their systematic progression through the closing school.

"Will you tell me something?" Ruth said suddenly. "Why did you leave U of T?"

"I don't understand."

"Is the question confusing? I remember Larissa saying you had tenure. There's been gossip, you know. Constantly."

Henry reordered the folders in his briefcase. "Well, I'm sorry to disappoint your desire for mystery. There's nothing whatsoever gossip worthy behind it. I needed a change. It wasn't what I wanted anymore."

"After all the years of work that went into getting there?"

He shrugged.

That was it? After all these months of speculation, all that waiting for the perfectly timed confession, the clarifying turpitude, she had ended up with only this? At the core of it all was not some appalling, life-threatening shame but simply his own capriciousness? Ruth had been—they had all been—so certain that there was a dark secret. She supposed that she had wanted to think this, that to believe him debauched in some spectacular way was not materially different from heroicizing him. Although she had not actively planned, over the course of their affair, on exhuming the secret, she saw now that its projected presence had bestowed on him a grandeur, had rendered him instantly, undeservedly intriguing.

She thought of that first night in the staff room: the reverent darkness of the school, their cocoon of exclusive light, the mesmerized compliance of her shocked body, the thrill, equal to the raw pleasure of the kiss itself, of knowing that her life could still take turns, that it was not, after all, entirely arranged. She had not known that the experience, even had it ended there, would become necessary to her sustenance. An insane leap, she knew, but the closest parallel she could summon for the way she felt with Henry that night was her moody elation when she discovered that she was pregnant. That concurrence of foreboding and euphoria—not merely the connection, but the symbiosis, of fear and hope.

"Tell me," she pressed. "Tell me what happened."

He looked towards the window, and she was certain that she saw something in his face: a hardness that aged him, the pulse of bitterness.

"Don't I deserve to know, after all this?"

"Ruth, don't be facile. I can't think why on earth it matters anyway."

"Why did you start this with me, Henry?"

He took a small step towards her, his palms upturned but not outstretched. He seemed at a loss, a state that only made everything worse. He had become wary rather than frustrated. Annoyance she would have welcomed. Antagonism would have offered at least some acknowledgment of her modicum of power, an assurance of some enduring conviction on his part.

"What do you want from me? A psychological examination of my *motives*?"

"You *just* got married."

"There are no reasons, Ruth."

What had she hoped for? A philandering father? A murmured confession that he had never learned to be better than this, and that he chosen her because he had seen, even before she did, that she wasn't better than it either? She walked down an aisle towards the back of the room and crossed her arms, ostensibly studying the arrangement of wilted, faux-antique brownish maps of the continents. For a second she thought that she could hear Larissa's voice travelling through the grid of hallways—so distant it sounded like a television left on at low volume. "I envy you your restraint," she said.

· "Restraint?" he replied with a smile. "We wouldn't be here if I had any. We both know that."

"But you know better than to talk about love."

She thought that now was the safest time to float that idea, even to say it, flat out, when he was sure to say nothing back. She had not planned on ever bringing that word into their vocabulary. Whatever she felt she would feel privately. But Henry's distance made her push for something she didn't quite understand. She turned to face him, and he looked at the clock, then to his watch, assessing their synchronicity, as if to throw onto an imaginary screen before them the image of Clayton in the parking lot, jingling her keys in her hand, heading to the door under the cover of the low evening clouds.

"Let's be dignified about this," he said.

She searched his face for some sign that there was something he wanted to say to her, a softening at the corner of his lips, a cautious dip of his eyelids, an allusion to affection, somewhere, but she found nothing. He clicked shut the clasp of his briefcase: the insignificant sound of dismissal.

He regarded her for a moment, relenting. "You were so nervous that first night. So nervous and lovely. Your nervousness made you more lovely."

The words were brutally elegiac.

"Maybe you should meet Clayton outside," she said.

Nodding, he grabbed his briefcase and was gone with a bashful backwards wave, gone to the warm, waiting car, its private swish through the gathering congestion of the city streets to the gritty freedom of the train station, which would take him farther, still, from this classroom, where it seemed she would wait forever, wondering what had just happened.

Chapter Sixteen

MS. MCALLISTER'S DARK FORM was silhouetted against the too-bright window when Audrey opened the door and stepped into her office on Thursday afternoon. The summons had been sent during final period, and Audrey had spent the remainder of French class in a flap. Unsuccessfully, she tried to pay even closer attention to the lesson, as though at the eleventh hour she could make up for her academic apathy. All her alarm focused on her grades: another midterm report card loomed, and she had made little improvement since the fall term. She had a vision of Ms. McAllister poring over her results with an enormous magnifying glass.

With a sideways flick of her wrist, Ms. McAllister motioned for Audrey to sit, then continued to gaze out the window for a moment, her profile precisely outlined again the dusty glass. Audrey had the impression of forced calm—not leisure but the performance of it. At length, she made a stiff and slow revolution, fixing her eyes on Audrey as she sank into the commodious recesses of her stately chair. A file was open before her and she leafed through it with reflective gravity. Finally she folded her hands and spoke. "You worked very hard to get into this school."

Audrey nodded.

"Although the process of test design certainly has its own rewards, the entrance examinations are not simply a difficult test I design for my own fancy," Ms. McAllister began. "They serve a critical function you and I have discussed before. In many respects, they are the linchpin of George Eliot Academy's success. What is a school but an amalgamation of its principles and its people?" She looked at Audrey as if waiting for a response, then continued. "This is why I allow prospective girls to try the tests only twice. In your case, as you know, an exception was made. For this, I blame myself. I allowed personal feelings and the obligations of a long-standing professional relationship to override my better judgment. And now, I fear, we are all suffering the consequences of my misguided, and dare I say foolish, compassion. I have never so heartily wished to be proven wrong. "

The sound of rowdy male voices shouting outside roused Ms. McAllister from her desk. She pulled back the half-drawn curtain and peered outside in curiosity and consternation. Even with her back turned, her eyes were trained on Audrey, immobile but seemingly alive, staring out from the enormous portrait of her that hung on the wall to the right of the desk. Although painted a decade before, to mark the occasion of Eliot's opening, it might have been a likeness of her appearance that day. It made words, the lecture or punishment intended to set Audrey on the right path, almost unnecessary, so clearly did it convey her message of authority and disappointment.

Ms. McAllister cleared her throat and turned back around. "What have you to say for yourself?" she asked.

Audrey swallowed hard. "I know I can do better."

"I shouldn't think it possible to do much worse."

"I'm trying really hard. I am. My mom's getting me a math tutor.

I'm just starting to catch up. Everything was different at my old school. It was a lot easier, obviously. And I mean, I love how challenging it is here. I'm really getting used to it now. I know that by the end of the year, you'll see how hard I'm working."

Ms. McAllister frowned and held up her hand. "I must stop you here, for I can't comprehend the purpose of this vile charade. If there's one way to redeem oneself, it's through honesty and repentance. Evasion is an extension of the original sin. To commit such an inexcusable offence is bad enough. But to show no desire, no ability, for atonement is quite unthinkable."

It was at this point that Audrey realized they weren't talking about the same thing. Dizziness washed over her, a nostalgia that was avoidant but entirely without comfort; every ounce of her wanted to return to a time, even just seconds before, when she had considered bad marks a problem of any magnitude. It didn't occur to her to wish for the chance to do everything differently, but simply to revisit the hour when she didn't know the outcome would be this: the restoration not of innocence, but of ignorance. She felt her face crumpling. "I don't—"

"Enough. Do you truly propose to deny the charges against you?"

"I don't know what you're talking about." Her quivering voice allowed her no dignity and was a reasonable enough indication of guilt.

"Dr. Winter caught you in the act you now mean to disown. Caught you red-handed at your victim's locker."

Audrey fought the insight threatening to submerge her.

"Ah. Now we're getting to it." Smiling spitefully, Ms. McAllister exited her chair and began to pace stiffly in front of the bookcases. "Do you have anything to say for yourself?"

Audrey muttered a hushed no. Even this single, inadequate word took considerable effort to get out.

In the middle of Ms. McAllister's desk was the remainder of a reheated Lean Cuisine lasagne, sitting in its plastic dish on top of a chipped white plate, emitting a powerful smell of tomato sauce and cheese. Nausea swelled inside Audrey. Ms. McAllister was standing to the side and just slightly behind her, so that Audrey could feel, but not see, Ms. McAllister staring at her. She turned, compelled to witness the loathing she would find there. Ms. Mc-Allister's lips were pursed and the studied restraint in her face had been replaced not by simple antipathy, but by triumph. She seemed not merely satisfied to have caught the culprit, but pleased at the outcome, at locating the trouble in Audrey, about whom she had always had doubts. There was a resurgent gleam in her eyes, a twitching at the corner of her lips that suggested a smile suppressed. She was vindicated: Audrey's crime was proof not of the failure of her instincts, but their success, her distaste for the girl evidence not of pettiness, the random targeting of snobbery, but of her powerful insight. The exams, the interview—the meticulously erected structures of assessment—were proven effective, Audrey's multiple failures clear warning signs that she did not heed for one reason only.

A quiet knock came at the door.

"Enter," called Ms. McAllister.

In the doorway stood Ruth.

"Oh!" she said, spotting Audrey.

"Take a seat, Ruth."

Ruth obeyed swiftly and solemnly, as though already under the weight of punishment. She looked at Audrey searchingly, but Audrey refused connection.

"It is my unfortunate and unusual burden to call you here today," Ms. McAllister said. "I won't waste time on preamble. The culprit has been identified in the recent crimes that have victimized our school. She sits before you."

Ruth's face was as blank as if nothing had been said. Audrey dared to look at her mother, but saw no cascading recognition, no identifiable emotion. Ms. McAllister seemed content to witness Ruth's immobility. Firmly rooted, she made no movement, even as the phone on her desk rang.

In the jarring silence that followed, Ruth finally awoke. "No," she said, a laugh skirting the edges of her tone, as though a joke had been made that she didn't quite get.

Ms. McAllister was visibly annoyed. "Did I ask a question?"

"No, it's just … Audrey? No. She can't have."

"I'm afraid she did."

"It's totally unlike her."

"I don't doubt that your maternal bias prevents you from being able to accept this news with equanimity. However, accept it you must."

Now Ruth appeared to have altogether forgotten Audrey's presence. A strength was gathering in her body. She raised her eyes from the large mole on Larissa's right knee, visible through her tan pantyhose, to her expectant face. Ruth's voice was tight. "I won't accept any such thing. Not until you give me good reason."

"Mom, I—"

Ruth put out a hand to silence her daughter. "Larissa, I'm—"

"Ms. Brindle, don't forget yourself."

Ruth smiled angrily. "I'm quite certain there's some sort of explanation here for whatever conclusion you've drawn. Ms. Mc-Allister."

"This isn't about any conclusion *I've* drawn. Audrey was caught red-handed in the act."

"You must be confused."

"Dr. Winter witnessed the atrocity himself."

Ruth's eyes cast around confusedly, as though scrambling to spot an alternative. "Henry?" she said.

"I'm sure you'll agree that he's as reliable a witness as can be."

"Henry." Ruth nodded slowly.

"I don't know if I've ever felt so personally attacked by misbehaviour," Ms. McAllister said. "For months, Audrey has terrorized not just one girl, but an entire school. In the history of Eliot, no comparable villainy has been perpetrated against us. Clearly, this act will not be treated as mere sophomoric hijinks."

Ruth was still clinging to the fight, Audrey could see, but she herself had let it go. She was exhausted by the decade-long struggle that had been her relationship with Eliot. Late one afternoon about a month into fall term, she had gone into the grade one classroom to see if the desk Ruth had marked so many years earlier was still there. Of course it wasn't. All the old schoolhouse desks had been replaced with roomier, more practical models. At first she had remarked the changes bleakly. But then another part of that old memory—the part she usually excised—surfaced. On their way out of the room, her mother had hoisted Audrey up to a world map on the wall. "How many countries does the Danube run through?" Ruth asked. All the excitement Audrey had been feeling drained out of her. "I don't remember," she replied, squirming to be put down. What telling throb of intuition had she forced herself to ignore?

"I can't begin to understand what motivated you. You came here from an ordinary public school, true, but you were given the chance to make yourself more than ordinary. To take your place in a league of exceptional females. To be elevated by them. You could have been part of something great."

Ms. McAllister continued to speak, but Audrey was barely listening. What she didn't want—what she couldn't bear—was for Ruth to ask her why. From the beginning, she had avoided directing too much insight towards the Seeta notes, her own desire to participate. She had always known what Arabella and the group's professed reasons might be, or at least what they would tell each other, but that crude patchwork of logic still only covered the surface of it. Audrey wasn't sure she even wanted to place it in the clear light of her scrutiny, to understand what was best left ignored. All year, there had been signs of an ugliness she wanted to deny. Seeta repelled her, repelled all of them, but the nature of that repulsion was a tricky thing. It was imperative that the cause be insignificant, that it should stem from nothing more malignant than Seeta's refusal to recognize the rules that governed them.

Audrey could see Ms. McAllister gluttonously suspecting, desiring, the worst. It was clear in her thinly victorious smile, that septic pleasure. How desperately she wanted it on her own behalf, how plainly the desire shimmered in that vampiric face.

"Not everyone is capable of elevation, of course," Ms. McAllister was saying. "The lowest common denominator will seek to drag others to its level."

Ruth shook her head. "I understand, of course I do, that there must be some punishment, some atonement. But Audrey can't have been alone in this. Ms. McAllister, all this mess can't have been the work of one girl."

"You must open your eyes, Ms. Brindle," Ms. McAllister replied. "Really, you must."

"My eyes are open. Are yours?"

Ms. McAllister smiled coldly. "That Audrey was not an appropriate candidate for George Eliot Academy was clear from the beginning. For years, I chose to spare you the full assessment of her entrance exam results. Suffice to say, my judgment is unerring."

Audrey looked her mother. "I'm sorry."

"No. No!" Ruth exclaimed, standing up quickly. "You're not sorry for anything!"

"Think about what you are saying, Ms. Brindle."

Roughly, Ruth swung Audrey's knapsack onto her own shoulder, accidentally knocking onto the floor a row of framed photographs of Eliot that adorned the edge of Ms. McAllister's desk.

"Get up, Audrey. We're leaving."

Ms. McAllister's polished penny loafers formed a perfect *plié* as she stood by the door, looking very much as though she were hearing music in her head. Audrey looked down at the jumble of photographs by the principal's feet. On top was Martha McKirk, before a screen of library books, smiling blandly for the picture-day photographer, the dates of her birth and death inscribed on the cream mat. Another Eliot girl of the past.

Ms. McAllister was waiting to escort her into the disgrace of her expulsion. But Audrey had already vanished into her future.

THE IMPRESSIONISTIC FORMS OF the known landscape sailed past, but Ruth remarked none of it. Her sightline had become a tunnel. Her hands gripped the steering wheel at some distance in front of her, but she couldn't have said how near or far they were. In this distortion, reminiscent of a childhood fever, the only thing she was truly aware of was the acrid odour of the antibacterial soap from the school bathroom, where she had stopped before leaving. The drive home, away from this place, had seemed impassable—all at once too long and too short. How would she manage the mechanics of driving? Hurtling vehicles, red stop-lights, weaving bicycles—the world was full of things that required her to command and coordinate her senses, which seemed to exist just outside of her reach. But the alternative, actually being at home, was equally incomprehensible. What would she tell Richard?

There had been no reason to linger at school, there was every reason to get out, but she had stayed as long as she could in the cold brilliance of the empty staff bathroom turning her hands under the warm water. How was she to return to her ordinary life and eat cilantro-encrusted halibut for dinner as if nothing was wrong? No, she would rather stay in the school, as odious as it now was, because entering the aftermath meant admitting that the events had happened, that they were no longer unfolding, fluid, changeable. It meant that the outcome was settled.

So she had turned her hands under the water, pumping that awful soap again and again, and looking at her face, studying it even though she knew she couldn't really see it. She could never see what others saw, never see her true face, only its reflection. She stared and stared, the way she stared at herself as a girl, thinking she'd discover the trick of how to be beautiful, the angle that would show her as her best self, her true self. But she had never mastered the control that consistent beauty required. The best she could do was accept familiarity. And sometimes in rooms with lighting this awful she could bear how ugly she was, sometimes she could ignore it and go about her day, sometimes she could forget about the shadows and wrinkles, the incipient drooping, the failing radiance. And sometimes she couldn't.

She could only get used to things.

What things had Audrey grown used to? Across the car, she was silent, whether in shame or in anger Ruth couldn't say. There was no telling what Audrey was thinking. Her daughter had become as opaque to her as any girl on the street—more, in fact. Girls revealed something of their desires, as they rode their bicycles in sweet summer dresses, as they rambled down the sidewalk in cut-offs–clad packs. Even the hidden ones, clothed drably, blemished faces cast down, betrayed a flicker of selfhood, a prejudice, a proclivity, in their hiding. Ruth had spent her life around young people. Yet the most basic drift of her daughter's mind was a mystery to her. Audrey still looked like Audrey, but the face Ruth had once considered so expressive—too expressive (how helpless she had felt, observing its dazzling nakedness)—had gone blank. Somehow Audrey had disappeared behind the cloak of her school uniform.

As they descended the Bayview Extension, cars sped past on the right, a white suv bore down from behind. At the light, Ruth glanced at Audrey staring out the passenger window, and her heart began to thud wildly. A fearful, cornered feeling overtook her. Was life as she knew it over?

She turned onto Pottery Road. Just past the small bridge over the Don River, she pulled abruptly into the gravelly crescent fronting the converted stables of Todmorden Mills. There she got out of the car and paced for a moment by the bumper before going around to Audrey's side and opening the door.

"Get out," Ruth said. "I don't trust myself to drive while we're having this conversation."

Looking stunned, Audrey obeyed.

In the distance behind them, the hazy grey rectangles of downtown, relieved by the peak of the CN Tower, spread across the horizon. Restlessly, Ruth took several steps away, then back, churning the gravel under her silly stilettos. "Tell me," she said.

For a moment, Audrey looked chastened, perhaps on the brink of tears, but then a flicker of resolve steeled her features. "As if any of it matters now anyway."

"Tell me! I know you weren't alone in this."

Audrey looked around, as though fearing witnesses, but the only people nearby were faceless figures contained in the cars slowly ascending the long hill. A cyclist, made safely anonymous, androgynous, by a spandex one-piece and a bike helmet, whizzed down the opposite side of the road at breakneck speed. "Ms. McAllister already told you everything," she said.

"Do you think I'm buying that?"

The only response Audrey produced was one infuriating shrug.

"God!" Ruth exclaimed. "Can this apathy be real?" She felt a flash of rage, but too quickly it was succeeded by despair. Was Audrey's neutrality not final confirmation of her own irrelevance? How could Audrey not feel as trapped and petrified as she did? In mere months, she'd overturned the life they'd spent years building towards. Did she not balk at the unknown that lay before her? Ruth threw her arms up. "I can't believe it. I don't! Do you completely lack the capacity for forethought? Have you not thought about going back to your old school, months before the end of the year? Are you not aware of how that smacks of failure? Have you considered what it will be like to tell your father? You're acting like you just got fired from the Gap!"

The more listless Audrey's expression, the more Ruth felt her own pulse quickening. She couldn't tell whether Audrey was even listening to her. No word seemed to penetrate. "We worked so hard to get you into Eliot," she continued.

"Did *we*?" And now it seemed that Audrey might even be smirking.

"Oh, wonderful!" Ruth said. "I'm so glad my emotion has provided you with some pleasure on one of the worst days of my life!"

"The worst day of *your* life?" Audrey laughed. "Look, you think there's so much to say. But there's nothing to say. Let it go."

"How can I do that? I don't even care, not really, about the notes. Seeta's a pain. I see that. But why do you have to be so unemotional? Why are you so secretive?"

"I really think it would be best for you to let this go," Audrey said in a low voice.

Ruth wrung her hands. "Just tell me who else was in on it. We can start from there. Why are you making me beg? Does it give you pleasure to see me this way? Are you trying to be honourable? I think you're well past that."

Audrey rolled her eyes.

"Was it really the only way you could make friends?"

Audrey looked at the ground, and Ruth thought perhaps she had scored a victory. But then Audrey raised her eyes again. In them had awakened an anger unlike any Ruth had ever seen in her daughter. Without a word, Audrey turned around and slammed her car door so hard that Ruth expected the window glass to shatter. Then she turned on her heel and began walking up the hill.

"What are you doing?" Ruth yelled.

Audrey didn't break her powerful stride.

Tripping over the gravel, Ruth started to run after her daughter. But on the most basic level, this was problematic. Those heels again. How was she to run in them? Certainly not with dignity, if running after one's daughter could ever be done with dignity. At the end of the driveway, she took the shoes off and, holding one in each hand, started up the hill in her stocking feet.

"Stop!" she shouted. "Audrey!"

To Ruth's surprise, Audrey did stop, though her desire to avoid a scene was the clear motivation for this obedience. Glaring, she gestured for Ruth to be quiet.

"What are you doing?" Ruth called.

"I'm going home."

"You're walking home? From here?"

"I refuse to sit in that car with you for one more second."

"That's ridiculous!"

"No," Audrey said. "You're the one who's ridiculous."

"Don't speak to me that way, Audrey. I don't deserve that. You know I've only ever wanted the best for you."

Audrey laughed again, that dismal, knowing little laugh. "The best for me? It's amazing to me that you can still make that argument."

Audrey's face danced with defiance. Ruth prayed that this was just empty bravado.

"Is that what you've been doing these past months, Mother? Working on what's best for me?"

"I don't know what you're getting at." But her voice was always her undoing. She had no control over its strange electricity, its pre-teen male disorder, its haywire leaps and somersaults.

"Oh, give it up," Audrey said. "I know about Henry Winter."

Ruth paused. "Whatever you think you know, you're mistaken."

"I saw you in the library. At the dance. I'm not an idiot."

Ruth was about to deny the charge, but denial suddenly seemed useless on so many levels. She knew she should fight for her life, as any sane person would, but she had that queer, floating feeling she sometimes got during arguments. A portion of her cared about nothing. If she was found out, then so be it. She looked at the sky with damp eyes. "What do you want from me, Audrey? I'm a horrible person, okay?"

"I don't want anything from you. I just want you to leave me alone."

"How can I leave you alone?

"I'm not a child. I can get home by myself."

"And then what? You have to talk to me sometime. Look, I'm sorry for everything I've done, but the Henry thing...it has nothing to do with you."

Audrey's cheeks flushed. "You're a liar! How can that have nothing to do with me?"

Now came Ruth's turn to smirk. "I'm sorry, I had no idea honesty was the value you held most dear."

"You made me go to that school! Whatever happened there—"

"Oh, yes, it's all my fault," Ruth interrupted. "Audrey, you wanted to go to Eliot."

"How could I even know what I wanted?" Tears had begun to pour down Audrey's face, and she took rapid, clumsy swipes at them. "Just leave me alone. Leave me alone!"

A woman, looking discreetly down, moved to the side of the walkway to pass them. From behind, Ruth watched her steady ascent. The woman's straight brown hair was tied into a ponytail, loosened like a sagging mood, and over her hunched shoulder was slung a heavy-looking black leather purse. But there was purpose in her march, a sturdy metre that spoke to Ruth of efficiency, dependability, despite the unattractive black-heeled boots (poor quality, uncomfortable, polished and repolished, made to last beyond their lifespan) that suggested an outdated sense of style. A narrow flash of light blinked for a second at the side of the woman's head: a dangling silver earring catching the sun. Ruth had an urge to overtake the woman and glimpse her face. Something about the twinkle of the earring against the general drabness. She felt as though she had just missed something she was supposed to see, that the woman's face would somehow have given her strength, that, in embodying everything unlike her, it would be something she could hold on to, like the sight of a Muskoka chair at the end of a long dock by the lake, an image she could recall later when she needed to manage her disordered feelings. A restorative breath. Not emotion recollected in tranquility, but tranquility, recollected in emotion.

"It's over, you know, with Henry," Ruth said.

Audrey was silent.

"Are you planning to tell your father?"

Still swatting at her wet eyes, Audrey glanced down to the valley below, her face bounding with uncertainty.

Ruth shielded her eyes against the setting sun and its blinding reflection off the hard surface of the cars still moving past. "I used to know you," she said.

"Just leave me alone."

Ruth sighed. She supposed she had no choice but to let Audrey walk. "Do you want my scarf?" she asked.

Audrey shook her head and set off up the hill towards Broadview.

Ruth waited for a minute, hoping Audrey would relent, then put her shoes back on and returned to the car. Her hands trembled as she started up the engine, but she couldn't bring herself to drive away. She saw that from the beginning, she had worried about all the wrong things: child killers, car accidents, rare diseases. She worried about what would happen to Audrey if she didn't go to Eliot, if she went to Eliot. She worried that Audrey was too conventional, not conventional enough. She should have been worrying about herself. What pain she would cause to the being she had created. What damage she would do in the name of love.

She craned around to the back to retrieve her gloves, but they were lost in the chaos of papers spread across the seats. She searched the floor, dug around in the piles. So much work, the accumulation of everything she'd been ignoring. Just that afternoon, Sheila had delivered a folder of *Pomegranate* submissions to Ruth's desk. She had gotten her class to write their own version of William Carlos Williams's "This Is Just to Say," and she had excitedly asked Ruth to look at the poems then and there. Ruth had nearly dumped the entire pack into the garbage.

The thick folder lay on top of the others, held shut by a long blue elastic. Even as she opened it, Ruth reminded herself how little she cared. She would just take the smallest peek. The poem on top was written in tiny, neat, green cursive. Ruth's eyes passed over the words once quickly, then again more slowly, then again, and again.

> This is just to say
> I cut off all the hair
> of your favourite Barbie
>
> the one you
> had hidden
> in the back of your closet

Forgive me
I always hated that doll
and the hair looked like gold
coming away in my hands

Chapter Seventeen

AUDREY RETURNED TO ELIOT for the last time at the end of the week. Her parents would have forbidden the trip, had they known, but Ruth was out doing errands as Audrey boarded the bus and set forth. The day had been mild, a half-hearted struggle between rain and sunshine, and spreading across the sky over the top of Eliot were heavy charcoal thunderclouds made dazzling by blurry golden outlines from the sun they obstructed. The grounds were quiet: it was after four o'clock already.

From her position on the sidewalk, Audrey couldn't get a clear view of the school. And perhaps she didn't need to see it after all, its elegant stance on that minor hill, waiting for her in the compromised light of late day. Had she been closer, she might have seen the dirty snow melting in the troughs on each side of the driveway. She might have seen the softball game the Eliot girls would never win. Her own reflection in the windows, her eyes taking a measure of everything she was leaving behind. A part of her was glad she could no longer get this view. She wanted to keep it as it was, as it never was. The windows just washed. The red balloon floating overhead. The weather verging on autumn, on the beginning. If she had approached, she might have seen the little girl on her knees, drawing a chalk hopscotch board as her friends looked on. The girl that was never her. Already memory was forming a protective seal around imprecision. With her merciful removal in time, what could ever correct her? How easy it was to fall out of your own tiny history.

A black car swished out through the open gates. Through its rear window, an old English sheepdog regarded her dolefully. Two prefects came down the driveway, carrying props from a morning skit. Seeing Audrey there, they cast their eyes away. She was about to turn and leave when she noticed, at the far end of the driveway, a known figure, approaching with light, pretty precision, as though her feet didn't quite touch the ground. Retreat was the smartest option, the only option for someone of her criminal condition, but Audrey was stupefied, as ever, by the radiant force of that figure. It put her in mind of a fairy tale character, stepping tenuously out of the pages of a storybook into the fallen world she couldn't quite resist.

"What are you doing here?" Arabella said cautiously, drawing near.

In Arabella's face for the first time was fear. Never before had her glow faltered, never had it been smothered even for a second by the tenebrous unease that crossed her face now. The sight of it filled Audrey with new strength. It was the one thing that had never occurred to her during the accumulating humiliations of the past days. All of her focus had been on the fitting injustice of the fact that she had been caught on the one occasion she had tried to do the right thing. But she saw now that she was not exclusively the pathetic picture of herself presented in Ms. McAllister's office. She was not as powerless as she had believed.

"You'll get in trouble if someone notices you," Arabella continued.

Audrey made a face. "I'm on a public sidewalk."

"Why are you even here?" She glanced around, as though to summon psychic support from her absent entourage. "It's not like anyone misses you or wants to say goodbye."

"Why do you care what I do?" Audrey said.

"I don't!"

Audrey wanted to laugh, so little did Arabella's contempt touch her. For her, it was over. Yet Arabella still had everything to lose. It should have been so obvious all along. The notes, for her, were a love letter to Eliot—yes, they went against what the institution stood for, but wasn't it the nature of love to go awry? The notes only revealed how intimately involved she was in every miniscule pulse of life within the place, how ardently she needed to create a whole dramatic life for herself there. Without Eliot, she was just a girl. A pretty girl. But not an Eliot girl.

"No one will believe you, if you try to give the rest of us away," Arabella said too vehemently.

Audrey knew that this was probably true. But she also recognized the power an accusation would have. Ms. McAllister would dismiss it, in all likelihood. But it would be out there, a lasting disgrace, a malignancy no one could quite eradicate.

"You hope no one would believe me," Audrey said.

"No one likes you enough to listen to you."

The angrier Arabella sounded, the more liberated Audrey felt. She seemed to have poured all her fear into the girl facing her. She knew well that the worst thing to face was the unknown. Would Arabella be afraid for a week, a month? Always looking over her shoulder now?

"Enjoy your glory days," Audrey said. "They'll be over soon." She began to move away, then stopped. "Oh, and tell Henry I said hi." She reached into her pocket and pulled out a book, *The Rainbow*. "My mom, too. Actually, could you give this back to him for her? I guess he lent it to her when they were fucking."

Audrey turned into the wind, her face as vivid and purified as if she had just splashed cold water on it.

THROUGH THE LONG OVAL window of the front door, Audrey could see to the lit kitchen. Richard was cutting vegetables at the island, and Ruth was standing by the stove in her ratty old University of Toronto sweatshirt. Their backs were to each other, but their lips were moving. Soon they would sit down to dinner together, Ruth and Richard at either end, Audrey in the centre, at the spot some part of her thought she'd be sitting at for the rest of her life.

One day, she knew, she would probably long for just this. The time when she was still with them, contained in the perpetual childhood of the kitchen table. When she was barely able to remember the particulars of this life—the rhythms of the dogs' sleep-breathing on the couch, the water stain in the middle of the kitchen table, the smell of pencil shavings in her Eliot classroom, the configuration of veins on Ruth's hands—she would call for her mother. In history, they had learned about the soldiers dying on the beaches at Normandy: through the fog of confusion, the thicket of duress, from the deathbed comes the anguished request. That long-suppressed ache for a lost time, a phantom time: it always surfaces. Perhaps it only intensifies once you have finally forgotten your mother's distinctive tactility. The time past. The time that never was. Would Audrey's last thoughts be of her?

Audrey watched her parents, twisting the bottom of a lock of hair around her index finger. She realized Ruth was doing the same. The silhouette, in profile, was a familiar sight—a hip jutted, that restless hand—but for a second, the refrigerator light collaborated with Richard's penumbral form to turn Ruth into a reflection, a prediction.

Then Richard turned to the island and adjusted the volume button on the radio. He pulled Ruth away from the stove and into a clumsy embrace. A wooden spoon fell from her hand, and she bent to retrieve it, but he stopped her, pulling her body against his as he swayed. Grabbing her hand, he twirled her under the arch of his arm. She was shaking her head, but laughing too, probably protesting that she felt like an idiot. Dancing in the kitchen was for others, people who could let go of their pride enough to be foolish together, if only for the length of a song. Audrey imagined that when she opened the door, she would hear the tinny warmth of Edith Piaf singing "La Vie en Rose." If she tried, she could almost make it out.

Marlow lay by the front door, his dozing head twitching slightly on his paws. Sensing her approach, he lifted his head. She knew exactly the way he smelled, the soft wave of his fur under her hands. She waved to let him know that she saw him there, that she loved him too, and his tail began to wag, welcoming her home.

Acknowledgments

MY DEEP GRATITUDE TO my parents, Jill Bridge and Ed Bridge, who've been more supportive, both as readers and parents, than any grown child could reasonably expect. Thank you to Chris Labonté at Douglas & McIntyre for his wisdom and his belief in me. Thank you to Barbara Berson, whose talent and dedication as an editor pushed me further and kept me going. Thank you to my agent Martha Magor Webb for her invaluable support. Thank you to Pam Robertson for meticulous copy editing.

Thank you to the Canada Council for the Arts and the Ontario Arts Council for providing important financial assistance during the period I was writing this book. And thank you to the team at Harbour Publishing for giving Douglas & McIntyre a second chance at life.

Most of all, thank you to my husband, Peter Wambera, whom I will spend a lifetime trying to deserve.

PHOTO CREDIT: Jacklyn Atlas

KRISTA BRIDGE HAS PUBLISHED fiction in numerous magazines and anthologies, including *Toronto Life, Best Canadian Stories,* and *The Journey Prize Stories,* and she has been a finalist for both the Writer's Trust of Canada/McClelland and Stewart Journey Prize and a National Magazine Award. Her first book, a collection of stories called *The Virgin Spy,* was shortlisted for the Danuta Gleed Literary Award and the Relit Award. She lives in Toronto with her husband and two sons.